THE
DRAGON'S
PATH

Marcus rubbed his chin with a callused palm.

"Yardem?"

"Sir?" rumbled the Tralgu looming at his side.

"The day you throw me in a ditch and take command of the company?"

"Yes, sir."

"It wouldn't be today, would it?"

The Tralgu crossed his thick arms and flicked a jingling ear.

"No, sir," he said at last. "Not today."

"Pity."

THE
DRAGON'S
PATH

BOOK ONE OF THE DAGGER AND THE COIN

DANIEL
ABRAHAM

www.orbitbooks.net

ORBIT

First published in Great Britain in 2011 by Orbit
This paperback edition published in 2012 by Orbit
Reprinted 2013

Copyright © 2011 by Daniel Abraham

Map by Chad Roberts

Excerpt from *The Black Prism* by Brent Weeks
Copyright © 2010 by Brent Weeks

The moral right of the author has been asserted.

A CIP catalogue record for this book
is available from the British Library.

ISBN 978-1-84149-888-1

Printed and bound by CPI Group (UK) Ltd, Croydon, CR0 4YY

Papers used by Orbit are from well-managed forests
and other responsible sources.

MIX
Paper from
responsible sources
FSC
www.fsc.org   FSC® C104740

Orbit
An imprint of
Little, Brown Book Group
100 Victoria Embankment
London EC4Y 0DY

An Hachette UK Company
www.hachette.co.uk

www.orbitbooks.net

To Scarlet

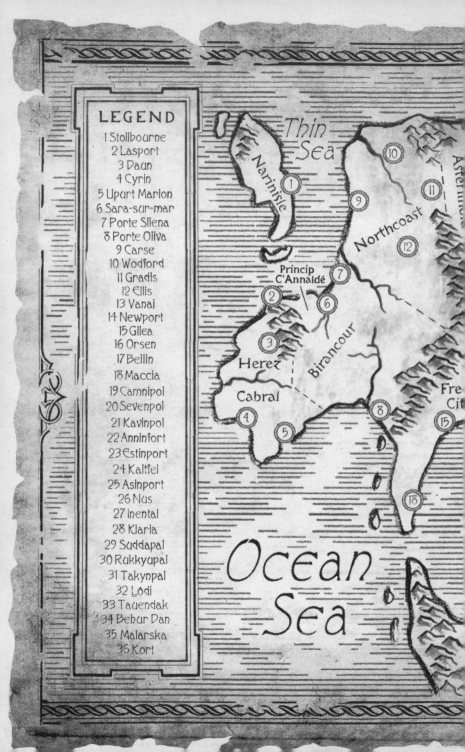

LEGEND

1 Stollbourne
2 Lasport
3 Daun
4 Cyrin
5 Upurt Marion
6 Sara-sur-mar
7 Porte Silena
8 Porte Oliva
9 Carse
10 Wodford
11 Gradis
12 Ellis
13 Vanai
14 Newport
15 Gilea
16 Orsen
17 Bellin
18 Maccia
19 Camnipol
20 Sevenpol
21 Kavinpol
22 Anninfort
23 Estinport
24 Kaltfel
25 Asinport
26 Nus
27 Inentai
28 Kiaria
29 Suddapal
30 Rukkyupal
31 Takynpal
32 Lòdi
33 Tauendak
34 Behur Dan
35 Malarska
36 Kort

Thin
Sea

Narinisle

Asterilhold

Northcoast

Princip
C'Annaldé

Birancour

Herez

Cabral

Fre
Cit

Ocean
Sea

Hallskar

Antea

Dry
astes

Sarakal

Borja

the
Keshet

Elassae

Pût

nner
Sea

oneia

Prologue

The Apostate

The apostate pressed himself into the shadows of the rock and prayed to nothing in particular that the things riding mules in the pass below him would not look up. His hands ached, the muscles of his legs and back shuddered with exhaustion. The thin cloth of his ceremonial robes fluttered against him in the cold, dust-scented wind. He took the risk of looking down toward the trail.

The five mules had stopped, but the priests hadn't dismounted. Their robes were heavier, warmer. The ancient swords strapped across their backs caught the morning light and glittered a venomous green. Dragon-forged, those blades. They meant death to anyone whose skin they broke. In time, the poison would kill even the men who wielded them. All the more reason, the apostate thought, that his former brothers would kill him quickly and go home. No one wanted to carry those blades for long; they came out only in dire emergency or deadly anger.

Well. At least it was flattering to be taken seriously.

The priest leading the hunting party rose up in his saddle, squinting into the light. The apostate recognized the voice.

"Come out, my son," the high priest shouted. "There is no escape."

The apostate's belly sank. He shifted his weight, preparing to walk down. He stopped himself.

Probably, he told himself. *There is* probably *no escape. But perhaps there is.*

On the trail, the dark-robed figures shifted, turned, consulted among themselves. He couldn't hear their words. He waited, his body growing stiffer and colder. Like a corpse that hadn't had the grace to die. Half a day seemed to pass while the hunters below him conferred, though the sun barely changed its angle in the bare blue sky. And then, between one breath and the next, the mules moved forward again.

He didn't dare move for fear of setting a pebble rolling down the steep cliffs. He tried not to grin. Slowly, the things that had once been men rode their mules down the trail to the end of the valley, and then followed the wide bend to the south. When the last of them slipped out of sight, he stood, hands on his hips, and marveled. He still lived. They had not known where to find him after all.

Despite everything he'd been taught, everything he had until recently believed, the gifts of the spider goddess did not show the truth. It gave her servants something, yes, but not *truth*. More and more, it seemed his whole life had sprung from a webwork of plausible lies. He should have felt lost. Devastated. Instead, it was like he'd walked from a tomb into the free air. He found himself grinning.

The climb up the remaining western slope bruised him. His sandals slipped. He struggled for finger- and toeholds. But as the sun reached its height, he reached the ridge. To the west, mountain followed mountain, and great billowing clouds towered above them, thunderstorms a soft veil of grey. But in the farthest passes, he saw the land level. Flatten. Distance made the plains grey-blue, and the wind on the mountain's peak cut at his skin like claws. Lightning flashed on the horizon. As if in answer, a hawk shrieked.

It would take weeks alone and on foot. He had no food, and worse, no water. He'd slept the last five nights in caves and under bushes. His former brothers and friends—the men he had known and loved his whole life—were combing the trails and villages, intent on his death. Mountain lions and dire wolves hunted in the heights.

He ran a hand through his thick, wiry hair, sighed, and began the downward climb. He would probably die before he reached the Keshet and a city large enough to lose himself in.

But only *probably*.

In the last light of the falling sun, he found a stony overhang near a thin, muddy stream. He sacrificed a length of the strap from his right sandal to fashion a crude fire bow, and as the cruel chill came down from the sky, he squatted next to the high ring of stones that hid his small fire. The dry scrub burned hot and with little smoke, but quickly. He fell into a rhythm of feeding small twig after small twig into the flame, never letting it grow large enough to illuminate his shelter to those hunting and never letting it die. The warmth didn't seem to reach past his elbows.

Far off, something shrieked. He tried to ignore it. His body ached with exhaustion and spent effort, but his mind, freed now from the constant distraction of his journey, gained a dangerous speed. In the darkness, his memory sharpened. The sense of freedom and possibility gave way to loss, loneliness, and dislocation. Those, he believed, were more likely to kill him than a hunting cat.

He had been born in hills much like these. Passed his youth playing games of sword and whip using branches and woven bark. Had he ever felt the ambition to join the ranks of the monks in their great hidden temple? He must have, though from the biting cold of his poor stone shelter, it was hard to imagine it. He could remember looking up with awe at the high wall of stone. At the rock-carved sentries from all the thirteen races of humanity worn by wind and rain until all of them—Cinnae and Tralgu, Southling and First-blood, Timzinae and Yemmu and Drowned—wore the same blank faces and clubbed fists. Indistinguishable. Only the wide wings and dagger teeth of the dragon arching above them all were still clear. And worked into the huge iron gate, black letters spelled out words in a language no one in the village knew.

When he became a novice, he learned what it said. BOUND IS NOT BROKEN. He had believed once that he knew what it meant.

The breeze shifted, raising the embers like fireflies. A bit of ash stung his eye, and he rubbed at it with the back of his hand. His blood shifted, currents in his body responding to something that was not him. The goddess, he'd thought. He had gone to the great gate with the other boys of his village. He had offered himself up—life and body—and in return…

In return the mysteries had been revealed. First, it had only been knowledge: letters enough to read the holy books, numbers enough to keep the temple's records. He had read the stories of the Dragon Empire and its fall. Of the spider goddess coming to bring justice to the world.

Deception, they said, had no power over her.

He'd tested it, of course. He believed them, and still he had tested. He would lie to the priests, just to see whether it could be done. He'd chosen things that only he could know: his father's clan name, his sister's favorite meals, his own dreams. The priests had whipped him when he spoke false, they had spared him when he was truthful, and they were never, *never* wrong. His certainty had grown. His faith.

When the high priest had chosen him to rise to novice, he'd been certain that great things awaited him, because the priests had told him that they did.

After the nightmare of his initiation was over, he'd felt the power of the spider goddess in his own blood. The first time he'd felt someone lie, it had been like discovering a new sense. The first time he had spoken with the voice of the goddess, he'd felt his words commanding belief as if they had been made from fire.

And now he had fallen from grace, and none of it might be true. There might be no such place as the Keshet. He believed there was, so much so that he had risked his life on flight to it. But he had never been there. The marks on the maps could be lies. For that matter, there might have been no dragons, no empire, no great war. He had never seen the ocean; there might be no such thing. He knew only what he himself had seen and heard and felt.

He knew *nothing*.

On violent impulse, he sank his teeth into the flesh of his palm. His blood welled up, and he cupped it. In the faint firelight, it looked nearly black. Black, with small, darker knots. One of the knots unfurled tiny legs. The spider crawled mindlessly around the cup of his hand. Another one joined it. He watched them: the agents of the goddess in whom he no longer believed. Carefully, slowly, he tipped his hand over the small flame. One of the spiders fell into it, hair-thin legs shriveling instantly.

"Well," he said. "You can die. I know *that*."

The mountains seemed to go on forever, each crest a new threat, each valley thick with danger. He skirted the small villages, venturing close only to steal a drink from the stone cisterns. He ate lizards and the tiny flesh-colored nuts of scrub pine. He avoided the places where wide, clawed paws marked paths in the dirt. One night, he found a circle of standing pillars with a small chamber beneath them that seemed to offer shelter and a place to recover his strength, but his sleep there had been troubled by dreams so violent and alien that he pushed on instead.

He lost weight, the woven leather of his belt hanging low around his waist. His sandals' soles thinned, and his fire bow wore out quickly. Time lost its meaning. Day followed day followed day. Every morning he thought, *This will probably be the last day of my life. Only probably.*

The *probably* was always enough. And then, late one morning, he pulled himself to the top of a boulder-strewn hill, and there wasn't another to follow it. The wide western plains spread out before him, a river shining in its cloak of green grass and trees. The view was deceptive. He guessed it would still be two days on foot before he reached it. Still, he sat on a wide, rough stone, looked out over the world, and let himself weep until almost midday.

As he came nearer to the river, he felt a new anxiety start to gnaw at his belly. On the day, weeks ago, when he had slipped over the temple's wall and fled, the idea of disappearing into a city had been a distant concern. Now he saw the smoke of a hundred cookfires rising from the trees. The marks of wild animals were scarce. Twice, he saw men riding huge horses in the distance. The dusty rags of his robe, the ruins of his sandals, and the reek of his own unwashed skin reminded him that this was as difficult and as dangerous as anything he'd done to now. How would the men and women of the Keshet greet a wild man from the mountains? Would they cut him down out of hand?

He circled the city by the river, astounded at the sheer size of the place. He had never seen anything so large. The long wooden buildings with their thatched roofs could have held a thousand people. The roads were paved in stone. He kept to the underbrush like a thief, watching.

It was the sight of a Yemmu woman that gave him courage. That and his hunger. At the fringe of the city, where the last of the houses sat between road and river, she labored in her garden. She was half again as tall as he was, and broad as a bull across the shoulders. Her tusks rose from her jaw until she seemed in danger of piercing her own cheeks if she laughed. Her breasts hung high above a peasant girdle not so different from the ones his own mother and sister had worn, only with three times the cloth and leather.

She was the first person he had ever seen who wasn't a Firstblood. The first real evidence that the thirteen races of humanity truly existed. Hiding behind the bushes, peeking at her as she leaned in the soft earth and plucked weeds between gigantic fingers, he felt something like wonder.

He stepped forward before he could talk himself back into cowardice. Her wide head rose sharply, her nostrils flaring. He raised a hand, almost in apology.

"Forgive me," he said. "I'm...I'm in trouble. And I was hoping you might help me."

The woman's eyes narrowed to slits. She lowered her stance like a hunting cat preparing for battle. It occurred to him that it might have been wiser to discover if she spoke his language before he'd approached her.

"I've come from the mountains," he said, hearing the desperation in his own voice. And hearing something else besides. The inaudible thrumming of his blood. The gift of the spider goddess commanding the woman to believe him.

"We don't trade with Firstbloods," the Yemmu woman growled. "Not from those twice-shat mountains anyway. Get away from here, and take your men with you."

"I don't have any men," he said. The things in his blood roused themselves, excited to be used. The woman shifted her head as his stolen magic convinced her. "I'm alone. And unarmed. I've been walking for . . . weeks. I can work if you'd like. For a little food and a warm place to sleep. Just for the night."

"Alone and unarmed. Through the mountains?"

"Yes."

She snorted, and he had the sense he was being evaluated. Judged.

"You're an idiot," she said.

"Yes," he said. "I am. Friendly, though. Harmless."

It was a very long moment before she laughed.

She set him to hauling river water to her cistern while she finished her gardening. The bucket was fashioned for Yemmu hands, and he could only fill it half full before it became too heavy to lift. But he struggled manfully from the little house to the rough wooden platform and then back again. He was careful not to scrape himself, or at least not so badly as to draw blood. His welcome was uncertain enough without the spiders to explain.

At sunset, she made a place for him at her table. The fire in the pit seemed extravagant, and he had to remind himself that the things that had been his brothers weren't here, scanning for signs of him. She scooped a bowl of stew from the pot above the fire. It had the rich, deep, complex flavor of a constant pot; the stewpot never leaving the fire, and new hanks of meat and vegetables thrown in as they came to hand. Some of the bits of dark flesh swimming in the greasy broth might have been cooking since before he'd left the temple. It was the best meal he'd ever had.

"My man's at the caravanserai," she said. "One of the princes s'posed to be coming in, and they'll be hungry. Took all the pigs with. Sell 'em all if we're lucky. Get enough silver to see us through storm season."

He listened to her voice and also the stirring in his blood. The last part had been a lie. She *didn't* believe that the silver would last. He wondered if it worried her, and if there was some way he could see she had what she needed. He would try, at least. Before he left.

"What about you, you poor shit?" she asked, her voice soft and warm. "Whose sheep did you fuck that you're begging work from me?"

The apostate chuckled. The warm food in his belly, the fire at his side, and the knowledge that a pallet of straw and a thin wool blanket were waiting for him outside conspired to relax his shoulders and his belly. The Yemmu woman's huge gold-flecked eyes stayed on him. He shrugged.

"I discovered that believing something doesn't make it true," he said carefully. "There were things I'd accepted, that I believed to my bones, and I was...wrong."

"Misled?" she asked.

"Misled," he agreed, and then paused. "Or perhaps not. Not intentionally. No matter how wrong you are, it's not a lie if you believe it."

The Yemmu woman whistled—an impressive feat, considering her tusks—and flapped her hands in mock admiration.

"High philosophy from the water grunt," she said. "Next you'll be preaching and asking tithes."

"Not me," he said, laughing with her.

She took a long slurp from her own bowl. The fire crackled. Something—rats, perhaps, or insects—rattled in the thatch overhead.

"Fell out with a woman, did you?" she asked.

"A goddess," he said.

"Yeah. Always seems like that, dunit?" she said, staring into the fire. "Some new love comes on like there's something different about 'em. Like God himself talks whenever their lips flap. And then..."

She snorted again, part amusement, part bitterness.

"And what all went wrong with your goddess?" she asked.

The apostate lifted a scrap of something that might have been a potato to his mouth, chewed the soft flesh, the gritty skin. He struggled to put words to thoughts that had never been spoken aloud. His voice trembled.

"She is going to eat the world."

Captain Marcus Wester

Marcus rubbed his chin with a callused palm.

"Yardem?"

"Sir?" rumbled the Tralgu looming at his side.

"The day you throw me in a ditch and take command of the company?"

"Yes, sir."

"It wouldn't be today, would it?"

The Tralgu crossed his thick arms and flicked a jingling ear.

"No, sir," he said at last. "Not today."

"Pity."

The public gaol of Vanai had once been a menagerie. In ancient days, the dragons themselves had stalked the wide square and bathed in the great fountain at its center. At the perimeter, a deep pit, and then great cages rising three stories high. The dragon's jade façades were carved with figures of the beasts that had once paced behind the iron bars: lions, gryphons, great six-headed serpents, wolves, bears, great birds with breasts like women.

Between them, pillars in the shapes of the thirteen races of mankind: tall-eared Tralgu, chitinous Timzinae, tusked Yemmu, and on and on. The Dartinae even had small braziers hidden in its eyeholes to mimic the glow of their gaze, though no one lit them anymore. The figures were unworn by time and rain, marred only by the black, weeping streaks where the bars had rusted away — nothing eroded dragon's jade and nothing broke it. But the animals themselves were gone, and in their place, people.

Sullen or angry or bored, the guests of Vanai's justice were displayed in their shame for ridicule and identification while they waited for the sentence of the appointed magistrate. Good, upstanding citizens could parade through the square where few bronze pennies would buy offal from a stand, usually wrapped in a sling of rags. Boys would make a show of showering loose shit, dead rats, and rotting vegetables over the prisoners. A few tearful wives and husbands would bring cheese and butter to throw across the void, but even if the gift reached the intended hand, there was no peace in prison. As they watched from the low wall at the pit's edge, Marcus saw one such lucky man — a Kurtadam with clicking beads in his close, otter-smooth pelt — being beaten for his round of white bread while a pack of Firstblood boys laughed and pointed at him and called out, *Clicker, clicker, ass-licker* and other racial insults.

In the lowest row of cells, seven men sat. Most had the build and scars of soldiers, but one kept himself apart, thin legs stuck between the bars, heels swinging over the pit. The six soldiers had been Marcus's men. The other, the company cunning man. They belonged to the prince now.

"We're being watched," the Tralgu said.

"I know."

The cunning man raised an arm in a rueful wave. Marcus responded with a false smile and a less polite gesture. His former cunning man looked away.

"Not him, sir. The other one."

Marcus shifted his attention away from the cages. It only

took a moment to see the man Yardem meant. Not far from the wide space where the street spilled into the square, a young man in the gilt armor of the prince's guard slouched at ease. A tug at his memory brought Marcus the man's name.

"Well, God smiles," Marcus said sourly.

The guard, seeing himself noticed, gave a rough salute and walked toward them. He was thick-faced and soft about the shoulders. The smell of bathhouse cedar oil came off him like he'd been dipped in it. Marcus shrugged the way he did before a fight.

"Captain Wester," the guard said with a nod. And then, "And Yardem Hane. Still following the captain, are you?"

"Sergeant Dossen, isn't it?" Marcus said.

"Tertian Dossen now. The prince keeps to the old titles. Those your men?"

"Who, those?" Marcus asked with feigned innocence. "Worked with lots of men, one time and another. Shouldn't be surprised if I knew men in every gaol in the Free Cities."

"That bunch there. We herded them up last night for being drunk and causing trouble."

"Men will do that."

"You don't know anything about it?"

"I wouldn't want to say anything that might get back to the magistrate," Marcus said. "He might not take it the way I meant."

Dossen spat into the wide air of the ditch.

"I can respect you wanting to keep them out of trouble, Captain. But it wouldn't make a difference. War's coming, and the prince needs men. That lot has training. Experience. They'll be impressed into the army. Might even get ranks."

Marcus felt the anger growing, the warmth in his chest

and belly, the sense he had grown an inch taller. Like all things that felt good, he distrusted it.

"You sound like there's something you want to say."

Dossen smiled like a river snake.

"You've still got a reputation. Captain Wester, hero of Gradis and Wodford. The prince would notice that. You could take a fair commission."

"Princes, barons, dukes. They're all just little kings," Marcus said, a degree more hotly than he'd intended. "I don't work for kings."

"You will for this one," Dossen said.

Yardem scratched his belly and yawned. It was a signal that reminded Marcus to keep his temper. Marcus took his hand off the pommel of his blade.

"Dossen, old friend," Marcus said, "a good half of this city's defense is hired men. I've seen Karol Dannian and his boys. Merrisan Koke. Your prince will lose all of them if the word gets out that he's impressing professional soldiers who are under contract—"

Dossen's jaw actually dropped in astonishment.

"You aren't under contract," he said.

"I am," Marcus said. "We're guard on a caravan for Carse up in Northcoast. Already paid."

The guard looked across the gap at the incarcerated men, the dejected cunning man, and the rust-streaked jade. A pigeon landed on the carved foot of a gryphon, shook its pearl-grey tailfeathers, and shat on the cunning man's knee. An old man behind them brayed out a laugh.

"You don't have any men," Dossen said. "Those are your caravan guards right there. You and the dog-boy can't guard a 'van by yourselves. The papers call for eight sword-and-bows and a company cunning man."

"Didn't know you'd read our contract," Yardem said. "And don't call me dog-boy."

Dossen pressed his lips together, eyes narrow and annoyed. His armor clinked when he shrugged, too thin a sound for the metal to be much more than show.

"Yes, I saw it."

"But I'm sure it had nothing to do with those particular men getting rounded up," Marcus said.

"You'd best come along, Captain. The city of Vanai needs you."

"The caravan leaves in three days," Marcus said. "And I leave with it. Under contract."

Dossen didn't move, but his face flushed red. Marcus suspected that a member of the prince's guard wasn't used to being refused.

"You think you're above men like me?" Dossen said. "You think you can dictate terms and the world's going to listen? Wake up, Wester. You're a long way from the fields of Ellis."

Yardem grunted like he'd taken a body blow and shook his massive head.

"I wouldn't have mentioned Ellis," he said, his voice a low rumble.

Dossen looked up at the Tralgu with contempt, then at Marcus, and then, nervously, away.

"Didn't mean disrespect to your family, Captain," he said.

"Walk away," Marcus said. "Do it now."

Dossen stepped back. Just out of thrusting range, he paused.

"Three days until the 'van leaves," he said.

The rest was clear. *Fail to meet the terms of the contract, and answer to the prince. Like it or no.* Marcus didn't answer. Dossen turned and strode into the square.

"That's a problem," Yardem said.

"It is."

"We need men, sir."

"We do."

"Any thoughts on where we find them?"

"No."

Marcus took one more despairing look at the men who had once been his, shook his head, and left the menagerie behind.

The city of Vanai had once been a seaport at the mouth of the river Taneish, but centuries of silt had slowly pressed the river mouth away until now it lay a full morning's ride to the south. Canals and waterways laced the city, and flatboats still came there on the way to and from the smaller, younger city of Newport carrying grain and wool, silver and timber from the countries to the north.

Like all the Free Cities, Vanai had a history of conflict. It had been a republic led by a lottery-chosen council, the private holding of a monarch, the ally or enemy of Birancour or the Severed Throne depending on which way the wind blew. It had been a center of religion, and of revolt against religion. Every incarnation had left its mark upon the white wood buildings, the greasy canals, the narrow streets and open squares.

Here, ancient gates still hung at rest, prepared to protect the halls of the Common Council though the last councilmen were all generations dead. There, a noble bronze statue showed the wise and solemn countenance of a robed and mitred bishop streaked with verdigris and pigeon shit. The streets had signs in wood and stone from a thousand years of history, so that a single alley might be called by a dozen names. Iron gates marked the twenty tiny political districts, allowing the prince to remake the pathways through the city at his whim, protection against riots and conspiracy.

But even more than the architecture, Vanai wore its past in the character of its people.

Timzinae and Firstblood were most common, but glow-eyed, hairless Dartinae, the reed-thin, snow-pale Cinnae, and bronze-scaled Jasuru all had districts within the city's wide white walls. Time and experience had given them all a sophisticated, cynical edge. Walking through the narrow streets beside rich green canals, Marcus could see all the small signs of it. Firstblood merchants, loyalists to the prince, offered the soldiers discounts on goods that had been marked higher for the purpose. The beer houses and physicians, tanners and cobblers and professionals of every sort prepared fresh signs in Imperial Antean script so that business could go on unabated after the war was lost. Old Timzinae men, their dark scales greying and cracked, sat cross-legged at quayside tables talking about the last revolution when the prince's father had taken power from the republic. Their granddaughters walked in groups wearing thin white skirts of an almost imperial cut, black-scaled legs showing through the cloth like shadows.

Yes, some soldiers would die. Yes, some buildings would burn. Some women would be raped. Some fortunes would be lost. It was an evil that the city would weather, as it had before, and no one expected the disaster would come to them in particular. The soul of the city could be summarized with a shrug.

In a green-grass common, a weathered theatrical cart had dropped its side, the shallow stage hanging with dirty yellow ribbons. The small crowd standing before it looked curious and skeptical in equal measure. As Marcus walked past, an old man stepped out from behind the ribbons. His hair stood high on his head, and his beard jutted.

"Stop!" the man cried in a deep and resonant voice. "Stop now, and come near! Hear the tale of Aleren Mankiller and the Sword of the Dragons! Or if you are faint of heart, move on. For our tale is one of grand adventure. Love, war, betrayal, and vengeance shall spill out now, upon these poor boards, and I warn you..."

The actor's voice seemed to drop to a whisper, though it still carried as clearly as the shouting.

"...not all that are good end well. Not all that are evil are punished. Come close, my friends, and know that in our tale as in the world, *anything* may happen."

Marcus didn't realize he'd stopped walking until Yardem spoke.

"He's good."

"Is, isn't he?"

"Watch for a bit, sir?"

Marcus didn't answer, but like the rest of the small crowd stepped closer. The play was a standard enough tale. An ancient prophecy, an evil rising from the depths of hell, and a relic of the Dragon Empire destined for the hand of the hero. The woman who played the maiden fair was perhaps a bit too old, and the man who spoke the hero's part a little too soft. But the lines were well delivered, and the troupe was professionally rehearsed. Marcus picked out a long-haired woman and a stick-thin youth in the crowd who laughed at all the right times and put down hecklers: spare players planted in the audience. But each time the actor who had called the introduction came onstage, Marcus lost his train of thought.

The old man played Orcus the Demon King with such a sense of evil and pathos that it was easy to forget it was all for show. When Aleren Mankiller swung the Dragon Sword and blood gouted down the Demon King's chest, Marcus had to stop himself from reaching for his blade.

In the end, and despite the actor's warnings, the good triumphed, the evil were vanquished, and the players took their bows. Marcus was startled by the applause; the crowd had doubled without his noticing. Even Yardem was thumping his plate-wide palms together and grinning. Marcus dug a silver coin out of the pouch hung under his shirt and tossed it onto the boards. It landed with a hard tap, and a moment later Orcus the Demon King was smiling and bowing in a small rain shower of money. He thanked them for their generosity and their kindness with such warmth that even walking away, Marcus found himself thinking of people as generous and kind.

The early autumn sun was lowering, the pale city glowing gold. The audience unwound itself from around the stage, breaking off in groups of two and three to walk across the sward. Marcus sat on a stone bench under a yellow-leafed oak and watched as the actors reassembled their cart. A pack of Firstblood children descended upon the players, laughing, and were chased away with grins. Marcus leaned back and considered the darkening sky through the tree's boughs.

"You have a plan," Yardem said.

"Do I?"

"Yes, sir."

It had been a fine little play. Not a huge cast. Alaren Mankiller and his companion. The maiden fair. Orcus the Demon King. The one man who'd taken all the small business as villager or demon or nobleman, depending on his hat. Five people for a full play's work. And the two leading the crowd...

Seven people.

"Ah," Marcus said. "So I do."

Seven people sat at the wide round table drinking beer and eating cheese and sausage paid from Marcus's diminishing funds. The two from the crowd were the thin boy Mikel and the long-haired woman Cary. The youth who'd played the hero was Sandr, the elderly maiden fair was Opal, the hero's companion was Hornet, and the jack-of-all-roles was Smit. Yardem sat with them, a wide, gentle smile on his face, like a mother hound surrounded by puppies.

Marcus sat apart at a smaller table with Orcus the Demon King.

"And I," Orcus said, "am called Kitap rol Keshmet, among other things. Most often, Master Kit."

"I'm not going to remember all those names," Marcus said.

"We'll remind you. I don't think anyone is likely to take offense," Master Kit said, "especially if you keep buying the drinks."

"Fair point."

"Which brings us to the question, doesn't it, Captain? I can't think you've brought us all here out of your overflowing love of the stage?"

"No."

Master Kit raised his eyebrows in an unspoken question. Off the stage and out of makeup, he was an interesting-looking man. He had a long face and steel-grey hair. The deep olive tone of his skin reminded Marcus of the First-blood men who lived in the deserts across the Inner Sea, and his eyes were so dark, Marcus suspected there might be Southling blood in his heritage somewhere not too far back.

"The prince wants to press me into his army," Marcus said.

"I understand that," Master Kit said. "We lost two of our company that way. Sandr's our understudy. He's been getting up before the sun reciting lines."

"I'd rather not work for the prince," Marcus said. "And as long as I have a legitimate contract, the issue won't arise."

"The issue?"

"Refusing a press gang ends you up on the field or in a grave. And I'm not going in the field for Vanai."

Master Kit frowned, great brows curving in like caterpillars.

"I hope you'll forgive me, Captain. Did you just tell me this is a matter of life and death for you?"

"Yes."

"You seem very calm about that."

"It's not the first time."

The actor leaned back in his chair, fingers laced over his flat belly. He looked thoughtful and sober, but also interested. Marcus took a swig of the beer. It tasted of yeast and molasses.

"I don't think I can hide both of you," Master Kit said. "You, perhaps. We have ways of making a man not seem himself, but a Tralgu this far west? If the prince knows to look for you, I'm afraid keeping with your friend is like hanging a flag on you. We'd be caught."

"I don't want to join your troupe," Marcus said.

"No?" Master Kit said. "Then what are we talking about?"

At the other table, the long-haired woman stood on her chair, struck a noble pose, and began declaiming the Rite of

St. Ancian in a comic lisp. The others all laughed, except Yardem, who smiled amusedly and flicked his ears. Cary. Her name was Cary.

"I want your troupe to join me. There's a caravan to Carse."

"We call ourselves a traveling company," Master Kit said. "I think Carse is a good venue, and we haven't been there in years. But I don't see how putting us in your 'van helps you."

"The prince took my men. I need you to replace them. I want you to act as guards."

"You're serious."

"I am."

Master Kit laughed and shook his head.

"We aren't fighters," he said. "All that onstage is dance and show. Faced with a real soldier, I doubt we would acquit ourselves very well."

"I don't need you to *be* guards," Marcus said. "I need you to *act* as them. Raiders aren't stupid. They calculate their chances just the way anyone would. Caravans fall because they don't have enough bodies in armor or they're carrying something that makes it worth the risk. If we put your people in leather and bows, no one is going know whether they can use them. And the cargo we're hauling isn't worth a fight."

"No?"

"Tin and iron. Undyed wool. Some leatherwork," Marcus said. "A man in the Old Quarter called Master Will put together an association of merchants to send out their goods as near the battle as they can and hope the fighting's over before payment comes. It's small and low-risk. If I were a raider, I wouldn't look at it twice."

"And the pay is good?"

"Very good," Marcus said.

Master Kit crossed his arms, frowning.

"Well, it's decent," Marcus said. "For what it is. And it will get your people out of harm's way. Even soft little gentlemen's wars like this spill some blood, and you have women in your troupe."

"I think Cary and Opal can look after themselves," Master Kit said.

"Not if the city's sacked. Princes and empires don't care if a few actors get raped and killed. People like you are beneath their notice, and the foot soldiers know that."

The actor looked at the larger table. Several conversations seemed to be going on simultaneously, some of the actors taking part in all of them. The older man's gaze softened.

"I believe you, Captain."

They sat in silence for a moment, only the roar of the fire in the grate, other voices raised in conversation, and the chill evening wind rattling the doors and windows. The chimney draw was poor, and it belched occasional puffs of smoke into the rooms. The actor shook his head.

"May I ask you something?" Master Kit said.

"Go ahead."

"I know your reputation. And I have the sense that you are a man with experience. Well bruised by the world. Guarding small caravans in the Free Cities seems to me an odd place to find you."

"That's not a question," Marcus said.

"Why are you doing this?"

Marcus shrugged.

"Too stubborn to die," he said, trying to make it sound like a joke.

Master Kit's smile would have been pitying if it hadn't carried some hidden suffering of its own.

"I believe that too, Captain. Well. You need nine soldiers to protect the last caravan from free Vanai?"

"Eight," Marcus said. "Eight soldiers and a cunning man."

Master Kit looked up at the soot-darkened ceiling.

"I have always wanted to play a cunning man," he said.

Sir Geder Palliako
Heir of the Viscount of Rivenhalm

If Geder Palliako hadn't been thinking about his translation, he would have saved himself. The book in question
was a speculative essay on the Drowned by a semi-discredited
philosopher from Princip C'Annaldé. Geder had found it in a
scriptorum in Camnipol, and, preparing for the long march
south to the Free Cities, he had left out a spare pair of boots
to make room for it. The dialect was ancient and obscure.
The leather binding wasn't original. Its pages were almost
brown with age, and the ink was faint.

He loved it.

The waxed cloth of his tent was cheaper than good field
leathers, but it kept the worst of the cold at bay. His legs and
back ached from riding. His inner thighs were chafed, and
he had untied his vest to give his belly some room. His father
had the same build. The family curse, he called it. Geder
had an hour, perhaps, before he had to sleep, and he was
spending it on a folding stool, hunched close over his book,
piecing out each word and phrase.

Unlike the animals of the field, humanity need not resort to
an abstract, mythological God to discover its reason for
being. With the exception of the unmodified, bestial Firstblood, each race of humanity is the artifact of some purpose. The eastern races — Yemmu, Tralgu, Jasuru — were

clearly fashioned as beasts of war; the Raushadam as objects of amusement and entertainment, the Timzinae—youngest of the races—as a race of beekeepers or some such light use, the Cinnae, myself included, as the conscious lens of wisdom and philosophy, and so on.

But what of the Drowned? Alone of the races of humanity, the Drowned show design without purpose. Common opinion places these, our lesser siblings, as akin to plants or the slow-moving beasts of the western continents. Their occasional gatherings in tidepools indicate more about the ocean's currents than anything of human will. Some romantics suggest that the Drowned are themselves working on some deep, dragon-inspired plan that continues to unfold even after the death of its planners. A romantic thought, and one which must be forgiven.

Instead, I think it is clear, the Drowned are the clearest example of humanity as artistic expression, and as such—

Or would *aesthetic intention* be more accurate than *artistic expression*? Geder rubbed his eyes. It was late. Too late. Tomorrow was another long ride to the south with another day of the same following it. If God was kind, they'd reach the border in a week, spend a day or at worst two choosing the field of battle, a day to crush the local forces, and he could be in a real bed, eating real food, and drinking wine that didn't taste of the skin it had been carried in. If he could only make it that far.

Geder put the book aside. He combed his hair, pleased by the absence of lice. He washed his face and hands, then laced up his vest for the short trek to the latrines as a last stop before bed. Outside his tent, his squire—another gift from his father—slept curled in a ball after the Dartinae fashion, eyes glowing a dull red behind their lids. Beyond him, the army lay on the countryside like a moving city.

Cookfires dotted the nearby hills and filled the air with the smell of lentils. The carts were gathered in the center of the camp, and the mules, horses, and slaves were all in separate corrals beside them. A cold wind blew from the north. It was a good sign. No rain. The moon had crawled halfway up the sky, its crescent offering the idea of light more than actual illumination, so Geder made his way to the latrine carefully.

The essay kept turning itself in his mind. He wished there was someone on the march with whom he could discuss the matter, but speculative essay wasn't considered a manly art. Poetry. Riding. Archery. Swordplay. Even history, if it was done with sufficiently apt turns of phrase. But speculative essay was a guilty pleasure, best hidden from his companions. They laughed at him enough for the size of his belly. No need to give them more stones for their slings. But if not *aesthetic intention*...was the Cinnae author *really* saying that the Drowned were only brought into existence because they made the shoreline pretty?

The latrine was empty, a small cloth tent with two rough planks spanning a pit. Geder took down his hose, his mind still turning on the fine points of the book. He noticed the sweet smell under the reek of shit, but didn't put importance on it. He sat his bare ass on the planks, sighed, and wondered a moment too late why the latrine smelled of sawdust.

The planks gave way, and Geder shrieked as he tipped backwards and down into the foul-smelling swamp of turds and piss. One of the planks bounced against the side of the pit and gouged his arm. The force of his landing blew the breath out of him. He lay stunned in the stinking darkness, his jacket and hose soaking up the sewer wetness and the cold.

Laughter came from above him. And then light.

Four lanterns shed their hoods, glowing in the sky above him. The light hid the faces of the men who held them, but the voices were clear enough. His so-called friends and companions of the sword. Jorey Kalliam, son of the Baron of Osterling Fells. Sir Gospey Allintot. Sodai Carvenallin, secretary to the High Marshal. And, worst of all, Sir Alan Klin, captain of the company, Geder's immediate superior, and the man to whom he would have reported the poor behavior of his fellows. Geder stood up, his head and shoulders peeking above the pit while the other men howled their mirth.

"Very funny," Geder said, holding shit-stained hands up to them. "Now help me out of this."

Jorey took him by the arm and hauled him up. He had to give the man some credit for not shying away from the mess they'd tipped him into. Geder's hose hung at his knees, soaked and filthy. He stood in the lantern light considering whether to put them back on or go naked from the waist down. With a sigh, he pulled up the hose.

"You were our last hope," Klin said, pounding Geder's shoulder. There were tears of hilarity running down his cheeks. "Everyone else noticed something wrong. Well, except Sodai, but he was too skinny to break the boards."

"Well, it was an excellent joke," Geder said sourly. "Now I'm going to go find something clean to—"

"Ah, no," Sodai said in his nasal, high-town accent. "Please, my friend. Don't spoil the night. It was a jest! Take it as it was meant."

"It's truth," Klin said, putting an arm around Geder's

shoulder. "You must let us apologize. Come, my friends! To the tents!"

The four men stumbled off through the darkness, hauling Geder along with them. Of the four, only Jorey seemed genuinely sympathetic, and then only in his silence.

All through his childhood, Geder had imagined what it would be to serve the king, to ride on campaign, to prove his cleverness and his strength in arms. He read stories of the great warriors of old, heard his father's wine-soaked anecdotes about the friendship and camaraderie of the sword.

Reality disappointed.

The captain's tent was heavy leather strung on iron frames. Inside, it was more luxurious than Geder's home. Silk hung from the ceiling, and a great fire roared in the pit, smoke channeled up and out by a hanging chimney of finely wrought chain and blackened leather. The heat was like walking into the worst of summer, but at least there was a bath drawn, and Geder didn't shiver as he pulled off his soiled clothes. The others shed the gloves and jackets that had been contaminated by touching Geder, and a Timzinae slave boy took it all away.

"We, my friends, are the pride and hope of Antea," Klin said as he filled a deep flagon with wine.

"To King Simeon!" Gospey said.

Klin pressed the flagon into Geder's hand and stood with the wineskin in his own.

"To Kingdom and Empire," he said. "And confusion to the upstart in Vanai!"

The others rose. Geder stood in his bath, water running down him, because to stay seated would have been a petty treason. It was the first toast of many. Sir Alan Klin was many things, but stingy with his wine wasn't one. And if Geder had the sense that his flagon was always a little more filled than the other men's, it was surely only a sign of the captain's contrition, an apology for the evening's prank.

Sodai declaimed his latest sonnet, a bawdy tribute to one of the more popular road whores who followed the campaign. Klin topped the performance by extemporizing a speech on the manly virtues of strength at arms, cultured arts, and sexual prowess. Jorey and Gospey pounded out a merry song on drum and reed organ, their voices harmonizing beautifully. When the turn came to Geder, he rose from the tepid bath, recited an explicit rhyme, and did the little jig that went with it. It was something his father had taught him once when they were deep in their cups, and Geder had never shared it outside the family. It wasn't until he finished, the other men helpless in their laughter, that it occurred to him how very drunk he must be to have repeated it here. He smiled to hide the sudden stab of anxiety. Had he just become complicit in his own humiliation? The smile goaded them on to new hilarity, until Klin, breathless, pounded the floor and gestured that Geder should sit.

There was cheese and sausage, more wine, flatbread and pickles, more wine. They talked about things that Geder could hardly follow at the time, much less recall later. At some point, he found himself going on with a drowsy gravity about the Drowned as artistic expression, or possibly aesthetic intention.

He woke in his own waxed-cloth tent, cold and aching and without memory of coming back to it. The thin, unkind light of the coming dawn pressed in through the cloth. A breeze whistled. Geder pulled his blanket up around his head like a fishwife's kerchief and willed himself back to sleep for just a few minutes more. The lingering tendrils of dream teased his mind, but the blare of the assembly call ended all hope of rest. Geder struggled up, put on a fresh uniform, and pulled back his hair. His guts were in riot. His head was in a debate between pain and illness. If he vomited inside the tent, no one would see it, but his squire would have to clean it up before they struck down for the day's ride. If he went outside, he'd almost certainly be seen. He wondered how much he'd drunk the night before. The second assembly call came. No time for it now. He gritted his teeth and set out once again for the captain's tent.

The company stood in order, Kalliam, Allintot, and two dozen other knights, many of them already in chain and show plate. Behind each, their sergeants and men-at-arms arranged in five ranks deep. Geder Palliako tried to stand straight and true, knowing that the men behind him were judging their chances of glory and survival by his competence. Just as his depended on the captain, and above him Lord Ternigan, the High Marshal who commanded the whole of the army.

Sir Alan Klin stepped out of his tent. In the cool light of morning, he looked like the perfect warrior. His pale hair was drawn back. His uniform was a black so deep it seemed like a sheet cut from midnight. His broad shoulders and jutting chin were a memorial statue brought to life. Two camp slaves brought a speaking dais and set it at the man's feet. The captain stepped up.

"Men," he said. "Yesterday, Lord Ternigan sent new orders. Vanai has entered into alliance with Maccia. Our reports are that six hundred sword-and-bows are on the march to reinforce Vanai even as we speak."

The captain paused to let that sink in, and Geder frowned. Maccia was an odd sort of ally for Vanai. The two cities had been at each other's throats over the spice and tobacco trades for more than a generation. Vanai was built of wood, he'd read, mostly *because* Maccia controlled the quarries while timber floated down the river from the north. But perhaps there was something more going on than he knew.

"These reinforcements will not save Vanai," Alan said. "Especially because when they arrive, they shall find us in control of the city."

Geder felt his frown deepen, and a sense of sick foreboding rise in his gut. It was perhaps five days by water from Maccia to Vanai, and they were at least a week from the border. To reach Vanai before the reinforcements meant...

"Today, we begin a hard march," Alan said. "We will sleep in our saddles. We will eat while we walk. And in four days' time, we will take Vanai by surprise and show her what the power of the Severed Throne means! To the King!"

"To the King!" Geder said in chorus with the others, raising his hand in salute even as he tried not to weep.

They had known. Last night, they had known. Already, Geder could feel the ache growing in his spine and his thighs. The throbbing in his head redoubled. As the formation broke, Jorey Kalliam met his eyes and then looked away.

Here was the prank. Being tipped into the sludge of the latrine had only been the start. After that, insist on the buffoon accepting apology. Get him in warm water. Fill him full of wine. Make him dance. The memory of reciting his father's dirty rhymes and dancing the little jig came back like a knife in his back. And all so that they could announce the forced march while fat idiot Palliako tried not to puke himself at formation. They'd taken his last night of sleep, and for days they would have the pleasure of watching him suffer.

The camaraderie of the sword. The brotherhood of the campaign. Warm, meaningless words. It was no different here than back home. The strong mocked the weak. The handsome pitied the plain. Everywhere and aways, the powerful chose who was in favor and who could be made light of. Geder turned and stalked back to his tent. His squire had the slaves ready to strike it. He ignored them and walked into his last moment's privacy before the battle that was still days away. He reached for his book.

It wasn't where he'd left it.

A chill that had nothing to do with autumn ran down his spine.

He'd been drunk when he came back. He might have moved it. He might have tried to read it before he slept. Geder searched his cot, then under his cot. He looked through his uniforms and the wood and leather chest that held all his other things. The book wasn't there. He found himself breathing faster. His face felt hot, but whether it was shame or anger, he couldn't let himself think. He stepped out of his tent, and the slaves jumped to attention. The rest of the camp was already being loaded onto wagons and mules. There wasn't time. Geder nodded to his Dartinae squire, and the slaves got to work putting his things in order. Geder walked across the camp again, his steps slowed by fear. But he had to have his book back.

The captain's tent was already struck, the leather unfastened from the frames, the frames broken down and stowed. The bare patch of earth where Geder had capered last night was like a thing from a children's story, a fairy castle that vanished with the dawn. Except that Sir Alan Klin was there, his leather riding cloak hanging from his shoulders and his sword of office at his hip. The master of provender, a half-Yemmu mountain of a man, was taking orders from the captain. Geder's rank technically gave him the right to interrupt, but he didn't. He waited.

"Palliako," Klin said. The warmth of the previous night was gone.

"My lord," Geder said. "I'm sorry to bother you, but when I woke up this morning...after last night..."

"Spit it out, man."

"I had a book, sir."

Sir Alan Klin closed his noble, long-lashed eyes.

"I thought we'd finished with that."

"We did, sir? So you know the book? I showed it to you?"

The captain opened his eyes, glancing about at the ordered chaos of the breaking camp. Geder felt like a boy bothering a harried tutor.

"Speculative essay," Klin said. "Palliako, really? Speculative essay?"

"More for the exercise in translation," Geder lied, suddenly ashamed of his true enthusiasm.

"It was...courageous of you to admit the vice," Klin said. "And I think you made the right decision in destroying it."

Geder's heart knocked against his ribs.

"Destroying it, sir?"

Alan looked at him, surprise on his face. Or possibly mock surprise.

"We burned it last night," the captain said. "The two of us together, just after I took you back to your tent. Don't you remember?"

Geder didn't know whether the man was lying or not. The night was a blur. He remembered so little. Was it possible that, lost in his cups, he had forsworn his little failure of sophistication and permitted it to be set to fire? Or was Sir Alan Klin, his captain and commander, lying to his face? Neither seemed plausible, but one or the other had to be true. And to admit not knowing was to confess that he couldn't hold his wine and prove again that he was the joke of the company.

"I'm sorry, sir," Geder said. "I must have been a little muddled. I understand now."

"Be careful with that."

"It won't happen again."

Geder saluted, and then, before Klin could respond, stalked off to his mount. It was a gelding grey, the best his family could afford. He lifted himself to the saddle and yanked the reins. The horse turned sharply, surprised by his violence, and Geder felt a stab of regret through his rage. It wasn't the animal's fault. He promised himself to give the beast a length of sugarcane when they stopped. If they stopped. If this twice-damned campaign didn't drag on to the end of all days and the return of the dragons.

They took to the road, the army moving at the deliberate pace of men who knew the walk wouldn't end. The hard march began, rank following rank down the wide, dragon's jade road. Geder sat high in his saddle, holding his spine straight and proud out of sheer will and anger. He had been humiliated before. Likely he would be humiliated again. But Sir Alan Klin had burned his book. As the morning sun rose, the heat drawing cloaks from shoulders, the glorious leaves of autumn glowing around them, Geder realized that he had already sworn his oath of vengeance. And he'd done it standing before his new and mortal enemy.

It won't happen again, he'd said.

And it wouldn't.

Cithrin Bel Sarcour
Ward of the Medean Bank

Cithrin's only vivid memory of her parents was being told of their deaths. Before that, there were only wisps, less than ghosts, of the people themselves. Her father was a warm embrace in the rain and the smell of tobacco. Her mother was the taste of honey on bread and the thin, graceful hand of a Cinnae woman stroking Cithrin's leg. She didn't know their faces or the sounds of their voices, but she remembered losing them.

She had been four years old. Her nursery had been painted in white and plum. She'd been sitting by the window, drinking tea with a stuffed Tralgu made of brown sacking and stuffed with dried beans. She'd been straightening its ears when her Nanné came in, face even paler than usual, and announced that the plague had taken master and mistress, and Cithrin was to prepare herself to leave. She would be living somewhere else now.

She hadn't understood. Death was something negotiable to her then, like whether or not to wear a particular ribbon in her hair, or how much sweet oats to eat in the morning. Cithrin hadn't cried so much as felt annoyance with the change of plan.

It was only later, in her new, darker rooms above the banking house, that she realized it didn't matter how loud she screamed or how violently she wept. Her parents would never come to her because, being dead, they didn't care anymore.

You worry too much," Besel said.

He reclined, splayed out, looking utterly comfortable on the worn wooden steps. He looked comfortable anywhere. His twenty-one summers made him four years older than Cithrin, and he had dark, curly hair and a broad face that seemed designed for smiling. His shoulders were as thick as a laborer's, but his hands were soft. His tunic, like her own dress, was dyed the red and brown of the bank. It looked better on him. Cithrin knew he had half a dozen lovers, and she was secretly jealous of every one of them.

They were sitting on a wooden bench above the Arched Square, looking down at the bustle and clutter of the weekly fresh market, hundreds of tightly packed stalls of bright cloth and thin sticks growing out from the buildings at the square's edge like new growth on an old tree. The grand canal of Vanai lapped at the quay on their right, the green water busy with narrow boats and pole barges. The market buzzed with the voices of the fishmongers and butchers, farmers and herb-men, all hawking their late summer harvest.

Most were Firstblood and black-chitined Timzinae, but here and there Cithrin caught sight of the pale, slight body of a full-blooded Cinnae, the wide head and mobile, hound-like ears of a Tralgu, the thick, waddling gait of a Yemmu. Growing up in Vanai, Cithrin had seen at least one example of nearly every race of mankind. Once, she had even seen one of the Drowned in a canal, staring up at her with sorrowful black eyes.

"I don't understand how the bank can side with Imperial Antea," she said.

"We're not siding with them," Besel said.

"We're not siding with the prince. This is a *war*."

Besel laughed. He had a good laugh. Cithrin felt a moment's anger, and then immediately forgave him when he touched her hand.

"This is a theater piece," he said. "A bunch of men are going to meet on a field outside the city, wave sticks and swords at each other, tumble about enough to satisfy honor, and then we'll open the gates to the Antean army and let them run things for a few years."

"But the prince—"

"Exiled. Or imprisoned, but probably exiled. This goes on all the time. A baroness in Gilea marries a prince in Asterilhold, and King Simeon decides Antea needs a counterbalance in the Free Cities. So he finds a reason to declare war on Vanai."

Cithrin frowned. Besel seemed so amused, so unconcerned. By his light, her fear seemed naïve. Foolish. She dug in her heels.

"I've read about wars. The history tutor doesn't make it sound like that at all."

"Maybe real wars are different," Besel said with a shrug. "If Antea ever marches on Birancour or the Keshet, I'll pull all wagers. But this? It's less than a spring storm, little bird."

A woman's voice called Besel's name. A merchant's daughter wearing a deep brown bodice and full skirts of undyed linen. Besel rose from Cithrin's side.

"My work's before me," he said with a glimmer in his eye. "You should get back to the house before old Cam starts getting anxious. But seriously, trust Magister Imaniel. He's been doing this longer than any of us, and he knows what he's about."

Cithrin nodded, then watched as Besel took the steps two

at a time, down to the dark-haired girl. He bowed before her, and she curtseyed, but it all looked false to Cithrin. Formality used as foreplay. Likely Besel didn't think Cithrin knew what foreplay was. She watched sourly as he took the woman by the elbow and led her away into the pale streets and bridges of the city. Cithrin plucked at her sleeves, wishing—not for the first time—that the Medean bank had adopted colors that flattered her more. Something green, for instance.

If her parents had both been Firstblood or Cinnae, she might have had family to take her in. Instead, her father's titles in Birancour had been reclaimed by the queen and awarded to someone else. Her mother's clan in Princip C'Annaldé had politely declined to take a half-blood child.

If not for the bank, she would have been turned into the streets and alleys of Vanai. But her father had placed a part of his gold with Magister Imaniel, and as inheritor, Cithrin became the bank's ward until she was old enough to press her bloodied thumb to contracts of her own. Two more summers, it would be. She would see her nineteenth solstice, become a woman of property, and move, she supposed, out of the little apartments near the Grand Square where the Vanai branch of the Medean bank did its business.

Assuming, of course, that the invading army left the city standing.

Walking through the fresh market, she saw no other particular signs of fear on the faces around her. So perhaps Besel was right. God knew the man seemed sure of himself. But then, he always did.

She let herself wonder whether Besel would see her differently when she wasn't the bank's little girl any longer. She paused at a stall where a Firstblood woman sold perfumes, oils, and colored hair-cloths. A mirror hung on a rough wood post, inviting the customers to admire themselves. Cithrin considered herself for a moment, lifting her chin the way women with real families might.

"Oh, you poor thing," the woman said. "You've been sick, haven't you? Need something for your lips?"

Cithrin shook her head, stepping back. The woman snatched her by the sleeve.

"Don't run off. I'm not afraid. Half my clients are here because they've been unwell. We can wash that pale right off you, dear."

"I haven't," Cithrin said, finding her voice.

"Haven't?" the woman said, steering her toward a stool at the stall's inner corner. The scent of roses and turned earth made the air almost too thick to breathe.

"I'm not sick," she said. "My mother's Cinnae. It's...it's normal."

The woman cast a pitying look at her. It was true. Cithrin had neither the delicate, spun-glass beauty of her mother's people nor the solid, warm, earthy charms of a Firstblood girl. She was in between. The white mule, the other children had called her. Neither one thing nor the other.

"Well, all the more, then," the woman said consolingly. "Just sit you down, and we'll see what we can do."

In the end, Cithrin bought a jar of lip rouge just so she could leave the stall.

You could just let him have a bit," Cam said. "He is the prince. It isn't as if you won't know where to find him."

Magister Imaniel looked up from his plate, his expression pleasant and unreadable. The candlelight reflected in his eyes. He was a small man with leathery skin and thin hair who could seem meek as a kitten when he wished, or become a demon of cold and rage. In all her years, Cithrin had never decided which was the mask. His voice now was mild as his eyes.

"Cithrin?" he said. "Why won't I lend money to the prince?"

"Because if he doesn't want to pay you back, you can't make him."

Magister Imaniel shrugged at Cam. "You see? The girl knows. It's bank policy never to lend to people who consider it beneath their dignity to repay. Besides which, who's to say we have the coin to spare?"

Cam shook her head in feigned despair and reached across the table for the salt cellar. Magister Imaniel took another bite of his lamb.

"Why doesn't he go to his barons and dukes, borrow from them?" Magister Imaniel asked.

"He can't," Cithrin said.

"Why not?"

"Oh, leave the poor girl alone for once," Cam said. "Can't we have a single conversation without it turning into a test?"

"We have all their gold," Cithrin said. "It's all here."

"Oh dear," Magister Imaniel said, his eyes widening in false shock. "Is that so?"

"They've been coming for months. We've sold letters of exchange to half the high families in the city. For gold at first, but jewels or silk or tobacco...anything worth the trade."

"You're sure of that?"

Cithrin rolled her eyes.

"Everyone's sure of that," she said. "It's all anyone talks about at the yard. The nobles are all swimming away like rats off a burning barge, and the banks are robbing them blind while they do it. When the letters of credit get to Carse or Kiaria or Stollbourne, they aren't going to get back half of what they paid for them."

"It is a buyer's market, that's true," Magister Imaniel said with an air of satisfaction. "But inventory becomes an issue."

After dinner, Cithrin went up to her room and opened her windows to watch the mist rise from the canals. The air stank of the autumn linseed oil painted onto the wood buildings and bridges against the coming snow and rain. And beneath that, the rich green bloom of algae in the canals. She imagined sometimes that all the great houses were ships floating down a great river, the canals all connected in a single vast flow too deep for her to see.

At the end of the street, one of the iron gates had come loose from its stays, creaking back and forth in the breeze. Cithrin shivered, closed the shutters, changed for bed, and blew out her candle.

Shouts woke her. And then a lead-tipped club banging on the door.

She threw open the shutters and leaned out. The mist had cleared enough that the street was plain before her. A dozen men in the livery of the prince, five of them holding pitch-reeking torches, crowded the door. Their voices were loud and merry and cruel. One looked up, his dark eyes catching hers. The soldier broke into a grin. Cithrin, not knowing what was happening, smiled back uneasily and retreated. Her blood felt cold even before she heard the voices—Magister Imaniel sounding wary, the guard captain laughing, and then Cam's heartbroken cry.

Cithrin ran down the stairway, the dim light of a distant lantern making the corridors a paler shade of black. Part of her knew that running toward the front door was lunacy, that she should be running the other direction. But she'd heard Cam's voice, and she had to know.

The guards were already gone when she reached the door. Magister Imaniel stood perfectly still, a lantern of tin and glass glowing in his hand. His face was expressionless. Cam knelt beside him, her wide fist pressed against her mouth. And Besel—perfect Besel, beautiful Besel—lay on the stone floor, bloody but no longer bleeding. Cithrin felt a shriek growing in the back of her throat, but she couldn't make a sound.

"Get me a cunning man," Magister Imaniel said.

"It's too late," Cam said, her throat thick with tears.

"I didn't ask. Get me a cunning man. Cithrin, come here. Help me carry him in."

There was no hope, but they did as they were told. Cam pulled on a wool cloak and hurried off into the gloom. Cithrin took Besel's heels, Magister Imaniel his shoulders. Together, they hauled the body into the dining room and laid him on the wide wooden table. There were cuts on Besel's face and hands. A deep gouge ran from his wrist almost to his elbow, the sleeve torn by the blade's passage. He didn't breathe. He didn't bleed. He looked as peaceful as a man asleep.

The cunning man came, rubbed powders into Besel's empty eyes, pressed palms to his silent chest, called the spirits and the angels. Besel took one long, ragged breath, but the magic wasn't enough. Magister Imaniel paid the cunning man three thick silver coins and sent him on his way. Cam lit a fire in the grate, the flames giving Besel the eerie illusion of motion.

Magister Imaniel stood at the head of the table, looking down. Cithrin stepped forward and took Besel's cold and stiffening hand. She wanted badly to cry, but she couldn't. Fear and pain and terrible disbelief raged in her and found no escape. When she looked up, Magister Imaniel's gaze was on her.

Cam spoke. "We should have given it over. Let the prince take what he wants. It's only money."

"Bring me his clothes," Magister Imaniel said. "A clean shirt. And that red jacket he disliked."

His eyes were moving now, darting as if reading words written in the air. Cam and Cithrin exchanged a glance. Cithrin's first, mad thought was that he wanted to wash and dress the body for burial.

"Cam?" Magister Imaniel said. "Did you hear me? Go!"

The old woman heaved herself up from the hearth and trundled quickly into the depths of house. Magister Imaniel turned to Cithrin. His cheeks were flushed, but she couldn't say if it was rage or shame or something deeper.

"Can you steer a cart?" he asked. "Drive a small team? Two mules."

"I don't know," Cithrin said. "Maybe."

"Strip," he said.

She blinked.

"Strip," he said. "Your night clothes. Take them off. I need to see what were working with."

Uncertainly, Cithrin lifted her hands to the stays at her shoulders, undid the knots, and let the cloth fall to the floor. The cold air raised gooseflesh on her skin. Magister Imaniel made small noises in the back of his throat as he walked around her, making some evaluation she couldn't fathom. The corpse of Besel made no move. She felt the echo of shame. It occurred to her that she had never been naked in front of a man before.

Cam's eyes went wide when she returned, her mouth making a little O of surprise. And then, less than a heartbeat later, her expression went hard as stone.

"No," Cam said.

"Give me the shirt," Magister Imaniel said.

Cam did nothing. He walked over and lifted Besel's shirt and jacket from her. She didn't stop him. Without speaking, he dropped the shirt over Cithrin's head. The cloth was soft and warm, and smelled of the dead man's skin. The hem dropped down low enough to restore some measure of modesty. Magister Imaniel stood back, and a bleak pleasure appeared at the corners of his eyes. He tossed Cithrin the jacket and nodded that she should put it on.

"We'll need some needlework done," he said, "but it's possible."

"You mustn't do this, sir," Cam said. "She's just a girl."

Magister Imaniel ignored her, stepping close again to pull Cithrin's hair back from her face. He tapped his fingers together as if trying to remember something, bent to the fire grate, and rubbed his thumb through the soot. He smudged Cithrin's cheeks and chin. She smelled old smoke.

"We'll need something better, but..." he said, clearly speaking only to himself. "Now...what is your name?"

"Cithrin?" she said.

Magister Imaniel barked out a laugh.

"What kind of name is that for a fine strapping boy like yourself? Tag. Your name is Tag. Say that."

"My name is Tag," she said.

Magister Imaniel's face twisted in scorn. "You talk like a girl, Tag."

"My name is Tag," Cithrin said, roughening her voice and mumbling.

"Fair," he said. "Only fair. But we'll work on it."

"You can't do this," Cam said.

Magister Imaniel smiled. It didn't reach his eyes.

"The prince has crossed a line," he said. "The policy of the bank is clear. He gets nothing."

"You *are* the policy of the bank," Cam said.

"And I am *clear*. Tag, my boy? A week from now, you are going to go to Master Will, down in the Old Quarter. He's going to hire you to drive a cart in a caravan bound for Northcoast. Undyed wool cloth he's moving to keep from losing it in the war."

Cithrin didn't nod or shake her head. The world was spinning a little, and everything had the sense of being part of a terrible dream.

"When you reach Carse," Magister Imaniel continued, "you take the cart to the holding company. I'll give you a map and directions. And a letter that will explain everything."

"It's weeks on the road!" Cam shouted. "Months, if there's snow in the pass."

Magister Imaniel turned, rage lighting his eyes. His voice was low and cold.

"What would you have me do? Keep her here? She's no safer in our beds than passing for a carter in a caravan. And I will *not* simply accept the loss."

"I don't understand," Cithrin said. Her voice sounded distant in her ears, as if she were shouting over surf.

"The prince's men are watching us," Magister Imaniel said. "I must assume they're watching anyone in the bank's employ. And, I expect, the bank's ward, Cithrin the half-Cinnae. Tag the Carter, on the other hand..."

"The carter?" Cithrin said, echoing him more than thinking thoughts of her own.

"The cart's false," Cam said, her voice thick with despair. "Besel was set to take it. Smuggle out all the money we can."

"The gold?" Cithrin said. "You want *me* to take the gold to Carse?"

"Some, yes," Magister Imaniel said. "But gold's heavy. We're better sending gems and jewelry. They're worth more. Spices. Tobacco leaf. Silk. Things light enough they'll pack tight and won't break the axles. And the account books. The real ones. As for the coins and ingots...well, I'll think of something."

He smiled like the mask of a smile. Besel's corpse seemed to shift its shoulders in the flickering light. A draught of cold air rubbed against her bare thighs, and the knot in her belly tightened until she tasted vomit in the back of her mouth.

"You can do this thing, my dear," Magister Imaniel said. "I have faith in you."

"Thank you," she said, swallowing.

Cithrin walked through the streets of Vanai, her stomach in knots. The false mustache was the sort of thin, weedy thing a callow boy might cultivate and be proud of. Her clothes were a mix of Besel's shirts and jackets resewn in the privacy of the bank and whatever cheap, mended rags could be scrounged. They hadn't dared to buy anything new. Her hair was tea-stained to an almost colorless brown and combed forward to obscure her face. She walked with the wider gait Magister Imaniel had taught her, a knot of uncomfortable cloth held tight against her sex to remind her that she was supposed to have a cock.

She felt worse than foolish. She felt like a mummer in clown face and comic shoes. She felt like the most obvious fraud in the city, or the world. And every time she closed her eyes, Besel's corpse waited for her. Every voice that called out started her heart skipping faster. She waited for the knife, the arrow, the lead-tipped cudgel. But the streets of Vanai didn't notice her.

Everywhere, the final preparations for the war were being made. Merchants nailed their windows closed. Wagons clogged the streets as families who had chosen not to flee to the countryside changed their minds and left and others that had gone changed their minds and returned. Criers in the service of the prince announced the improbable thousand men on the march now from their new allies, and the old Timzinae men by the quayside laughed and said they'd all be better off Antean than married to Maccia. Press gangs scattered people before them like wolves snapping at hens. And in the Old Quarter, the tall, dark, richly carved doors of Master Will's shop were flung wide. The street was jammed with carts and wagons, mules and horses and oxen. The caravan was forming in the square, and Cithrin made her way through the press of the crowd toward the wide, leather-capped form of Master Will.

"Sir," she said in a soft, low voice. Master Will didn't answer, and so uncertainly she tugged at his sleeve.

"What?" the old man said.

"My name's Tag, sir. I've come to drive Magister Imaniel's cart."

Master Will's eyes went wide for a moment and he glanced around to see if they'd been heard. Cithrin cursed silently. Not Magister Imaniel's cart. The bank didn't have a cart. She was driving the wool cart. It was her first mistake. Master Will coughed and took her by the shoulder.

"You're late, boy. I thought you might not come."

"Sorry, sir."

"For God's sake, child, try not to talk."

He led her quickly through the press to a deep, narrow cart. The weathered wood planks looked sturdy enough, and a canvas tarp over the top would keep the rain off the bolts of tight-packed grey cloth. The axles were thick iron, and the wheels bound with steel. It looked to Cithrin like obviously more of a wagon than mere cloth would need. The two mules in harness hardly seemed enough to pull a thing that big. Surely, *surely* they could all see through the sham. The prince's guards hardly needed to glance at her to understand everything. Her gut tightened harder, and she thanked the angels she hadn't been able to eat that morning. She didn't know how well her false whiskers would survive vomiting. Master Will leaned close to her, his lips brushing against her ear.

"The first two layers are wool," he said. "Everything beneath that's in sealed boxes and casks. If the tarp fails and things get wet, just let them stew."

"The books—" she muttered.

"The books are in enough sheepskin and wax you could drive this bastard into the sea. Don't worry about them. Don't think about what you're hauling. And do not under any circumstances dig down and have a look."

She felt a passing annoyance. Did he think she was stupid?

"You can sleep on top," Master Will continued. "No one will think it odd. Do what the caravan master says, keep the mules healthy and fed, and keep to yourself as much as you can."

"Yes, sir," she said.

"Right, then," the old man said. He stood back and clapped her on the shoulder. His smile was forced and mirthless. "Good luck."

He turned and walked back toward his shop. Cithrin had

the powerful urge to call after him. This couldn't be all there was. There must be something else she was supposed to do, some preparation or advice she should have. She swallowed, hunched forward, then walked around the cart. The mules met her eyes incuriously. They, at least, weren't frightened.

"I'm Tag," she said into their long, soft ears. And then, whispering, "I'm really Cithrin." She wished she knew their names.

She didn't catch sight of the soldiers until she'd climbed up to the driver's bench. Men and women in hard leather, swords at their sides. They were Firstblood, apart from one Tralgu with rings in his ears and a huge bow slung on his shoulder. The captain of the troop, the Tralgu, and an older man in long robes and tightly knotted hair were talking animatedly with the Timzinae caravan master. Cithrin gripped the reins, her knuckles aching and bloodless. The captain nodded toward her, and the caravan master shrugged. She watched in horror as the three soldiers came toward her. She had to run. She was going to be killed.

"Boy!" the captain said, his pale eyes on her. He was a hard-faced man younger than Magister Imaniel and older than Besel. He wore his sandy hair too short for Antean style, too long for the Free Cities. He leaned forward, his eyebrows rising. "Boy? You hear me?"

Cithrin nodded.

"You aren't dim, are you? I didn't sign on to guard boys who are likely to wander off on their own."

"No," Cithrin croaked. She coughed, careful to keep her voice husky and low. "No, sir."

"Right, then," the captain said. "You're driving this cart?"

Cithrin nodded.

"Well. Good. You're the last to come, so you missed the

introductions before. I'll keep it brief. I'm Captain Wester. This is Yardem. He's my second. And that's our cunning man, Master Kit. We're guard on this 'van, and I'd be obliged if you did whatever we said, whenever we said it. We'll get you through safe to Carse."

Cithrin nodded again. The captain mirrored her, clearly not yet convinced she wasn't dim.

"Right," he said, turning away. "Let's get going."

"Anything you say, sir," the Tralgu said in a deep, gravelly voice.

The captain and the Tralgu turned and walked back toward the caravan master, their voices quickly lost in the cacophony of the street. The cunning man, Master Kit, stepped closer. He was older, his hair more grey than black. His face was long and olive-complected. His smile was surprisingly warm.

"Are you all right, son?" he asked.

"Nervous," Cithrin said.

"First time driving on a 'van?"

Cithrin nodded. She felt like an idiot, nodding all the time like a mute in the streets. The cunning man's smile was reassuring and gentle as a priest's.

"I suspect you'll find the boredom's the worst thing. After the third day seeing just the cart in front of you, the view may get a bit dull."

Cithrin smiled and almost meant it.

"What's your name?" the cunning man asked.

"Tag," she said.

He blinked, and she thought his smile lost a degree of warmth. She bent her head forward, her hair almost covering her eyes, and her heart began to race. Master Kit only sneezed and shook his head. When he spoke, his voice was still comforting as soft flannel.

"Welcome to the 'van, Tag."

She nodded again, and the cunning man walked away. Her heart slowed to a more human pace. She swallowed, shut her eyes, and willed her shoulders and neck to relax. She hadn't been found out. It would be fine.

The wagons started out within the hour, a great wide feed wagon lumbering along at the head, then a covered wagon that clanked loud enough Cithrin could hear it from her perch three back. The Timzinae caravan master rode back and forth on a huge white mare, tapping wagons and drivers and beasts with a long, flexible rod, half stick and half whip. When he came to her, she shook the reins and called out to the mules the way Besel had taught her back when he'd been alive and smiling and flirting with the poor ward of the bank. The mules started forward, and the caravan master shouted at her angrily.

"Not so fast, boy! You're not in a damned race here!"

"Sorry," Cithrin said, pulling back. One of the mules snorted and looked back at her. She had a hard time not imagining annoyance in the slant of its ears. She moved them forward again more slowly. The caravan master shook his head and cantered back to the next wagon. Cithrin held the reins in a fierce grip, but there was nothing she had to do. The mules knew their work, following the cart before them. Slowly, with many shouts and imprecations, the caravan took form. They moved from the wide streets of the Old Quarter, past the canals that led down to the river, across the Patron's Bridge, the prince's palace high above them.

Vanai, the city of her childhood, slipped past her. There was the road that led to the market where Cam had bought her honey bread for her birthday. Here, the stall where an apprentice cobbler had stolen a kiss from her and been whipped by Magister Imaniel for his trouble. She'd forgotten that until now. They passed the tutor's house where she'd gone to study numbers and letters when she was just a girl. Somewhere in the city were the graves of her mother and father. She had never visited the corpses, and she regretted it now.

When she came back, she told herself. When the war was over and the world safe, she'd come back and see where her family was buried.

Too soon, the city wall loomed up before them, pale stone as high as two men standing. The gate was open, but the traffic on the road slowed them. The mules seemed to expect it and stood patiently as the caravan master rode to the front to clear the way, whipping at whatever was in the 'van's path. High on the tower gate, a man stood in the bright armor of the prince's guard. For a sickening moment, Cithrin thought it was the same grinning face that had looked up at her the night Besel died. When the guard called out, it was to the captain.

"You're a coward, Wester!"

Cithrin caught her breath, shocked by the casual insult.

"Die of the pox, Dossen," the captain sang back, grinning, so perhaps the two were friends. The idea made her like Captain Wester less. The prince's guard didn't stop them, at least. The carts rolled and bumped and creaked their way out of the city and onto the road where they left the stone cobbles for the wide green of dragon's jade. Carse lay far to the north and west, but the road here tracked south, echoing the distant curve of the sea. A few other carts passed, traveling in toward the city. The low hills were covered with trees in the glory of their autumn leaves; red and yellow and gold. When the sun struck them at the proper angle, it looked like fire. Cithrin hunched on her bench, her legs growing colder, her hands stiff.

Over the long, slow miles her anxiety faded, lulled by the rumble and rocking of the cart. She could almost forget who she was, what was behind her, and what was in the cart with her. As long as the world was her, the mules, the cart before and the trees beside, it was almost like being alone. The sun tracked lower, shining into her eyes until she was as good as blind. The caravan master's call slowed the carts, then stopped them. The Timzinae rode down the line of carts as he had in Vanai, pointing each of them to a place in a low, open field. The camp. Cithrin's place, thankfully, was near the road where she didn't need to do anything fancy. She turned the mules, brought the cart where she'd been told, and then climbed down to the earth. She unhitched the mules and led them to a creek where they stuck their heads down to the water and kept them there so long she started to grow nervous. Would a mule drink enough to make itself sick? Should she try to stop them? But the other animals were doing the same. She watched what the other carters did and tried not to stand out.

Night came quickly and cold. By the time she'd fed her animals, scrubbed them, and set them in the 'van's makeshift corral, a mist had risen. The caravan master had set up a fire, and the smell of smoke and grilling fish brought Cithrin's stomach suddenly and painfully to life. She joined the carters laughing and talking in the line for food. She kept her head bowed, her eyes downcast. When anyone tried to bring her into the conversation, she grunted or spoke in monosyllables. The 'van's cook was a short Timzinae woman so fat the chitin of her scales seemed ready to pop free of her sausage-shaped arms. When Cithrin reached the front of the line, the cook handed her a tin plate with a thin strip of pale trout-flesh, a heaping spoonful of beans, and a crust of brown bread. Cithrin nodded in a mime of gratitude and went to sit at the fire. The damp soaked her leggings and jacket, but she didn't dare move in nearer to the warmth. Better to keep to the back.

As they ate, the caravan master pulled a low stool out from his own cart and stood on it, reading from a holy book by the light of the fire. Cithrin listened with only half her attention. Magister Imaniel was a religious too, or else thought it wise to appear so. Cithrin had heard the scriptures many times without ever finding God and angels particularly moving.

Quietly, she put down plate and knife and went out to the creek. How to visit the latrine without giving herself away had been a haunting fear, and Magister Imaniel's dismissive answers—*All men squat to shit*—hadn't reassured her. Alone in the mist and darkness, leggings around her ankles and codpiece stuffing in hand, she felt relief not only in her flesh. Once. She'd gotten away with it once. Now if she could only keep the charade up for the weeks to Carse.

Coming back to the fire, she saw a man sitting beside her plate. One of the guards, but thankfully not the captain or his Tralgu second. Cithrin took her seat again and the guard nodded to her and smiled. She hoped he wouldn't talk.

"Quite the talker, our 'van master," the guard said. "He projects well. Would have made a good actor, except there aren't many good Timzinae roles. Orman in the Fire Cycle, but that's about it."

Cithrin nodded and took a bite of cold beans.

"Sandr," the guard said. "That's me. My name's Sandr."

"Tag," Cithrin said, hoping that between mumbling and her full mouth, she'd sound enough like a man.

"Good meetin' you, Tag," Sandr said. He shifted in the darkness, hauling out a leather skin. "Drink?"

Cithrin shrugged the way she imagined a carter might, and Sandr grinned and popped the stopper free. Cithrin had drunk wine in temple and during festival meals, but always with water, and never very much. The liquid that poured into her mouth now was a different thing. It bit at the softest parts of her lips and tongue, slid down her throat, and left her feeling as if she'd been cleaned. The warmth that spread through her chest was like a blush.

"Good, isn't it?" Sandr said. "I borrowed it from Master Kit. He won't mind."

Cithrin took another drink then reluctantly handed it back. Sandr drank as the caravan master reached the end of his reading, and half a dozen voices rose up in the closing rite. The moon seemed soft, the mist scattering its light. To her surprise, the wine was untying the knot in her stomach. Not much, but enough that she could feel it. The warmth in her chest was in her belly now too. She wondered how much of the skin she'd have to down to bring the feeling to her shoulders and neck.

She couldn't be stupid, though. She couldn't get herself drunk. Someone shouted out Sandr's name and the guard leapt to his feet. He didn't pick up the skin.

"Over here, sir," Sandr said, walking in toward the fire. Wester and his Tralgu were gathering up their soldiers. Cithrin looked out into the grey and shifting darkness, in toward the fire, and then carefully, casually scooped up the wineskin, tucking it into her jacket.

She walked back to her cart, avoiding the others as she went. Someone was singing, and another voice lifted to join the song. A night bird called out. Cithrin clambered up. Dew was forming on the wool cloth, tiny droplets catching the glow of the moon. She wondered whether she ought to lower the tarp, but it was dark, and she didn't particularly want to. Instead, she snuggled into among the bolts, snuck the wineskin out of her jacket, and had just one more drink. A small one and only one.

She had to be careful.

Dawson Kalliam
Baron of Osterling Fells

The sword's arc changed at the last second, the steel blade angling up toward his face. Had Dawson been as young as his opponent, the move would have had its intended effect: he would have flinched back from it, turned, and left himself open. But he had been dueling for too many years. He shifted his own blade an inch to the side and pushed the unexpected thrust a hair's breadth wide of its mark.

Feldin Maas, Baron of Ebbinbaugh and Dawson's opponent in this little battle as in everything, spat on the ground and grinned.

The original slight had been a small one. Despite Dawson having a greater landholding, Maas had demanded to be served before him at the king's court three days before on the strength of having been named Warden the Southern Reach. Dawson had explained Maas's mistake. Maas had made an insult of his concession. The pair of them had come near blows there in the great hall. And so the question was to be resolved here, in the fashion of old.

The dueling yard was a dry, dusty ground long enough for jousting and narrow enough for a meeting like this one: short blades and dueling leathers. To one side, the great walls and towers of the Kingspire rose up, taller than trees. To the other, the Division a thousand feet deep that split the city and gave the Severed Throne its name.

They disengaged and resumed the slow, tense circling. Dawson's right arm was so tired it felt as if it was burning, but the tip of his sword didn't waver. It was a point of pride that after thirty years on the field of honor, he was still as strong as the first day he'd stepped in. The younger man's blade was slightly less steady, his form apparently more careless. It was a physical lie, and Dawson knew better than to believe it.

Their leather-soled boots hushed against the earth. Feldin thrust. Dawson parried, counterthrust, and now Feldin stepped back. The grin was less certain, but Dawson didn't let himself feel pleasure. Not until the bastard wore a Kalliam scar. Feldin Maas swung low and hard, twisting the blade fast from the wrist. Dawson parried, feinted to the right and attacked to the left. His form was perfect, but his enemy had already shifted away. They were both too experienced on the battlefield for the old tricks to carry much effect.

Something unexpected was called for.

In a true battle, Dawson's thrust would have been suicidal. It left him open, off balance, overextended. It was artless, and so it had the effect he'd intended. Feldin leaped back, but too slowly. The resistance of metal cutting skin translated through Dawson's blade.

"Blood!" Dawson called.

In the space of a heartbeat, Dawson saw Feldin's expression go from surprise to rage, from rage to calculation, and from calculation to a cool, ironic mask. For an instant, he still prepared a counterattack. There would be no parrying it. Young Feldin was tempted, Dawson realized. Honor, witnesses, and rule of law aside, Feldin Maas had been tempted to kill him. It made the victory taste all that much better. Feldin stepped back, put his hand to his ribs, and lifted bloodied fingers. The physicians ran forward to assess the damage. Dawson sheathed his sword.

"Well played, old man," Feldin said as they stripped off his shirt. "Using my honor as your armor? That was almost a compliment. You wagered your life on my gentle instincts."

"More your fear of breaking form."

A dangerous glint came to the younger man's eyes.

"Here, we've just finished one duel," the chief physician said. "Let's not have another."

Dawson drew his dagger in salute. Feldin pushed the servants aside and drew his own. The blood pouring down his side was a good sign. This newest scar would be deep. Dawson sheathed his dagger, turned, and left the dueling ground behind him, his honor intact.

Camnipol. The divided city, and seat of the Severed Throne.

From the time of dragons, it had been the seat of First-blood power in the world. In the dim, burned ages after the great war had brought the former lords of the world low and freed the slave races, Camnipol had been the beacon of light. Black and gold and proud upon her hill, the city had called home the scattered Firstblood. Fortunes might have waxed and waned through the centuries, but the city stood eternal, split by the Division and held by the might of the Kingspire, now the home of King Simeon and the boy prince Aster.

The Silver Bridge spanned the Division from the Kingspire to the noble quarter that topped the western face. The ancient stone rested on a span of dragon's jade no thicker than a hand's width, and permanent as the sun or the sea. Dawson rode in a small horse-drawn carriage, eschewing the newer tradition of being pulled by slaves. The wheels rattled and flocks of pigeons flogged the air below him. He leaned out his window, looking down through the strata of ruins and stone that made the Division's walls. He'd heard it said that the lowest of the ancient buildings, down in the huge midden at the great canyon's base, were older than the dragons themselves. Camnipol, the eternal city. His city, at the heart of his nation and his race. Apart from his family, Dawson loved nothing better.

And then he had crossed the great span of air, and the driver turned into his narrow private square. His mansion rose up, its clean, sweeping lines elegant free of the gaudy filigree with which upstarts like Feldin Maas, Alan Klin, and Curtin Issandrian tarted up their homes. His home was classic and elegant, and it looked out over the void to the Kingspire and the wide plain beyond it, the noblest house in the city, barring perhaps Lord Bannien of Estinford's estate.

His servants brought out the steps, and Dawson waved away the offered hands as he always did. It was their duty to offer, and his dignity required that he refuse. The ritual was the important thing. The door slave, an old Tralgu with light brown skin and silver hair at the tips of his ears, stood by the entryway. A silver chain bound him to the black marble column.

"Welcome home, my lord," the slave said. "A letter has come from your son."

"Which son?"

"Jorey, my lord."

Dawson felt a twist in his gut. Had it been from one of his other children, he could have read the news with unalloyed pleasure, but a letter from Jorey was a letter from the loathed Vanai campaign. With trepidation, he held out his hand. The door slave turned his head toward the door.

"Your lady wife has it, my lord."

The interior of the mansion was dark tapestry and bright crystal. His dogs bounded down the stairway yipping with excitement; five wolfhounds with shining grey fur and teeth of ivory. Dawson scratched their ears, patted their sides, and walked back to the solarium and his wife.

The glass room was a consolation he gave his Clara. It spoiled the lines of the building on the north side, but she could cultivate the pansies and violets that grew in the hills of Osterling. The reminder of home made her more nearly content during the seasons in Camnipol, and she kept the house smelling of violets all through the winter. She sat now in a deep chair, a small desk at her side, the tables of dark blooms arrayed around her like soldiers on parade. She looked up at the sound of his steps and smiled.

Clara had always been perfect. If the years had taken some of the rose from her cheeks, if her black hair was shot with white, he could still see the girl she had been. There had been rarer beauties and sharper poets when Dawson's father had chosen the womb that would carry his grand-children. But instead he had picked Clara, and it had taken Dawson no time at all to appreciate the wisdom of that choice. She was good at heart. She might have been a para-gon in all other things, but if she had not been good, those other virtues would have turned to ash. Dawson leaned down, kissing her lips as he always did. It was a ritual like refusing the footman's help and scratching the hounds' ears. It gave life meaning.

"We've heard from Jorey?" he said.

"Yes," she said. "He's fine. He's having a wonderful time in the field. His captain is Adria Klin's boy Alan. He says they're getting along quite nicely."

Dawson leaned against a flower table, arms crossed. The twinge in his belly grew worse. Klin. Another of Feldin

Maas's cabal. It had been like a bone in the throat when the king had placed Jorey under the man, and it still brought a little taste of anger thinking of it.

"Oh, and he says he's serving with Geder Palliako, but that can't be right, can it? Isn't that the strange little pudgy man with the enthusiasm for maps and comic rhyme?"

"You're thinking of Lerer Palliako. Geder's his son."

"Oh," Clara said with a wave of her hand. "That makes much more sense, because I couldn't see him going out in the field again at his age. I think we're all well beyond that. And then Jorey also wrote a long passage about horses and plums that's clearly some sort of coded message for you that I couldn't make head or tail of."

After a moment's rooting through the folds of her dress, she held out the folded paper.

"Did you win your little fight?" she asked.

"I did."

"And did that awful man apologize?"

"Better than that, dear. He lost."

Jorey's script dotted the pages like well-regulated bird scratches, neat and sloppy at the same time. Dawson skimmed through the opening paragraphs. A few bluff comments about the rigors of the march, an arch comment about Alan Klin that Clara had either not seen or chosen to misunderstand, a brief passage about the Palliako boy who was apparently something of the company joke. And then the important part. He read it carefully, parsing each phrase, picking out the words he and his son had chosen to represent certain key players and strategems. *There aren't any windfall plums this year.* Meaning Sir Klin was not the client of Lord Ternigan. Klin took his orders because Lord Ternigan was marshal of the army and not through any particular political alliance. That was useful information to know. *My own horse is in real danger of developing a limp on his right side.* Horse, not mount. Limp, not lameness. Right side, not left. So Klin's company was favored to remain in conquered Vanai, and Klin himself the likely temporary governor. Ternigan wasn't planning to take rule of the city on himself. All the more important, then, that the army stall.

Only *stall*, of course. Not *fail*. Never fail. Everything would be in place, if Ternigan's forces could just withhold victory for a season. That difference between postponement and failure kept his private negotiations with Maccia from crossing the line into treason. As long as the conquest of Vanai was delayed until the spring season, there would be time to get Klin recalled to the court and Jorey put in his place. Governing Vanai would be Jorey's first step up within the court, and it would take some prestige away from Maas and Klin and their type.

Dawson had worked through the most obscure channels he could, had sent letters to agents in Stollbourne who sent letters to merchants in Birancour who had business in Maccia. Discretion was critical, but he had managed it. Six hundred soldiers would reinforce the free city of Vanai until such time as it was convenient that they not. In spring, they would retreat, Vanai would fall, and by summer Dawson would be drinking with King Simeon and laughing together at his cleverness.

"My lord?"

The servant stood in the solarium's doorway, bowing his apology. Dawson folded the letter and handed it back to Clara.

"What is it?"

"A visitor, sir. Baron Maas and his wife."

Dawson snorted, but Clara stood and adjusted her sleeves.

Her face took on an almost serene calm, and she smiled at him.

"Now love," she said. "You've had your play at war. Don't begrudge us our play at peace."

Objections sprang to mind like dogs after a fox: dueling wasn't a game, it was honor; Maas had earned the scar and the humiliation that went with it; receiving him now was empty etiquette, and on and on. Clara hoisted an eyebrow and canted her head to the side. All his bluster drained away. He laughed.

"My love," he said, "you civilize me."

"Oh not that, surely," she said. "Now come along and say something pleasant."

The receiving room swam in tapestry. Clothwork images of the Last Battle with the dragon's wings worked in silver thread and Drakis Stormcrow in gold. Sunlight spilled through a wide window of colored glass worked in the heraldic gryphon-and-axe of Kalliam. The furnishings were among the most elegant in the house. Feldin Maas stood by the door as if at attention. His dark-haired, sharp-faced wife flowed forward as Dawson and Clara entered the room.

"Cousin!" she said, taking Clara's hands. "I am so happy to see you."

"Yes, Phelia," Clara said. "I'm sorry that we only ever seem to visit one another when our boys have been misbehaving."

"Osterling," Feldin Maas said, using Dawson's more formal title.

"Ebbinbaugh," Dawson replied, bowing. Feldin retuned the bow with a stiffness that said the pain of his new cut still bothered him.

"Oh stop it, both of you," Clara said at the same moment Feldin's wife said, "Sit down and have some wine."

The men did as they were told. After a few minutes of chatter, Feldin leaned over, speaking low.

"I hadn't heard whether you were joining the king's tourney."

"Of course I am. Why wouldn't I?"

"I thought you might be leaving some glory for your sons, old friend," Feldin said. "That's all. No offense intended. I don't think I can afford much more of your offense. At least not until I've healed."

"Perhaps next time we should duel with words. Insulting couplets at ten paces."

"Oh, blades will be fine. Your couplets do permanent damage. People still call Sir Lauren the Rabbit Knight because of you."

"Me? No. I could never have done it without his teeth and that ridiculous helmet of his. I know they were supposed to be wings, but by God they looked like ears to me," Dawson said and took a drink. "You acquitted yourself well today, my boy. Not as well as I did, but you're a fighter and no doubt."

Clara rewarded him with a smile. She was right; it wasn't so hard being magnanimous. There was even a kind of warmth in it. The wine was rich, and the servants brought in a plate of dry cheese and pickled sausages. Clara and her cousin gossiped and touched each other's arms and hands at every chance, like children flirting. It was much the same thing, he supposed. First insult, then violence, and reassurance afterward. It was women like theirs who kept the kingdom from bursting apart in a war of ego and manliness.

"We are lucky men," Dawson said, "to have wives like these."

Feldin Maas startled, considered the two women deep in conversation about the difficulty of maintaining households in Camnipol and their family holdings both, and gave a rough half-smile.

"I suppose we are," he said. "How long are you staying in Camnipol?"

"Until the tourney, and then another week or two. I want to get home again before the snows."

"Yes. Nothing like the Kingspire in winter for catching every breath of wind off the plain. It's like his majesty had a sailmaker for an architect. I've heard the king's thinking of touring the reaches just so he can spend some time in a warm house."

"It's the hunting," Dawson said. "Ever since we were boys, he's loved the winter hunts in the reaches."

"Still, he's getting old for it, don't you think?"

"No. I don't."

"I bow to your opinion," Feldin said, but his smile was thin and smug. Dawson felt a tug of anger, and Clara must have seen it. Part of peacekeeping, it appeared, was to know how to stop playing at friends before the illusion faded. She called for the servants, gathered a gift of violets for her cousin, and they walked together to the entry hall to say their farewells. Just before he turned away, Feldin Maas frowned and raised a finger.

"I forget, my lord. Do you have family in the Free Cities?"

"No," Dawson said. "Well, I think Clara has some obscure relations in Gilea."

"Through marriage," Clara said. "Not blood."

"Nothing in Maccia, then. That's good," Feldin Maas said.

Dawson's spine stiffened.

"Maccia? No," he said. "Why? What's in Maccia."

"Apparently the Grand Doge there has decided to throw in with Vanai against his majesty. 'Unity in the face of aggression' or some such."

Feldin knew about Vanai's reinforcements. And if he knew, so did Sir Alan Klin. Did they know whose influence had brought Vanai its new allies, or did they only suspect? They must at least suspect, or Feldin wouldn't have brought it up. Dawson smiled the way he hoped he would have if he'd had no stake in the matter.

"Unity among the Free Cities? That seems unlikely," he said. "Probably just rumor."

"Yes," Feldin Maas said. "Yes, I'm sure you're right."

The dog-faced, small-cocked, hypocrite bastard son of a weasel and a whore bowed and escorted his wife from the house. When Dawson didn't move, Clara took his hand.

"Are you well, dear? You look pained."

"Excuse me," he said.

Once in his library, he locked the doors, lit the candles, and pulled his maps from their shelves. He'd marked the paths from Maccia to Vanai and the roads the army was sure to take. He measured and made his calculations, fury rising like waves whipped by a storm. He'd been betrayed. Somewhere along the chain of communications, somebody had said something, and his plans had been tipped to the ground. He had overreached, and it left him exposed. He'd been outplayed. By Feldin Maas. One of the dogs whined and scratched at the door until Dawson unlocked it and let it in.

The dog climbed onto the couch, wrapping its haunches in close and looking up at Dawson with anxious eyes. The Baron of Osterling Fells sank down beside the beast and scratched its ears. The dog whined again, pressing its head up into Dawson's palm. A moment later, Clara appeared in the doorway, her arms folded, her eyes as anxious as the hound's.

"Something's gone wrong?"

"A bit, yes."

"Does it put Jorey in danger?" she asked.

"I don't know."

"Does it put us in danger?"

Dawson didn't reply because the answer was *yes,* and he couldn't bring himself to lie.

Geder

A mist lay on the valley, white in the morning sun. The banners of the houses of Antea hung limp and damp, their colors darkened and greyed by the thick air. The world smelled of trampled mud and the cold. Geder's horse shook its head and grunted. He reached forward a gauntleted hand and patted the beast's shoulder.

His armor had been his father's once, the bright steel of the plate dimmed a little now where the smith had bent it to more nearly fit Geder's back. The straps pinched even through the brigandine. The march had been a long, weary foretaste of hell. The pace had never been fast, but it was relentless. From that first hungover morning, he had ridden and walked for four days without more than two short hours' rest at a time. In the night, he draped a blanket across his shoulders and shivered against the cold. During the day, he sweated. The army passed down the wide green dragon's road, the tramp of feet against the jade becoming first an annoyance, then a music, then an odd species of silence, before cycling around to annoyance again. With only one horse, he had to spend a fair part of each day walking. A richer man would have brought two or three, even four mounts on the campaign. And plate that hadn't seen decades of use before he was born. And a tent that kept out the cold. And, just perhaps, a little respect and dignity.

The other titled nobles rode in groups or with their personal retinue. Geder shared their place at the head of the column, but significantly at the rear of the grouping. The supply carts came just behind him, and the infantry and camp followers behind them, though there weren't many camp followers these days. It said something when a march was too much trouble to be worth a whore's time.

The order to stop had come last evening an hour before sunset. Geder's squire had erected his little tent, brought a tin plate of lentils and cheese, and curled up into a small Dartinae ball just outside Geder's tent flap. Geder had crawled onto his cot, pressed his eyes shut, and prayed for sleep. His dreams had all been about marching. With the first light of dawn, the new order had come: prepare.

All through his boyhood, he had imagined this day. His first real battle. He'd imagined the wind of the charge, the heat and speed of the horse beneath him, the fierce cries of battle in his throat. He hadn't thought about the numbing hours sitting in the saddle, his armor cooling against him, while the infantry formed, shifted, and re-formed. The noble line of knights, sword and lance at the ready, was a clump of men laughing, trading dirty jokes, and complaining that the food was either sparse or spoiled. It felt less like the noble proving ground of war than the ninth day of an eight-day hunt. Geder's spine was a single burning ache from his ass to the base of his skull. His thighs were chapped raw, his jaw popped every time he yawned, and his mouth tasted like sour cheese. His squire stood by his side, Geder's battle lance in his hands, shield slung across his back, and a wary expression on his hairless face.

"Palliako!"

Geder shifted. Sir Alan Klin rode a huge black charger, the steel of its barding all enameled red. The man's armor glittered with dew and the silver worked into a dragon's wing design. He could have stepped out of an ancient war rhyme.

"My lord?" Geder said.

"You're with the charge on the west. The scouts report it as the mercenary forces Vanai's bought, so it should be the easiest fighting."

Geder frowned. That seemed wrong, but fatigue made it hard to think through. Mercenaries were professional fighters and veterans to a man. And that was where the fighting would be *easy*? Klin read his expression, leaned to the side, and spat.

"They aren't protecting their homes and wives," Klin said. "Just follow where Kalliam goes and try not to knock your horse into anyone. Knees get broken that way."

"I know that."

Klin's pale eyebrows rose.

"I mean...I mean I'll be careful, my lord."

Klin made a clicking sound, and his beautiful charger shook its head and turned. Geder's squire looked up at him. If there was any amusement in the Dartinae's glowing eyes, it was well hidden.

"Come on," Geder said. "Let's get in place."

The hell of it was, what Klin said might be true. Perhaps he was sending Geder and the youngest Sir Kalliam into the easiest part of the coming battle. A charge, a few sword strokes to one side and another, and the paid forces call surrender before anyone got too badly hurt. It would be a mark of Klin's ability if he could have all his knights alive, and increase his own glory by keeping the fiercest fights for himself. Anything to impress Lord Ternigan and stand out from the marshal's other captains. Or perhaps Klin wanted Geder to die in the battle. Geder thought he might be ready to die if it meant not riding anymore.

Jorey Kalliam sat high on his saddle, speaking to his bannerman. His plate was simple steel, unadorned and elegant. Six other knights were with him, their squires all close and ready. Kalliam nodded solemnly to Geder and he returned the salute.

"Come close," he called. "All of you. To me."

The knights shifted their mounts in. Sir Makiyos of Ainsbaugh. Sozlu Veren and his twin brother Sesil. Darius Sokak, the Count of Hiren. Fallon Broot, Baron of Suderling Heights, and his son Daved. All in all, a pretty sad bunch. He could see from their own expressions that they'd drawn similar conclusions from his arrival.

"The valley narrows about half a league from here," Kalliam said. "The Vanai are there, and they're entrenched. The scouts are saying the banners here on the western edge belong to a mercenary company under a Captain Karol Dannian."

"How many men's he got?"

"Two hundred, but mostly sword-and-bows," Kalliam said.

"Brilliant," Fallon Broot said, stroking the mustache that drooped down past his weak chin. "That should leave enough for all of us to have our turn."

Geder couldn't tell if it was meant as a joke.

"Our work," Kalliam said, "is to hold tight to the edge of the valley. The main thrust will be on the eastern end where Vanai's forces are thickest. Lord Ternigan has all his own knights and half of ours. All we need is to be sure no one flanks them. Sir Klin is giving us three dozen bows and twice as many swords. I've sent the bows ahead. At the signal, they'll start the attack and try to draw out their cavalry. When we hear the charge, we'll go in with the swords following."

"Why are they here?" Geder asked. "I mean, if I were them, I'd try to be behind a wall someplace. Make it a siege."

"Can't hire mercenaries for a siege," one of the Sir Verens said, contempt for the question dripping from his words. "They take contract for a season, and Vanai can't raise money to renew."

"The city's less than an hour's ride from here," Kalliam said, "and there's no place more defensible until you reach it. If they hope to keep us from reaching Vanai, this is the first defense and the last."

A distant horn sang. Two rising notes and one falling. Geder's heart started beating a little faster. Kalliam smiled, but his eyes were cold.

"My lords," Kalliam said. "I believe that's the first call. If you have any last business, it's too late for it now."

The mist hadn't vanished, but enough had burned off that the landscape was clear before them. To Geder's unpracticed eye, it looked like any of the other small valleys they'd passed on their way through the low, rolling hills north of the Free Cities. The enemy was a dark, crawling line like ants from a hill. The other knights' squires began the final preparation, strapping shield to arms, handing up the steel-tipped lances. Geder suffered the same. The Dartinae finished with him, then nodded and prepared his own arms for the battle; light leather and a long, wicked knife. And not half a league away, some other squire or low soldier was cleaning another knife just as wicked to push through Geder's throat if the chance came. The horn sang again. Not the charge, but the warning of it.

"Good luck, my lord," his squire said. Geder nodded awkwardly in his helm, turned his mount to follow the others, and started down toward the battle. His little gelding whickered nervously. The ants grew larger, and the enemy banners grew clear. He saw where Kalliam's archers were set, hiding behind blinds of wood and leather. Kalliam raised his shield, and the knights stopped. Geder tried to twist back, to see the swordsmen behind them, but his armor forbade it. He squeezed his eyes closed. It was just like a tourney. Joust first, then a little melee. Even a rich mercenary company wasn't likely to have many heavy cavalry. He'd be fine. He needed to piss.

The horns blew the martial doubled note of the charge. Kalliam and the other men shouted and spurred their mounts. Geder did the same, and the tired old gelding that had carried him for days and weeks became a beast made of wind. He felt himself shouting, but the world was a single roar. The archers' blinds flickered by him and were gone, and then the enemy was there; not knights or heavy cavalry, but pikemen bringing their great spears to bear. Sir Makiyos barreled into the line, smashing it, and Geder angled his own attack to take advantage of the chaos.

A horse was screaming. Geder's lance struck a pikeman, the blow wrenching his shoulder, and then he was past the line and into the melee. He dropped his lance, drew his sword, and started hewing away at whatever came close. To his right, one of the Veren twins was being pulled from his horse by half a dozen mercenary swordsmen. Geder yanked his mount toward the falling knight, but then his own swordsmen appeared, pouring through the broken line. He saw his squire loping along, head low and knife at the ready, but there were no men in plate to knock over and let his Dartinae finish. The mass of fighting men pushed to the south. Geder turned again, ready to find someone, but the mercenaries seemed reluctant to press the attack.

He didn't see where the bolt came from. One moment, he was scanning the battle for a likely target, the next a small tree had taken root in his leg, the thick black wood punching through the plate and into the meat of his thigh. Geder dropped his sword and screamed, scrabbling at the bolt in agony. Something hit his shield hard enough to push him back. A drumbeat rolled from the south, low and deep as thunder. The gelding shifted unexpectedly, and Geder felt himself starting to slide out of his saddle. The hand that steadied him was Jorey Kalliam's.

"Where did you come from?" Geder asked.

Kalliam didn't answer. There was blood on the man's face and spattered across his sheild, but he didn't seem injured. His eyes were fixed on the battle, or something beyond it, and his expression was carved from ice. Trying to put aside his pain, Geder followed the boy's gaze. There, dancing above the fray, new banners were flying. The five blue circles of Maccia.

"Never mind you," Geder squeaked. "Where did *they* come from?"

"Can you ride?"

Geder looked down. His gelding's pale side was red with blood, and the flow coming from the bolt in his leg looked wide as a river. A wave of dizziness made him clutch at his saddle. Men could die of leg wounds like that. He was sure he'd heard of men dying from leg wounds. Was he about to die, then?

"Palliako!"

He looked up. The world seemed to swim a little. Jorey Kalliam glanced from the line of battle now surging back toward them to Geder's face.

"I'm hurt," Geder said.

"You are a knight of the empire," Kalliam said, and the power in his voice wasn't anger. "Can you ride, sir?"

Geder felt some part of the other man's strength come into him. The world steadied and Geder steadied with it.

"I can...I can ride."

"Then go. Find Lord Ternigan. Tell him the Maccian banners are flying on the west end of the line. Tell him we need help."

"I will," he said and picked up his reins. Kalliam's mount shifted toward the fight, snorting, but the young knight paused.

"Palliakio! Go directly to Lord Ternigan. *Directly.*"

"Sir?"

"Not to Klin."

Their eyes met for a moment, and an understanding passed between them. Kalliam didn't trust their captain any more than he did. Relief and gratitude surged in Geder's heart, and then surprise at the feelings.

"I understand," he said. "I'll bring help."

Kalliam nodded, turned, and charged for the melee. Geder spurred his horse, riding east across the field. He struggled to unstrap his shield, gauntleted fingers and jouncing horse making the leather and buckles unwieldy. He managed to free his arm at last, and leaned forward, urging the beast faster. An hour ago, the valley had been grass and autumn wildflowers. Now it was churned mud and the roar of brawling men.

Geder squinted. The mist was gone now, but the wet banners were still darkened and clinging to their poles. He had to find the gold and crimson of House Ternigan. He had to do it now. All around him, men lay in the muck, dead or wounded. The screams of soldiers and horses cut through the air. But the banner of the king's marshal was nowhere.

Geder shouted curses, shifting his gaze one way then the other. He felt cold. His bleeding leg was heavy, blood soaking his brigandine as quickly as the strength left his flesh. Every minute that passed made it less likely Kalliam and the others would survive, and his vision was starting to dance gold and darkness around the edges. He tried to stand higher in his stirrups, but his injured leg couldn't support him. He drove his horse forward. There were the banners of Flor and Rivercourt, Masonhalm and Klin...

Klin. There, not fifty yards from where he sat, the banner of Sir Alan Klin flew wet and limp over a knot of fighting men. And there among them, the huge black warhorse with its red barding. Geder felt a tug. If it was a mistake, if Klin hadn't *meant* to send them to the slaughter, then help was there. Right there. But if it had been his intention, and Geder went to him now, Kalliam and the others were dead. He rode on. His leg was numb. His mouth was dry. There, the banners of Estinford, Corenhall, Dannick.

Ternigan.

He spurred his horse and the gelding leapt forward, running toward the knot of battle that swirled around the banner. He cursed Ternigan for leading the charge instead of hanging back to direct the battle from the rear. He cursed Sir Alan Klin for sending him and Kalliam into the enemy's trap. He cursed himself for having taken off his shield, and for having been wounded, and for not moving fast. An enemy swordsman lurched up out of the muck, and Geder rode him down. He smelled pine smoke. Something, somewhere was burning. The gelding was shaking under him, exhausted, trembling. He apologized silently to the beast and put spurs to it again.

He barreled into the fighting men like a stone thrown through a window. Swordsmen scattered around him, as many of them Antean as Vanai. Ten feet from the bannerman, Lord Ternigan stood high in his saddle, his sword shining in his hand, and soldiers five men deep keeping the enemy from reaching him.

"Lord Ternigan!" Geder shouted. "Ternigan!"

The roar of battle drowned him out. The marshal moved forward, in toward the line where the battle was thickest. A deep crimson rage rolled over Geder's vision. Kalliam and the others were fighting, dying, for this man. The least the bastard could do was pay some attention. He pushed his shuddering mount forward, pressing through the marshal's guard by raw determination. The battlefield narrowed to the one lord on his mount. The edges of Geder's vision contracted, like he was riding through a tunnel that led to the world. When he came within three yards, he shouted again.

"Maccia, my Lord Ternigan. Maccia's come on the west end, and they're killing us!"

This time, the marshal heard. His head snapped toward Geder, the high, noble forehead furrowed. Geder waved his arms and pointed to the west. *Don't look at me. Look at Maccia.*

"Who are you, sir?" Lord Ternigan said. His voice was as deep as a drum and echoed a bit. The world around it seemed quieter than it should have.

"Sir Geder Palliako. Jorey Kalliam's sent me. West end's not just mercenaries, my lord. Maccia's there. Can't hold them back. Kalliam…Kalliam sent me. You have to help him."

Ternigan shouted something over his shoulder, and the horns blared again, close by and powerful as being slapped in the jaw. Geder opened his eyes again, surprised to find that he'd closed them. People were moving around him. Knights rode past him, streaming toward the west. At least he thought that was west. Lord Ternigan was beside him, holding him hard by one elbow.

"Can you fight, sir?" the Marshal of the Kingdom of Antea asked him from a long way away.

"I can," Geder said, turning in his saddle. Slick with blood, his foot slipped free of the stirrup. Churned mud rose up, but the world went black before it reached him.

Marcus

For the midday meal, the caravan stopped at a clearing with a wide, slow brook. The thin boy, Mikel his name was, sat on the fallen log at Yardem's side. Like the Tralgu, he wore his leathers open at the throat. They both leaned forward over their plates of beans and sausage. The boy's shoulders were set as if bound by muscle they didn't possess and his movements had a slow, deliberate power that his frame didn't justify. Yardem tilted his head down a degree to look at Mikel. With the same gravity, the boy tilted his head up.

"Captain," Yardem said, his ears pressed back. "Make him stop."

Marcus, cross-legged on the ground, fought back a smile. "Stop what?"

"He's been doing this for days, sir."

"Acting like a soldier, you mean?"

"Acting like *me*," Yardem said.

Mikel made a low noise in his throat. Marcus had to cough to cover his laugh.

"We hired these people to act as guards," Marcus said. "They're acting as guards. Only natural they'd look to us for the details."

Yardem grunted and turned to face the boy. When the boy met his gaze, the Tralgu deliberately flicked an ear.

The forest around them now was oak and ash, the trees taller than ten men. A scrub fire had come through within the last few years, scorching the bark and burning down the underbrush without ever reaching the wide canopy above. Marcus could imagine smoke rising up through green summer leaves. Now the roadside litter was damp, the fallen leaves black with mold and on their way to becoming soil for the next year's weeds. Only the leaves on the road itself were dry. At the eastern end of the clearing, a wide-eyed stone Southling king in battle array and a six-pointed crown was half entombed in an oak. The old bark had swallowed half of the solemn face, roots tilted the wide stone pediment a degree. Vines draped the stone shoulders. Marcus didn't know what the marker had been meant to commemorate.

For almost a week, the caravan had been making good progress. The road was well traveled, local farmers keeping it for the most part clean, but there had still been whole leagues where their way was covered in newly fallen leaves. The rustling of horses' hooves and the crackle of the cart wheels had been loud enough to drown out conversation. The 'van master wasn't bad for a religious. For the most part, Marcus could ignore the scriptures read over the evening meals. If the Timzinae happened to pick something particularly hard to listen to—sermons on family or children or the assurances that God was just or anything that touched too closely on what had happened to his wife and daughter—Marcus ate quickly and took a long private walk out ahead on the road. He called it scouting, and the 'van master didn't take offense. Other travelers had joined with the 'van and parted company again without more than a look from Yardem or himself to keep the peace. Except that they weren't yet a quarter of the way to the pass that marked the edge of Birancour, the job was going better than expected.

Marcus chewed his last bite of sausage slowly. The dozen carts filled half the clearing, horses and mules with feedbags over their heads or else being led to and from the brook to drink. The carters knew their business for the most part. The old man driving the tin ore was a little deaf and the boy with the high cart of wool cloth was either new to the trade or an idiot or both, but they were the worst. And his acting troupe had worked out magnificently. If he looked at the trees, not considering the people at all, he could still pick out the guards in the sides of his vision, just by their swagger.

By the side of the road, the long-haired woman, Cary, stood with her arms crossed and a huge horn-and-sinew bow slung across her back. Likely she couldn't have drawn the damn thing, but she wore it like the companion of years. Sandr, the young lead, walked among the carts, head high and brow furrowed. He'd been telling stories to the carters about how he'd broken a foot jousting in an Antean tourney, and had become so familiar with the tale he'd adopted a barely noticable limp to go with it. And then there, sitting with the 'van master's fat wife, was his cunning man, Master Kit, without whom Yardem would even now be failing to keep Vanai from falling. Without whom Marcus would have been jailed or killed.

The 'van master's whistle brought Marcus back to himself, and he squinted up into the thin patch of high, white cloud that showed through the canopy above them. Time was harder to judge in the shadows of a forest, but he guessed the meal had run long. Well, his contract was to get them all into Carse safely. On schedule wasn't his problem. Marcus cleaned his plate with a crust of bread and pulled himself up to standing.

"Rear or fore?" Yardem asked.

"I'll take fore," Marcus said.

The Tralgu nodded and lumbered toward the iron merchant's wagon that brought up the rear of the 'van. It would be the last to leave. Marcus checked his blade and his armor with the same care he did before going into battle—an old habit—and went to the 'van master's tall, broad feed wagon. He climbed up beside the master's wife and settled in for the afternoon's trek. The Timzinae woman nodded to him and blinked her clear inner eyelids.

"That was a fine meal, ma'am," Marcus said.

"You're kind to say so, Captain."

Their conversation complete, she shouted at her horses, flicking her whip lightly at shoulder and haunch to direct them. The wagon lurched forward up onto the road, and then to the west. As they passed into the deep shadows again, Marcus wondered whether Vanai had fallen yet, and if not, how many more days the free city had left. Not many. Another problem not his own.

The rotation was a simple one. Rear and fore were Yardem or Marcus. Master Kit drove his own cart in the center of the 'van with the gaudy colors of the theater draped in cloth. The others rode three on either side of the carts, keeping their eyes on the trees. If anyone saw something suspicious, they'd call out, and Yardem or Marcus would go and look. In a week, the only call they'd had was when Smit, the jack-of-all-roles, had spooked himself with stories about bands of feral Dartinae assassins. Marcus let his eyes narrow, his back rest against the hard wood of the driver's rig. The world smelled of rotting leaves and coming weather, but he couldn't decide yet if it would be rain or snow.

The road made a tight turn at the base of a densely wooded hill. A tree had fallen across the road, its base still white where the axe had cut it. Marcus felt his body tense almost before he knew why.

"Call the stop," he said.

Even before the Timzinae woman could ask why, Smit, Sandr, and Opal all shouted. Marcus turned, scrambling to the top of the wagon. There shouldn't have been bandits. They didn't have anything worth taking. The 'van master's white mare was racing up the side of the carts toward the front. He saw four figures in leather and light chain step out from the trees, bows at the ready. They had hoods covering them, but from the width of their build, Marcus guessed Jasuru or Kurtadam. Four in plain sight could mean the bandits were bluffing. Or that there were a dozen more still in the trees.

At least they hadn't announced themselves with an arrow.

"Hai!" a raspy voice called from the road ahead. "Who speaks for you?"

Four men on horses had appeared in front of the fallen oak. Three were either poorly groomed Cinnae or badly underfed Firstbloods riding nags, but the one in front rode a grey stallion with good lines and real strength in his legs. He also had a steel breastplate and chainmail. His bow was horn, his sword was curved in the southern style, and his face had the broad, thick-boned jaw and bronze scales of a Jasuru.

The Timzinae caravan master pulled his mare up in front of the supply wagon's team.

"I speak for this 'van," he shouted. "What is the meaning of this?"

Marcus shrugged his shoulders to loosen them. Eight men they could see. Half of those mounted. He had eight men, and six of them on horse. It was a damn small advantage, and if it came to blows, they wouldn't last five long breaths together. He hoped the Timzinae wasn't going to press the bandits too hard.

"I am Lord Knightly Tierentois," the bandit captain said loud enough to carry. "You are traveling in my road, and I have come to collect my due tribute."

Marcus slipped back down to the driver's rig, the impulse to roll his eyes warring with the tightness in his belly. The horseman might be a fake and a blowhard, but he had blades and bows.

"These are dragon's roads," the 'van master shouted. "And you're a half-wit, jumped-up thief in stolen armor. Birancour doesn't have any Jasuru knights."

Well, that wasn't as politic as Marcus had hoped. The bandit captain's laughter was hearty and false. Marcus put his hand on the pommel of his sword and tried to think of a way out of this that left the fewest people dead. If the actors charged the bowmen at the sides of the 'van, they might spook them into running. Leaving only four men on horse for him. Yardem appeared at his side, silent as a shadow. The Tralgu's bow was in his hand. So two horesmen each. Unless there were more in the trees.

"The day you mutiny and take the company?" Marcus murmured.

"Not today, sir."

The caravan master was shouting now, and the false knight's face was taking the green-bronze cast that spoke of rage among the Jasuru. Marcus slipped off the wagon and walked forward. The men on horse didn't seem to notice him until he was almost even with the 'van master's mare.

"How much do you want?" Marcus said.

Timzinae and Jasuru both shifted to stare down at him with equal anger.

"Pardon my interrupting your fine and spirited debate, but how much do you want?"

"You should show me some respect, boy," the Jasuru said.

"How much do you want, *my lord*," Marcus said. "Because if you'll look at the 'van here, we don't have much. Unless his lordship and his lordship's noble compatriots are willing to accept tribute in tin ore and iron, there may not be a great deal we can offer."

"Don't speak for me," the Timzinae hissed.

"Don't get us killed," Marcus said, equally softly.

"And who are you, Firstblood?" the Jasuru said.

"Marcus Wester. I'm guard captain of this 'van."

The laughter this time was less forced, and the men on the other horses joined in. The Jasuru shook his broad head and grinned. His tongue was black, and his teeth needle sharp.

"You're Marcus Wester?"

"I am."

"Ah. And I suppose that one back there is Lord Harton returned from the dead. Tell you what, I'll be Drakis Storm-crow."

"No less likely than Lord Knightly Whatever-it-was," the 'van master said.

Marcus ignored him. "You've heard of me, then."

"I was at Wodford, and I am about done being insulted," the Jasuru said. "All your coin. All your food. Half your women. The rest of you can crawl back to Vanai."

"Eat shit," the 'van master said.

The Jasuru reached for his sword, and a new voice boomed out behind them.

"We. Shall. Pass."

Master Kit stood on the top of the feed wagon. The black and purple robes of Orcus the Demon King draped from him like shadows made solid, and he held a staff with a skull on its end. When the actor spoke again, his voice carried to them all as if it came from the dim air.

"My protection is on these men. You cannot harm them."

"What the sweet hell is this?" the Jasuru said, but his voice had taken a worried tone.

"You cannot harm us," Master Kit said. "Your arrows will stray from us. Your swords will not break our skins. You have no power here."

Marcus turned back to the Jasuru. Confusion and anxiety twisted the bandit's face.

"This is shit," one of the three behind him said, but his voice lacked conviction.

"Who is that?" the Jasuru said.

"My cunning man," Marcus said.

"*Hear me*," Master Kit shouted, and the forest itself seemed to go quiet. "The trees are our allies and the shadow of oak protects us. You cannot harm us, boy. And we *shall* pass."

A chill ran up Marcus's spine. He could see that Orcus the Demon King was having much the same effect on the bandits. He felt a small, tentative hope. The Jasuru pulled his bow from its sling and nocked a vicious-looking arrow.

"Say that again, you bastard!" the bandit captain shouted.

Even in the dimness, Marcus saw Master Kit smile. The actor raised his arms, the dark folds of the costume seeming to twist on their own accord, just as they'd done during the play in Vanai. It was something to do with uneven stitching, but with Master Kit's sepulchral voice and defiant posture, the effect was unsettling. Master Kit spoke again, slow and clear and utterly confident.

"You cannot harm me. Your arrow will miss its mark."

The Jasuru scowled and drew back the string. The horn bow creaked.

Well, Marcus thought, *it was worth the try.* And then, a second later: *God damn. He is going to miss.*

The arrow sped through the gloom. Master Kit didn't flinch as the shaft flew past his ear. The Jasuru licked his lips with a wide, black tongue. His gaze shifted from Marcus to Master Kit and back. There was real fear in his eyes now.

"And for what it carries, I really *am* Marcus Wester."

The silence lasted four long breaths together, before the Jasuru turned his horse to the side and raised his arm. "There's nothing here, boys," the bandit shouted. "These little turds aren't worth the effort."

The horsemen sprang away into the forest. Marcus stood in the road, listening to their hoofbeats fade and realizing that he wasn't going to die today after all. He clasped his hands behind him to keep them from trembling and looked up at the 'van master. The Timzinae was shaking too. At least Marcus wasn't the only one. He stepped to the side of the road, leaning to see that the bowmen at the treeline had also vanished.

Yardem walked to him. "That was odd," the Tralgu said.

"Was," Marcus said. "Don't suppose we have a winch? We're going to have to move that tree."

That night, the 'van master's wife cooked meat. Not sausage, not salt pork, but a fresh-killed lamb the 'van master bought from a farm at the forest's edge. The meat was dark and rich, seasoned with raisins and a sharp-tasting yellow sauce. The carters and drivers and most of Marcus's guard sat around a roaring bonfire at the side of the road. All except the wool-hauler, Tag, who never seemed to eat with anybody. And sitting at a separate fire away from all the others, Marcus ate with Master Kit.

"It's how I've made my living since…well, not since before *you* were born, I suppose," the actor said. "I stand before people, usually on a wagon, and I convince them of things. I tell them that I am a fallen king or a shipwrecked sailor on an unknown shore. I presume they know it isn't truth, but I see my work as making them believe even when they know better."

"What you did back there, then?" Marcus said. "Talking the bastard with the bow out of his confidence? It wasn't magic?"

"I think talking a man into believing in his own failure is close enough to magic. Don't you?"

"I don't really, no."

"Well, then perhaps we disagree on the point. More wine?"

Marcus took the proffered skin and squirted the bright-tasting wine into his mouth. In the light of the two fires— the small one at their knees, the large one fifteen yards away—shadows clung to the old actor's cheeks and in the hollows of his eyes.

"Captain. If it's any comfort to you, I'll swear this. I can be very convincing, and I can tell when someone is trying to convince me. That is all the magic I possess."

"Cut thumbs on it?" Marcus said, and Master Kit laughed.

"I'd rather not. If I get blood on the costumes, it's hard to get out. But what about you? What exactly did *you* intend, facing the man down like that?"

Marcus shrugged.

"I didn't intend anything. Not in particular," he said. "Only I thought the 'van master was going about it badly."

"Would you have fought?" Master Kit asked. "If it had come to swords and arrows?"

"Of course," Marcus said. "Probably not for very long, given the odds, but I'd have fought. Yardem too, and I hope your people along with us. It's what they pay us for."

"Even though you knew we couldn't win?"

"Yes."

Master Kit nodded. Marcus thought a smile was lurking at the corners of the actor's lips, but in the flickering light he couldn't be sure. It might have been something else.

"I want to start drilling your people," Marcus said. "An hour before we ride in the morning, and an hour after we stop. We can't do much, but they ought to know more about a sword than which end to hold it by."

"I think that's wise," Master Kit said.

Marcus looked up at the sky. The stars glowed like snowfall, and the moon, newly risen, sent long, pale shadows across black ground. The forest was behind them, but the air still smelled like weather. Rain, Marcus decided. Most likely it would be rain. Master Kit was chewing his lamb, his eyes on the little fire and his expression distant.

"Don't worry. Today was the worst of it," Marcus said. "We've got our excitement behind us."

Master Kit didn't look at him, making his polite smile to the flames instead. For a moment, Marcus thought the old man wasn't going to speak. When he did, his voice was low and abstracted.

"Probably," Master Kit said.

Geder

Geder had imagined Vanai would be more like Camnipol or Estinport: a great city of stone and jade. The close-built wooden structures and wide canals felt both smaller than he'd expected and larger. Even the Grand Square of the conquered city was small compared to the wide commons of Camnipol, and the richest sections of Vanai were as thick with humanity as the better slums at home. Camnipol was a city. Vanai was a child's scrapwood playhouse that had spread. It was beautiful in its way, strange and foreign and improbable. He wasn't sure yet whether he liked it.

He limped down the rain-darkened streets of occupied Vanai, leaning on the blackwood-and-silver walking stick with every step. Lord Ternigan's address was to begin soon, and while his wound would forgive his absence, Geder had missed too much already. The prospect of going home to regale his father with stories of how he'd collapsed in the battle and spent the two-day sack with a cunning man tending his leg was bad enough.

The canal on the eastern edge of the modest Grand Square was choked with fallen leaves, gold and red and yellow remaking the surface of the dark water. As Geder watched, a turtle rose from below, its black head sticking out of the water. A single bright red leaf adhered to its shell. The turtle made its stately way past what looked at first like a log, but was in fact a corpse wearing the drenched colors of the former prince: a soldier of Vanai hauled in a cart from the battlefield and dropped in the canal as a message to the locals. Other bodies hung from the trees in the parks and along the colonnades. They lay on the stairs of the palaces and the markets and the square of the public gaol where the former prince now ate and shat and shivered before his subjects. The smell of rotting flesh was only kept in check by the cool weather.

Once the prince entered exile, the dead would be gathered up and burned. They had been men once. Now they were political sculpture.

"Palliako!"

Geder looked up. From halfway across the Grand Square, Jorey Kalliam scowled and waved him on. Geder turned away from turtle and corpse, limping manfully across the pavement. The nobles of Antea stood in martial array, waiting only for the few stragglers like himself. Before them, on the bare ground, sat what high officials of the city had been spared. Timzinae merchants and guildsmen, Firstblood artisans and pragmatic noblemen. They wore their own clothing—much of it with a notably imperial cut—and held themselves more like the polite attendees of a religious function than the debased and the conquered. Sodai Carvenallin, the secretary to Lord Ternigan, stood alone on the stone platform they all faced and looked forward with folded arms. Geder hadn't seen the man to speak to since the night they'd gotten drunk together. The night Klin had burned his book. Geder shook the memory away and took his place.

He tried not to notice the new finery around him, but it was impossible. Sir Gospey Allintot's cloak was closed with a broach of worked silver and brilliant ruby. Sozlu Veren had his sword sheathed in a scabbard of dragon's jade and yellowed ivory that could have been made a thousand years before. A chain of gold looped around Jorey Kalliam's neck that looked to be more than a month's rent from all the holdings of Rivenhalm. Their clothes were freshly laundered, their boots shone even in the grey overcast light. The warrior aristocrats of Antea wore their conquest proudly. Geder looked down at his little walking stick. It was the nearest thing he had to spoils of war, and he tried to be proud of it.

"Quite a day," Geder said, nodding toward the low grey clouds. "It was snowing for a bit this morning. Glad we aren't marching in this. Though I suppose we will be soon, eh? Taking tribute to the king."

Jorey Kalliam made a low, affirming sound in his throat but didn't meet Geder's eyes.

"My leg's doing well. All laudable pus," Geder said. "But you heard about Count Hiren? Cut to the arm went septic. He died last night when they tried to amputate. Damn shame. He was a good man."

"He was," Jorey agreed.

Geder tried to follow the man's gaze, but Jorey seemed focused on nothing. Or, no. His eyes moved restlessly, searching for something. Geder searched too, uncertain what he was looking for.

"Something wrong?" Geder asked, his voice low.

"Klin's not here."

Geder looked through the crowd, his attention more focused now. There were gaps in the form, men killed or injured or called away on the Lord Marshal's business. Kalliam was correct. Sir Alan Klin should have stood at the head of the group, the men under his command arrayed behind him. Instead, Sir Gospey Allintot had the place, his chin held high.

"Ill, maybe?" Geder said. Jorey chuckled as if it had been a joke.

The drums announced the Lord Marshal. The collected nobility of Antea lifted their hands in salute, and Lord Ternigan let them remain there for a moment before he returned the gesture. Between them, the powerful men of Vanai accepted their ritual humiliation with polite silence. Jorey grunted, his expression sour. He wasn't searching any longer. Geder followed his gaze, and found Klin standing at the rear of the platform beside the Lord Marshal's secretary. Klin wore a silk tunic and hose of somber red and a black-dyed woolen cloak. The cut spoke less of blades and battle than governance.

Geder felt his belly drop. "Are we staying here?" he asked quietly. Jorey Kalliam didn't answer.

"Lords of Antea," Ternigan said, his voice echoing through the square not quite so loudly as it might have. The Lord Marshal appeared to be coming down with a cold. "I thank you all in the name of King Simeon. Through your valor, the empire has been made again secure. It is my decision that we return now to Camnipol with the tribute which Vanai owes the throne. It's late in the season, and the march is a long one, I'd rather we didn't spend all week getting our boots on. I have asked Sir Alan Klin to remain as Protector of Vanai until such time as King Simeon names a permanent governor. All of you who followed him in battle will follow him in this as well."

His orders given, Ternigan nodded to himself and turned his attention to the men seated on the pavement. As he retold the history of Antean claims upon Vanai, justified the occupation in terms of wars and agreements made six hundred years before between dynastic lines and independent parliaments long since dissolved, Geder's mind stumbled through what had just happened to him.

There would be no return to Camnipol for him, not this season. Possibly not for years. He looked around at the close-built wooden buildings with their steep-pitched roofs crowding the narrow streets, the grand canal where barges and boats made their way through the city and back out to the river, the low grey sky. This wasn't an exotic adventure any longer. This was where he would live. A thousand half-formed plans for his return to Camnipol, to Rivenhalm, to his father's hearth fell apart before him.

Ternigan stepped back from the platform's edge, took a sealed letter from his secretary, and presented it to Alan Klin, Protector of Vanai. Klin stepped forward, opened the letter, and read his charge from the Lord Marshal aloud. Geder shook his head. The despair that grew with every phrase showed him how deeply he'd been anticipating the campaign's end and his freedom from Alan Klin.

The ache in Geder's leg throbbed as Klin assured the men of Vanai that he would treat all races with equanimity, that loyalty to Antea would be rewarded and treachery punished swiftly and terribly. The glory of King Simeon in particular and Antea in the large took up the better part of an hour. Even the others in Geder's cohort were growing restless by the end. Then Klin thanked the Lord Marshal for his service and formally accepted this new charge. His salute was met with a rousing cheer, the men pleased as much that the ceremony had ended as with anything Klin had said. The citizens of Vanai rose to their feet, shaking limbs gone numb and talking among themselves like merchants at a fresh market.

Geder saw mixed reactions among the men of the empire. Some envied Klin and his men their new role. Sir Gospey

Allintot was grinning so widely, he seemed to glow. Jorey Kalliam walked away with a thoughtful expression, and Geder struggled to keep up with him.

"We're exiled," Geder said when they were away from the greater mass of their companions. "We won the battle, and in return they exiled us just as sure as the damned prince of the city."

Jorey looked at him with annoyance and pity. "Klin's been aiming for this from the start," he said. "This was always what he hoped for."

"Why?" Geder asked.

"There's power in being the king's voice," Jorey said. "Even in Vanai. And if Klin makes himself useful, when the time comes to trade the city away again, he'll have a place at that table as well. Excuse me. I have to write to my father."

"Yes," Geder said. "I should tell my family too. I don't know what I'll say."

Jorey's laughter was low and bitter.

"Tell them you didn't miss the sack after all."

If there was any question of who among Alan Klin's men were favored, it was answered when Lord Ternigan left the gates of the city. Klin's new secretary, the son of an important Timzinae merchant, took Geder from his bed in the infirmary to his new home: three small rooms in a minor palace that had been storage and still smelled of rat piss. Still, there was a small hearth, and the winds didn't blow through the walls the way they had in his tent.

Each day brought Geder a new order from Lord Klin. A channel gate that was to be locked and disabled, a marketplace in which each of the merchants was to pay for an Antean permit to continue their businesses, a loyalist of the deposed prince to be taken to the jail cells as an example to others. It might be common soldiers who announced the demands and enforced their execution, but a nobleman's presence was required; a face to show that the aristocracy of Antea was present and involved with the business of its new city. And given the tasks assigned him, Geder suspected that he'd be the most hated man in Vanai before the winter passed.

Closing a popular brothel? Geder led the force. Turning the widow and children of a loyalist out of their hovel? Geder. Arresting a prominent member of the local merchant class?

"May I ask the charge?" said Magister Imaniel of the Medean bank in Vanai.

"I'm sorry," Geder said. "I'm ordered to bring you before the Lord Protector, willing or no."

"Ordered," the small man said sourly. "And parading me through the street in chains?"

"Part of my instructions. I'm sorry."

The house of the Medean bank in Vanai was in a side street, and little larger than a well-to-do family's home. Even so, it seemed somehow bare. Only the small, sun-worn magister and a single well-fed woman wringing her hands in the doorway. Magister Imaniel rose from the table, considered the soldiers standing behind Geder, and then adjusted his tunic.

"I don't imagine you know when I'll be able to return to my work," he said.

"I'm not told," Geder said.

"You can't do this," the woman said. "We've done nothing against you."

"Cam," the banker said sharply. "Don't. This is only business, I'm sure. Tell anyone that asks there's been a mistake, and I'm speaking with the very noble Lord Protector to correct it."

The woman—Cam—bit her lips and looked away. Magister Imaniel walked quietly to stand before Geder and bowed.

"I don't suppose we can overlook the chains?" he asked. "My work depends to a great wise on reputation, and…"

"I'm very sorry," Geder said, "but Lord Klin gave—"

"Orders," the banker said. "I understand. Let's be done with this, then."

A crowd had gathered on the street, word of Geder's appearance at the house traveling, it seemed, faster than the birds could fly. Geder walked in the middle of his guardsmen, the prisoner in his clinking iron just behind him. When he looked back, the man's leathery face was a mask of amusement and indulgence. Geder couldn't say if the man's fearlessness was an act or genuine. All along their route past the canals and down the streets, faces turned to see the banker in chains. Geder marched, his walking stick tapping resolutely against the streets. He kept his expression sober, to hide the fact that he didn't know why he was doing the things he did. He had no doubt that by morning the whole city would know he had taken the man in. That it was clearly Klin's intention didn't reassure him.

Sir Alan Klin met them in the wide chamber that had once been the prince's audience hall. All signs of the former government were gone or else covered over by the Antean banners of King Simeon and House Klin. The air smelled of smoke, rain, and wet dogs. Sir Alan rose, smiling, from his table.

"Magister Imaniel of the Medean bank?"

"The same, Lord Protector," the banker said with a smile

and a bow. His voice was amiable. Geder might almost have thought Klin hadn't just humiliated the man in front of the city. "It appears I may have given your lordship some offense. I must, of course, apologize. If I might know the nature of my trespass, I will, of course, guard against it in the future."

Klin waved a hand casually.

"Not at all, sir," he said. "Only I spoke with your former prince before he left in exile. He said that you had refused to fund his campaign."

"It seemed unlikely that he would repay the debt," Magister Imaniel said.

"I understand," Klin said.

Geder looked from one to the other. The tone of the conversation was so calm, so nearly collegial, it confused him. And yet there was a hardness in Klin's eyes that—along with the chains still around the banker's wrists and ankles— made everything he said a threat. Klin walked slowly back to the table where the remains of his midday meal were still sitting on a silver plate.

"I have been looking over the reports of the sack," Klin said. "I saw that the tribute to King Simeon taken from your establishment . . . Well, it seems surprisingly light."

"My former prince may have an exaggerated opinion of my resources," Magister Imaniel said.

Klin smiled. "Is it buried, or have you smuggled it out?"

"I don't know what you mean, my lord," Magister Imaniel said.

"You wouldn't object to my factor auditing your books, then?"

"Of course not. We are pleased that Antea has taken the authority that rightly belonged to it, and look forward to doing business in a more friendly and ordered city."

"And access to your house?"

"Of course."

Klin nodded. "You understand that I will have to hold you until I find the truth of all this? Whatever money your bank holds here is now subject to Antean review."

"I expected as much," Magister Imaniel said, "but I trust you won't take offense that I had hoped for better."

"It's a fallen world. We do what we must," Klin said, and then to the captain of the guard at Geder's left, "Take him to the public gaol. Put him on the lower level, where everyone can see him. If anyone tries to talk with him, take note of what they say and detain them."

Geder watched as the small man was led away. He wasn't sure whether he was intended to follow along or not. But Klin wasn't glaring at him, so perhaps he'd been meant to stay after all.

"Did you follow that, Palliako?" Klin asked when the banker and guards had gone.

"The bank had less money than expected?" Geder said.

Klin laughed in a way that left Geder unsure whether he was being mocked.

"Oh, it's there," he said. "Somewhere. And from what the prince said, there was quite a bit of it. Enough to pay the mercenary forces to outlast a siege. Enough to buy the Maccian forces twice over. Maybe more than that."

"But he kept it from his prince," Geder said.

"Not out of loyalty to us," Klin said. "Bankers answer to no throne. But if they drowned the money, someone will have helped cart it to a canal. If it's buried, someone held the spade. If it's smuggled, someone arranged it. And when that person sees the head of the bank in gaol, they may panic and try to buy their way free."

"Ah," Geder said.

"You're the man associated with the arrest, so you'll need

to be available these next few days," Klin said. "Approach-
able. And whatever you hear, you bring to me."

"Of course, sir."

"Excellent," Klin said. The silence between them stretched,
and Geder realized that he'd been dismissed.

He walked back out to the square, found a stone bench
under a black-barked tree almost bare of its leaves, and sat.
His leg ached, but there was no coolness on his thigh where
fresh blood or pus had leaked. Across the street, a group of
youths—Firstblood and Timzinae mixing together as if the
races were at perfect ease—pretended not to watch him. A
flock of crows conversed among themselves in the branches
of the trees and then rose like winged smoke into the air.
Geder tapped his walking stick against the pavement, the
little shock against his fingers oddly reassuring.

For the next few days, he was bait on a hook. He understood that. Perhaps the banker's conspirators would take the
chance to buy themselves the good opinion of Antea. Or
perhaps they'd stay quiet. Or, quite possibly, they'd arrange
an accident for the man most associated with the problem.
Klin had put him in danger without so much as making the
threat he was under explicit.

And still, it was a handful of days that Geder could make
his way through the streets and markets and call it Klin's
order. His squire had brought him rumor of a bookseller in
the southern quarter. He could make his way there at last.
And if he had to go armed and under guard, at least he
could go.

For two days Geder wandered the streets and cafés and
beer halls of Vanai, but carefully. In church, with the voices
of the choir spiraling in the wide air above him, he was still
careful not to let anyone sit too near him in the pew. At the
fresh market, he picked through the half-rotten volumes in

a bookseller's cart, but with a soldier at his back. Then on the third day, a carter named Olfreed came to his rooms with talk of a caravan organized by a well-known ally of the Medean bank called Master Will.

For the first time, Geder heard the name Marcus Wester.

Cithrin

Distracted by the rigors of her disguise and the wealth hidden in her cart, Cithrin had not been careful.

"What were you *thinking*, boy?" the caravan master demanded. Cithrin looked at his feet, her cheeks burning and her throat thick with shame. The red dust of the caravanserai's yard caked their boots, and fallen leaves rimed with frost littered the ground.

"I'm sorry," she said, the cold turning her words white.

"They're mules," the caravan master said. "They need caring for. How long has this been going on?"

"A few days," she said, her lips hardly moving.

"Speak up, boy! How long?"

"A few days," she said.

A pause.

"All right. The feed cart can get by with three on the team. You tie the sick one to a tree out there, and I'll bring you one to take its place."

"But if we leave him, he'll die," Cithrin said.

"That's the thought, yes."

"But it's not his fault. You can't just leave him to die all by himself."

"All right. I'll bring you a knife, and you can bleed him out."

Cithrin's outraged silence was eloquence enough. The

caraban master's clear interior eyelids slid closed and open again, blinking without looking away from her.

"If you'd rather drop out of the 'van, you're welcome," he said. "We're going too slow already. I'm not going to stop everything because you can't keep your team. You let me know what you decide."

"I won't leave him," she said, surprised by her own words. Horrified that she meant them. She couldn't drop out of the 'van.

"He's a *mule*."

"I won't leave him." The words felt better that time.

"Then you're an idiot."

The caravan master turned, spat, and walked away. Cithrin watched him as he stalked back to the stone walls and thin-thatched roof of the shelter. When it became clear he wasn't coming back, she went back to the stable. The larger of her mules stood in his stall, his head lowered. His breath was thick and ragged. Cithrin stepped in beside him, her hand stroking his thick, wiry coat. The mule raised his head, flicked an ear, and sagged down again.

She tried to picture herself tying the animal to a tree and leaving him there for sickness and snow to kill. She tried to imagine slitting his warm, fuzzy throat. How would she get the money to Carse now?

"I'm sorry," Cithrin said. "I'm not really a carter. I didn't know."

She'd thought at first that the slowness of her cart was her own fault, that the gap that opened in the afternoons between her and the cart before hers meant she wasn't pushing the team when she should, or that some fine point of negotiating turns was beyond her. It was only when the larger mule had coughed—a wet, phlegmy sound—that she realized he was ill. Magister Imaniel had kept a religious household, but Cithrin prayed that the animal would recover on his own.

He hadn't.

The caravanserai—a ruin barely maintained by those who passed through it—was on the side of a wide, sloping hill, the first foothill of the high, snow-peaked mountain range that marked the end of the Free Cities and the beginning of Birancour. Even now, distance-blued peaks rose from the horizon. The pass through them marked the shortest path between Vanai and Carse.

Carse. The word itself had taken on almost religious significance for her. Carse, the great city of Northcoast overlooking the peaceful sea. The home of white towers above chalk cliffs, of the Council of Eventide, of the Grave of Dragons. The seat of the Medean bank, and the end of her career as a smuggler and refugee. She had never been there, but her longing for it was like wanting to go home.

She could go alone. She'd have to. Only she didn't know the way. Or how to nurse a sick mule back to health. Or what she'd do if another bandit crew stepped out of the forest. The mule heaved in a huge breath and then coughed: deep, wet, and rasping. Cithrin stepped forward and rubbed his wide, soft ears.

"We can find a way," she said as much to herself as the animal. "It'll be all right."

"Probably, it will," a man's voice said.

The cunning man, Master Kit, stood at the stable door, the woman called Opal at his side. Cithrin moved half a step in toward her mule, her arm around its sloping neck as if to protect it. Or be protected by it. An anxious thrill quickened her breath.

"This is the poor thing, then?" Opal said, pushing past the cunning man. "Tired-looking, ain't he?"

Cithrin nodded, looking down to avoid their eyes. Opal slipped into the stall, walked around the mule once, pausing to press her ear to the beast's side. Then, singing a low song in words Cithrin didn't recognize, she knelt before its head and gently pried open its lips.

"Opal takes care of our team, when we have one," Master Kit said. "I've come to put my trust in her when it comes to things with hooves."

Cithrin nodded, torn between a rush of gratitude and discomfort at being so close to the guardsmen. Opal rose and sniffed carefully at the mule's ears.

"Tag, is it?" she said, and Cithrin nodded. "Well, Tag, can you tell me if the old boy was listing to one side? Did you have to correct him?"

Cithrin tried to remember, then shook her head no.

"That's something," Opal said, and then over her shoulder to Master Kit, "I don't think it's in his ears, so that's for the best. He's wheezing, but he doesn't have water in his lungs. At a guess, keep him warm a couple of days, he'll stand true as sticks. Needs more blankets, though."

"Two days," Master Kit said. "I would be surprised if Captain Wester were comfortable with that."

The mule's labored breath and the murmur of the morning breeze through the boughs roughened the silence. Cithrin felt the knot in her belly tightening into something like nausea.

"One fewer guard won't make any damn difference," Opal said. "I'll stay with Tag, and when the old boy's well enough, we'll catch you up. Won't be more than a day or two, and one cart with a good team moves faster than a full 'van."

The cunning man crossed his arms, considering. Cithrin felt a rush of hope.

"Can you do that?" Master Kit asked her. His eyes were gentle, his voice as soft as old flannel.

"I can, sir," Cithrin said, keeping her voice low and masculine. The cunning man nodded.

"I don't suppose there's any harm in suggesting it," he said. "But perhaps you would allow *me* to approach them, Tag?"

She nodded, and the old man smiled. He turned and walked back toward the quarters, leaving Cithrin, Opal, and the animals to themselves.

The relief took the edge off her fear. And perhaps it wasn't such a bad thing, in its way. With Opal dressing in her leathers and Cithrin disguised as a man, they weren't likely to arouse suspicion. It would be a few days away from the greater company, so she would only have to avoid discovery by Opal. And their supposedly different sexes would give a plausible excuse for privacy.

And yet the fear didn't entirely fade. It came, she told herself, from knowing more than the people around her. She could almost hear Magister Imaniel now, sitting at the evening meal with Cam and Besel, dissecting exactly how a merchant or prelate had behaved differently than expected, and what it implied that they had. Cithrin knew that Tag the Carter carried enough wealth to buy a small army, but no one else did. The risk of lagging behind the body of the 'van was no more than she would have faced if she'd truly carried a load of undyed wool. Her chances only seemed worse because she knew the stakes of the bet were high. She was undiscovered. No one was searching for her or what she carried, the mule would be made well, and she wouldn't face a journey to Carse by herself. Everything would be fine.

"First time out?" Opal said.

Cithrin glanced at her and nodded.

"Well, don't let it worry you, dear," the guard said. "We take care of our own."

It didn't occur to Cithrin for hours to wonder exactly why a mercenary guard would include a semi-competent carter in *our own,* and by then the plan was set and the caravan with Captain Wester and Master Kit was gone down the road to the mountains and to Carse.

They passed the day in caring for the sick beast: warming the stable, rubbing down the mule, forcing an odd concoction that smelled of tar and licorice into its mouth. By nightfall, the mule held its head higher and its cough seemed less violent. That night, Cithrin and Opal slept in the stables, wrapped in thin blankets. An ancient iron brazier between them threw off enough heat to keep the room from freezing, but only just. In the darkness outside, something shrieked once and then not again. Cithrin closed her eyes, resting her head on one arm, and willed herself to sleep. She envied Opal's slow, even breath. Her own body tensed and shivered, her mind jumped from one fear to another, conjuring a hundred possible disasters. The bandits who had attacked the 'van before might arrive in the night, rape and murder them both, and make off with the bank's money. Opal might discover her secret and, mad with avarice, slit her throat. The mule might relapse and leave her stranded in the autumn cold.

When a low, grey dawn finally came, Cithrin hadn't slept. Her head ached, and her back felt as if someone had beaten her with a hammer. Opal, humming to herself, rebuilt the fire, boiled a pan of water with a sprinkling of leaves in it, and checked on their patient. When Cithrin joined her, the mule felt cooler to the touch, his eyes looked brighter, his head stood at its more usual angle. In the next stall, the other mule cleared her throat and grumbled.

"Is she getting sick too?" Cithrin asked. The very idea made her want to weep.

"She may, but she hasn't yet," Opal said. "Probably just jealous that the old boy here's getting all the attention."

"Should we go, then? I mean, is it safe to get back to the 'van?"

"This afternoon, maybe," Opal said. "Better that he have his strength back. Start him with a half day's work."

"But—"

"We've been this way before. We'll catch them up before they go over the pass. They'll stop at Bellin, send up scouts."

Cithrin knew the name, but she couldn't place it. Opal glanced over at her.

"Bellin," Opal said. "Trading town just before the pass. You really don't know much about hauling in a caravan, do you?"

"No," Cithrin said, both sullen and embarrassed at being sullen.

"Bellin's not much, but they're friendly to travelers. Master Kit took us there for a month once. New people coming through the road every few days, no one staying long. It was like being a traveling company without the traveling."

A breath of cold wind stirred the straw. In the brazier, the coals brightened and the thin flame danced. Cithrin's mind felt slow and sodden with fatigue. What would a guard company do with a month of passing traders and merchants and missionaries? Protect them inside the town walls where they needed it the least?

"I should go," Cithrin said. "Check the...check the cart."

"Make sure it hasn't gone anywhere," Opal said, as if she was agreeing.

In practice, being only with Opal was better than being with the full 'van. With just one person to keep track of, Cithrin could find moments to let her guard down, be herself instead of Tag. When the time came and they harnessed the mules, it wasn't all that different from being alone. Opal did most of the talking, and that was for the most part about how to manage the team. Cithrin knew that Tag should have been bored by the lectures, but she drank them in. In the first half day, she learned a hundred things she'd been doing wrong. When they bedded down that night in a wide meadow beside the road, she was a better carter than she'd been in all the long weeks since Vanai.

She wanted to thank the guard for all she'd done, but she was afraid that if she started she might not stop. Gratitude would become friendship, and friendship confession, and then her secrets would be spilled. So instead she made sure that Opal got the best food and the softer place to sleep.

In the darkness, the two of them lay on the soft wool. The moon and stars were gone, wrapped in clouds, and the darkness was absolute. Cithrin's mind skittered and shifted, thin with exhaustion. And still, sleep was slow to come. In the middle of the night, she felt Opal's body pressing next to her own and woke up in a panic, afraid that the guard was attacking her or seducing her or both, but she was only cold and half asleep. She spent the rest of the night drawn by the warmth of Opal's body and trying to hold herself apart for fear of compromising her disguise.

In the dark, the weeks between her and Carse seemed eternal. She imagined that she could feel the casks and boxes hidden just beneath her. The books and ledgers, silk and tobacco leaf and spice. Gems and jewelry. The weight of responsibility and fear was like someone pressing on her chest. When, just before dawn, she finally slept deeply enough to dream, she found herself at the edge of a cliff, trying to keep a hundred stumbling babies from pitching into the abyss.

She woke with a cry, and she woke to snow.

Wide, fat flakes dropped from the sky, grey against the white of clouds. The trees caught it, the bark seeming to turn black by contrast. The dragon's jade of the road was gone, their path marked only by a clear space between the trunks. The horizon had been erased. Opal was already fixing the mules in their harness.

"Can we really go in this?" Cithrin asked, forgetting to deepen her voice.

"Better had. Unless you'd prefer to settle here."

"It's safe, though?"

"Safer than the option," Opal said. "Help me with this buckle. My hand's half frozen."

Cithrin clambered down from the cart and did as she was told. Before long, they were forging ahead. The wide iron cartwheels became caked with wet snow and the mules began to steam. Without discussion, Opal had taken the reins and the whip. Cithrin huddled beside her, miserable. Opal squinted into the weather and shook her head.

"The good news is there won't be bandits."

"Really? And what's the bad?" Cithrin said bitterly.

Opal looked over at her, eyes wide with surprise and delight. Cithrin realized it was the closest thing to a joke she'd made since the caravan left Vanai. She blushed, and the guard beside her laughed.

Bellin had only half a dozen buildings. The rest of the town crouched inside a wide cliff, doorways and windows carved into the grey stone thousands of years before by inhuman hands. Soot stained the wall where chimneys slanted out into the world. Snow clung to huge runes carved into the mountainside, a script Cithrin had never seen before. The peaks themselves were invisible apart from a sense of looming darkness within the storm. The familiar carts of the 'van were black dots against the white, horses and carters already sheltered within the rock. She helped Opal set their cart in place, unhitch the mules, and guide them safely into the stable where the 'van's other animals were already tucked away.

The guards were there, sitting around a banked smith's furnace, Mikel and Hornet, Master Kit and Smit. Sandr grinned at them both as they came in, and the Tralgu second in command lifted a wide hand without turning from his conversation with the long-haired woman, Cary. Opal's pleasure at seeing them almost made Cithrin happy too.

"There must be something," Cary said, and Cithrin could tell it wasn't the first time she'd said it.

"There's not," Yardem rumbled. "Women are smaller and weaker. There's no weapon that can make that an advantage."

"What are we talking about?" Opal asked, sitting by the open furnace. Cithrin sat on the bench at her side, only realizing afterward that it was the same position they'd held on the cart. Master Kit chuckled and shook his head.

"I think Cary would prefer to train with weapons that better exploit her natural abilities," Master Kit said.

"Like being small and weak," Sandr said. Without looking over, Cary flicked a clod of earth at his head.

"Short bow," Cary said.

"Takes power to pull back a bow," Yardem said. He seemed on the edge of apology. "With a sling and stone, it matters less, but it still matters. A spear has better reach, but takes more muscle. A blade needs less strength, but calls for more reach. A strong, big woman's better than a small, weak man, but there's no such thing as a woman's natural weapon." The Tralgu shrugged expansively.

"There has to be *something*," Cary said.

"There doesn't," Yardem said.

"Sex," Sandr suggested with a grin. Cary threw another clod at his head.

"How are your mules, Tag?" Master Kit asked.

"Better," Cithrin said. "Much better. Thanks to Opal."

"It was nothing," Opal said.

"I'm pleased it worked out," Master Kit said. "I was beginning to worry that we'd leave you behind."

"Wouldn't have happened," a voice said from behind them.

Cithrin twisted in her seat, and her chest went tight with anxiety. Captain Wester stalked into the room. Snow caked his wide leather cloak and matted his hair. His face was so bright, it looked like the cold had slapped him. He walked to the heat, scowling.

"Welcome back, sir," the Tralgu said. The captain didn't so much as nod.

"I take it the scouting went poorly, then," Master Kit said.

"No worse than expected," Marcus Wester said. "The 'van master's breaking it to the others right now. There's no getting through that pass. Not now, not for months."

"*What?*" Cithrin said, her voice sharp and unexpected. She tried to swallow the word as soon as she'd said it, but the captain took no particular notice of her.

"Snow came early, we took too long, and we didn't get lucky," he said. "We'll get some warehouse space for the goods and bunks for the rest of us. Not much room, so it'll be close quarters. We'll make for Carse in the spring."

Spring. The word hit Cithrin in the gut. She looked at the flames dancing in the furnace, felt a trickle of snowmelt tracing its way down her spine. Despairing laughter bubbled at the back of her throat. If she let it out, it would turn to tears, and it wouldn't stop. A season spent in disguise. Moving everything in her cart to a warehouse and back without being discovered. Months to Carse instead of weeks.

I can't do this, she thought.

Marcus

Nightfall came early. Only half of the carts had been emptied, and the caravan master was all but chewing his own wrists over it. Marcus didn't think it would be a problem. The storm had come from the west, and the mountains would squeeze the worst of the snow out. They might be tunneling up from the roofs in Birancour, but Bellin was in the rain shadow. They'd be fine. At least when it came to snow.

Yardem had arranged a separate barracks for the so-called guards. Two small rooms with a shared fire grate, but in the town proper, tucked snugly in the living rock. Carved swirls and whorls caught the firelight, and the walls seemed to breathe and dance. Marcus pulled off the soaked leather of his boots and leaned back, groaning. The others were about him, lounging and talking and negotiating for the best sleeping spaces. The ease the actors took in close company wasn't all that different from real sword-and-bows, and the jokes were better. Even Yardem seemed half relaxed, and that wasn't a common thing.

Still, Marcus's work wasn't done.

"Meeting," he said. "Our job's changed now. Best that we talk that through, not find ourselves surprised later."

The chatter stilled. Master Kit sat beside the fire, his wiry grey hair standing like smoke gone still.

"I don't see how the 'van can afford this," the actor said. "Even with small quarters, it's going to cost having us kept and fed for a full season."

"Likely they'll lose money," Marcus said. "But that's the caravan master's problem, not ours. We aren't here to see a profit turned. Just everyone kept safe. On the road, that means bandits. Holed up for a winter, that means no one gets stir crazy or starts sleeping with someone, makes someone else jealous, or gets in mind to cheat too much at cards."

Smit, the jack-of-all-roles, pulled a long face. "Are we playing guards or nursemaids?" the man said.

"We're doing whatever gets the 'van to Carse safe," Marcus said. "We'll protect them from ourselves if we have to."

"Mmm. Good line," Cary, the thin woman, said. "*Protect them from ourselves if we have to.*"

Marcus narrowed his eyes, frowning.

"They're writing a new play," Master Kit said. "A comic piece about an acting troupe hired to pretend they're caravan guards."

Yardem grunted and flicked an ear. Maybe annoyance, maybe amusement. Likely both. Marcus chose to ignore it.

"We've got a dozen and a half carters," Marcus said. "Add the 'van master and his wife. You've traveled with these people for weeks. You've watched them. You know them. What problems are we going to have?"

"The man hauling the tin ore," Smit said. "He's been spoiling for a fight since those raiders. He's not going to last a season without one unless someone starts sharing his bed or puts him down hard."

"I'd thought the same," Marcus said, allowing himself a moment's pleasure. The actors were much more perceptive than his usual men. Given the circumstances, that would help. "What else?"

"The quarter-Dartinae," Opal, the older leading woman, said. "He's been avoiding the 'van master's sermons almost as much as you have, Captain. A constant diet of scripture isn't going to sit well with him."

"The girl in the false whiskers," Mikel, the thin boy, said. "She's looking mightily fragile."

"Oh, yes. *Her*," Cary said.

"And God knows what she's really hauling," Opal said, her tone all agreement. "Gets jumpy as a cat whenever anyone gets too near her cart. Won't talk about it either."

Marcus raised a hand, commanding silence.

"*Who?*" he said.

"The girl in the false whiskers," Master Kit said. "The one that calls herself Tag."

Marcus looked at Yardem. The Tralgu's expression mirrored his own blank surprise. Marcus lifted an eyebrow. *Did you know?* Yardem shook his head once, earrings jingling. *No.*

And God knows what she's really hauling.

"With me, Yardem," Marcus said, pulling his boots back on.

"Yes, sir," the Tralgu rumbled.

The carters and and 'van master were in a separate network of rooms and tunnels. Marcus went through the smoke-hazed halls and common rooms, Yardem looming at his side. The other guards or actors, or whatever they were, trailed along behind like children playing follow-me-follow-you. With every room that Tag wasn't in, Marcus felt the hair on the back of his neck rising. His mind ran back over everything that had happened on the road, every time he'd spoken to the boy, everything that the 'van master had said about him. There was very little. Almost nothing. Always, the boy had kept himself—and, more the point, his cart— to himself.

The last of the rented rooms looked out over the dark and snow-carpeted hills. Behind him, Marcus heard the high, excited voices of the carters asking what was happening. The chill, wet air smelled as much of rain as snow. Lightning sketched the horizon.

"He's not here, sir."

"I see that."

"She can't have gone," Opal said from behind them. "Girl hardly knew how to steer the cart without something in front for the mules to follow."

"The cart," Marcus said, walking out into the gloom.

The carts that hadn't been unloaded were near the low stone warehouses. Half a foot of snow covered them, making them all seem taller than they truly were. Marcus stalked among them. Behind him, someone lit torches, the fires hissing in the still-falling snow. Marcus's shadow shuddered and danced on the wool cart. The snow on its bench was hardly an inch thick. Marcus hooked a foot on the iron loop beside the wheel and hauled himself up. Once atop it, he pulled back the tarp. Tag lay curled in a ball like a cat. Now that the words had been said, Marcus could see where the whiskers were unevenly placed, the dye in the hair patchy. What had been an underfed, half-dim Firstblood boy resolved into a girl with Cinnae blood.

"Wh-what—" the girl began, and Marcus grabbed her shoulder and pulled her to her feet. Her lips were blue from the cold.

"Yardem?"

"Here, sir," the Tralgu said from the cart's side.

"Catch," Marcus said and shoved her over. The girl yelped

as she fell, and then Yardem had her in a headlock. Her cries were wild and Yardem grunted once as a lucky blow struck. Marcus ignored the struggle. The wool was damp and stank of mildew. He lifted up bolt after bolt, letting them drop to the ground. The girl's cries became sharper, and then quiet. Marcus's hand found something hard.

"Pass me a torch," he called.

Instead, Master Kit scrambled up beside him. The old man's face expression said nothing. In the torchlight, Marcus pulled up the box. Blackwood with an iron fastener and hard leather hinges. Marcus drew his dagger and slashed at the hinges until there was enough play to let him push the blade between lid and box.

"Be careful," Master Kit said as Marcus bore down on the knife.

"Late for that," Marcus said, and the lock gave with a snap. The box hung open, limp and broken. Inside, a thousand bits of cut glass glittered and shone. No. Not glass. Gems. Garnets and rubies, emeralds and diamonds and pearls. The box was full to the brim with them. Marcus looked down into the hole he had left in the wool and snow. There were more boxes like it. Dozens of them.

He looked at Master Kit. The old man's eyes were wide with shock.

"All right," Marcus said shortly, letting the box fall closed. "Come on."

On the ground, the other guards were clustered around Yardem and the girl. Yardem still held the girl in his wide arms, ready to choke her asleep. Tears were flowing down her cheeks. The set of her jaw was all defiance and grief. Marcus pinched off a bit of the whiskers from her cheek, rubbed them between his fingers, and let them drop to the ground. Beside the Tralgu's bulk, she seemed barely more than a child. Her eyes met Marcus's, and he saw the plea there. Something dangerous shifted in his chest. Not rage, not indignation. Not even sorrow. Memory so vibrant and bright it was painful. He told himself to turn away.

"Please," the girl said.

"Kit," he said. "Take her inside. Our quarters. She doesn't talk to anyone, not even the 'van master."

"As you say, Captain," Master Kit said. Yardem loosened his grip and stood a half step back. His eyes were locked on the girl, ready to incapacitate her again if she attacked. Master Kit held out a hand to her. "Come along, my dear. You're among friends."

The girl hesitated, her gaze jumping from Marcus to Yardem to Master Kit and back again. Tears filled her eyes, but she didn't sob. He'd known another girl once who'd cried the same way. Marcus pushed the thought aside. Master Kit led her away. The others, as if by habit, followed the master actor and left the soldiers to themselves.

"The cart," Marcus said.

"No one comes near it, sir," Yardem said.

Marcus squinted up into the falling snow. "How old do you think she is?"

"Part Cinnae. Makes it hard to tell," Yardem rumbled. "Sixteen summers. Seventeen."

"That was my thought too."

"Same age Merian would have been."

"Near that."

Marcus turned back toward the cliff. Light glimmered in the stone-carved windows, and the ancient, snow-filled script carved into the cliffside above shone deep grey against the black.

"Sir?"

Marcus looked back. The Tralgu was already sitting on

the cart's bench and wrapping the wool around himself in the style of Pût nomads to keep his body warm and his sword arm free.

"Don't let what happened at Ellis affect your judgment. She's not your daughter."

The emotion in Marcus's chest shifted uneasily, like a babe troubled in its sleep.

"No one is," he said and walked into the darkness.

A cup of warm cider, Master Kit's sympathetic ear, and half an hour got the full tale. The Medean bank, the original carter's death, the desperate smuggler's run to Carse. The girl wept through half of it. She'd left the only home she'd known and the nearest she had to family. Marcus listened to it all with arms crossed, the scowl etching into his face. What caught him were the small things about her — the way her voice grew stronger when she talked about letters of exchange and the problem of capital transport, the habit she had of pushing her hair out of her eyes even when it wasn't there, the protective angle of her shoulders and her neck. Tag the Carter had been beneath his notice. Cithrin bel Sarcour, amateur smuggler, was a different matter.

When she was done, Marcus left her with the actors, took Master Kit by the elbow, and steered him out through the thin stone corridors that laced the stones of Bellin. The darkness was broken by candles at each turning; enough light to see where they were going, if not the individual steps that would get there. But walking slowly fit Marcus's needs at the moment.

"You knew about this?" Marcus said.

"I knew the girl was traveling in disguise."

"You never mentioned it."

"I didn't think it was odd. In my experience, people take

on roles and put them off again quite often. Consider my own position with the caravan."

Marcus took a long, slow breath.

"All right," he said. "I'll have to take this to the 'van master. We can't stay here."

"No offense meant, Captain, but why not? It seems to me that the caravan's mission remains what it was before. Now that we know the situation, perhaps we could help the girl maintain her illusion. We could hide her cargo until spring, and carry on as if nothing were different."

"Doesn't work that way."

"What doesn't work that way, Captain?" Master Kit asked. Marcus paused at a sharp turn. The single candle gave the carved lines of the wall the aspect of life and awareness. In the dim light, the actor's face was dull gold and blackness.

"*World* doesn't work that way," Marcus said. "You never have that much money without blood coming out of it. Eventually one of us would get greedy. And even if we didn't, there's someone looking for that cart."

"But how would they find it, if they didn't also know to look for us?" Master Kit asked. Marcus noted that the man hadn't argued against the dangers of greed and betrayal.

"At a guess? They'd hear stories about a 'van being guarded by the hero of Gradis and Wodford. And with a cunning man who can turn aside arrows and command the power of the trees."

The chagrin on the actor's face told Marcus that his point was clear.

"This isn't what I hired you on for," Marcus said, "but I need you to stay with me."

Master Kit pursed his lips, hesitated for a long moment,

then turned and walked farther into the darkness between candles, heading toward the 'van master's lodging. Marcus followed him. For almost a minute, their footsteps were the only sounds.

"What are your plans?" Master Kit said, his voice cautious. Marcus nodded to himself. At least it hadn't been *no*.

"Go south," Marcus said. "West is snowbound, east is back toward whoever follows us. North is the Dry Wastes in winter. We let it be known we're taking the goods to Maccia or Gilea, trying to sell at the markets there instead of wait for Carse. Move off east, then cut south."

"I don't know of any roads going south until—"

"Not roads. We have to get off the dragon's roads and take farm tracks and local paths down to the Inner Sea. There's a pass along the coast hardly ever freezes. Put us into Birancour in four weeks if it stays cold. Five, if it thaws enough to get muddy. They don't take well to armed bands crossing the border, so anyone following us might be turned back. Another week and we're in Porte Oliva. It's a big enough city to disappear into for the winter. Or if the roads are decent, we can push on for Northcoast and Carse."

"It seems like the long way around," Master Kit said. The hallway opened out into a wider chamber where several passages came together and an oil lamp hung from a worked iron bracket, and Master Kit stopped in the light, turning to face him. The man's face was gentle and sober. "I wonder whether you've considered the other option?"

"Don't see there is one."

"We could all visit the cart, fill our pockets and purses, and vanish like the dew. Anything left, we could put in a warehouse as someone else's problem."

"That might be the wise thing," Marcus said. "But it's not the job. We keep the 'van safe until it gets where it's going."

Marcus could see the skepticism in the actor's long face, and the grim amusement. It was, Marcus knew, the moment that would decide all the rest. If the actor refused, there weren't many options left.

Master Kit shrugged.

"Then I suppose we should tell the 'van master that his plans have changed."

The caravan left just before midday under low, grey skies. Marcus rode fore. His head still ached from a night of dreams as familiar as they were vicious. Blood and fire. The dying screams of a woman and a child who were both twelve years' dust now. The smell of burning hair. It had been years since he'd woken calling for his wife and daughter. For Alys and Merian. He'd hoped the nightmares had passed forever, but clearly they had returned, at least for the time.

He'd lived through them before. He could again.

The 'van master sat at his side, their white-plumed breaths falling in and out of time. Crows watched them from snow-caked trees, shifting their wings like old men. The snow was wet, but not more than a foot thick on the road. It would be worse once they turned off the dragon's roads.

"Can't believe we're doing this," the 'van master said for the hundredth time. "They didn't even *tell* me."

"They didn't think of you as a smuggler," Marcus said.

"Thought of me as a dupe."

"Me too," Marcus said. And then to the Timzinae's out-raged look, "No, *they* also thought *I* was a dupe. Not that *I* also thought *you* were."

The 'van master sank into a bitter silence. The cliffs of Bellin faded behind them. It promised to be a miserable winter. When they stopped for the night, putting up tents in the fast-fading twilight, Marcus walked through the camp with

Yardem at his side. Conversations paused when they came near. Smiles grew false and unconvincing. Resentment soaked the caravan like oil on a wick. He'd have to be sure nothing happened to light it. It was no worse than he'd expected. When he came to his own tent, she was waiting for him.

Tag the Carter was gone, vanished from the world as if he'd never been. The actors had helped her wash the worst of the dye from her hair, and without the lichenous whiskers her face seemed almost unnaturally clean. Youth and her Cinnae blood conspired to make her coltish, but a few years would change her into a woman.

"Captain Wester," she said, then swallowed nervously. "I didn't get to say how much I appreciate this."

"It's what I do," Marcus said.

"All the same, it's more than I could have asked, and... Thank you."

"You aren't safe yet," Marcus said, more sharply than he'd meant. "Save your gratitude until you are."

The girl flushed, her cheeks like rose petals on snow. She half bowed, turned, and walked away, footsteps crunching in the snow. Marcus watched her go, shook his head, and spat. Yardem, still at his side, cleared his throat.

"This girl's not my daughter," Marcus said.

"She's not, sir."

"She doesn't deserve my protection more than any other man or woman in this 'van."

"She doesn't, sir."

Marcus squinted up into the clouds.

"I'm in trouble here," he said.

"Yes, sir," Yardem said. "You are."

Dawson

T he King's Hunt pressed through the thick-falling snow, the calling of the hounds made fainter and eerie by the grey. Dawson Kalliam leaned in toward his horse's steaming neck, feeling the great animal launch itself into the air. He saw the icy ditch as a blur beneath them, and then it was gone, and the impact of their landing gave way again to the wind-swift chase. Behind him, half a dozen voices rose, but not the king's. Dawson ignored them. To his left, a grey horse with red leather hunter's barding loomed out of the snow. Feldin Maas. Others rode close behind, nothing more than snow-drowned shadows. Dawson leaned closer to his mount, digging heels into its flanks, urging it faster.

The hart had run long and hard, nearly outwitting the hunstmen and their dogs twice. But Dawson had ridden the hills of Osterling Fells in all weather since he was a boy, and he knew the traps of them. The hart had turned down a blind canyon, and it would not return from it. The kill, of course, would be King Simeon's. The race now was to be the first to reach their prey.

The lower branches of a pine stood startling green against the void, marking where the hart had passed. Dawson turned, feeling Feldin Maas and the others crowding close behind him. Someone was shouting. The howls and yaps of the hounds grew louder. He set his teeth, willing himself forward.

Something surged on his right. Not the grey. A white horse without barding. Its rider had no helmet or cap, and the long red-gold hair announced Curtin Issandrian as clearly as a pennant. Dawson dug his heels again, and his horse leapt forward. Too fast. He felt the drumming, pounding rhythm of the gallop roughen and the horse struggled to keep its feet. The white surged forward, passing him, and a moment later the grey with Feldin Maas was at his shoulder.

If the hart had gone another thousand yards, Dawson might have retaken the position of honor, but the doomed beast stood at bay in a clearing too near. Two dogs lay dead at its feet, and the huntsmen held back the rest of the pack with their voices and short whips. A point had broken off the hart's rack, and blood marked its side. Its left hind leg was blood-soaked where an overeager hound had ripped off its dewclaw, and its patchy winter coat gave it the aspect of a traveler at the end of a journey. It turned toward them, breath white and exhausted, as Curtin Issandrian pulled to a stop, Dawson and Feldin Maas just behind him.

"Well played, Issandrian," Dawson said bitterly.

"It's a beautiful thing, isn't it?" the victor said, ignoring him. Dawson had to admit the hart had an air of real nobility to it. Exhausted, beaten, and facing death, there was no sense of fear from it. Resignation, perhaps. Hatred, certainly. Issandrian drew his sword and saluted the beast, and it lowered its head as if in acknowledgment. The second group of riders pelted into the clearing, six together each with the sigils of their houses. The hounds leaped and barked, the huntsmen shouted and cursed.

And then the king.

King Simeon rode into the clearing on a huge black charger, the black leather reins braided with scarlet and gold. Prince Aster rode a pony at his father's side, the child's spine straight with pride and his armor still a little too large for his frame. His personal master of the hunt rode behind and behind him: a huge Jasuru in green-gold armor that matched his scales. King Simeon himself wore dark leathers studded with silver and a black helm that hid the beginnings of jowls and his skewed nose.

Dawson had been on hunts with him since they had both been boys younger than Maas and Issandrian, and he could see the weariness in the king's spine, even if no one else could. The rest of the hunting party rode behind him, the casual hunters more interested in gossip and a clean day's ride than the sport of it. The banners of all the great houses were present, the court of Camnipol come to a clearing in Osterling Fells.

The Jasuru huntsman lifted a spear from his back and held it out to King Simeon. In the king's hands, it seemed longer. The Jasuru huntsman called, and the dogs surged forward, leaping at the hart. Distracting it. King Simeon set the spear, spurred his mount, and charged. At the impact, the hart staggered back, the spear's point deep in its neck. As it fell, Dawson had the visceral sense that the beast was surprised more than pained. Death, however clearly foretold, still came unexpectedly. King Simeon's arm was as strong as ever, his eyes as keen. The hart died fast and without the need for an arrow's grace. When the huntsmen called back the hounds and lifted fists to confirm that the beast was dead, a cheer rose from the noblemen, Dawson's voice among them.

"So who took honors?" King Simeon asked as his huntsman went about unmaking the hart. "Issandrian? Or was it you, Kalliam?"

"It was so near at the end," Issandrian said, "I would say the baron and I arrived together."

Feldin Maas dropped down from his horse with a smirk and went to examine the killed dogs.

"Not true," Dawson said. "Issandrian arrived a good length ahead of me. The honors go to him."

And I will not carry a debt to you, even something as small as that, he thought but did not say.

"Issandrian will have the horns, then," King Simeon said, and then, shouting, "Issandrian!"

The others raised fists and swords, grinning in the snow-fall, and called out the victor's name. The feast would come the next day, the venison cooked at Dawson's own hearth, and Issandrian given the place of honor. The thought was like a knot in his throat.

"Are you all right?" the king said, softly enough that the words would not carry.

"Fine, Highness," Dawson said. "I'm fine."

An hour later, as they rode back to the house, Feldin Maas trotted alongside him. Since Vanai's fall and the defeat of the Maccian reinforcements, Dawson had pretended that the news from the Free Cities meant nothing particular to him, but the charade chafed.

"Lord Kalliam," Maas said. "Something for you."

He tossed a twig to Dawson. No, not a twig. A bit of broken horn, red with the dog's blood.

"Small honor's better than none, eh?" Maas said with a grin, then chucked to his mount and moved forward.

"Small honor," Dawson said bitterly and under his breath, the words white as fog.

As they rode back to the holding, the snowfall turned from deep, feathery flakes to mere specks, and the mountains to the east reappeared as the low clouds thinned and broke. The scent of smoke touched the air, and the spiraling towers of Osterling Fells stood in the south. The stone — granite and dragon's jade — glowed with sunlight, and the garlands that hung from the battlements left the impression that the buildings themselves had come to welcome the moment's brightness.

As host, Dawson was to oversee the preparation of the hart. It meant little more than standing in the kitchens for half an hour looking jolly, and still his soul rebelled. He couldn't bring himself to descend into the chaos of servants and dogs. He stalked to the wide stone stairs beside the ovens and stood on the landing that overlooked the preparation tables. Along the wall, pies and loaves of bread cooled, and an ancient woman pressed peacock feathers into a pork loaf that had been sculpted to resemble the bird and candied until it shone like glass. The smell of baked raisins and chicken filled the hot air. The huntsmen arrived with the carcass, and four young men fell to preparing the meat, rubbing salt, mint leaves, and butter into the flesh, carving out the glands and veins that the unmaking had left in. Dawson scowled and watched. The beast had been noble once, and watching it now —

"Husband?"

Clara, behind him, wore the pleasant expression she adopted in the early stages of exhaustion. Her eyes glittered, and the dimples that framed her mouth dug just a fraction deeper than usual. No one would know who hadn't spent a lifetime looking at her. He resented the court for putting that look in her eyes.

"Wife," he said.

"If we might?" she said, taking half a step toward the back hall. Annoyance tightened his mouth. Not with her, but with whatever domestic catastrophe required him now.

He nodded curtly and followed her back toward the shadows and relative privacy. Before he left the landing a new voice stopped him.

"Sir! You've dropped this, my lord."

One of the huntsmen stood at the stair. A young man, wide-chinned and open-faced, wearing Kalliam livery. He held out the bit of broken, blood-darkened horn. A servant, calling Baron Kalliam back like a child for a lost bauble.

Dawson felt his face darken, his hands clench.

"What is your name," he said, and the huntsman went pale at the sound of his voice

"Vincen, sir. Vincen Coe."

"You are no man of mine, Vincen Coe. Get your things and leave my house by nightfall."

"M-my lord?"

"Do you want to be whipped in the bargain, boy?" Dawson shouted. The kitchen below them went silent, all eyes turning to them, and then quickly away.

"No, my lord," the huntsman said.

Dawson turned and stalked into the gloom of the corridor, Clara at his side. She didn't rebuke him. In the shadows of the stair, she leaned in speaking quietly and almost into his ear.

"Simeon asked for a warm bath when he came in, and instead of kicking everyone else out of the blue rooms, I had the janitor prepare Andr's house. The one by the eastern wing? It's a more pleasant space anyway, and it has those clever little pipes to keep the water hot."

"That's fine," Dawson said.

"I've left orders that no one else be let in except you, of course. Because I knew that you wanted a moment with him."

"I can't intrude on the king's bath," Dawson said.

"Of course you can, dear. Only tell him I didn't remember to warn you. I was very careful to mention that it was the place you've always preferred after a hunt, so it won't be at all implausible. Unless, of course, he asks the servants and they say you actually use the blue rooms. But prying like that would be rude, and Simeon's never struck me that way, has he you?"

Dawson felt a weight he'd only been half aware of lift from him.

"What did I do to deserve a wife as perfect as you?"

"It was luck," she said, a faint smile penetrating her polite façade. "Now go before he finishes his bath. I'll tend to that poor puppy of a huntsman you just kicked. They really should know better than to approach you when you're in a temper."

Andr's house sat within the walls of the holding proper, tucked beside the chapel hall and otherwise apart from the main buildings. The Cinnae poet whose name it bore had lived in it when Osterling Fells had been the seat of a king with a penchant for the art of lesser races, and Antea only the name of a minor line of noblemen half a day's ride to the north. None of Andr's poems had survived the centuries. The only marks that she had left on the world were a small house that bore her name and a carving in the stone doorway — DRACANI SANT DRACAS — whose meaning was itself forgotten.

King Simeon lay in a bath of worked bronze shaped into a wide Dartinae hand, the long fingers turned back to the palm and dribbling steaming hot water from channels just beneath the claws. A stone bowl of soap rested in a shelf on the thumb. A window of stained glass turned the warm air green and gold. The body servants stood at the back wall with soft cloths to dry the king and black swords to defend him. The king looked up as Dawson stepped into the room.

"Forgive me, sire," Dawson said. "I hadn't known you were here."

"It's nothing, old friend," Simeon said, gesturing to the body servants. "I knew I was intruding on your private haunts. Sit. Enjoy the heat, and I'll make way for you as soon as I have feeling back in my toes."

"Thank you, sire," Dawson said as the servants brought a stool for him. "As it happens, I was hoping to discuss a matter with you in private. About Vanai. There's something it would be best you hear from me."

King Simeon sat up, and for a moment, they weren't lord and subject noble, but Simeon and Dawson again. Two boys of blood and rank, full of their own pride and dignity. Dawson's disdain for the Vanai campaign and outrage at his own son being set to serve under Alan Klin were well-known matters. Still, Dawson rehashed them, building up his anger and self-righteousness to a speed that would carry him through his confession. Simeon listened and the body servants ignored everything with equal care. Dawson watched the old, familiar face as it passed from curiosity to surprise to disappointment and settled at the end in a species of amused despair.

"You have to stop playing games like that with Issandrian's cabal," the king of Imperial Antea said, leaning back in his bath. "And still, I wish to God it had worked. Would have saved me half a world of trouble. You've heard about the Edford Charter?"

"The what?"

"Edford Charter. It's a piece of parchment a priest found in the deepest library of Sevenpol that names the head of a farmer's council under King Durren the White. There's a petition in the north to name a new farmer's council on the strength of it. Any landholder with enough crops to pay in would have a voice in court."

"You can't be serious," Dawson said. "Are they going to drive mules through the palaces? Keep goats in the Kingspire gardens?"

"Don't suggest it to them," the king said, reaching for the bowl of soap.

"It's a gambit," Dawson said. "They'll never do it."

"You don't understand how split the court is, old friend. Issandrian is well loved by the lowborn. If they gain power, he gains with them. And now with Klin as his purse in Vanai, I don't see that I have a great deal of leverage."

"You can't mean—"

"No, there can't be a farmer's council. But there's peace to be made. At midsummer, I'm sending Aster to be Issandrian's ward."

The great bronze fingertips dripped. A passing cloud dimmed the light. King Simeon sat quietly lathering his arms, expressionless as the implications unfolded themselves between them.

"He'd be regent," Dawson said, his voice thick and strangled. "If you died before Aster came of age, Issandrian would be regent."

"Not a sure thing, but he'd have a claim to it."

"He's going to have you killed. This is treason."

"This is politics," Simeon said. "I had hoped Ternigan would keep the city for himself, but the old bastard's independent-minded. He knows Issandrian's cabal is on the rise. Now he's done them a favor without quite throwing himself in their camp. I'll have to woo him. They'll have to woo him. He'll be sitting in Kavinpol getting kissed on both cheeks."

"Curtin Issandrian will *kill* you, Simeon."

The king lay back, dark water running up his arms and darkening his hair. A scum of soap floated and spun on the water.

"He won't. As long as he has my son, he can call my tunes without the bother of sitting on a throne."

"Then break him," Dawson said. "I'll help you. We can build a cabal of our own. There are men who haven't forgotten the old ways. They're *hungry* for this. We can rally them."

"We can, yes, but to what end?"

"Simeon. Old friend. This is the moment. Antea needs a true king now. You have it in you to be that man. Don't send your boy to Issandrian."

"The time's not right. Issandrian's on the rise, and opposing him now will only add to the strife. Better to wait until he stumbles. My work now is to see that we don't follow the dragon's path along the way. If I can give Aster the kingdom without a civil war, it will be legacy enough."

"Even if it's not the true Antea?" Dawson said, an ache gathering behind his eyes. "What honor is there in a kingdom that's lost its heritage to these preening, self-important children?"

"If you'd said it before Ternigan handed him Vanai, I might have agreed. But where's the honor in fighting a battle you can't win?"

Dawson looked at his hands. Age had thickened his knuckles and cold chapped his skin. The smell of soap mocked his nose. His boyhood friend, his lord and king, sighed and grunted, shifting in his bath like an old man. Somewhere in Osterling Fells, Curtin Issandrian and Feldin Maas were drinking his wine, toasting each other. Laughing. Dawson's cheeks ached, and he forced himself to relax his jaw.

Where's the honor in fighting a battle you can't win? hung in the air between them. When he could keep the disappointment out of his voice, Dawson spoke.

"Where else would it be, my lord?"

Cithrin

The dragon's roads behind them, the world turned to snow and mud. The cart beneath her lurched through ruts and holes, the mules before her strained and slipped, and the wheels grumbled and spat through the churn the carts ahead of her had left. Cithrin sat, reins in her numbed fingers, her breath making ghosts, and watched the low hills give way to plains, the forests thin and snow-sheeted scrub and brambles take their place. In springtime, the land surrounding the Free Cities might be green and alive, but now it seemed empty and eternal.

They passed a field with stacks of rotting hay that testified to some farmer's tragedy. A vineyard where row after row or trellis supported black, dead-looking woody vines. Now and again, a snow hare would bound along, almost too far away to see. Or a deer would stray near until one of the carters or the guards shot an arrow toward it in hope of fresh venison. From what she could tell, they never hit.

Mostly it was cold. And the days were still getting shorter.

The caravan master stopped them for the night at an abandoned mill. Cithrin pulled her cart to a stop beside the ice sheet of the pond, unhooked her mud-spattered mules, and rubbed them clean as they ate. The sun hung low and bloody in the west. Opal came to check on her, and the woman's mild eyes seemed pleased by what she saw.

"We'll make an honest carter of you yet, my dear," she said.

Cithrin's smile hurt her cold-burned cheeks. "A carter, maybe," she said. "Honest is another question."

The older woman's eyebrows rose. "More humor," Opal said. "The world may stop turning. Are you coming to the meal?"

"I don't think so," Cithrin said, looking at one of the mules' hoofs. The small sore she'd seen the day before was still there, but hadn't gotten worse. "I don't like being with them."

"Them?"

"The others. I don't think they like me. If it wasn't for me, they'd all be in Bellin sitting around a fire grate. And the captain..."

"Wester? Yes, he is a bit of a bear, isn't he? I still don't know quite what to make of him myself," Opal said, her voice dry and speculative and on the edge of flirtation. "Still, I'm sure he wouldn't bite unless you asked him."

"All the same," Cithrin said. "I think I'll stay with the cart."

"I'll bring you a plate, then."

"Thank you," Cithrin said. "And Opal?"

"Yes?"

"Thank you."

The guard smiled and dropped a small, ironic curtsey. Cithrin watched her walk back toward the mill house. Someone was lighting a fire in there, thin smoke rising from the stone chimney. Around her, the snow glowed gold and then red, and then between one moment and the next, grey. Cithrin laid blankets on her mules and lit a small fire of her own. Opal returned with a plate of stewed greens and wheat cakes, then went back to the voices and music. Cithrin stood to follow her and then sat back down.

As she ate, the stars came out. Snow made the pale blue light of a three-quarter moon seem brighter than it should have been. The cold grew, and Cithrin huddled closer to her small fire. The chill seeped in, pressing on her. Narrowing her. Later, when the captain and the Tralgu had gone out scouting and the others had gone to sleep, she'd sneak into the mill house and find a corner to curl up in. At breakfast, she'd avoid the stares and curiosity of the other carters and come back to her mules as quickly as she could. Daylight was scarce, and the caravan master didn't leave much time for idle banter. These long, dark, cold hours between work's end and sleep were the worst part of her day. She passed them by retreating into her mind.

She might begin by singing herself songs or recalling plays and performances she'd gone to as part of the bank. Before long, though, she found herself returning to Magister Imaniel and his constant dinner-table testing. The difference between a gift given for a consideration and a formal loan, the paradox of two parties following reason and yet coming to a solution to no one's advantage, the strategies of a single contract and the strategies of a contract that is continually renewed. The puzzles were the playthings of her childhood, and she came to them now for comfort and solace.

She found herself estimating the worth of the caravan as a whole, how much they might have gained in Carse and how much more or less they would have to offer in Porte Oliva to make the two journeys balance. She thought about Bellin, and whether taxation on passage or on boarding would make the township richer. At what point it would make as much sense to abandon the carts as to keep on. Whether Magister Imaniel had been wise to invest in a brewery and also insure it against fire. In the absence of real information, it was no more than a game, but it was the game that she knew best.

Banking, Magister Imaniel said, wasn't about gold and silver. It was about who knew something no one else did, about who could be trusted and who not, about seeming one thing and being another. With the questions she asked herself, she could conjure him and Cam and Besel. She could see their faces again, hear their laughter, and sink into another time and place. One where she was loved. Or no, not truly. But at least where she belonged.

Even as the night around her grew colder, the knot in her belly loosened. Her tight-curled body grew softer and more at ease. She fed larger sticks into the fire, watching the flames first dim under the weight of the wood, and then brighten as it caught. The heat touched her face and hands, and the wool wrapped around her kept the worst of the night at bay.

What would happen, she wondered, if a bank offered a greater loan to those who'd repaid an old one before the set time? The borrowers would gain more gold by the arrangement, and the bank would see its profits more quickly. *And yet,* Magister Imaniel said in her mind, *if everyone benefits, you've overlooked something.* There was some consequence that she was missing...

"Cithrin."

She looked up. Sandr, half crouched, scuttled from the shadows between the carts. One of the mules lifted his head, snorted a great plume of white breath, and went back to his rest. As Sandr sat, she heard an odd clanking of metal and the telltale sloshing of wine in a skin.

"You didn't," she said, and Sandr grinned.

"Master Kit won't mind. He stocked up again as soon as we reached Bellin, getting ready for the winter. Only now he's got to haul it through the back end of the world. We'll be doing him a favor, lightening the load."

"You are going to get in so much trouble," she said.

"Never happen."

He opened the skin with a gloved hand and held it out to her. The smell of the fumes warmed her almost before the wine. Rich and strong and soft, it washed her mouth and tongue, flowed down her throat. The warmth of it lit her like she'd swallowed a candle. There was no sweetness to it, but something deeper.

"*God,*" she said.

"It's good, isn't it?" Sandr said.

She grinned and took another long drink. Then another. The warmth spread into her belly and started pressing out toward her arms and legs. Reluctantly, she passed it back.

"That's not all," he said. "I've got something for you."

He pulled a canvas bag out from beneath his cloak. The cloth reeked of dust and rot, and something in it shifted and clanked as he put it on the snow. His eyes sparkled in the moonlight.

"They were in the back storeroom. And a bunch of other things. Smit found them really, but I thought of you and I traded him."

Sandr pulled out a cracked leather boot laced with string. A complication of rusted metal clung to the sole, dark and dingy except for a knifelike blade running the length that shone bright and new-sharpened.

"Ever skated?" Sandr asked.

Cithrin shook her head. Sandr pulled two pairs of boots out of the sack, the ancient leather grey in the dim light. She took another long drink of the wine.

"They're too big," he said, "but I put some sand inside.

Sand's good because it shifts to fit the shape of your foot. Cloth just bunches up. Here, try them."

I don't want to, Cithrin thought, but Sandr had her foot in his hand, stripping off her boot, and he was so pleased with himself. The skate was cold and the bent leather bit into the top of her foot, but Sandr pulled the string laces tight and started on her other foot.

"I learned how in Asterilhold," Sandr said. "Two...no, God, three years ago. I'd just joined the troop and Master Kit had us in Kaltfel for the winter. So cold your spit froze before it hit the ground, and the nights went on forever. But there's a lake in the middle of the city, and the whole time we were there, you could cross it anywhere. There's a winter city they build on the ice every year. Houses and taverns and all. Like a real town."

"Really?" she said.

"It was brilliant. There. I think that's done it. Let me get mine on."

She took another mouthful of the fortified wine, and it pressed its heat out toward her fingers and toes. Somehow, they'd already gone through half the skin. She felt it in her cheeks. And the fumes made her head feel muzzy and bright. Sandr struggled and grunted, the knife-shoe of the skates creaking and rattling. It seemed impossible that anything so awkward would actually work until he had the last strap in place, half walked and half wobbled to the pond, and then pressed himself out onto the ice. Between one breath and the next, he became grace made flesh. His legs scissored and shifted, the blades hissing as they scored the ice. His body shifted and swooped as he slid across the pond and then back, his arms graceful as a dancer's.

"They're not bad," he called. "Come on. You try."

Another drink of wine, and then one more for luck, and

Cithrin maneuvered herself out. Cold air bit at her, but only with dull teeth. Her ankles shifted as she fought to make sense of this new way of balancing. She tried to push off the way Sandr did, and fell hard on the ice. Sandr laughed his delight.

"It's hard the first time," he said, hissing to her side. "Give me your hand. I'll show you."

Within minutes, her knees were bent, her arms widespread, and her feet chopping at the ice. But she didn't fall.

"Don't try to walk," Sandr said. "Push with one foot, glide on the other."

"Easy for you," she said. "You know what you're doing."

"This time. I was worse than you when I started."

"Flatterer."

"Maybe you're worth flattering. No, like that. That's it. *That's* it!"

Cithin's body caught the trick, and she found herself gliding. Not quite as gracefully and certainly as Sandr, but closer. The ice sped under her, white and grey and black in the moonlight. The night tasted like the fortified wine and moved like a river flowing around her. Sandr whooped and took her hand, and together they raced the length of the mill pond, the grooves of their skates tracing white lines in the dim.

From the banks, one of the mules commented with a grunt and flick of his haunch. The wind of Cithin's passage whuffled in her ears. She felt herself grinning and spinning. The knot in her belly was a memory, a dream, a thing that happened to another person. She fell twice more, but it only seemed funny. The ice was cloud and sky, and she had learned how to fly. It creaked and groaned under her weight, and Sandr clapped his hands as she made an elaborate and awkward curtsey in the center of the pond.

"Race me," he shouted. "There and back."

Like an arrow from a bow, Sandr sped for the far bank, and Cithrin followed him. Her legs ached, and her heart beat like a boulder rolling down a hill, her numb face made itself a mask. Sandr reached the edge of the ice, pushed off from the snow, and sped past her, going back toward her cart. Cithrin turned too, pushing faster, harder. In the middle of the pond, the ice darkened and complained, but then she was over it, almost at Sandr's back, skating beside him, past him. Almost past him.

Her skate slammed into the snow and the dead, winter-killed reeds. The moon-blued ground rose up and hit her so hard she couldn't breathe. Sandr lay beside her, his eyes wide, his cheeks as red as if she'd pinched them. The look of surprise and concern on his face was so comic that, when she could, Cithrin started laughing.

Sandr's laughter twinned with hers, and he threw a handful of snow in the air, the flakes drifting down around them like dandelion fluff. And then he rolled to her, resting his weight against her side. His lips were on hers.

Oh, she thought. And then, half a breath later, she tried kissing him back.

It wasn't as awkward as she'd expected it to be. His arms shifted around her, his body entirely on hers now, pressing her into the snow that didn't seem cold at all. His hand fumbled at her jacket, and then the thick wool sweater. His fingers found her skin. She felt herself arching up, pressing herself into the touch almost as if she were watching it be done. She heard her breath grow ragged.

"Cithrin," Sandr said. "You need to... You need to know..."

"Don't," she said.

He stopped, pulling back. His hand retreated from her

breasts. Contrition narrowed his face. She felt a flare of impatience.

"Don't *talk*, I mean," she said.

She'd always known about sex in a general way. Cam had talked about it in dour, stern, and warning tones. She'd seen the mummers in the spring carnival dancing through the torchlit streets in masks and nothing more. Perhaps there should have been no mystery. And still, as she undid her belt and pushed down the rough pants, she wondered whether this was what Besel had done with all those other girls. All the ones that weren't her. Had it been like this for them? She'd heard it hurt the first time. She wondered what that would feel like. Sandr's bare flanks shone nearly as pale as the snow. Concentration possessed him as he tried to pry off his skates without rising up.

I hope it's all right that I don't love him, she thought.

A roar came out of nowhere, deep and violent and sudden. Sandr rose up into the air, his weight gone, his eyes round in surprise. Cithrin grabbed for her waistband. Her first thought was that a monstrous bird had come down from the sky and plucked him away.

Captain Wester threw Sandr out onto the ice, where he landed awkward and skidding. The captain's sword hissed out of its scabbard, and he moved toward Sandr, cursing in three languages. Cithrin rose to her knees, tugging at her clothing. Sandr stumbled back, his still-erect penis bobbing comically, and slipped.

"I wasn't forcing her," Sandr squeaked. "I wasn't forcing."

"Do I care?" Wester shouted, pointing with his sword at the wineskin half covered by snow. "You get her stupid drunk to get her knees apart, and you want a good-conduct medal?"

"I'm not drunk," Cithrin said, realizing that she likely was. Wester ignored her.

"Touch her again, son, and I cut something off you. Best pray it's a finger."

Sandr opened his mouth, but only a high whine came out.

"Stop it!" Cithrin shouted. "Leave him alone!"

Wester turned to her, rage in his eyes. Taller than she was, twice as broad, and with naked steel in his hand, he made the small, still part of her mind tell her to be quiet. Wine and embarrassment and anger washed her forward.

"Who are you to tell him what he can and can't?" she said. "Who are you to tell *me*?"

"I am the man who's saving your life. And you will do as I say," Wester shouted, but she thought there was a new confusion in his eyes. "I won't have you turning into a whore."

The word bit. Cithrin balled her fists until her knuckles ached. Blood lit her cheeks and roared in her ears. When she spoke, she shrieked.

"I wasn't going to *charge him*!"

Wester looked at her as if seeing her for the first time. The confusion deepened, knitting his brow, and something like amusement plucked at his mouth. And then—inexplicably—anguish.

"Captain," a new voice growled, and the Tralgu loomed out of the darkness.

"Not a good time, Yardem," Wester said.

"Took that from the shouting, sir. There's soldiers."

Wester changed between one heartbeat and the next. His face cleared, his body pulled back a degree. Their confrontation evaporated, and Cithrin felt herself unnerved by the sudden shift. It seemed unfair that the captain had abandoned their conflict with things still unsettled.

"Where?" Wester asked.

"Camped over the ridge to the east," the Tralgu said. "Two dozen. Antean banner, Vanai tents."

"Well, God smiled," Wester said. "Any chance their scouts overlooked us?"

"None."

"Did they see you?"

"No."

Cithrin's rage collapsed as the words fought through the wine fumes and trailing remnants of anger. Wester was already pacing the length of her cart. He considered Sandr still wobbling on his skates, the half-buried wineskin, the pond with the white scoring of blade tracks still on the ice.

"Sandr," he said. "Get Master Kit."

"Yes, sir," Sandr said and awkwardly scampered off toward the mill house.

Wester sheathed his sword absentmindedly. His eyes shifted across the landscape, searching for something. Cithrin waited, her heart in her throat. They couldn't run. Against two dozen, they couldn't fight. Any goodwill she might have expected from Wester was certainly gone now.

The seconds stretched by endlessly. Wester took a deep breath and let it out slowly.

"We'll need a broom," he said.

Geder

The bitterly cold predawn breeze murmured through the walls of Geder's tent and set the flame on his oil lamp dancing. He leaned closer, then cursed softly and turned up the wick. The flame brightened and then smoked. He backed it down slowly until the smoke disappeared. In the brighter light, the pale ink grew, if not clear, at least legible. He stuck his hands into his armpits for warmth and leaned in closer.

And so it came that in these final days, the three great factions entered into a war of both blood and terrible cunning such that measureless stone ships flew through the skies with great iron thorns that slaughtered dragons as they flew and also deep pods found manners to hide themselves from their enemies until they should be forgotten that they might attack an unprotected enemy and also swords envenomed to slay both master and slave. The mighty silver-scaled Morade, maddest and mightiest of the warring clutch-mates, fashioned a tool more devious than the world had known, and in the high mountains south of Haakapel (which, Geder thought, would be Hallskar now) and east of Sammer (which Geder was almost certain was the fifth-polis name for the Keshet), he forged the Righteous Servant to whom none could lie nor no one could long disbelieve, and its sigil

was of cardinal and intercardinal showing the eight directions of the world in which no falsehood could hide, and in
this great Morade found his subtlest power.

He rubbed his eyes. The thick, yellowed pages of the book
smelled of dust and mold and the odd sweet binder's glue
that no one had used in half a thousand years. When he'd
found it in the deep shadows of a rag-and-bone shop in
Vanai, it delighted him. As he struggled through his translation, his enthusiasm waned.

The author claimed to have copied and translated a much
older scroll, long since lost, that dated back to the first generations after the fall of the Dragon Empire. That was, for
the first part, a framing device for speculative essay so trite
and overdone that Geder's heart sank when he read it. In the
second part, it meant that everything else in the essay was
presented as legitimate history, which he found less interesting. And finally, the author had embraced long sentences
and complex grammar in an attempt to make the text feel
authentic, and it made every page an endurance test. By the
time Geder reached the verbs, he had to turn back and
remind himself what they were talking about.

If he'd been back in Vanai, he would have put the work
aside. But Sir Alan Klin, Protector of Vanai, had heard of
the caravan smuggling out the secret wealth of the city and
made its recovery his first priority. This meant sending his
favorites along the dragon's roads to Carse, and every man's
status after that took his search party farther and farther
from the likely hunting grounds until Jorey Kalliam was left
with the Dry Wastes, Fallon Broot on the sea road to Elassae, and Geder Palliako leading two dozen half-mutinous
Timzinae soldiers through the icy mud of the southernmost
of the Free Cities.

In their weeks on the farmer's tracks and game trails, they'd found three caravans. Small affairs hardly more than three carts each, and all of them tracking winter goods between local cities and towns. In between, days of mud and nights of nagging cold wore on Geder. And as poor a companion as his essay on the powers of dragons to unmake lies might be, it outshone the soldiers. At the end of the day, he curled into his bed, sleeping while the others drank and sang and cursed the snow. In the mornings, he rose with the cook, reading and translating and pretending that he was anywhere besides here.

A discreet scratch came at the door, and his squire stepped in along with the Timzinae who acted as his second. The squire carried a tray with a shaped-bone bowl of stewed oats with raisins and an earthenware bottle of hot, dark, oily water that pretended to be coffee. The Timzinae made a formal salute. Geder closed the book as the squire laid his food out before him.

"What are the scouts saying?" Geder asked.

"The carts haven't moved," his second said. "They aren't more than two hours' march."

"Well, no hurry then," Geder said with more cheer than he felt. "Tell the men we'll break camp after we eat and have this done with by midday."

"And after?"

"South and west," Geder said around a mouthful of oats. "That's where the road goes."

The second nodded and saluted again, turned on his heel, and left. Geder had the feeling that there was contempt in the movement, but he might only have been seeing what he expected to see. As he ate, the seams of his tent began to grow more distinct. Voices rose, men calling to each other, horses complaining, the chopping sound of planks coming down from the cooking platform. Outside, the sky moved from darkness to grey to a blue-and-white daybreak more light than warmth. By the time the weak sun had taken the worst chill from the air, Geder was mounted, and his men ready to march. According to the scouts, the newly sighted caravan was at least a decent size.

Still, Geder didn't have any real hope for more than another disappointing search and sullen locals until he saw the Tralgu.

It was sitting on the outermost cart, its ears pricked forward with an interest that didn't show in the rest of its face. Wester's second was supposed to be a Tralgu. Geder swept his eyes over the carts huddled around the old mill, counting under his breath. Information was always sketchy, memory unreliable, and carts in a rough group could be hard to count, but it was near enough to what they'd been searching for that Geder's heart began to beat a little faster.

A Timzinae in a thick wool robe walked down the road toward them. Geder motioned, and his six archers fanned out on the road behind him. The Tralgu sat forward and flicked an ear.

"You're master of this 'van?" Geder asked.

"I am," the Timzinae said. "Who the fuck are you?"

"I am Lord Geder Palliako of Rivenhalm and representative of King Simeon and Imperial Antea," Geder said. "Where are you coming from?"

"Maccia. Going back there too. Bellin's snowed over."

Geder stared down at the black eyes. The nictatating membranes slid closed and open again, blinking without blinking. Geder wasn't sure if it was a lie. It was possible, of course, that there was more than one 'van in the Free Cities with a Tralgu guard. This might still be a false alarm.

"You've stopped here?"

"Axle came loose on one of the carts. Only just got it strapped back in place. What's this all about?"

"Who's your guard captain?" Geder asked.

The 'van master, turned, spat, and pointed to a man leaning against one of the carts. A Firstblood with a blank, friendly face and an air of restrained violence. Wheat-colored hair touched by grey. Broad across the shoulder. It might have been Marcus Wester. It might have been a thousand other men.

"What's his name?"

"Tag," the 'van master said.

One of the soldiers in the road behind him spoke, his voice too low for Geder to make out the words. Another replied. He felt a blush crawling up his neck. Either the man was lying to him or he wasn't, and every moment that Geder hesitated, he felt more like a fool.

"Get your guards out onto the road," he said. "Put the carters with their carts."

"And why would I do that?"

Someone chuckled. Geder's embarrassment turned to rage.

"Because if you don't, I'll have you killed," he shouted. "And because you had the temerity to question me, I'll have every weapon and piece of armor in a pile on the road ten paces from your guardsmen. And if I find so much as a work knife overlooked, I'll leave your corpse for the *crows*."

The nictatating membrane slid open and closed. The caravan master turned around and trudged back toward the carts. Geder motioned his second closer.

"Send men around the sides. If anyone tries to sneak away, bring them back alive if you can. Dead if you have to. We're searching this place down to the pegs and nails."

"The mill house too?" the second asked.

"Everything," Geder said.

The Timzinae nodded and moved back, calling to his men. Geder watched the carts, anger and embarrassment giving way to anxiety. The captain and the caravan master exchanged a few words, and the captain looked up. He frowned at Geder, shrugged, and turned away. If there was going to be resistance, it would come now and it would come hard. Geder shifted in his saddle, the still-healing wound in his leg aching in anticipation. Movement came from the mill house, from every cart. How many soldiers would they have? If the full wealth of the Medean bank was sitting in those carts, every carter would be a swordsman or an archer. Geder's scalp began to crawl. If they had bowmen hidden in those carts, he'd be sprouting arrows. Fear shifted in his belly like he'd eaten bad fish. Trying to seem casual, he turned his horse and trotted to the rear of their formation.

To judge by the expressions of the soldiers, he hadn't fooled anybody.

The first of the guards lumbered out from the carts, half a dozen swords in her arms like firewood. She dropped them on the ground where Geder had ordered. Then a thin boy hardly old enough to be a soldier with two unstrung bows and a backload of quivers. Slowly, the unpromising parade went on, the sad pile of arms and armor growing until ten guards and a wild-haired cunning man marched out to the road in wool and cotton, counted ten paces from the heap, and stood in the clear, hugging themselves against the cold.

"Move in," Geder said.

The soldiers walked forward, blades drawn. The carters stood by their carts and smiled or frowned or looked around in confusion. Geder rode a slow turn around the little encampment. The sound of the search seemed to follow him— voices fierce and querulous, wood clacking, metal clanging against metal. He watched as his men pulled ingots of pig iron out of a cart and dropped them to the ground. One man scratched at the metal to be sure it was only what it seemed, then spat and turned back to the search.

Midday came and went. A chill wind picked up, setting the snow to skitter and swirl around their ankles. The soldiers unloaded each cart, looked under them, examined the horse and mules, and began going through the mill house. Geder got off his horse at the edge of the mill pond and looked at the bare carts, the frigid carters, the ineffectual sun in the watery sky. One of the carters—a sickly-looking girl with pale hair and skin—crouched by bolts of fallen wool and pretended not to watch Geder. He knew what she saw. A puffed-up nobleman bullying her and her friends. He wanted to go to her, to explain that it wasn't like that. That he wasn't like that.

Instead, he turned away. The shifting dust of snow moved over the ice like ripples on water. Geder walked along the edge, trying not to feel the girl's gaze on him. Some idiot had been skating. White marks showed where blades had cut across the thin ice. Lucky they didn't break through. He'd read an essay once outlining the time it took each of the thirteen races to die in icy water. Well, twelve, really. The Drowned weren't…

Geder stopped almost before he knew what stopped him. On the edge of the pond, a long, low drift of snow swept out onto the ice. The white blade marks vanished into it, and then out of it again as if the skater had passed directly through the little drift. Or it hadn't been there until after the skater had passed. Geder walked closer. The snow itself looked odd. It didn't have the ice-crust he expected, and it was smooth as broom-swept sand. Geder looked up. The guards were on the far side of the caravan. His own soldiers grouped at the mouth of the mill house. He walked around the curious snow.

Deep scores and marks marred the surface of the ice. Poking out just at ankle height, something black and square. He squatted, brushing the snow away. A box, half drowned in recently cut ice and then covered over. And others beside it, all of them crusted over with thin ice and hidden by the carefully arranged snowdrift. He looked up. The girl carter was standing now, craning her neck to see him, her hands knotted at her belly. Geder took out his knife and forced the latch. Topaz, jade, emerald, pearl, gold and silver filigree as delicate as frost. Geder pulled back like the gems had stung him, and then, as he understood what he was seeing, felt a sunrise in his chest, relief and pleasure rushing through him, unknotting his muscles and bringing a grin to his face.

He'd done it. He'd found the missing caravan and the hidden wealth of Vanai. No more of Geder Palliako, the expendable idiot. No more apologizing for what he liked to read or the roundness of his belly. Oh, no. His name would be carried back to Camnipol and King Simeon on a carriage of gold by horses with rubies on their reins. He would be the talk of the court, praised and honored and celebrated in the highest circles of the kingdom.

Except, of course, that he wouldn't. The name that would be celebrated in Camnipol was Alan Klin's.

Alan Klin, who'd humiliated him. Who'd burned his book.

Geder took a long, deep breath, let it out slowly, and closed the lid. A moment later, he opened it again, dug two double handfuls of gems out, and poured them down his shirt. The lovely little stones gathered around his belly where his belt cinched tight. He closed his jacket to cover the lumps, lowered the lid again, and scraped the snow back over it. As he stood, a wide, black joy filled him and made his first pleasure seem weak. When he walked back to the carts, he didn't need to remind himself to hold his head high. The girl watched him approach. Geder grinned at her like he was greeting an old friend or a lover. An accomplice. Briefly, he lifted a single finger to his lips. *Don't tell.*

The girl's eyes went wide. Half a breath later she nodded, only once. *I won't.* He could have kissed her.

When he found his second, the Timzinae had finished leading the common soldiers through the mill house. Geder noticed that the conversation among the soldiers stopped when he walked in the room, but this time it didn't bother him. The interior of the house smelled of mold and smoke, and the signs of the caravan's night in the shelter marked the stones of the flooring. A broom leaned against the far wall. Its head was wet, and a thin puddle of water darkened the stones beneath it. Geder pointedly ignored it.

"What have you found?" he asked.

"Nothing, my lord," the second said.

"We're wasting time here," Geder said. "Gather the men. We should move on."

The second looked around. One of the soldiers—a young Timzinae with black scales that shone like he'd polished them—shrugged.

"My lord, we haven't turned the basement. If you'd like—"

"Do you really think there's a point to it?" Geder asked. When the second didn't reply at once: "Honestly."

"Honestly, no."

"Then let's get the men together and go."

The caravan master, sitting on a stool, made a rough impatient noise in the back of his throat. Geder turned to him.

"On behalf of empire and king, I apologize for this inconvenience," he said with a bow.

"Think nothing of it," the 'van master said sourly.

Outside, the soldiers fell into position as they had every time before. Geder lifted himself to his own saddle carefully. His belt held. The gems and jewels dug at his skin, pinching a little at his sides. None fell out. The caravan guards watched with well-feigned lack of interest as Geder drew his sword in salute, turned his horse, and moved forward at a gentle walk. With every step they took away from the caravan, he felt his spine relax. The sun, already sliding down toward the horizon, half blinded him, and he craned his neck, counting the soldiers behind him to make sure no one had doubled back or been left behind. None had.

At the top of the ridge, Geder paused. His second came to his side.

"We can make camp at the same place as last night, my lord," he said. "Strike out south and west in the morning."

Geder shook his head. "East," he said.

"Lord?"

"Let's go east," Geder said. "Gilea's not far, and we can spend a few days someplace warm before we go back to Vanai."

"We're going back?" the second asked, his voice carefully neutral.

"May as well," Geder said, struggling against his smile. "We aren't going to find anything."

Dawson

*W*inter business.

The words themselves reeked of desperation. From the longest night to first thaw, noblemen took to their estates or they followed the King's Hunt. They took stock of what sort of men their sons were becoming, reacquainted themselves with wives and mistresses, looked over the tax revenue from their holdings. To the highborn, winter meant domesticity and the work of the hearth. Much as he loved Camnipol, passing through the wind-chilled, smoke-stinking streets put Dawson in the company of professional courtiers, merchants, and other men of uncertain status. But his cause was just, and so he bore the insult to his dignity.

Nor was he the only one to suffer it.

"I don't understand why you hate Issandrian so deeply," said Canl Daskellin, Baron of Watermarch, Protector of Northport, and His Majesty's Special Ambassador to Northcoast. "He's entirely too pretty and full of himself, it's true, but if you take being self-impressed and ambitious as sinning, you won't find any saints in this court."

Dawson sat back in his chair. Around them, the Fraternity of the Great Bear seemed almost empty. Seats and cushions upholstered in raw silk or Cabral damask sat empty. Black iron braziers squatted in rooms built to be cool in midsummer. The servant girls, so often hard-pressed to tend the needs of the fraternity members, haunted the shadows and doorways, waiting for a sign that something might be wanted. At summer's height, there might be a hundred men of the best breeding in the empire drinking and smoking and conducting affairs of court in these grand and comfortable rooms. Now, if Dawson spoke too loud, it echoed.

"It isn't the man," Dawson said. "It's the philosophy behind him. Maas and Klin are no better, but Issandrian holds their leashes."

"Philosophical differences hardly seem to justify...What? Conspiracy?"

"Philosophy always becomes action. Issandrian and Maas and the others are willing to play to the lowest kind of man in order to gain power."

"You mean the farmer's council."

"That's one place," Dawson said. "But if they are willing to champion rabble, how long is it before the rabble choose to champion themselves? Already we have restrictions on slavery, on bed servants, on land service. All of that within our lifetimes. And all from men like Issandrian, courting favor from laborers and merchants and whores."

Canl Daskellin gave out a low grunt. Between the thin winter light silhouetting him and the almost Lyoneian darkness of his skin, Dawson could hardly make out his expression. Still, he hadn't disagreed. And if he hadn't had concerns of his own, he wouldn't have come.

"It's time for the true spirit of Antea to put things right," Dawson said. "These hounds think they run the hunt. They must be broken, and if we wait until Prince Aster is living under Issandrian's roof..."

The silence finished his thought more eloquently than any words could. Daskellin shifted forward in his chair, muttering something obscene under his breath.

"You're sure the king intends to take that step?"

"I heard it from his own mouth," Dawson said. "Simeon is a good man, and he could be a good king too, but not without our loyalty. He's waiting for his chance to put Issandrian in his place. And I am going to provide that chance."

Soft voices came from the passage beyond, and then faded again. From the street, the clacking of steel-shod hooves. Canl drew a small clay pipe from his jacket and lifted his hand. A servant girl scurried over with a taper. With the first fragrant blue cloud of smoke, she retreated. Dawson waited.

"How?" Daskellin asked. His voice had taken on the firmness of an interrogator. Dawson smiled. The battle was half won.

"Deny Issandrian his strength," Dawson said. "Recall Alan Klin from Vanai. Alienate Issandrian from the farmers. Shatter his circle."

"Meaning Maas and Klin."

"To start, but he has other adherents as well. But that isn't enough. They gained influence because the men who understand what noble blood means are divided."

Daskellin took a long draw on his pipe, the ember glowing bright and then fading as he exhaled.

"And thus your conspiracy," he said.

"Loyalty to the king is no conspiracy," Dawson said. "It's what we should have been doing all along. But we slept, and the dogs snuck in. And, Canl, you *know* that."

Daskellin tapped the clay stem against his teeth. His eyes narrowed.

"Whatever it is," Dawson said, "say it."

"Loyalty to King Simeon is one thing. Becoming the tool of House Kalliam is something else. I am ... *disturbed* by the changes Issandrian and his cabal are suggesting. But trading one man of ambition for another is no solution."

"You want me to show I'm not Issandrian?"

"I do."

"What proof do you want?"

"If I help to recall Klin from Vanai, you cannot profit from it. Everyone's quite aware that your son is under Klin's command there. Jorcy Kalliam cannot take the protectorship of Vanai."

Dawson blinked, opened his mouth, closed it again.

"Canl," he began, but Daskellin's eyes narrowed. Dawson took a deep breath and let it out slowly. When he spoke, his voice was harder than he'd meant it to be. "I swear before God and the throne of Antea that my son Jorey will not take protectorship of Vanai when Alan Klin is called home. Further, I swear that no one of my house will take profit from Vanai. Now, will you swear the same, old friend?"

"Me?"

"You have a cousin in the city, I think? I'm sure you wouldn't want to give the impression that your own support of the throne is merely self-serving?"

Daskellin's laughter boomed and rolled, a deep sound and warm enough to push back the teeth of winter, if only for a moment.

"God wept, Kalliam. You'll make altruists of us all."

"Will you swear?" Kalliam said. "Will you make common cause with the men who are loyal to King Simeon and to put the restoration of tradition ahead of your own glory?"

"True servants to the throne," Daskellin said, half amused.

"Yes," Dawson said. There was no room for lightness in his voice. He was hard as stone, his intentions fashioned from steel. "True servants to the throne."

Daskellin sobered.

"You *mean* this," he said.

"I do," Dawson said.

The dark eyes flickered over Dawson's face, as if trying to penetrate a disguise. And then as it had with half a dozen men before him — men whom Dawson had chosen because he knew they were as hungry for it as he himself was — pride bloomed in the dark face. Pride and determination and a sense of becoming part of something greater and good.

"Then yes," Daskellin said softly, "I will."

The Division was the most obvious of the partitions within the city, but it was far from the only one. On both sides of the bridges, nobility held to their mansions and squares while the lesser people lived in smaller, narrower ways. Living north of the Kestrel Square meant you were of high stature. Having your stables by the southern gate meant you had good blood, but a squandered fortune. The city was complex in ways that only her citizens could know. The streets were not the only dimension in which class could be measured. The poorest and most desperate tunneled down to coax new life out of the ruins of previous ages on which the modern city was built, living in darkness and squalor, but saving them at least from the indignities of winter.

Ice and snow turned the dark cobbles white. Carts went slowly, and mules carefully. Horses walked haltingly for fear of slipping, breaking a leg, and being slaughtered on the street where they fell. The Camnipol winter stole even the dignity of a waiting carriage, but the meeting with Daskellin had left Dawson so pleased with himself that he barely minded. He let the servant girl belt on his overcoat of dark leather with silverwork seams and bloodstone hooks, put on the broad-brimmed hat that matched it, and marched himself out into the streets toward his home and Clara.

He'd spent his boyhood in Camnipol, following his father through the rituals of power during the day and then drinking, singing, and carousing with the other highborn boys through the nights. Even now, decades later, the snow-caked stone held memories under it. He passed the thin alley where Eliayzer Breiniako had run naked after losing a bet with him the night they'd both turned fourteen. Then the wide turning that led to the streets where all the Timzinae and Jasuru made their homes: the quarter of bugs and pennies. He passed under Morade's Arch, where the last, mad Dragon Emperor had died in his clutch-mate's talons; the arc of the dragon's jade rose up almost as high as the Kingspire itself and so thin and finely worked it seemed any wind would tip it over. He passed the Chancel of Sorrial, with its soot-blackened southern wall. The cathouse where his father had taken him on his tenth birthday and bought him his first night with a woman.

The single white cloud of the sky glowed beneficently on the city, dispelling shadows. A baker's cart coming back from the market square dropped a crate of almonds, and a dozen children seemed to appear from no place, grabbing at the nuts before the carter could stop them. On the western wall, he could look down over the great plains of Antea like God looking down on the world. The wind through the streets bit and rasped on his lips and cheeks. It was the perfect city. Everything had happened here, from the fall of dragons, to the elevation of the White Prophet, to the slave riots that had brought House Antea to refound a Firstblood empire in the city that dragons built. The stones stood witness to centuries, to ages.

And now, perhaps for the first time, Dawson was taking his place in the city that he loved. He had begun the work for which Camnipol would remember him. Dawson Kalliam,

Baron of Osterling Fells, who purified the court and guarded Antea on the right and proper path. Kalliam, who gathered the defenders of righteousness. Who destroyed the agents of chaos and change.

The Undying City invited him to get drunk on his memories and the vision of a future bent to his will—a future where Curtin Issandrian and Feldin Maas were left to scuttle through filthy snow on winter business instead of him—and Dawson succumbed. If there were any warning signs before the attack, he missed them entirely.

The road curved, following the shape of the promontory's edge, and in the triangular park where two wide streets became one, three men in dark wool overcoats and leggings stood together in deep conversation. Their breath came out white as feathers, white as the sky. Dawson strode toward them, expecting them to give way before a Baron of the Court. Hard eyes met his. The men didn't move.

Annoyance intruded on Dawson's revery, then the thought that they might not recognize his rank and station. The nearest of the men opened his coat and drew a wide, curved knife. The others moved to flank. Dawson barked out a short laugh of disdain and disbelief, and the knife man rushed him. Dawson danced back, trying to draw his own sword. Even before he had his blade clear of the scabbard the thug on his left struck his elbow with a weighted club. Dawson's hand went numb and his sword fell silently to the icy ground. The knife man swung, his blade slicing through the leather overcoat and into the flesh of Dawson's chest. Dawson yelped and jumped back.

It was the farthest thing from a duel. There was no beauty in the men's movements or style, no sense of honor. Not even the grace of formal training. The knife man held his blade like a butcher, and his partners with their clubs penned

Dawson in as if he might turn and flee, squealing like a frightened sow. Dawson drew himself to his full height, pressing fingers to the torn coat. The fingers of his gloves came away bloody.

"You have just made your last mistake," Dawson said. "You have no idea who you're facing."

The knife man smiled.

"Think I do, m'lord," he said, and struck again. The blade would have sunk deep into Dawson's belly if decades of training hadn't pulled him back and to the side. The club man on the left swung hard, catching him on the shoulder. As Dawson sank to his knees, it occurred to him for the first time that these were not simple street toughs looking for a few coins. It was a trap, and it was meant for him.

The club man on his right danced back and forward and back on the balls of his feet, weapon raised high and ready to come down with a skull-shattering blow. Dawson raised his arm, and the attacker vanished with a grunt. The assassins turned. A new man in grey hunter's wool rolled on the cobbles, locked in the club man's violent embrace. When they broke, the new man leapt up. His clothes were soaked in red, as was the short sword in his hand. The thug didn't rise.

"Lord Kalliam," the new man shouted, and tossed his blade. Dawson watched it arc through the air, blood and steel. Time seemed to slow. The grip was dark leather, well used. The blade itself had a blood channel running down its center. Dawson reached out, plucking the sword from the air. The remaining club man swung at him, and, still on his knees, Dawson parried the attack.

The fallen attacker groaned, lifted himself with one hand, then slipped back into the spreading pool of red.

Dawson rose. The two assassins glanced at each other,

and Dawson read the fear in them. True, he was hurt and his rescuer now unarmed. True, the numbers were merely even. And still, to go so suddenly from three men and a victim to an almost equal battle shook their confidence. The club man took a step back, half turning as if he might flee. Dawson felt his lips curl. These men were cowards.

He swung his borrowed sword fast, low, and hard. The man danced back, parrying awkwardly. To Dawson's right, the knife man shouted and leapt for Dawson's unarmed ally. The pain of Dawson's wounds faded, the chill of his own blood freezing on his chest brought a feral grin to his mouth. The club man fell back a step, and Dawson pressed in, his knees bent, his weight low, his body balanced and ready. When the weighted club made its next swing, Dawson pushed inside its arc, taking the blow on his ribs as he thrust the blade forward. The club man's breath went out of him in a white, feathery rush. There was armor under that overcoat. The assassin wasn't dead, but he was staggered. Dawson turned, brought a heel down on the man's instep, swung the pommel of his sword in a short, hard jab at his face. The unmistakable crunch of breaking cartilage transferred itself to Dawson's wrist.

The assassin bent low and rushed him, trying to bowl him over by main force. Dawson slid back, his boots finding little purchase on the icy street. The thug weighed more than him, and he was counting on that to save him in the grapple. He had misjudged Dawson's character.

Dawson dropped the sword, grabbed the thug's dark hair in his left hand, not to pull the man's head away but to steady it. He drove his thumb deep in the man's eye socket, bending at the knuckle. Something soft and terrible happened, and the man shrieked high and pained and frightened. Dawson pushed him away, and the man stumbled to his knees, hands pressed to his ruined eye and shattered nose.

The knife man and Dawson's rescuer were circling one another. The rescuer's arms were spread and weaponless. A cut on his left arm bled, scattering droplets of scarlet on the white ice and black cobbles. A crowd was gathering on the street. Men, women, children with eyes wide and hungry taking in the violence without daring to intervene. Dawson kicked the mewling club man to the pavement and pulled the strap of his club from around his wrist. The knife man's glance spoke panic, and Dawson drew the weighted club whirring through the air, testing its balance and weight.

The knife man bolted, dark boots throwing bits of snow up behind him as he pelted away. The crowd parted, letting the thug escape rather than risk a swing of his little blade. Peasants, commoners, and serfs making way for one of their own. He wanted to feel some outrage that the simple citizens of Camnipol would allow the man to flee, but he didn't. Cowardice and the safety of the herd was the nature of the lowborn. He could as well blame sheep for bleating.

The first assassin to fall lay perfectly still, the blood around him steaming. The second club man was growing quiet too, slipping into shock. Dawson's rescuer squatted on bent ankles, considering his wounded arm. He was young, thick arms and shoulders and rough, knife-cropped hair. The shape of his face was familiar.

"It seems I owe you my thanks," Dawson said. To his surprise, he was out of breath.

The new man shook his head.

"I should have come sooner, my lord," the young man said. "I stayed too far back."

"Too far back?" Dawson said. "You've been tracking me?"

The man nodded and would not meet his eyes.

"Why is that?" Dawson asked.

"Your lady wife, my lord," the man said. "She took me into service after you turned me out. She tasked me with keeping you safe, sir. I'm afraid I've done a poor job."

Of course. The huntsman from the kitchens who'd returned the bit of horn soaked in dog's blood and insult. Vincen Coe, the name had been. He'd never asked Clara what she'd done to see to the boy, but of course she couldn't simply reinstate him over her husband's express words. And certainly it would be beneath him to say he'd been unjust with the boy.

"You're mistaken," Dawson said.

"Lord?"

"I've never seen you before, and I wouldn't have turned a man of your courage and talent out of my service."

"Yes...I mean, no, my lord."

"That's settled, then. Come along with me, we'll get these little scratches daubed."

Coe stood.

"My sword, my lord?"

"Yes. We may have need of that," Dawson said, gesturing to where it lay, grimed with blood and snow and soot. "It seems I'm frightening all the right men."

Marcus

Fire and blood. Merian shrieked her pain and fear and indignation as only a child could blend them. Her eyes were fixed on him, her arms reaching out. Marcus fought his paralysis, forced his arms to reach for her, and in moving them, woke himself.

The screams of the dead lingered in the cool air as he lifted himself up, still expecting in his half-dream to see the wheat fields and high, stately windmills of Ellis. Instead, the wide star-crowded sky of Birancour arched above him, the looming darkness of the mountains behind him to the east without even the suggestion of dawn. The burning smell of memory gave way to the sweet, astringent scent of ice lily and the distant presentiment of salt that was the sea.

He lay back in his bedroll and waited for the dream to fade. By long habit, he attended to his body. The constricting tightness in his throat eased first, then in his chest. The gut-punch ache in his belly faded slowly and vanished. Soon there was only the permanent hollow beneath his ribs, and he knew it was safe to stand.

They were battle scars. Some men lost a leg or a hand. Some men lost their eyes. Marcus had lost a family. And just as old soldiers knew when rain was coming from the ache of healed bones, he suffered now. It didn't mean anything. It was just his own private bad weather, and like bad weather, it would pass. It was only for the moment that the dreams were getting worse.

The caravan slept, carters and mules both, in the deep night. The watch fire glittered on the hillside above him, no brighter than a star, but orange instead of blue. Marcus made his way toward it. The dry grass hushed against his boots and field mice skittered away. Yardem Hane sat silhouetted by the small fire, back turned to keep the light from blunting his eyes. Beside him sat a less familiar form. Marcus moved close enough to make out their words.

"The *shape* of a soul?" Master Kit asked. "I think I don't understand what you mean."

"Just that. A soul has a shape," Yardem said. His wide hands patted the air in front of him. "And fate is formed by it. Whatever the world delivers to you, the shape of your soul determines what you do with it, and the actions you take make your destiny."

Marcus turned his foot, scraping the ground loud enough to announce himself.

"Morning, Captain," Yardem said without turning to look.

"You filling our cunning man's head with your superstitious hairwash?"

"I am, sir."

"Be careful, Kit," Marcus said, walking into the dim circle of light. "Yardem used to be a priest, you know."

Master Kit's eyebrows rose and he looked his question from Marcus to Yardem. The Tralgu shrugged eloquently.

"Ended poorly," Yardem said.

"It's not a faith I'd heard of before," Master Kit said. "I have to say I find the ideas fascinating. What shape is your own soul?"

"I've never seen my soul," Yardem said.

Marcus sat. The warmth of the fire touched his back. High above them, a falling star streaked from east to west, fading almost before Marcus saw it. The silence felt suddenly awkward.

"Go ahead," Marcus said. "Tell him if you want to."

"Tell me what?" Master Kit asked.

"I have seen the captain's. I was at Wodford the day of the battle. The captain rode by, taking count of the troop, and... I saw it."

"And what shape was it?" Master Kit asked

"A circle standing on its edge," Yardem said.

"What did you take that to mean?"

"That he rises when brought low and falls when placed high," Yardem said.

"He needed magical visions to see that," Marcus said. "Most people just take it as given."

"But always?" Master Kit said. "Surely if God wanted to change the shape of a man's soul—"

"I've never seen God," Yardem said.

"But you believe in him," Master Kit said.

"I'm reserving judgment," Yardem said. Master Kit considered that.

"And what about you, Captain?" he asked. "Stories are you were a pious man once."

"I choose not to believe in any gods as an act of charity," Marcus said.

"Charity toward whom?"

"Toward the gods. Seems rude to think they couldn't make a world better than this," Marcus said. "Do we have any food left?"

The dawn crept in softly, the outline of the mountains to the east growing clearer against the stars, then the few finger-thin clouds began to glow pink and gold and light seemed to come from nowhere, to rise up from the earth like a mist. The carts changed from near-invisible hulks to wood and iron. Pot metal clanked from across the camp as the caravan master's wife began cooking the morning's mash of stewed grain and honeyed pork. The landscape changed from endless featureless darkness to hills and trees, scrub and stream. Yardem ran the guards through their morning drills while Marcus walked through the camp and pretended there was no cart in the caravan he cared about more than another.

The girl, Cithrin, followed the same routine as the others. She cared for her mules, she ate her food, she scraped the mud out of her axle holes. If she needed help, she asked Opal or Master Kit. Never the caravan master, never Marcus himself. But never Sandr either, and the boy had been avoiding her like his life depended on it, so that was for the best. Marcus watched her without being obvious. She'd gotten better since they'd left Vanai. Since they'd left Bellin, for that. But there were dark pouches under her eyes and the awkwardness of exhaustion in her movements.

Marcus found the caravan master squatting beside the lead cart, a wide scroll of inked parchment on the dirt before him: a map of south Birancour probably centuries out of date, but it would still show where the dragon's roads were. His wife, breakfast duties finished, was putting their team in harness.

"Day," the caravan master said. "Day and a half at most, and we'll get onto a real road again."

"That's good."

"Another three, and we'll be in Porte Oliva. You've been there before?"

"A time or two," Marcus said. "It's a good winter port. Doesn't get too cold. The queen's governor isn't too heavy a tax hand."

"We'll stop there, then."

"Roads should be clear to Carse by early spring," Marcus said.

"Not for me," the caravan master said, folding the map. "We reach Porte Oliva, and we're done. The 'van stops there."

Marcus frowned and crossed his arms.

"There are some problems with that," he said. "The job is to see all this to Carse."

"Your job is to protect the caravan," the Timzinae said. "Mine is to say where it goes and when it stops. Porte Oliva has a market. Road trade to Cabral and Herez, not to mention the rest of the cities in Birancour. Ships to Lyoniea, and the blue-water trade to Far Syramys. The cargo I was contracted to haul will sell well enough there."

"The cargo you were contracted for," Marcus repeated, turning the words over like they tasted wrong.

"Is there something else I should care about?" The caravan master's chin jutted forward. "You're worried I might inconvenience the smuggler?"

"Last I heard, the Medean bank doesn't trade in Birancour," Marcus said. "You'll be sitting that girl on a pile of money high as a tree with nothing to protect her. Might as well hang a sign on her neck."

The 'van master tossed his folded map on the seat of his cart and began hauling himself up beside it. His wife blinked a silent apology to Marcus and looked away.

"*That girl* and her drinking and smuggling and sinning with your guardsmen can watch out for herself," the 'van master said. "We were blind lucky with that Antean bastard. There's no reason to expect we'll be as fortunate next time."

And there will be a next time, he didn't say. He didn't need to.

"If you take my advice," the 'van master went on, "you'll take your fee, turn your horse, and ride away from that girl until she's less than a memory. People like that are only trouble."

Marcus bristled.

"What kind of people do you mean?"

"Bankers," the 'van master said, and spat.

Porte Oliva nestled on a land spur that pressed out into a wide, shallow bay. Even at low tide, the sea protected her on three sides. Reefs and sandbars made the approach from the ocean dangerous enough that local boatmen could earn their living guiding ships from the deep ocean safely into port and then out again. In the thousand years since its foundation, the city had never been taken by force, though twice it had been seduced. The dragon's road led to it, the green pathway curving up over hills long since washed away, so that the carts traveled across the tops of wide-sloping arches as the ground dropped away beneath them.

As they drew nearer the city, the road became more crowded. Where Vanai had been rich with the black-chitined Timzinae, the crowd here showed the pale, ethereal faces of Cinnae and the oily, short, bead-adorned fur of Kurtadam in greater numbers even than Firstblood. The press of carts and bodies thickened, and Marcus started to see swordsmen in with copper torcs and the green and gold of Birancour. Queensmen. The guardians of the city, though the queen herself kept to the greater cities of Sara-su-mar and Porte Silena in the north. Marcus watched the caravan master approach one of the older queensmen, lean forward as if to speak above the chirr and murmur of the crowd. A few coins traded hands, and without any obvious change, the carts soon found themselves moving faster than before, passing the foot traffic and hand barrows. Marcus knew they had reached the Porte Oliva proper when the beggars and mendicants appeared.

Please, my lord, I have a child.

My husband is a sailor. His ship is three months late, and there's no money for food.

God tells us to be generous.

Marcus paced alongside the carts, ignoring the words and gestures, watching for the thieves and cutpurses who always lived in crowds like these. The other guards followed his example, and likely knew more about sleight of hand than he did. It was odd how well suited the players were to every part of guarding a 'van besides the actual guard duty. He reached the last cart and turned to start for the front again. Three carts ahead, Master Kit leaned down and pressed a coin into an old man's hand.

"Don't encourage them," Marcus called. "They're all liars."

"Not all, Captain," Kit called back with a grin. "Only most."

He passed the wool cart where the smuggler girl, still in her rough carter's clothes, drove her team. Put beside the full-blood Cinnae on the road, it was easier to see her as something besides a frail Firstblood girl. Her hair wasn't as fine as theirs, her features were thicker, her skin had more color, but the resemblance was there. She noticed him watching her, and tried out a smile. He ignored her with the same studied intention as the beggars, and for similar reasons.

Riding on, the sense of anticipation and dread sat in his gut. The conversation would come, and it would be today, and the wise thing—the right thing, the thing that would let his nightmares fade again—was to refuse the girl. At the lead cart, Yardem met his gaze impassively.

Once, centuries before, the city had ended at the great stone embattlements. Now the towering white stone walls were in the middle of a busy market quarter. Fishmongers shouted out their catch on the north side of the arched tunnel that led to the inner city, and after they passed through, indistinguishable men and women called out the same fish. The architecture of war slept in the middle of a living community like a great hunting cat torpid from the kill. Beyond it, the dragon's road widened and stopped at a huge open square.

The crowd pressed here as thick as they had on the road. A great marble temple high as five men standing one atop the other loomed on the eastern end, the governor's palace of red brick and colored glass on the west. God's voice and the law's arm, twin powers of the throne. And between them, scattered through the square, wooden platforms rose with prisoners suffering their punishments. A Kurtadam man with rheumy eyes and severed hands held a sign between his stumps announcing himself a thief. A Firstblood woman smeared in shit and offal sat under the carved wooden symbol of a procuress. Three Cinnae men hung dead from a gallows, flies darkening the soft flesh around their eyes; a murderer, a rapist, and a child-user respectively. Together, the platforms served as a short, effective introduction to the local laws.

The caravan master left them standing for the better part of an hour as he vanished into the governor's palace, returning with small stone figures on leather thongs to place on the carts as proof the road taxes had been paid. With a shout, he led them down a side road of hard, pale brick to the yard.

Journey's end. Marcus made his way to the front cart. The caravan master had a cloth sack waiting for him. It jingled when he held it out.

"You can count it," the Timzinae said.

"That's fine," Marcus said.

The 'van master's brows lifted, then he shrugged.

"Suit yourself. But don't come later saying it was short."

"Won't."

"All right, then."

Marcus nodded and turned away. He took out his share and Yardem's, then despite what he'd said, he counted the rest. It was all there.

The players were at their own cart, still wearing their armor and swords. The road had changed them and it hadn't. They were harder now, and each of them could handle a sword like a soldier. On the other hand, they laughed and joked now as much as they had in the tavern in Vanai. Sandr and Smit were competing now to see who could hold a handstand longest. Cary, Opal, and Mikel traded quips and barbs as they saw to their mules. Master Kit sat on the cart's high bench, watching over it all like a benevolent saint from the old stories. Marcus went to him.

"It appears we've managed the trick, then," Master Kit said. "I hadn't expected it to be quite so eventful."

"Make a fine comedy," Marcus said,

"I think the world is often like that."

"Like what?"

"Comic, but only at the right distance."

"Likely true," Marcus said as he handed the money to Master Kit. "What are you going to do now?"

"I suspect Porte Oliva's as good a venue as any, and suppose we'll try our luck at our original trade. After a bit of a rest, maybe. There's a long tradition of puppeteers here, and I'm hoping we might be able to recruit a new actor or two with those skills."

"It was good working with you," Marcus said. "Went better than I expected, considering. I expect I'll see you about the city. We'll stay until thaw."

"Thank you for not emasculating Sandr. I still hope to make a decent leading man of him one day."

"Luck with that," Marcus said.

"Take care of yourself, Captain Wester," Master Kit said. "I find you a fascinating man."

And that was over as well. To his left, the caravan master was passing to each cart in turn, taking signatures and inventories. Yardem appeared at Marcus's side.

"We'll need men," the Tralgu said.

"And a cunning man. But there's not a war on here. We'll find some."

The Tralgu flicked a jingling ear.

"Are you going to let the girl hire us, sir?"

Marcus took a deep breath. The city smelled of horse shit, fish, and brine. Haze left the sky more white than blue. He exhaled slowly.

"No," he said.

They stood together. The 'van master reached her cart. Cithrin stood before him like a prisoner before a magistrate, spine straight, eyes ahead of her. Alone in a city she didn't know, without protector or path.

"We could leave now," Yardem said.

Marcus shook his head.

"She deserves to hear it."

The 'van master moved on. Marcus looked to the Tralgu, the girl, spat, and went to her. *Do it,* he told himself, *and get the worst behind and on to the next thing.* The girl looked up as he came, her eyes unfocused and glassy with exhaustion, her skin even paler than usual. And yet she lifted her chin a degree.

"Captain," she said.

"Yes," he said. "Yardem and I. We can't work for you."

"All right," she said. For all her reaction, he might have told her the sun rose in the morning.

"My advice, take as much as you can carry, leave the rest, and take ship out to Lyoniea or Far Syramis. Start over."

The 'van master whistled. The first cart pulled away. The caravan officially ended. The carts around them began to shift and squeak, each bound for its own market, its own quarter. Even the players were moving off now, Sandr and Smit walking with the mules to clear the way. Cithrin bel Sarcour, orphan and ward of the Medean bank, novice smuggler, almost woman, looked at him with tired eyes.

"Good luck," he said, and walked away.

The salt quarter of Porte Oliva was, as Master Kit had said, inhabited by puppets. Street performers seemed to be at every other corner, crouched behind or within boxes, hectoring the passersby in the voices of their dolls. Some were the standard race humor of PennyPenny the violent Jurasu and the clever Timzinae Roaches. Some were political like the idiot King Ardelhumblemub with his oversized crown. Some, Stannin Aftellin the perpetually lustful Firstblood in his traditional love triangle with a phlegmatic Dartinae and a manipulative Cinnae, were bawdy and racial and political all together.

Many more were more local. Marcus was pausing for a moment by a performance about a filthy butcher who smoked his meat with burning shit and ground maggots into his sausage when a Cinnae woman in the crowd started yelling at the puppeteer for taking gold from a rival butcher. At another, four queensmen with swords and copper torcs watched a story about plums and a fairy princess with scowls that suggested the allegory, whatever it was, might put the performer on the wrong side of the law.

The public house they stopped at had a courtyard that overlooked the seawall. The sun was sliding down the western sky, setting the white stucco walls glowing gold. The water of the bay was pale blue, the sea beyond an indigo so deep it was almost black. The smell of brine and roasting chicken wrestled with the incense smoke from a wandering priest. Sailors of several races, thick-shouldered and loud-throated all of them, sat at the wide tables under the bright embroidered canopies. Braziers burned between every table, bringing the memory of summer to the winter-chill air. Marcus sat and caught the serving girl's eye. She nodded a promise, and he leaned back in his chair.

"We'll need work."

"Yes, sir," Yardem said.

"And a new crew. A real one this time."

"Yes, sir."

"But there will be warehouses. Come the spring, caravans going inland."

"There will, sir."

"Any thoughts, then?"

The serving girl—a Kurtadam with the soft, pale pelt of an adolescent and gold and silver beads all down her sides— brought mugs of hot cider to them and hurried off before Marcus could pay her. Yardem lifted one. In his hands, it looked small. He drank slowly, his brow furrowed and his ears tucked back. Behind him, the sun glowed bright enough to hurt.

"What it is?" Marcus said.

"The smuggler girl, sir. Cithrin."

Marcus laughed, but he felt the anger behind it. From the shift in Yardem's shoulders, the Tralgu heard it too.

"You think it would be wise to put us between that cart and whoever wants to take it from her?"

"It wouldn't be," Yardem said.

"Then what's there to talk about? Job's done. Time to move forward."

"Yes, sir," Yardem said and took another sip. Marcus waited for him to speak. He didn't. One of the sailors—a Firstblood with close-cropped black hair and the slushy accent of Lyoneia—started singing a dirty song about the mating habits of Southlings. The large black eyes of that race often got them called *eyeholes,* which lent itself to certain rhymes. Marcus felt his jaw clench. He leaned forward, putting himself in Yardem's sight.

"You have something to say?"

Yardem sighed.

"If she were less like Meriam, you'd have stayed," Yardem said.

The dirty song went to a new verse, speculating on the sex life of Dartinae and Cinnae. Or glow-worms and maggots, as the lyrics put it. Marcus shot an annoyed glance at the singer. The tightness in his jaw was spreading down his neck and between his shoulder blades. Yardem put down his cider.

"If it had been a man driving that cart," Yardem said. "Or an older woman. Someone who looked less like Alys or wasn't the age Meriam would have been, you would have taken contract from them."

Marcus coughed out a laugh. The singer took a breath, preparing to launch into another verse. Marcus stood.

"You! Enough of that. There's grown men here trying to think."

The sailor's face clouded.

"Who the fuck are you?"

"The man telling you that's enough," Marcus said.

The sailor sneered, then blinked at something in Marcus's expression, flushed red, and sat down, his back toward Marcus and Yardem. Marcus turned back to his second.

"That cart is going to pull blades and blood to it, and we both know it," Marcus said softly. "That much wealth in one place is a call to murder. Now you're telling me that standing in front of it's the right thing?"

"No, sir. Damned foolish, sir," Yardem said. "Only you'd have done it."

Marcus shook his head. In his memory, Meriam reached out from the flames. He took her dying body in his arms. He could smell the burning hair, the skin. He felt her relax against him and remembered thinking that she was saved, that she was safe, and then realizing what the softness in her joints really meant. He didn't know anymore if it was the true memory of the events or his dreams.

Cithrin bel Sarcour. He pictured her cart. Pictured the middle-aged Firstblood tin hauler in her place. Or the 'van master and his wife. Or Master Kit and Opal. Anyone besides the girl herself.

He rubbed his eyes until false colors bloomed in front of him. The sea murmured. The sharp apple smell of his cider cut through the cold air. The anger in his chest collapsed, nothing more than paper armor after all, and he said something obscene.

"Should I go find her, sir?"

"We better had," Marcus said, dropping the coins for their drinks on the table. "Before she does something dangerous."

Geder

Geder might have found it more difficult to hide his subterfuge if his failure hadn't been assumed from the start. Instead, he and his half-loyal soldiers limped back into the city, gave their thin reports, and were dismissed. Geder returned to the weak stream of his duties; enforcing taxes, arresting loyalists, and generally harassing the people of Vanai in the name of Alan Klin.

"I can't pay this," the old Timzinae said, looking up from the taxation order. "The prince had us all pay twice over before the war, and now you want as much as he did."

"It isn't me," Geder said.

"I don't see anyone else in here."

The shop squatted in a dark street. Scraps of leather lay here and there. A brass tailor's dummy wrapped in soft black hide that still smelled slightly of the tanner's yard loomed near the oilcloth window. As armor, leather that thin would be useless. Barely better than cloth, and probably worse than good quilting. As court costume, on the other hand, it would look quite impressive.

"You want it?" the Timzinae asked.

"Sorry, what?"

"The cloak. Commissioned by the Master of Canals, then he vanished in the night just before"—he held up the taxation notice in his black-scaled hand—"our *liberation* by the noble empire. It's not done, and I've got enough of that dye lot left I could recut it to fit you."

Geder licked his lips. He couldn't. Someone would ask where he'd gotten it, and he'd have to explain. Or lie. If he said he'd bought it on the cheap, maybe while he was on the southern roads or from one of the little caravans they'd searched...

"Could you really recut it?"

The Timzinae's smile was a marvel of cynicism.

"Could you misplace this?" he asked, nodding at the paper.

For a moment, Geder felt the echo of his pleasure riding away from the smugglers, gems and jewels hidden in his shirt. One lost tax notice. At worst it would keep Klin's coffers a little more sparse, his reports back to Camnipol a little less promising. It would keep the leatherman in his shop for another season; if the man had asked, Geder would probably have "lost" the notice even without the promise of a good cloak.

Besides which, compared to what he'd already done, the twenty silver coins lost to Klin were like a raindrop in the ocean.

"Putting an honest man out of work can't be to anyone's benefit," Geder said. "I'm sure we can work this through."

"Stand up on that stool, then," the Timzinae said. "I'll make sure the drape's best for your frame."

Winter was dry season in Vanai. The walls of the canals showed high-water marks feet above the thin ice and sluggish, dark flow. Fallen leaves skittered along the bases of walls, and trees stood bare and dead in the gardens and arbors. The icicles that hung from the wooden eaves of the houses grew thinner by the day, and new snow didn't come.

The nights were bitter, the days merely cold. The city waited for the thaw, the melt, the rush of freshwater and life that came from a spring still months away. Everything was dead or sleeping. Geder walked through the street bouncing on his toes a little, his guardsmen following behind.

When he'd first returned, Geder had locked his doors, taken out the cloth pouch that he'd bought in Gilea, and spread the gems and jewels on his bed. Glittering in the dim light, they'd posed a problem. He had enough available wealth now to make his day-to-day life in Vanai more comfortable, but not as coin. He could sell them, of course, but giving them to gem merchants within the city risked someone recognizing a stone or a piece of metalwork. And if Klin or one of his favorites noticed that Geder had suddenly more coin than he should, nothing good could follow.

He'd answered the problem by sending his squire out to exchange only the most innocuous stones—three round garnets and a diamond in undistinguished silver. The purse of coins had silver and bronze, copper, and two thin rounds of gold frail enough to bend with his fingers. For his lifestyle, it was a fortune, and he carried a portion of it now in his satchel along with a book, ready for his last errand of the day.

The academy looked over a narrow square. In its greater days, it had been a center for the children of the lower nobility and the higher merchant class to hire tutors or commission speeches. The carved oaken archway that led into its great hall was marked with the names of the scholars and priests who had given lectures there over the century and a half since its founding. Within, the air smelled of wax and sandalwood, and sunlight filtered through high horizontal windows, catching motes of dust suspended in the

air. Somewhere nearby, a man recited poetry in a deep, resonant voice. He breathed the air of the place.

Footsteps padded up behind him. The clerk was a thin
Southling man, his huge dark eyes dominating his face. His
body spoke of deference and fear.

"May I help you, my lord? There isn't a problem?"

"I wanted to find a researcher," Geder said. "My squire
was told this was the place to come."

The Southling blinked his huge black eyes.

"I...That is, my lord..." The clerk shook himself.
"Really?"

"Yes," Geder said.

"You haven't come to arrest someone? Or levy fines?"

"No."

"Well. Just a moment, my lord," the Southling said. "Let
me find someone that might be of use. If you'll come
with me?"

In the side chamber, Geder sat on a wooden bench worn
smooth by decades of use. The recitation of poems went on,
the voice fainter now, the words made unintelligible. Geder
loosened his belt, shifting in his seat. He had the almost
physical memory of waiting for his own tutors, and pushed
back the irrational anxiety that he might not be able to
answer the scholar's questions. The door slid open, and a
Firstblood man sidled in. Geder popped to his feet.

"Good afternoon. My name is Geder Palliako."

"You're known in the city, Lord Palliako," the man said.
"Tamask said something about wanting a researcher?"

"Yes," Geder said, taking the book from his side and
holding it out. "I've been translating this book, only it's not
very well presented. I want someone to find more like it, but
different."

The scholar took the book gently, as if it were a colorful but unknown insect, and opened the pages. Geder fidgeted.

"It's about the fall of the Dragon Empire," he said. "It's couched as history, but I'm more interested in speculative essay?"

The sound of ancient pages hushing against each other competed with the distant voice and the murmur of a breeze outside the windows. The scholar leaned close to the book, frowning.

"What are you proposing, Lord Palliako?"

"I'll pay for any books you can find on the period. If they can be bought outright, I'll pay a reward. If they have to be copied, I can commission a scribe, but that means a smaller payment for the researcher. I'm looking particularly for considerations of the fall of the dragons, and especially there's a passage in there about something called the Righteous Servant? I'd like more about that."

"May I ask why, lord?"

Geder opened his mouth, then closed it. He'd never had anyone to talk with about the question, never had to explain himself.

"It's about...truth. And deceit. And I thought it was interesting," he said gamely.

"Would you also be interested in rhetorics on the subject? Asinia Secundus wrote a fine examination of the nature of truth during the Second Alfin Occupation."

"That's philosophy? I'll look at it, but I'd really rather it was an essay."

"You mentioned that. Speculative essay," the scholar said, the faintest sigh in his voice.

"Is that a problem?" Geder asked.

"Not at all, my lord," the scholar said with a forced smile. "We would be honored to help."

My contention is this: given the lack of primary documents from that time, our best practice is to examine those who later claimed the mantle of the Dragon Empire, and by considering their actions infer the nature of the examples they followed. The best example of this is the enigmatic Siege of Aastapal. Direct examination of the ruins there has failed to determine whether the destruction of the city was accomplished by the assaulting forces of the great dragon Morade or, more controversially, the occupying forces of his brother and clutch-mate, Inys.

Faced with this dearth of direct evidence, we may turn to better-known histories. As late as a thousand years after, we have the great Jasuru general Marras Toca in the fourth Holy Cleansing campaign. Also the Anthypatos of Lynnic, Hararrsin fifth of the name, at the battle of Ashen Dan. Also Queen Errathiánpados at the siege of Kázhamor. In each of these cases, a wartime commander claiming lineage with the last Dragon Emperor has chosen to destroy a city as a means of denying it to the enemy. If, as I will try to prove, this was done in conscious imitation of the last great war of dragons, it implies that the destruction of Aastapal was done by Inys as a tactical gambit to keep it from Morade's control rather than the generally accepted scenario.

Geder cocked his head. The argument seemed weak. For one thing, he'd never heard of two of the three examples. And then, out of all the battles and wars and sieges since the fall of dragons, he'd think you could pick instances of any strategy or decision you wanted. The case could be made just as well in the other direction by drawing different leaders, different battles. And God knew every third tyrant claimed some sort of lineage from the dragons.

And still, all specifics aside, it was a fascinating thought. When something can't be known, when the particulars are lost forever, to look at the events that followed from it, that echoed it, and trace backwards toward the truth. Like seeing the ripples in a pond and knowing where the stone fell in. He looked up at his little room, excited. His writing desk still had a bit of ink in the well, but he'd put his pen somewhere. He laid the book open and scurried to the stack of firewood near the grate, picked up a fallen splinter, and went back to his table quickly. Rough wood dipped into the darkness, and Geder carefully marked the margin of the book. *Looking at ripples to know where the stone fell.*

He sat back, pleased. Now if there was just some discussion of the Righteous Servant…

"Lord Palliako," his squire said from the doorway. "Lord Klin banquet?"

Geder sighed, nodded, and tossed the blackened splinter into the fire. His thumb and forefinger were stained. He washed his hands in the basin, his mind only half involved in his task. The squire helped him into his formal tunic and new black leather cloak and almost led him to the door and out to the street beyond.

At home in Camnipol, the one great event of the winter was the anniversary of King Simeon's ascension. Whatever favored noble family the king chose might spend half its year's income on one night, the court descending upon it like crows on a battlefield. Geder had been twice, and the richness of the food and drink had left him vaguely ill both times.

In Vanai, Sir Alan Klin echoed the event with a great banquet and an enforced public celebration.

Festive lanterns hung along the narrow streets casting strange shadows. Musicians played flutes and beat drums as reedy Timzinae voices rose and fell in song. A thick-faced woman rolled a barrel along the street, wood thundering on the cobbles.

Geder passed local men and women dressed in their finest, all wearing mildly amused expressions. The chill air left all the Firstblood faces rosy and noses running. Doors stood open all along the street, light blazing within, to invite passersby in, but without the flags and fireshows of Antea. Last year, none of these men and women had known or cared when King Simeon had taken his crown. If the soldiers of Antea went home, the date would be forgotten again as quickly and as cynically as it had been adopted. The whole enterprise struck Geder as the empty shell of a real celebration. Tin passing itself for silver.

At the palace of the former prince, Klin had appropriated a long audience chamber for the nobility of Antea to celebrate. Here, warm air pressed at the mouth and nose. Traditional Antean foods crowded the tables—venison in mint, trout paste on twice-baked toast, sausage links boiled in wine. The press of voices was like a storm, shouted conversations echoing against the great bronze-colored arches above them. Competing singers wandered between the tables cadging spare coins from the Antean revelers. An old servant with the red-and-grey armband of Klin's household led Geder to one of the smallest tables, far from the great fireplace where half a tree burned and popped. Geder kept his cloak. So far from the fire, it was cold.

Geder allowed a slave girl to give him a plate of food and a wide, cut-crystal glass of yeasty-smelling dark beer. In the midst of the revel, he ate by himself, mulling over questions of truth and deception, war and history. The high table—

Alan Klin, Gospey Allintot, and half a dozen of the others of Klin's favorites—was a ship on the horizon to him. He didn't notice Daved Broot being ushered to his table until the boy plopped down on a bench.

"Palliako," the younger Broot said with a nod.

"Hello," Geder said.

"Good cloak. New?"

"Recent anyway."

"Suits you."

Their conversation completed, Broot took a plate and began a campaign of systematically eating as much food as possible. He seemed to take no joy in it, but Geder felt a whisper of admiration for the boy's determination. Minutes later, when Jorey Kalliam and Sir Afend Tilliakin—two more of Klin's least favored—came to the table together, Broot had already called for a second plate.

"How does your father read the situation?" Tilliakin said as the pair took their seats.

Jorey Kalliam shook his head.

"I don't think we can draw any conclusions," he said, lifting a plate of venison and a flagon of wine out of a servant's waiting hands. "Not yet."

"Still, that little banker Imaniel won't be going free anytime soon. Lord Klin must be chewing his own guts that he didn't find that caravan, eh?"

All thought of dragons, ripples, and eating prowess fell away from Geder. He took a long drink of beer, hiding behind the glass, and tried to think how to ask what the pair were talking about without seeming obvious. Before he could come up with something clever, Broot spoke up.

"You talking about the letter from Ternigan?"

"Jorey Kalliam's father is seeing the whole thing from back home, but I can't pry details out with a crowbar."

Geder cleared his throat.

"Ternigan wrote a letter?" he said, his voice higher and more strained than he'd meant it to be. Tilliakin laughed.

"Half a book, the way I heard it," he said. "The war chests Klin's been sending home were a little light for some people's tastes. Ternigan wants to know why. The way I heard it, he's sending in one of his men to look over Klin's books, see if he's been taking more than his share."

"That's not happening," Jorey said. "At least it isn't happening yet."

Broot's eyebrows rose.

"So you *have* heard something," Tilliakin said. "I knew you were holding out."

Jorey smiled ruefully.

"I don't know anything certain. Father said that there's been some concern at court that the Vanai campaign hasn't done as well for the crown as expected. It's all grumbling in the court so far. The king hasn't said anything against the way Klin's managed things."

"Hasn't said anything *for* him either, though, has he?" Tilliakin asked.

"No," Jorey said. "No, he hasn't."

"Ternigan won't recall him," Broot said around a mouthful of sausage. "They'd both look bad."

"If he does, though, he'll do it quick. Be interesting to know who he'd put in his place, wouldn't it?" Tilliakin said, staring pointedly at Jorey.

Geder looked back and forth between the men, his mind bounding on ahead of him like a dog that has slipped its leash. Klin's steady stream of taxation demands suddenly took on more significance. Perhaps he wasn't only finding unpleasant tasks to occupy Geder's days. Those coins might be going back to Camnipol in place of the ones lost when the caravan vanished away. Klin buying back the court's good opinion.

The thought was too sweet to trust. Because if it was true, if *he* had put Sir Alan Klin in the bad graces of the king…

"I think Jorey would make a fine prince for Vanai," Geder said.

"God's wounds, Palliako!" Broot said. "Don't say that kind of thing where people can hear you!"

"Sorry," Geder said. "I only meant—"

A roar came from the high table. Half a dozen jugglers dressed in fool's costumes were tossing knives back and forth through the air, blades catching the firelight. The occupants of the high table had shifted, making room for the show, and Geder could see Alan Klin clearly now. Through the flurry of knives, he imagined there was an uneasiness about the man's shoulders. A false cheerfulness in his smiles and laughter. A haunted look to the bright eyes. And if it was true, then he—Geder Palliako—had put them there. And what was more, Klin would never know. Never follow back the ripples.

Geder laughed and clapped and pretended he was watching the performance.

Cithrin

After the night skating on the mill pond and the throat-closing fear of the day that came after, her nights took on a pattern. First, bone-deep exhaustion. Then, after she curled into the wool, a glorious hour of rest before her eyes popped open, her mind racing, her heart tight and nervous. Some nights, she would see the doughy Antean nobleman finding the hidden chests again, only this time he shouted out, and his soldiers came. Her mind spun through nightmare images of what had almost been. Sandr killed. Opal slaughtered. Master Kit riddled with arrows, his blood bright on the snow. Marcus Wester handing her over to the soldiers in exchange for the caravan's safe passage. And then what the soldiers might have done to her. That it hadn't happened gave the fear an almost spiritual power, as if her near escape had incurred a debt whose payment might be heavier than she could bear.

She fought back with memories of Magister Imaniel, the bank, the balances of trade and insurance, intrigue and subtle design that reminded her of home. It didn't bring rest, but it made the cold, dark, wakeful hours bearable, letting her pretend the world followed rules and could be tamed. Then the eastern sky would brighten, and the exhaustion would fall over her like a worked-metal coat, and she'd force herself up, out, and through another impossible day. By the time they reached Porte Oliva, she was living half in a waking dream. Small red animals shifted and danced in the corner of her vision, and the most improbable ideas—she had to swallow all the books to keep them safe, Master Kit could grow wings but didn't want anyone to know, Cary secretly planned to kill her in a jealous rage over Sandr—took on a plausibility they hadn't earned.

Everything she knew of Porte Oliva, she knew at second hand. She knew it sat at Birancour's southern edge and survived on what trade from the east didn't stop at the Free Cities and what from the west made the extra journey to avoid the pirates haunting Cabral. The greatest part of its wealth came as a wayport between Lyoneia and Narinisle. Magister Imaniel had called it everybody's second choice, but he'd said it as if that might not be such a bad role to play. She'd imagined it as a city of rough edges and local prides.

Her arrival itself had been uncanny. She remembered driving her team along hilly, snow-blown roads, and then a Kurtadam boy, sleek as an otter, trotted alongside her cart, his hand outstretched, asking her for coins, and a forest of buildings had sprouted around her. Porte Oliva was the first real city she'd seen apart from Vanai, stone where Vanai was wood, salt where Vanai was freshwater. Her first impressions of it were a blur of narrow streets with high white arches, the smells of shit and sea salt, the voices of full-blooded Cinnae chattering like finches. She thought they'd passed through a tunnel in a great wall, like the old stories of dead men passing from one life to another, but it was just as likely she'd dreamed it.

She remembered nothing about how she'd hired Marcus Wester and his second as her personal guard. Not even why she'd thought it was a good idea.

The captain padded across the stone floor. From the cot

against the wall, Yardem Hane snored. Cithrin let herself swim up from her nap and survey the dank little rooms again for the hundredth time. A small fire in the grate muttered, casting red-and-orange shadows on the far wall and belching pine smoke into the air. The window was scraped parchment, and it dirtied what sunlight it let in. The boxes—contents of the cart she'd carried so carefully from Vanai—were stacked along the walls like any cheap warehouse. Only the most valuable of the cart's contents had been put in the sunken iron strongbox. Hardly a tenth of what they carried would fit. Cithrin sat up. Her body felt bruised, but her head was almost clear.

"Morning," Marcus Wester said, nodding politely.

"How long was I asleep?" she asked.

"Half the morning. It's not midday yet."

"Is there any food?"

"Some sausage from last night," he said, nodding toward the small door of warped wood that led to the only other room.

Cithrin rose. For years in her life, half a morning's sleep would have been barely enough to see her through to evening. Now it felt like a luxury. The back room had neither door nor window, so Cithrin lit a thumb-sized stub of candle and carried it back with her. The books, soul and memory of the Vanai bank, hunkered on a wooden palette. A rough oak table supported a carafe of water and a length of greyish sausage. The overwhelming stink came from a tin chamberpot in the corner. Cithrin relieved herself, throwing a double handful of ashes in before putting the lid back in place. She cut a length of sausage and leaned against the table, chewing it. Apple and garlic seasoned the meat. It wasn't nearly as bad as she'd expected.

For almost two weeks, her life had been this. Marcus

watched the day, Yardem the night. They ventured outside as little as possible. The only privacy was in the smaller room, and the only light came from the dim window, the fire grate, and a few candles. The supplies were bought with the captain's money. What he'd earned selling the wool, cart, and mules was in a small leather purse by the door to the street. They'd taken less money for the mules than they could have gotten, but Cithrin thought the Firstblood woman who'd taken them in the end would treat them best.

She missed the mules.

Her hair felt greasy and lank. Her only clothes were the ones she'd been given when she became Tag the Carter. She finished the sausage and walked back out.

"I need clothes," she said. "I'm not wearing this until spring."

"All right," the captain said. "Only don't go far until you know the streets. And don't call attention to yourself. The fewer people realize we're here, the safer we are."

It was what he said every time, as if she would have forgotten since the day before. The Tralgu shifted in his sleep and sighed. She took the purse, tucked it in her pocket, and opened the door. The daylight was like a flood.

"Cithrin!"

She turned back. The captain was squatting by the fire, stirring the ashes with a blade, but his eyes were on her and full of concern.

"Be careful out there," he said.

"I know the stakes," she said, and stepped into the street.

The salt district was a maze. Buildings two stories high leaned over streets so narrow people couldn't pass without touching. The curve of the land shaped everything, making it impossible to see very far in any direction, and intersections that seemed to promise a wider path were as likely to end blind. Voices of men and women, Kurtadam, Cinnae, and Firstblood, filled the air. If a man shouted at his wife in this district, the echoes would carry the melody of his anger even as it washed away his individual words.

Children lurked in the windows and doorways, feral as cats. A few days' warm weather had melted the filthy snow and left black puddles lurking in the corners, covered with thin skins of ice. There might have been a thousand paths in and out, but Cithrin knew one, and she kept to it. A few minutes' walk and there was a five-way intersection with one pathway leading northeast. A wider swath of white-hazed sky glowed above it, and Cithrin followed it toward the market, the docks, and the flow of money that kept Porte Oliva alive.

The Grand Market wasn't an open square, but a network of covered walks. The rough cobbles of the street gave way to pale tiles. The archways sloped up like hands in folded prayer, great pale windows spilling light down between the stone and iron fingers. Men and women sang and played flutes. Pupeteers played through their little dramas, changed slightly to include a local merchant or political figure in the story. Servants from the great houses and palaces pushed along, enormous wicker baskets on their heads, to supply the dinners of the powerful. The small independent money-lenders—small fish compared to the leviathan of the Medean bank—set up their green felt boards and beam balances. Travelers and sailors came up from the docks to admire the chaos. Merchants called out their wares: bread and fish and meat, cloth and spice and spiritual guidance and never two days in the same configuration.

Every morning before the first light of dawn, merchants lined up at great kiosks waiting for the queensmen to arrive, escorting ornate iron chests from the governor's palace. Each merchant paid a fee and drew a ticket from the chest saying which of the thousands of alcoves and intersections would be theirs for the day. No moneylender, butcher, baker, or farmer could rely on making his fortune by holding a particular space. Or so it would be if the system weren't rigged. Cithrin had only been twice, but she doubted anything so carefully designed to give the appearance of fairness could keep from corruption.

She bought herself a burlap pocket of fire-warmed raisins and honey nuts, preparing herself for the search, but it wasn't long before she found the dressmaker she'd been hoping for, and only five alcoves from where she'd seen him last. The proprietor was a full-blood Cinnae man, thin and tall and pale, with rings on every finger and teeth that looked as if they'd been filed sharp. He had five tables arranged in a half circle with a sixth in the middle with his best wares on display. Cithrin paused, looking up at three dresses as if she were only passing time. The Cinnae stood at the side, shouting at a Firstblood woman who had her arms crossed and her face set in an almost godlike scowl. A crate lay between them, the pale wood soaked dark.

"Look! Look what the water's done to the dye!" the merchant said.

"I didn't drop them off the boat," the woman said.

"Neither did I."

"You signed papers for ten dresses. Here's ten dresses."

"I signed for ten dresses I could sell!"

Cithrin stepped closer. From what she could see, the dresses were simply cut. The seawater had run the dyes, yellow into blue into pale pink, and stippled all with spots of white like a handful of scattered sand. The Cinnae shot a look at her, annoyance narrowing his eyes.

"You need something?"

"A dress," Cithrin said around a mouthful of raisins. The merchant looked at her skeptically. Cithrin took her purse from her pocket and opened it. The silver caught the sunlight, and the merchant shrugged.

"Let me show you what we have," he said, turning away from the still-fuming Firstblood woman. From the center table, he took the first dress. Blue and white with embroidered sleeves, it seemed to breathe lavender petals. The merchant smoothed the cloth.

"This is our finest piece," he said. "Expensive, yes, but worth every coin. For a hundred and twenty silver, you won't find a better garment anywhere in the market. And that includes recutting it for your frame, of course."

Cithrin shook her head.

"That's not the one you sell," she said.

The merchant, replacing the dress on its stand, paused. Her phrase had struck him.

"You don't sell that one," Cithrin repeated. "It's not there to be sold. It's to make the next one seem reasonable. You offer the rose-colored one next? If you're starting at a hundred and twenty, you'll price it at... What? Eighty?"

"Eighty-five," the Cinnae said sourly.

"Which is too much," Cithrin said. "But I'll give you forty-five. That covers your cost and gives you a little profit."

"Forty-*five*?"

"It's a fair price," Cithrin said, taking another handful of raisins.

The merchant's jaw hung open an inch. The Firstblood woman beside the crate chuckled. Cithrin felt a sudden warmth in her belly, a release like the first drink of strong wine. She smiled, and for the first time in days, it came easily.

"If you give it to me for forty," Cithrin said, nodding at the ruined dresses, "I'll help you turn a profit on those."

The merchant stepped back, his arms crossed in front of him. Cithrin feared she'd overplayed him until he spoke.

"How would you propose that?" he said. His words had a touch of amusement.

"Forty," she said.

"Convince me."

Cithrin walked back to the crate and rifled through the dresses. They were all the same design. Cheap cloth with tin hooks and thread eyes, a bit of embroidery at the sleeve and collar.

"Where do you see the fewest goods from?" she asked. "Hallskar?"

"We don't see much from there," the merchant agreed.

"So switch out these hooks for silver," Cithrin said. "And put glass beads here at the collars. Three or four, but bright. Something to catch the eye."

"Why would I waste good silver and beads on trash like this?"

"You wouldn't," Cithrin said. "That's the point. If they have silver and beads, they must not be trash. Call them . . . I don't know. Hallskari salt dyes. New process, very rare. No other dresses like them in the Grand Market. Start them at two hundred silver, drop down to one hundred thirty."

"Why would anyone agree to pay that?"

"Why wouldn't they? When it's a new thing, no one knows its fair price. If nobody knows better, you can do anything."

The merchant shook his head, but it wasn't refusal. The Firstblood woman's eyebrows crawled toward her hairline. Cithrin dug out a honeyed nut. The roar and echo of voices around them was as good as silence. Cithrin waited for the space of four breaths as the merchant wrestled in his mind.

"If only one person in the whole Grand Market believed it," Cithrin said, "you'd cover the cost of all ten dresses. Hooks, beads, and everything. If *two* people did..."

The merchant was quiet for two breaths more.

"You know entirely too much about dresses," he said.

I don't know anything *about dresses,* she thought. The merchant barked out a laugh. He reached for the rose dress and tossed it at Cithrin in mock disgust.

"Forty," he said to her, then turned to the Firstblood woman. "Do you see this? Look at this face. That is a truly dangerous woman."

"I believe you," the Firstblood said as Cithrin, grinning, counted out coins.

An hour later, she was walking down the half-open ways of the Grand Market, her dress folded in a tight, rose-colored bundle under one arm, and the world around her a bright, benign place. The dress would need altering to make it fit her body, but that was a minor point. More than any object she'd gained, she enjoyed the idea of being *a truly dangerous woman.*

The sun had only just begun its slide into the west. Cithrin took herself toward the public baths, thinking of an hour's time in warm water and steam. Maybe even a few coins spent on a balm to drive away the fleas and lice that travel and her new, tiny rooms had given her. The baths sat at the northern edge of a wide public square. Pillars rose into the air, tall as trees, though whatever shelter they'd supported had been gone long enough that the rain had worn channels in the supports. Patches of brown, winter-killed grass lay like carpets in the open spaces, and twig-fingered bushes caught dead leaves and scraps of cloth. Cithrin walked past a cart selling hot soup and a weedy Kurtadam with a pair of marionettes dancing at his feet beside a beggar's bowl with a few bronze coins. Across the square, a troupe of players had changed their cart to a stage, edging out a pair of disgruntled puppeteers. Pigeons wheeled overhead. A group of Cinnae women walked together, pale and thin and lovely, their dresses flowing around their bodies like seaweed in the tide, and their voices all accents and music. Cithrin wanted to watch them, but without being seen. She'd never known a full-blooded Cinnae well. And yet her mother had been one, would have looked in place as part of just such a group.

The women turned up the wide steps that led to the baths, and Cithrin had started to follow when a familiar voice caught her up short.

"Stop!"

She turned.

"Stop now, and come near. Hear the tale of Aleren Mankiller and the Sword of Dragons! Or if you are faint of heart, move on."

On the players' stage, an older man strode across the planks, his voice ringing through the square. His beard jutted out, and his hair had been combed high. He wore gaudy theatrical robes, and his voice rang and slithered among the great pillars. There was no mistaking Master Kit, the cunning man. Cithrin walked toward the stage, wondering whether she was dreaming. Half a dozen other citizens of Porte Oliva had paused, drawn in by the patter, and the crowd itself drew a crowd. Cithrin stood on a patch of dead grass, amazed. Opal stepped out wearing a robe that made her seem ten years younger. Then Smit, wearing a simple laborer's cap and speaking in a broad Northcoast accent. Then Hornet in gilt armor, and behind him, striding onto the boards as if he owned the world and everything in it, Sandr. Cithrin laughed with delight, and other hands joined in her clapping. Mikel and Cary, both in among the crowd, nodded to her. Catching Cary's gaze, Cithrin pantomimed a drawing a sword and then gestured at the stage. *I thought you were soldiers, and you were this?* Cary shifted her head coyly and dropped a tiny curtsey before returning to the work of cheering Aleren Mankiller and hissing Orcus the Demon King.

The winter square was too cold. By the end of the first act, Cithrin's ears ached and her nose ran. She wrapped her arms around herself, huddling into her clothes, but nothing could have pulled her away. The story unfolded like a spring flower blooming, the caravan guards she'd known for months becoming actors before her, the actors becoming the parts they played until in the end Aleren Mankiller thrust the poisoned sword into the the belly of Orcus, Sandr and Master Kit half-forgotten echoes of men she used to know. The applause from the crowd was thin but heartfelt, and Cithrin dug out a few coins of her own to add to the shower dancing on the boards.

As the actors broke down the stage, Opal, Mikel, and Smit came out to grin at her and trade stories. Yes, they'd been actors from the start. They'd only played at being guards. Cary recited the opening of the comic piece they were making to commemorate the adventure. Cithrin told them— quietly so as not be overheard—about her rooms with Marcus and Yardem, and Opal made lewd jokes until Smit started to blush and they all lost track of themselves in laughing.

Sandr stood near the cart, frowning furiously and pointedly not looking at them all. Cithrin excused herself from the others and went to him, thinking that he might have been hurt that she was talking to the others and not to him.

"Imagine this," she said. "You never told me."

"Suppose not," Sandr said. He didn't meet her eyes.

"I didn't know," she said. "You were brilliant."

"Thank you."

Master Kit called from the far side of the cart, and Sandr hauled on a thick rope, pulling the stage up to lean against the cart's frame. Sandr tied off the rope, flickered his eyes to Cithrin and away, and nodded.

"I'm not done working. I need to go."

Cithrin stepped back, the pleasure in her heart going hollow.

"I'm sorry," she said. "I didn't mean to—"

"S'allright," Sandr said. "I just..."

Shaking his head, he walked away, ducking under a spar that Smit was bringing down to pack. Cithrin walked back into the square. The milk-colored sky seemed less benign than before. She didn't know whether to approach the players again or walk away, whether she was welcome here or an intrusion. She found herself suddenly aware of her tattered clothes and slept-on hair.

"It isn't you," a woman's voice said. Cary had looped around behind her. Cary, who'd demanded that Yardem tell her which weapon gave a woman advantage. Cary, who'd slung a bow over her shoulder and looked like a veteran of a dozen wars. Cary, who Cithrin didn't actually know.

"What isn't me?" she said.

"Sandr," Cary said, nodding toward a place down the square. "He's the new leading man. Leading men are always pigs for the first few years."

Sandr stood there, smiling. Three girls in rough clothes stood around him. One touched his arm, her fingers flickering on him like a butterfly unsure whether it was safe to land. Cithrin watched him smile at the girl, watched him glance down at her breasts.

"All I'm saying is, it's nothing to do with you," Cary said.

"I don't care," Cithrin said. "It's not as if I cared about him. But I didn't know that... I mean, I thought..."

"We all think that, the first few times," Cary said. "For what it draws, I'm sorry, and I promise I'll put sand in his beer in your name."

Cithrin forced herself to laugh. She didn't know when the knot had come back into her stomach, but it was there now.

"Nothing on my account," she said. "He's just what he is."

"Wise words, sister mine," Cary said. "Do you want to come out with us? We're trying another show outside the governor's palace at dusk."

"No," Cithrin said, too sharply. She tried again. "No, I was just going to the baths and then back to my rooms. Before the captain gets nervous."

"Luck with that. I think he was born nervous. Or watchful, at least," Cary said. "It was good seeing you."

Cithrin turned and walked up the broad steps. Steam billowed out of the bathhouse doors. Voices in argument and in song. Cithrin turned aside, walking past it all. Her jaw hurt, and she made herself unclench it. Part of her wanted to turn back, to go see who Sandr was talking with, whether he'd look her way. Maybe if...

Grit in the chilly air made her eyes water, and she wiped the tears away with the back of her hand. On the way home, she stopped at a public house and drank a mug of the same kind of fortified wine Sandr had brought her that day by the mill pond.

It didn't taste as good.

All well?" Captain Wester snapped as she came in. "You were gone a long time."

"Fine," she said shortly. "Everything's fine."

Dawson

Dawson Kalliam found Kavinpol ugly. The city squatted with one leg on either side of the river Uder, its buildings stuccoed a scabrous red-grey. The local food founded itself on onions and fish pulled from the same water into which the sewers emptied. Too many cycles of freeze and thaw cracked the streets, leaving pools of half-frozen mud to break the leg of an unwary horse. And in the center of it all, Lord Ternigan's estate with hunting grounds walled away from the city like a glorified lawn garden. In any other year, Dawson would have stayed on his estate with Clara and whichever of his sons chose to winter there rather than follow the hunt here.

This winter, though, the hunt had taken on a different meaning. Ternigan's tame deer and hand-raised quail weren't the prize Dawson tracked. And private audiences with the king were much easier to arrange when it was the king who wanted them.

"God *damn* it, Kalliam. I'm trying to keep peace, and you're killing people in the streets?"

The ceiling of the king's chamber vaulted up into the soot-muddied dimness above them. Great windows looked out over the city, boasts made of glass and iron. Overstated and gaudy, the architecture spoke of glory and power, and what it said was: *You may have these or comfort, but not both.*

Dawson looked at his childhood friend. The months of winter had etched a frown into the corners of his mouth and left grey at his temples like the first frost. Or perhaps the signs of age and weakness had always been there, and Dawson hadn't been willing to see them until now. The jewel-studded robes that Simeon wore—even the crown itself—looked less like the raiments of power and greatness than they had in the autumn. Instead, they were the empty form of it, like a dry pitcher waiting to be filled. Dawson knew the response that Simeon and etiquette expected. *Forgive me, sire.*

"Nobler blood's spilled in Camnipol every time someone slaughters a pig," Dawson said. "They were Issandrian's thugs."

"You have proof of that?"

"Of course I can't prove it, but we both know they were. His or Maas's, it hardly matters. And you wouldn't be pulling my leash if you believed they were street toughs with poor aim."

The pause weighted the air. Simeon rose. His boots scraped against the stone floor. Around them, the chamber's tapestries shifted, and the king's guard kept their silent watch. Dawson wished they could be truly alone. The guards were servants, but they were also men.

"Your Majesty," Dawson said, "I think you fail to understand the loyalty all around you. My own included. I have spent the season having private conversations with the highest-born men in Antea, and there is a wide support for you against Issandrian and his pack."

"Issandrian and his pack are also my subjects," Simeon said. "I can make the argument that feeding unrest is in itself acting against me."

"We are acting *for* you, Simeon. The men I have spoken

with are united in *your* name. I only wish you were with us."

"If I start declaring war on parts of the nobility only because they happen to be in ascendance at the moment—"

"Is that what you've heard me say? Simeon, I have spent months cajoling and promising everyone I could find with any influence on Ternigan. He is ready to pull Klin from Vanai. All he needs is a signal from you."

"If I take sides in this, it will end in blood."

"And if you don't the kingdom will have unending peace and light? You know better than that."

"The dragons—"

"The dragons didn't fall because there was a war. There was a war because there wasn't a leader. A family needs a father, and a kingdom needs a king. It is your duty to lead, and if you fail in that, the day will come when they follow someone else. *Then* we will be on the dragon's path."

Simeon shook his head. The firelight reflected in his eyes. Outside, a cold wind whirled, smelling of winter. Snow like a fall of ashes whirled past the windows.

"A family needs a father," the king said, as if the words were funny and bitter both. "When Eleora died, I promised her I'd take care of our son. Not the prince, our son."

"Aster *is* the prince," Dawson said.

"If he weren't, he would still be my son. You have children. You understand."

"I have three sons and a daughter. Barriath captains a ship under Lord Skestinin, Vicarian is studying for the priesthood, and Jorey's in Vanai. Elisia married Lord Annerin's eldest son three years ago, and I've barely heard of her since. And none of them, Simeon, have made me *timid*," Dawson said. And then, more softly, "What happened to you?"

Simeon laughed.

"I became king. It's all well and good when we were playing at it in the yards and on the battlefields, but then Father died. It wasn't play anymore. Issandrian's cabal isn't my only problem. Hallskar's begun harboring raiders again. Northcoast's aiming for another war of succession and Asterilhold's backing both sides. The tax revenues from Estinford aren't what they should be, so someone's either stealing them or the farms are starting to fail. And in a few years, Aster's to step up and run it all."

"Not so few," Dawson said. "We're not young, but we've got life in us yet. And you know the answer to this as well as I do. Find men you trust, and then trust them."

"Meaning you and your cabal instead of Issandrian and his?" the king asked dryly.

"Yes. Meaning that."

"I'd rather you backed away. Let Issandiran's movement collapse from within."

"It won't."

King Simeon looked up, and his eyes might have held anger or amusement or despair. Dawson sank deliberately to his knee, a man giving obeisance to his king. The angle of his chin and his shoulders made it a challenge. *Here is my loyalty. Deserve it.*

"You should go, old friend," the king said. "I need to rest before the feast. I need to think."

Dawson rose, bowed silently, and left for his own rooms. Lord Ternigan's estate sprawled. It had been built over the course of centuries by uncountable designers, each it seemed with his own conflicting vision. The result was a labyrinth. Every courtyard and square opened in some unexpected way, hallways angled and turned to avoid obstacles long since unmade. There was no better invitation for a quiet knife from the shadows.

He let the king's servant put him into his coat, drape the thick black wool cloak across his shoulders, and bow before stepping out into the white wind. Vincen Coe stepped behind him. Dawson didn't speak to the man, and the hunter offered no report. With only the creak of leather and their snow-muffled footsteps, they crossed the courtyard, passed through a series of overhung walkways, and across a wide, flat bridge where the wind threatened to whip them away like sparrows in a storm. There were warmer paths, but they were better peopled, and so more dangerous. If Issandrian and Maas wanted to strike at Dawson, they'd have to work for it.

The hospitality that Ternigan had offered House Kalliam included a private house that had once belonged to a king's favored concubine. The stonework had a vulgar sensuality, the gardens before it—no doubt lush in spring—were now hardly more than a collection of twigs and dead scrub. But it was defensible, and Dawson appreciated it for that. He shrugged off his cloak and his bodyguard at the door and entered the warm, dark inner rooms to the smell of mint tea and the sound of a woman weeping.

For a horrible moment, he thought the voice was Clara's, but the years had trained him to pick her sounds out from any others, and these sobs were not hers. Quietly, he tracked the weeping and, as he drew nearer, Clara's soothing voice to a sitting chamber where the long-dead concubine had once taken her ease. Now Clara sat there on a low divan, her cousin Phelia—Baroness of Ebbinbaugh and wife of the hated Feldin Maas—sitting on the floor before her, her head resting in Clara's lap. Dawson met his wife's gaze, and Clara shook her head without a pause in her soft litany of comfort. Dawson stepped back. He went to the private study to smoke his pipe, drink whiskey, and work on a poem he'd started composing until Clara came, an hour later, and dropped herself unceremoniously into his lap.

"Poor Phelia," she sighed.

"Domestic trouble?" Dawson asked, stroking his wife's hair. She plucked the pipe from his mouth and drew a deep lungful herself.

"It seems my husband is making her husband terribly unhappy," she said.

"Her husband is trying to kill yours."

"I know, but it hardly seems polite to point it out when the poor thing's broken down in front of me. Besides which, you're winning, aren't you? I can hardly see her asking mercy if the warm winds were blowing on Ebbinbaugh."

"Asking mercy was she?"

"Not in so many words," Clara said, relinquishing Dawson's lap but not his pipe. "But she wouldn't, would she? Terribly rude, and I'm fairly certain Feldin didn't know she'd come, so don't start figuring her into all your calculations and intrigues. Sometimes a frightened woman is only a frightened woman."

"And still, I don't plan to make her days any better," Dawson said. Clara shrugged and looked away. When he spoke next his tone was less playful. "I'm sorry about it. For you and for her. If that helps."

For a long moment, Clara was silent, sipping smoke from his pipe. In the dim light, she looked younger than she was.

"Our worlds are growing apart, husband," Clara said. "Yours and mine. Your little wars, my peaces. War is winning out."

"There's a time for war," Dawson said.

"I suppose," she said. "I...suppose. Still, remember that wars end. Try to be sure that there's something worth having at the other end. Not all your enemies are your enemies."

"That's nonsense, love."

"No it isn't," she said. "It's just not how you see the world. Phelia's no part of whatever you and Feldin hate in each other any more than I am. But she's at stake, as am I and our children. Phelia is your enemy because she has to be, not because she chose it. And when the end comes, remember that a great number of the people on the other side have lost a great deal and didn't pick the fight."

"Would you have me stop?" he asked.

Clara laughed, a deep, purring sound. The smoke rose from her mouth, curling in the candlelight.

"Shall I ask the sun not to set while I'm at it?"

"For you, I would," Dawson said.

"For me, you would try, and you'd batter yourself to nothing in the attempt," she said. "No, do what you think needs doing. And think about how you would want Feldin to treat me, if he won."

Dawson bowed his head. Around them, the beams and stones settled in the winter cold, popping and muttering to themselves. When he looked up again, her gaze was on him.

"I will try," he said. "And if I forget...?"

"I'll remind you, love," Clara said. "It's what I do."

The feast that night began an hour before sunset and was to last until all the candles had burned themselves out. Lord Ternigan sat at the high table with his wife and brother. Simeon sat at the far end, Aster beside him in red velvet and cloth-of-gold looking embarrassed whenever Lady Ternigan spoke to him. The rider who'd taken top honors in the hunt—the half-Jasuru son of a noble family from Sarakal who was traveling in Antea for God knew what reason—joined them, nodding at everything and contributing nothing.

The best tapestries of Ternigan's collection hung on the walls, beeswax candles burned in holders of sculpted crystal, and the dogs that lurked around the tables wore cloths on their backs in the colors of every noble house in Antea as a bit of levity to brighten the night. Dawson sat at the second table, near enough to hear what was said, and at the far end of the table with only five people between them, Feldin Maas. Ternigan once again evenhandedly marking that his allegiance was negotiable as a whore's virtue. Phelia Maas sat her husband's side stealing watery glances at Dawson. He ate his soup. It had too much salt, not enough lemon, and the fish still had bones in it.

"Lovely soup," Clara said. "I remember my aunt—not your mother, Phelia, dear, Aunt Estrir who married that awful fop from Birancour—saying that the best thing for river fish is lemon zest."

"I remember her," Phelia said, clutching at the connection almost desperately. "She came back for my wedding, and she affected that terrible accent."

Clara laughed, and for a moment things might almost have been at ease.

Behind Dawson, King Simeon cleared his throat. Dawson couldn't say what about the sound caught him, but the hair on the back of his neck rose. From the pinched, bloodless lips and the wineglass trapped halfway between table and mouth, it was clear Feldin Maas had heard it too.

"All of this is tribute from your man in Vanai?" Simeon asked with a forced casualness.

"No, Majesty. Most has been in my family for years."

"Ah, good. That squares better with what I'd heard about

Klin and his taxes. For a moment, I thought you'd been holding out on me."

Maas's face went pale. He lowered the wineglass to the table. Dawson took a bite of fish and decided that perhaps Clara was right. The lemon did add something to it. King Simeon had just joked that Klin's gifts from the conquered city wouldn't be enough to decorate a feast. The tone was light, the only response was laughter, and Sir Alan Klin would be back in Antea by the thaw.

"I hope you'll excuse me," Dawson said. "Nature."

"We understand," Feldin Maas said, biting the words. "Every bladder gets weak with age."

Dawson spread his hands in a gesture that could be read as an acknowledgment of the jest or as a provocation. *Do your worst, little man. Do your worst.*

By the time Dawson reached the edge of the feasting hall, Coe was silently walking behind him. In the wide stone hallway that led to the private retiring rooms, Dawson stopped and Coe stopped with him. It wasn't long before Canl Daskellin, Baron of Watermarch, appeared, silhouetted by the light from the feast.

"Well," Daskellin said.

"Yes," Dawson said.

"Come with me," Daskellin said. Together the two men walked to a private retiring room. Coe didn't remain behind, but he gave a greater distance between himself and his betters. Dawson wondered what would happen if he ordered Coe away. On one hand, the huntsman could hardly refuse. On the other, strictly speaking, Coe answered to Clara. Awkward position for the man. Dawson's mischievous spirit was tempted to try it and see which way the huntsman jumped, but Canl Daskellin spoke and brought his mind back to other matters.

"I've managed to catch Ternigan's ear. His loyalty's with us."

"Until the tide turns," Dawson said.

"Yes, and so we need to act quickly. I believe we can call the candidate for Klin's replacement. But..."

"I know."

"I've spoken with our friends in Camnipol. Count Hiren would have been the consensus choice if he'd lived."

"Issandrian's cousin? What did they like about him," Dawson said.

"Estranged cousin," Daskellin said. "But dead cousin in any case. His greatest strength was that he had no love for Issandrian and no direct ties to any of us."

Dawson spat.

"How is it we've come so quickly to the place where we don't want to seat one of our enemies or one of our own."

"It's the danger of conspiracy," Daskellin said. "Breeds a certain distrust."

Dawson crossed his arms. In his heart, he wanted his son Jorey in the prince's chair. He could rely on his own blood in a way that mere politics could never attain. Which was, of course, why he'd sworn against it. Vanai had to be denied to Issandrian. But it couldn't be taken by any single member of Dawson's still-fresh alliance without threatening its fracture. Dawson had foreseen the problem. He had his proposal ready.

"Hear me out, Canl. Vanai was always a small piece in this," Dawson said carefully.

"True."

"With Klin gone, Issandrian's lost the tribute, but the city is still his project. Maas agitated for taking it. Klin fought for it, and even controlled the city until now. If we don't put someone in power who is identified with us, it will remain Issandrian's in the general opinion."

"But who of ours can we put in?"

"No one," Dawson said, "that's what I mean. We can't take it from Issandrian in the mind of the court. But now we can control what it says about him. What if the governance of the city were to become a catastrophe? Lose the city to incompetence, and Issandrian's reputation suffers along with it."

Daskellin stopped. Between the dimness of the light spilling from the feast chamber and the darkness of the man's complexion, Dawson couldn't read his expression. He pressed on.

"My youngest son is there," Dawson said. "He's been sending reports. Lerer Palliako's son is in Vanai. Geder, his name is. Klin's been using him to do the unpopular work. No one likes or respects him."

"Why not? Is he dim?"

"Worse than dim, one of those men who *only* knows what he's read in books. He's the kind that reads an account of a sailing voyage and thinks he's a captain."

"And you want Ternigan to name Geder Palliako in Klin's place?"

"If half of what I've heard is true," Dawson said with a smile, "there's no one better suited to lose Vanai."

Marcus

Night in the salt district of Porte Oliva wasn't quiet. Even in the deep night when no moon lit the street, there were sounds. Voices lifted in song or anger, the scuttling and complaints of feral cats. And, in the rooms he and Yardem had hired, the slow, regular breath of the girl, sleeping at last. Marcus had come to know the difference between the way she inhaled when she was sleeping and when she was only willing herself to. It was an intimacy he never spoke of.

Yardem squatted on the floor by the glowing embers of the fire, ears forward, eyes focused on nothing. Marcus had seen the Tralgu sit through whole nights like that; motionless, waiting, aware without insisting upon awareness. Yardem never fell asleep on watch, and he never struggled to rest when he was off duty. Marcus, blanket-wrapped and sleepless, envied him that.

The cold of winter was still on the city, but it wouldn't be many more weeks before the sea lanes opened. A ship from Porte Oliva to Carse would be faster than going overland through Birancour. And as long as he could keep it from captain and crew what exactly they were hauling—

The scraping sound was soft, there and gone again in an eyeblink. Leather sole against stone. Yardem sat up a degree straighter. He looked over at Marcus, then pointed once toward the opaque parchment window, and then at the door.

Marcus nodded and rolled slowly off the cot, careful not to let the canvas creak beneath him. He took a slow step toward the window as Yardem shifted toward the door. When Marcus drew his knife, he kept his left thumb against the steel to keep it from singing when it cleared the scabbard. Cithrin snored delicately behind him.

Whoever they were, they'd done this before. The door burst open at the same instant a man leaped through the parchment window. Marcus kicked low, his boot slamming against the man's knee. While the man struggled to regain his balance, Marcus slit his throat, and two more men poured in after him. They had daggers. Swords would have been awkward in so small a space. Marcus had hoped they'd have swords.

Yardem grunted the way he did when he lifted something too heavy, and an unfamiliar voice cried out in pain. The knife man on Marcus's left made a flurry of short swings designed to catch his eye and force him back while the one on the right shifted to flank him. They were thickly built, but not massive. Firstblood or Jasuru rather than Yemmu or Haavirkin. Marcus ignored the false attack, feinting instead to keep the man on his right from getting around him. The first man took the opening and slid his blade in. Marcus felt the pain bloom on his ribs, but he ignored it. Behind him, a bone snapped, but no one screamed.

"We surrender," Marcus said, and slid forward, his ankle hooking behind the rightmost attacker's leg. When he brought his knife out, the man instinctively stepped back, stumbling. Marcus sank his blade in the man's groin, but the effort left him open again. The remaining attacker, having drawn blood once, swooped in for the kill. Marcus twisted, the enemy blade skittering across his shoulder. Marcus dropped his own knife and took a grip on the other man's elbow, but the attacker moved in close, bending Marcus back with a combination of weight and leverage. The hot breath stank of beer and fish. The embers glittered on scaled skin and evil, pointed teeth. Jasuru, then. Marcus felt the tip of the Jasuru's blade prick his belly. Another push and the knife would open him like a trout.

"Yardem?" Marcus grunted.

"Sir?" Yardem said, and then, "Oh. Sorry."

A dagger sprouted from the Jasuru's left eye, the blood sheeting down from the wound, black in the monochrome dimness. The attacker pressed forward even as he died, but Marcus felt the strength leave the man and stepped back to let the body fall.

Three men lay by the torn window, dead or bleeding dry. Another lay motionless on the floor, one arm sprawled into the fire grate and starting to burn, and the last slumped against the wall at Yardem's feet, head at an improbable angle. Five men. Strong and experienced. This, Marcus thought, was very, *very* bad.

"What's the matter?" Cithrin asked groggily. "Did something happen?"

"Outside," Yardem said, and Marcus heard it too. Retreating footsteps.

"Stay here," Marcus said, and bolted out the ruined window.

The night-black streets blinded him, but he loped forward, committing to each stride and hoping that his foot didn't come down on any icy puddle or unexpected step. Ahead of him, the footsteps slapped against cobbles. Something large and animal hissed as Marcus flew past. His lungs burned, and the blood on his shoulder and side chilled him. The fleeing footsteps skittered, lost balance, and pelted off toward the left. He was getting closer.

The street opened onto a wider square, and there, by starlight, Marcus caught sight of the fleeing figure. It was small and wrapped in a dark cloak with a hood that covered head and hair. The disguise was pointless. By the time he'd seen the fleeing woman take two steps, he knew her as well as if he'd seen her face.

"Opal!" he shouted. "You should stop."

The actress hesitated and then pressed on, pretending she hadn't been recognized. Marcus cursed, gritted his teeth, and kept running. The dark city ignored them. Opal shifted through streets and alleys, trying desperately to confuse or exhaust him. Marcus ignored his wounds and kept after her, one foot in front of the other, until by a wide cistern, Opal stopped, knelt, and put her head in her hands. Her chest was working like a bellows. Marcus tottered up beside her and sat. They were both wheezing like old men. Her pale hair caught the starlight.

"Not," Opal said between gasps. "Not what it looks like. You have to believe me."

"No," Marcus said. "I don't."

I didn't know," Master Kit said. "I should have, but I didn't."

Marcus's former cunning man was still in a striped wool sleeping shift and a close-fit nightcap. That and the fact that he'd been dead asleep in the back of the troupe's wagon when Marcus reached him argued for his innocence. Master Kitap rol Keshmet wasn't the picture of a man preparing to escape with his stolen gold. It was what Marcus had bet on.

The rooms they sat in now had been rented from a brewer. Most of the year, they warehoused the oats and malt of that trade, and the air was still thick with the smell of them. The table was three lengths of plank set across two piles of old brick, and the stools Marcus, Kit, and the disgraced Opal sat on were less than a milkmaid might use. In the flickering light of Master Kit's single candle, Opal's eyes had disappeared in pools of shadow. Her argument that it was all a misunderstanding, that she'd been there to protect Cithrin, vanished like the morning dew as soon as Master Kit had come into the room, and all that was left was her sullen silence.

"You mean to say she came to this herself and no one else in the company had a suspicion," Marcus said.

Master Kit sighed.

"I've traveled with Opal as long as I have with...well, anyone. I think she knows me, and I would guess well enough to know how to deceive me. Captain, if she had even lied about this, I'd have known."

"Leave him be, Wester," Opal said. "This wasn't his. It was mine."

It was the first confession she'd made. Marcus took no pleasure in it.

"But I don't understand why," Master Kit said. He wasn't talking to Marcus any longer. "I'd thought Cithrin was a favorite of yours."

"How many more years do I have?" Opal asked. Her voice was sharp as aged cheese. "You're already thinking of Cary for Lady Kaunitar roles. Another five years, and I'll be strictly witch-and-grandmother, and then the day will come when you and the others leave some shit-stinking village in Elassae and I don't."

"Opal," Master Kit began, but the woman raised a palm to stop him.

"I know how this goes. I've been a player since I was younger than Sandr is now. I've seen it happen. Made a kind of peace with it, really. But then the banker's girl appeared out of the air, and..." Opal shrugged, and it was an actor's movement made of weariness and resignation.

Weariness and resignation, Marcus thought, but not regret.

"All right," Marcus said. "Next problem."

Master Kit turned back toward him. There were tears in the man's eyes, but otherwise his expression was calm.

"I have five corpses," Marcus said. "Maybe three hours to first light. If I go to the queensmen, I have to explain what happened, and what we've got in those boxes that's worth killing over. Any hope of keeping quiet's gone then. Add to that, we'll have to move just in case any of Opal's friends have friends of their own. We've sold the cart. You still have one."

The cut in his shoulder had gone an uncomfortable sort of numb, but the scratch across his ribs tore open each time he took a deep breath. He knew that this was the point at which Master Kit might balk. Marcus had hoped he could avoid a long negotiation. He watched Master Kit's dark eyes as the man weighed his unpleasant options.

"I feel the company owes you something, Captain Wester," he said at last. "What would you have me do?"

An hour later, they were back in the small rooms of the salt quarter. The dead man had been pulled from the grate, and a new fire stoked. Hornet and Smit were somberly pasting lengths of cloth over the rips in the parchment while Cary, Sandr, and Mikel looked at the bodies piled like cordwood against the wall. Master Kit sat on an overturned handcart, his expression grim. Cithrin sat on the cot, her legs drawn up to her chest, her eyes empty. She didn't look at Opal, and Opal didn't look back. The room, small to begin with, felt dangerously crowded.

"There's an opening in the eastern seawall, not far from

baker's row," Master Kit said, thoughtfully. "I don't remember much cover, nor any way to explain being there, but I think I could find it again."

"Even in the dark?" Marcus asked.

"Yes. And if there's no reason for us to be there, I think there's little reason for anyone else either."

"They look peaceful," Mikel said. "I didn't think they'd look peaceful."

"All dead men are at peace," Marcus said. "That's what makes them dead. We've got five of these bastards to get rid of. We don't have much time. How far is this place?"

"We'll be seen," Cithrin said. "They'll find us. Ten people carrying five bodies? How does that...?"

The girl shook her head and looked down. Her face was paler even than usual. The others were quiet. If things had gone otherwise, there would only have been three bodies, and hers among them. Marcus could see the knowledge etching the girl's soul, but he didn't have time now to fix that, or any idea how he would have.

"Master Kit?" Cary said thoughtfully. "What about the festival scene in Andricore's Folly?"

"You can't be serious," he said.

"I think I am," Cary said. She turned to Yardem. "Can you carry one by yourself? Over your shoulder?"

The Tralgu crossed his arms, frowning deeply, but nodded. Master Kit's face was still pale, but he rose and turned the handcart back onto its wheels, considering it. By contrast, Cary's face was flushing rose.

"Yardem takes one," she said. "Smit and Hornet can take the small one there. Sandr and Cithrin, the poor fellow with the beard. That puts two on the handcart. Mikel can steady them, and you and the captain haul. Then Opal and I take torches and—"

"Not Opal," Master Kit said. "She stays with us."

"I'll take Cithrin, then," Cary said, hardly missing a breath. "Opal can help Sandr."

"You'll take Cithrin where, exactly?" Marcus said, his voice low.

"To make sure no one is looking at *you*," Cary said, and she stepped over to the cot, lowering herself beside Cithrin's slight frame. The dark-haired woman put an arm across Cithrin's shoulders and smiled at her gently. "Come on, sister mine. Are you ready to be brave?"

Cithrin blinked back tears.

"Kit?" Marcus said.

"Andricore's Folly. It's a comedy from a poet in Cabral," Master Kit said. "The city prince dies in a brothel, and they have to smuggle his body back into his wife's bed before she wakes."

"And they manage it how?"

"It's a comedy," Master Kit said, shrugging. "Help me with this cart, won't you?"

There were no torches, but two small tin lanterns in the back room came near enough. With a few pins and Cary's direction, their dresses had grown short in the skirt, and half undone at the neck and back. Their hair hung in loose curls, threatening to fall at any moment, like the ruins of some more respectable arrangement. Cary rouged Cithrin's lips and cheeks and the swell of her breast, and in the darkness of the night the pair seemed carved out of sunlight and the promise of sex.

"Count three hundred," Master Kit said to Cary. "Then follow. If I give the sign..."

"We'll start singing," Cary said, and then, to Cithrin, "Shoulders back, sister mine. We're here to be seen."

"Yardem?" Marcus said as the Tralgu hefted a dead man.

"Sir?"

"The day you throw me in a ditch and take the company?"

"I am the company, sir."

"Fair point."

They slipped into the darkness. The cold was bitter, and Marcus's breath fogged before him. The cobbles seemed made from ice, and the smell of death came from the cart, low and coppery and familiar as his own name. At his side, Master Kit pulled, the man's breath coming fast as panting. The living carried the dead through the black streets, guided by starlight and memory. Drying blood caked Marcus's side, plucking at his wounds with every step. He pressed himself forward. It seemed like a slow eternity, pain in his fingers giving way to numbness, and then pain again. Behind him, he heard Cary's voice suddenly rise in bawdy song, and then, like a river reed playing harmony to a trumpet, Cithrin's voice with hers. He looked over his shoulder. A block behind them, their lanterns held high above them, two scantily dressed women faced a patrol of queensmen. Marcus stopped, the handcart slowing as he dropped from the lead.

"Captain," Master Kit whispered urgently.

"This is idiocy," Marcus said. "This isn't your comedy, and that street's not a stage. Those are men with swords and power. Putting women in front of them and hoping for the best is—"

"What we've done, Captain," Master Kit said. "It's what we've done, and this is why. You should pull the cart now."

In the light of the lanterns, Cary twirled once, laughing. One of the queensmen draped a cloak over Cithrin's shoulders. Marcus realized he'd drawn his knife without knowing it. *They can't be trusted,* Marcus thought, looking at the guardians of civil peace in their cloaks of green and gold. *You can't trust them*.

"Captain?" Yardem asked.

"Go. Keep going," Marcus said and forced himself to turn away.

The break in the seawall was on the far eastern edge of the city. A stone walkway white with snow and gull droppings and black with ice and night looked out over an invisible ocean. Gulls nested in cracks in the walls around them and on the cliffs below. And there, a single crack, no wider than a doorway where the city had constructed a siege weapon long since turned to rust to defend it against an enemy as dead as the bodies Marcus hauled.

They moved quickly and in silence. Yardem strode to the edge and lofted the corpse from his shoulder and into the grey predawn mist. Then Smit and Hornet, like men helping a drunken companion over the threshold. Then, together, the handcart with its human cargo. And last, Sandr and Opal, the woman limping under the weight of her burden, came to the edge. The last of the knife men vanished. There was no splash. Only the hush of the wind, the complaints of the birds, and faraway muttering of the surf.

"Yardem," Marcus said. "Get back to the rooms. I'll find Cithrin."

"Yes, sir," the Tralgu said, and vanished into the gloom.

"We'll need money to pay their fines," Smit said. "Can we afford that?"

"Seems wrong to charge them for public lewdness," Sandr said. "Most places you have to pay extra for it."

"I think we can do what we must," Master Kit said shortly. "You all go back to the cart. I believe the captain and I have some last business. Opal, please stay with us."

The players stood for a moment and then walked slowly

away. Marcus listened to their footsteps fade. Sandr said something, and Smit replied darkly. Marcus couldn't make out the words. Master Kit and Opal stood, deeper black in the gloom all around. Marcus wished he could see their faces, and was also glad that he couldn't.

"I can't take her to the queensmen," Marcus said.

"I know," Master Kit said.

"I didn't tell anyone else," Opal said. "The only people who know about the banker girl's fortune are the ones who knew before."

"Unless one of your swimming friends down there told someone," Marcus said.

"Unless that," Opal admitted.

"It seems to me there are only two choices here, Captain. You won't appeal to the city's justice. Either Opal walks free, or she doesn't."

"That's truth," Marcus said.

"I would very much like you to let her walk away," Master Kit said. "She's already lost her place with me, and we've helped protect your work here. You're hurt, but Yardem Hane isn't. Or Cithrin. I won't say there's no harm done, but I hope there's room for mercy."

"Thank you, Kit," Opal said.

Marcus squinted up. The eastern sky had begun to show the first faint lightening of dawn. The stars in the great arch above him still glittered and shone, but the faintest of them had vanished. More would go out in the next few minutes. He'd been told that, in truth, the stars were always there, only during the day you couldn't see them. He'd heard the same thing said about the souls of the dead. He didn't believe that either.

"I'd need to know she wouldn't come after us again," he said.

"I swear it," Opal said, jumping at his words. "I swear to all the gods that I won't make another try."

Master Kit made a sudden, pained sound, as if someone had struck him. Marcus took a step toward him, but when the man spoke, his voice was clear and strong and unutterably sad.

"Oh, my poor, dear Opal."

"Kit," she said, and there was an intimacy in the way she formed the word that made Marcus reassess everything he thought he knew about the two and their past.

"She's lying, Captain," Master Kit said. "I wish that she wasn't, but you have my word that she is. If she leaves here now, it's with the intention to come back."

"Well, then," Marcus said. "That's a problem."

The shadow that was Opal turned and tried to bolt, but Marcus stepped in front of her. She clawed at his eyes and made an inexpert try to knee his groin.

"Please. He's wrong. Kit's wrong. *Please* let me go."

The desperation in her voice, the *fear,* made him want to step aside. He was a soldier and a mercenary, not the kind of feral thug who killed women for the joy of it. He moved half a step back, but then remembered Cithrin again, sitting on the cot with her legs drawn to her knees, facing the swords of the patrol with awkward song. He'd promised to protect her if he could. Not only when it was pleasant.

He knew what had to happen next.

"I'm sorry about this," Marcus said.

Geder

Geder had known, of course, that Klin's favorites had been given the better accommodations, and that men like himself had taken the leavings. The scale of the insult, however, hadn't been clear. He sat on a low divan upholstered in silk. High windows spilled light over the floors like God upending a milk jug. Incense touched the air with vanilla and patchai. The goldwork and gems that glowed over the fire grate hadn't been wrenched apart in the sack. Even before the soldiers of Antea had taken the streets below, it had been understood that the prince's house was sacrosanct. Not because it was the prince's, but because it was Ternigan's. And then Klin's. And now, unthinkably, his own.

"My Lord Protector?"

Geder jumped to his feet as if he'd been caught touching something he shouldn't. The chief of household was an old Timzinae slave, his dark scales greying and cracked. He wore the grey and blue of House Palliako now, or as close to them as could be scrounged.

"Your secretaries await, sir," the Timzinae said.

"Yes," Geder said, plucking at the black leather cloak he'd brought from his old rooms. "Yes, of course. Take me there."

The orders had come three days before. The Lord Marshal had called Alan Klin back to Camnipol, to the despair of some, the delight of others, and the surprise of no one. The astonishing development was who Ternigan had chosen as his replacement until such time as King Simeon named a permanent governor. Geder had read the order ten times at least, checked the seal and signature, and then read it again. Sir Geder Palliako, son of Viscount of Rivenhalm Lerer Palliako, was now Protector of Vanai. He had the order still, folded in a pouch at his belt like a religious relic: mysterious and awesome and entirely unsafe.

His first thought after the first wave of raw disbelief had passed was that Klin had discovered Geder's betrayal, and that this was his revenge. As he stepped into the meeting chamber, Klin's appointees peopling every seat except the one on the dais at the front reserved for himself, Geder had the suspicion again. His belly sloshed and he felt his hands trembling. His blood felt weak as water as he took the two steps up and lowered himself uncomfortably into the presentation seat. Once, the room had been a chapel, and the icons of gods in whom Geder didn't believe surrounded him. Unsympathetic eyes gazed up at him, expressions blank at best, openly contemptuous at worst. A handful of seats were empty. Loyalists of House Klin who had chosen to resign commission and return with him to Antea rather than submit to the new order. Geder wished he could have gone with them.

"Lords," Geder said. He sounded like someone was strangling him. He coughed, cleared his throat, and began again. "My lords, you will have read by now the orders of Lord Marshal Ternigan. I am, of course, honored and as surprised as I'm sure all of you are as well."

He chuckled. No one else made a sound. Geder swallowed.

"It's important that the city not suffer from a sense of unease during this change. I would like each of you to continue on with the directions and orders given by Lord Klin so that the...ah...change that we are—"

"You mean the policies that have him pulled back to Ternigan?" The questioner was Alberith Maas, eldest son of Estrian Maas and nephew of Klin's close ally Feldin.

"Excuse me?"

"The orders," the young man said. "They're the same ones that put Lord Klin in the crown's poor grace, and you want us to keep to them?"

"For now," Geder said, "yes."

"A bold decision, my Lord Protector."

Someone sniggered. Geder felt a rush of shame, and then anger. His jaw tightened.

"When I order a change, Lord Maas, I'll see that you know of it," he said. "We will all have to work to raise Vanai up from its present disorder."

So don't cross me, or I'll put you in charge of cleaning weeds out of the canals, Geder thought, but didn't say. The young man rolled his eyes but kept silent. Geder took a deep breath, letting the air curl slowly out through his nostrils. His enemies sat before him, looking up. Men of greater experience, with greater political connections, and who had not been given the power that Geder now held. For the most part they would be polite. They would say the right things, though often in the wrong tone of voice. In private, they would shake their heads and laugh at him.

Humiliation fueled his rage.

"Alan Klin was a failure." It was nothing he'd meant to say, and he threw the words out like a slap across the jowls. "The Lord Marshal gave him Vanai, and Klin pissed it away. And each of *you* were part of that failure. I know you are going to leave here and share your jokes and roll your eyes and tell yourselves it's all a terrible mistake."

He leaned forward now. The heat in his cheeks felt like courage.

"But, my very good lords, let me make this clear. *I* am the one Lord Ternigan chose. *I* am the one he picked to turn Vanai from an embarrassment into a jewel in King Simeon's crown. And I intend to do so. If you would rather make light of me and of the duty we are given, say it now, take your things, and crawl back to Camnipol on your bellies. But stand off *my path*!"

He was shouting now. The fear was gone, the humiliation with it. He didn't remember standing, but he was on his feet now, his finger pointing a general accusation at the group. Their eyes were wide, their brows risen. He could see unease in the angle of their shoulders and the way they held their hands.

Good, he thought. *Let them wonder who and what Geder Palliako is.*

"If Lord Klin has left pressing business, I'll hear it now. Otherwise, I will have reports from each of you by tomorrow on the state of the city in general, your particular responsibilities within it, and how you propose to do better."

There was silence for the space of four heartbeats together. Geder let himself feel a trickle of pleasure.

"Lord Palliako?" a man said from the back. "There's the grain taxes?"

"What about them?"

"Lord Klin was entertaining a proposal to change them, sir. But he didn't give a decision before he left. You see, fresh grain coming in from the countryside is taxed at two silver to the bushel, but sold from storage in the city runs two and a half. The local granaries appealed."

"Put them all at two and a half," Geder said.

"Yes, Lord Protector," the man said.

"What else?"

There was nothing more. Geder stalked from the room quickly, before the heat of his temper could fully cool. When the brief certainty of anger passed, it passed completely. By the time he returned to his drawing room—*his* drawing room—he was shaking from head to foot. He sat by the window, looking out on the main square of the city, and tried to guess whether he was on the verge of laughter or tears. Below him, dry leaves skittered. The canal lay bare and dry, a team of slaves of several races hauling armfuls of weeds and filth out of it. A handful of Firstblood girls ran across the square, screaming in their play. He told himself that they were his now. Slaves, girls, leaves. All of it. It frightened him.

"Geder Palliako, Lord Protector of Vanai," he said to the empty air, hoping that by speaking the words they would become plausible. It didn't work. He tried to imagine what Lord Ternigan had intended when he'd chosen him. Nothing made sense. He took the letter out again, unfolded it, read each word, each phrase, searching for something to reassure him. There was nothing there.

"My Lord Protector," the old Timzinae said. Geder jumped less this time. "Lord Kalliam has come, as you asked."

"Bring him in," Geder said. The old servant hesitated, as if on the verge of pointing out a breach of etiquette, but turned away after only a bow. Geder wondered if meeting in the private drawing room was supposed to be reserved for special occasions. He'd have to find a book on Vanai court etiquette. Next time he spoke to his hired scholars, he'd mention it.

Jorey Kalliam stepped into the room. He was in his best uniform, and bowed before Geder formally. Either Jorey was also exhausted and apprehensive, or else Geder was seeing all the world as a mirror. The Timzinae wheeled a cart in behind him laden with small shell dishes of pistachios and candied pears. Once the servant had poured them both crystal mugs of cool water, he retreated. The discreet click of the door latch left them alone.

"My Lord Protector wished to see me?" Jorey said.

Geder tried out a smile.

"Who'd have guessed it, eh? Me, Lord Protector of Vanai."

"I think we all would have put long odds," Jorey said.

"Yes. Yes, it's why I wanted to speak with you in particular," Geder said. "Your father's active in court, isn't he? And you write to him. You said that you write to him?"

"I do, my lord," Jorey said. His spine was stiff, his eyes set straight ahead.

"Yes, that's good. I was wondering if … that's to say, ah, do you know why?"

"Why what, my lord?"

"Why me?" Geder said, and his voice had a thin violin-string of whine at the back that embarrassed him.

Jorey Kalliam, son of Dawson Kalliam, opened his mouth, closed it, and frowned. The lines at his mouth and brow made him seem older. Geder took a small handful of pistachios from their dish, cracking the shells open and eating the soft, salty meat within less from hunger than for something to do with his hands.

"You put me in an awkward position, my lord."

"Geder. Please, call me Geder. And I'll call you Jorey. If that's all right. I think you're the nearest thing to a friend I have in this city."

Jorey took a long breath, and as he let it hiss out between his teeth, his eyes softened.

"God help you," Jorey said. "I think I am."

"Then can you tell me what's happening at court that Ternigan would put *me* here? I don't have a patron at court. It's my first campaign. I just don't understand it. And I hoped you might."

Jorey gestured to a chair, and Geder realized after a moment that he was asking permission to sit. Geder waved him on and sat across from him, hands clasped between his knees. Jorey's eyes shifted as if he were reading something from the air. Geder ate another nut.

"Of course, I don't know Ternigan's mind," he said. "But I know things at home are unsettled. Klin is allied with Curtin Issandrian, and Issandrian's been championing some changes that haven't all gone over well. He's made enemies."

"Is that why Ternigan called him back?"

"It's likely part, but if Issandrian's power at court is starting to waver, Ternigan might want someone who wasn't affiliated with him. You said you don't have a patron at court. That might be the reason he chose you. Because House Palliako hasn't taken a side."

Geder had read of any number of situations like it. The White Powder Wars, when Cabral had played host to exiles from Birancour and Herez both. Koort Neachi, the fourth Regos of Borja, who was supposed to have had a court so corrupt he named a random farmer as regent. Considered at that angle, Geder saw a way that his new position could be made explicable. And still...

"Well," he said with an awkward grin, "I suppose I should be grateful my father doesn't go to court, then. I'm sorry, though, that yours does. I really thought Ternigan might give the city to you."

Jorey Kalliam turned his face to the window. His brows were furrowed. In the grate, the fire murmured its secrets to itself, and in the square, a thousand pigeons rose as if they were part of a single body and whirled through the white winter sky.

"It wouldn't have been a favor," Jorey said at last. "Court games aren't fair, Palliako. They don't judge men by their worth, and they aren't about what's just. Guilty men can hold power their whole lives and be wept for when they pass. Innocent men can be spent like coins because it's convenient. You don't have to have sinned for them to ruin you. If your destruction is useful to them, you'll be destroyed. This, all of this? It isn't your fault."

"I understand," Geder said.

"I don't think you do."

"I know I didn't earn this," Geder said. "Raw luck's given me this chance, and now it's my work to deserve it. I didn't think Lord Ternigan put me over the city because he respected me. I'm convenient. That's fine. Now I can make him respect me. I can steer Vanai. I can *make* it work."

"Can you?" Jorey said.

"I can try," Geder said. "I'm sure my father's been bragging about this to everyone he can find. House Palliako hasn't taken a new title since my grandfather was Warden of Lakes. I know it's something my father wanted, and with me here now..."

"This isn't fair," Jorey said.

"It's not," Geder said. "But I swear I'll do what I can to make it up to you."

"Make it up to *me*?" Jorey said, as if Geder had suddenly dropped in from some other conversation.

Geder rose, took the two water mugs from the tray, and put one in Jorey's hand. With all the seriousness he could muster, he raised his glass.

"Vanai is mine," Geder said, and this time it sounded almost true. "And if there is anything within it that would do you the honor you deserve, I'll find it. This city should have been yours, and we both know it. But since it's dropped in my lap instead, I swear here, between the two of us, that I won't forget that it was luck."

The expression on Jorey Kalliam's face might have been pity or horror or raw disbelief.

"I need you beside me," Geder said. "I need allies. And on behalf of Vanai and House Palliako, I would be honored if you were one of them. You're a valiant man, Jorey Kalliam, and one whose judgment I trust. Will you stand with me?"

The silence left Geder apprehensive. He held his glass determinedly aloft and quietly prayed Jorey would return the salute.

"Did you practice that?" Jorey asked at last.

"A bit, yes," Geder said.

Jorey rose to his feet and raised his own glass. The water splashed and slid down his knuckles.

"Geder, I will do what I can," he said. "It may not be much, and God's witness, I don't see how this ends well, but I'll do what I can to make things right for you."

"Good enough," Geder said, and drank his water through a grin.

The rest of the day was as much a test of endurance as a parade of honors. The afternoon began with a congratulatory feast presented by the representatives of the major guilds of Vanai, two dozen men and women each pressing for his attention and favor. After that, he held audiences with a representative from Newport who was angling to make changes in the overland shipping charges, but over the course of a long, contentious hour wouldn't make it precisely clear what the changes were. Then, at Geder's request, the chief taxation auditor reviewed all of Klin's previous reports to Lord Ternigan and the crown. Geder had expected that meeting to be little more than a summation of how much gold had been sent north, but it ended up going twice as long as he'd intended with discussions of the difference between high- and low-function tariffs and "presentation on account" against "presentation in earnest" that left him feeling like he'd been reading something in a language that he hadn't yet mastered.

At the day's end, he retired to the bed chamber that had once belonged to the prince of Vanai. It could have fit Geder's previous accommodations in a corner and left room for two more like it. The windows looked out over a garden of leafless oaks and snowbound flowerbeds. In spring, it would be like having a private forest. Geder's new bed was warmed by an ingenious network of pipes that led to and from a great fire grate, the pump driven by the rising air. The contraption burbled to itself, sometimes directly beneath Geder, as if the feather mattresses had eaten something that disagreed with them. Geder lay in the dim, firelit room for almost an hour after the last servant had been dismissed. Though he was exhausted, sleep would not come. When he rose, it was with the delicious sense of doing something he ought not do, clear in the knowledge that he would get away with it.

He lit three candles from the fire, blackening the wax a bit with the smoke, and set them beside his bed. Then from the small cache of his own things brought here by his squire, he plucked the creaking binding of the book he'd most recently bought. He'd read it through already, and marked the section that he found most interesting so that he could find it easily.

Legends of the Righteous Servant, also called Sinir Kushku in the language of the ancient Pût, place it as the final and greatest weapon of Morade, though the degree to

which this is simple confabulation with the dragon's net-
work of spies and the curiously insightful nature of his final
madness remains unclear.

Geder put his finger over the words, fighting to remember
what he knew of the languages of the east.

Sinir Kushku.

The End of All Doubt.

Cithrin

I'm saying there is evil in the world," Master Kit said, hefting the box on his hip, "and *doubt* is the weapon that guards against it."

Yardem took the box from the old actor's hands and lifted it to the top of the pile.

"But if you doubt everything," the Tralgu said, "how can anything be justified?"

"Tentatively. And subject to later examination. It seems to me the better question is whether there's any virtue in committing to a permanent and unexamined certainty. I don't believe we can say that."

Captain Wester made a noise in the back of his throat like a dog preparing for the attack. Cithrin felt herself start to cringe back, but didn't let her body follow the impulse through.

"We can say," the captain said, "that wasting good air on the question won't get the work done any faster."

"Sorry, sir," the Tralgu said.

Master Kit nodded his apology and went back down the thin wooden stairs to the street. Sandr and Hornet, coming up with a box of gems between them, flattened themselves to the wall to let him pass. Cithrin shifted, giving them room enough to pass the new box to Yardem, and Yardem enough to find a place for it in the new rooms. A cold, damp breeze and the smell of fresh horse droppings wafted through the open windows along with the daylight. Cithrin thought it seemed like springtime.

"Was he a priest as a boy?" Marcus said, pointing down the stairway with his chin. "He starts talking about faith and doubt and the nature of truth, it's like we're back in the 'van getting a sermon with every meal."

"What he says makes sense," Yardem said.

"To you," Marcus replied.

"Suppose he might have been a priest. It's Master Kit," Hornet said with a shrug. "If he told us he'd walked up the mountainside and drank beer with the moon, I'd probably believe it. We've got two more boxes the size of that one, and then all those wax blocks."

"Wax?" Marcus asked.

"The books," Cithrin said, but the words came out as a croak. She coughed and began again. "The books and ledgers. They're sealed against the damp."

Which is a good thing, she thought, *since we sank them in a mill pond.* Immediately, she imagined a crack in the sealing wax. Pages and pages of smeared ink and rotting paper hidden by the protecting wraps. What if the books were ruined? What would she tell Magister Imaniel then? What would she tell the bankers in Carse?

"Well, bring them up," Marcus said. "We'll find a place for them somewhere."

Hornet nodded, but Sandr was already going down the stairs. He hadn't even looked at her. She told herself it didn't bother her.

Cithrin was very aware that the new rooms didn't entirely meet with Captain Wester's approval. Unlike the place in the salt quarter, these were on the second story with wood-plank floors that reported any motion to the floor below in a language of creaks and pops. The shop on the first floor was a gambler's stall, which meant any number of people of any status might come and go throughout the day. But the lock at the base of the stair was sturdy, surrounding streets less prone to the drunken and the lost, and the windows without balcony or simple access. Additionally, there was an alley window out which the pisspot could be emptied, and the change of location had landed her five doors down from a taproom where they could buy food and beer.

Cary and Mikel came up next. Cary was grinning.

"Boy on the street asked us what we were hauling," Cary said.

Cithrin could see the tension in Captain Wester's face as he walked to the window and peered out.

"What did you tell him?"

"Paste jewels for the First Thaw celebrations," Cary said. "Opened one of the boxes for him, too. You should have seen it. He looked so *disappointed*."

Cary laughed, not seeing the anger on Captain Wester's face. Or perhaps seeing it and not caring. During the days when they'd looked for new rooms and prepared to shift the smuggled wealth of Vanai to its new hiding place, Opal had only been mentioned once when Smit had joked that she'd found a way to keep from having to do any of the hard work. Nobody had laughed.

Cithrin still had to fight herself to believe that it had happened. That Opal had meant to slaughter her and take the money was hard enough to comprehend. That Captain Wester had killed her for it was worse. Of course the others were angry. Of course they resented the captain. And Yardem. And her. They had to. And here they were, hauling boxes and making jokes. Cithrin found that she trusted them—each and every one of them—not because they were trustworthy, but because she wanted them to be.

She'd made the mistake with Opal, and she was watching herself make it again. That knowledge alone twisted her badly enough she hadn't slept or eaten well since the night she'd woken up with five dead men around her.

Master Kit came up the stairs, a double armful of wrapped books before him. Then Sandr and Hornet with the last of the boxes. With everything from the cart, there wasn't much room left for them all. Sandr was trapped standing beside her. When he saw her looking at him, he blushed and nodded the bird-fast twitch he might use to greet someone in the street.

"I believe this is the last of it," Master Kit said as Yardem lifted the books from him.

"Thank you for this," Cithrin said. "All of you."

"It's the least we could," Smit said. "We're only sorry it happened this way."

"Yes, well," Cithrin said. She couldn't meet his eyes.

"Why don't the rest of you go on," Master Kit said. "I'll try to catch up in a bit."

The actors nodded and left. Cithrin heard their voices through the window as their cart pulled away. Captain Wester stalked around the room as if his restlessness and impatience would make the floorboards quieter and more certain. Yardem stretched out on the cot nestled between piles of boxes and closed his eyes, resting before the night came. Master Kit rose and held a hand out to her.

"Cithrin," he said, "I was hoping we might walk together."

She looked from the old actor's hand to Captain Wester and back.

"Where?" she said.

"I didn't have anyplace particularly in mind," Master Kit said. "I thought the walking might be enough."

"All right," Cithrin said, and let him help her to her feet.

Outside, the street traffic shifted like water; broad and slow in the wide square to the east, faster in the narrow channel of the street. A Cinnae man stood outside the gambler's stall, calling to the men and women walking past. Great fortune could be theirs. Luck favored the brave. They could soften the loss of business by wagering against themselves. Odds offered on any fair wager. He sounded bored.

Horse-drawn carts labored through the press, and a team of Timzinae walked behind them with flat-bladed shovels, picking up their droppings. Half a dozen children screamed and chased each other, splashing through puddles of mud and grime and worse. A laundry cart rattled by, pulled by a Firstblood girl no older than Cithrin, but with lines of hardship already forming in the angles of her mouth. Master Kit strode forth and Cithrin let him lead, unsure whether she was walking behind him or at his side.

The street opened into a square Cithrin hadn't seen before. A huge church loomed to the east. Voices raised in song wove through the chill air, praising God and working through harmonic puzzles as if the two pursuits were one. Master Kit paused when she did, listening with her. The smile on his face softened into something touched with sorrow.

"It is lovely, isn't it?" he said.

"What is?" Cithrin asked.

He leaned against a stone wall and gestured out. The square, the song, the sky above them.

"I suppose I meant the world. For all the tragedy and pain, I do, at least, find it beautiful."

Cithrin felt her lips press tight. She wanted to apologize for what had happened to Opal, but that would only put Master Kit in a position where he had to apologize again, and she didn't want to do that. Words and thoughts banged against each other, none of them quite right for the moment.

"What will you do now?" she said.

Kit took a deep breath and let it out slowly before turning away from the song.

"I expect we'll stay here for the time being. I don't think Cary's quite ready to take on the full burden of Opal's roles, but by the end of the summer, with some rehearsal and serious work, I expect she will be. Between the armies of Vanai and now Opal, the company's a bit thinner than I like. I hope we'll be able to recruit a few good people. I've found port cities often collect itinerant actors."

Cithrin nodded. Kit waited for her to speak, and when she didn't, went on.

"Besides which, I find myself rather fascinated by your Captain Wester."

"He's not *my* Captain Wester," Cithrin said. "He's made it perfectly clear that he's his own Captain Wester."

"Has he, then? I stand corrected," Master Kit said. The church song swelled, what could have been a hundred voices rising and falling, throbbing against each other until it seemed like some other voice threatened to speak through them. God whispering. It seemed to pull Master Kit's attention, but when he spoke he hadn't lost the conversation's thread. "I believe the dragons left a legacy in this world that is...destructive. Corrosive by nature, and doomed to cause pain. Unchecked, it will eat the world. Wester is one of the few people I've met who I thought might stand against it."

"Because he's so stubborn?" Cithrin asked, trying to make it a joke.

"Yes, because of that," Master Kit said. "And, I suppose, the shape of his soul."

"He was a general in Northcoast a long time ago," Cithrin said. "Something happened to his wife, I think."

"He led Prince Springmere's army in the succession. There were battles against the armies of Lady Tracian that should have been lost, but Captain Wester won them."

"Wodford and Gradis," Cithrin said. "But people also talk about... Ellis?"

"Yes. The fields of Ellis. They say it was the worst battle in the war, that no one wanted it and no one could back down. The story is he was so important that the prince grew afraid that another of the pretenders might seduce his loyalty. Convince him to change sides. Springmere had his family killed and his rival implicated. The captain's wife and daughter died in front of him, and badly even as these things go."

"Oh," Cithrin said. "What happened to Springmere? I know he lost the succession, but..."

"Our friend Marcus found out what had really happened, took his revenge, and then dropped out of history. I think most people assumed he died. In my experience, the worst thing that can happen to a man in that position is that he live long enough to see how little vengeance leaves after it. I don't think he has many illusions left to him, which is why he's..." Master Kit shook himself. "I'm sorry. I didn't mean to wander off like that. Getting old, I think. I had wanted to say again that I'm sorry for what happened, and I am deeply committed to seeing that it not happen again."

"Thank you," she said.

"I would also like to offer whatever help I can in seeing you safely to Carse. I feel we owe you more than a day's free labor. A bit odd, I know, but I think pretending to be soldiers for so long left us all with a bit of the camaraderie of the sword."

Cithrin nodded, but she felt her brow furrow even before she knew quite why. The church song sank in a final, conclusive cadence, and silence seemed to flow into the world like a wave. Seagulls looped through the high air, yellow beaks and steady, unflapping wings.

"Why do you apologize for everything you say?" she asked.

Master Kit turned to her, bushy eyebrows hoisted.

"I wasn't aware that I did," he said.

"You just did it again," Cithrin said. "You never say anything straight out. It's all *I believe* this or *I've found* that. You never say, *The sun rises in the morning.* It's always, *I think the sun rises in the morning.* It's like you're trying not to promise anything."

Master Kit went sober. His dark eyes considered her. Cithrin felt a chill run down her spine, but it wasn't fear. It was like being on the edge of finding something that she'd only guessed was there. Master Kit rubbed a palm across his chin. The sound was soft and intimate and utterly mundane.

"I'm surprised you noticed that," he said, then smiled at having done it again. "I have a talent for being believed, and I've found it to be problematic. I suppose I've adopted habits to soften the effect, and so I try not to assert things unless I'm certain of them. Absolutely certain, I mean. I'm often surprised by how little I'm absolutely certain of."

"That's an odd choice," Cithrin said.

"And it encourages me to take myself lightly," Master Kit said. "I find a certain value in lightness."

"I wish I could," she said. The despair in her voice surprised her, and then she was weeping.

The actor blinked, his arms shifting uncertainly, and Cithrin stood in the open street embarrassed by her own sobbing, but powerless to stop. Master Kit wrapped an arm around her and led her forward to the steps of the church. His cloak was cheap wool, rough and still smelling of lanolin. He draped it over her shoulders. She leaned forward, her head on her knees. She felt the fear and the sorrow, but only at a distance. But the landslide had begun, and there was nothing she could do now but let it go. Master Kit placed his hand on her back, just between her shoulder blades, and rubbed gently, like a man soothing a baby. After a while, the sobs grew less violent. The tears dried. Cithrin eventually found her voice.

"I can't do this," she said. How many thousand times had she told herself that since the day Besel died? But always to herself. This was the first time she'd said the words aloud to anyone. They tasted sour. "I can't do this."

Master Kit took his arm back, but still shared his rough, cheap cloak. A few of the people walking by stared, but most ignored them. The old actor's skin smelled like a spice shop. Cithrin wanted to curl up there on the cold stone steps, sleep, and never wake up.

"You can," Master Kit said.

"No, I—"

"Cithrin, stop. Listen to my voice," Master Kit said.

Cithrin turned. He looked older than she remembered him, and it took a moment to realize it was because he wasn't smiling, even in the corner of his eyes. There were pouches under his eyes. His jowls sagged, and the stubble of his beard was more white than black. Cithrin waited.

"You can do this," he said. "No, just listen to me. You can do this."

"You mean you think that I can," she said. "Or you expect that I will."

"No. I meant what I said. *You can do this.*"

Something in the back of Cithrin's mind shifted. Something in her blood altered, like the surface of a pond rippling when a fish has passed too close beneath it. The overwhelming sorrow was still there, the fear that she would fail, the sense of being at the mercy of a wild and violent world. None of it went away. Only with it, there was something else. Hardly brighter than a firefly in the darkness of her mind, there was a new thought: *Perhaps*.

Cithrin rubbed her eyes with the palms of her hands and shook her head. The sun had shifted farther and faster than she'd expected. She didn't know how long ago they'd left the new rooms.

"Thank you," she said softly.

"I felt I owed it to you," Master Kit said. He seemed tired.

"Should we go back?"

"If you're ready, I think we should."

Evening came later than Cithrin expected, another sign that winter was beginning to lose its grip. Yardem Hane sat on the floor, his huge legs crossed, and ate rice and fish from a plate. Captain Wester paced.

"If we pick the wrong ship," the captain said, "they'll murder us, throw our bodies to the sharks, and spend the rest of their lives living high in some port in Far Syramys or Lyoneia. But we'd only have the customs house here and the one in Carse to go past. On the road, we might have to weather half a dozen tax collectors."

Cithrin looked at her own plate of fish, her belly too knotted to eat. Every word Wester said made it worse.

"We could backtrack," Yardem said. "Go to the Free Cities, and north from there. Or back to Vanai, for that."

"Without a caravan to hide in?" Marcus said.

The Tralgu shrugged, conceding the point. Behind the

constant motion of the captain's legs, the wax-sealed books of the Vanai bank glowed in the candlelight. Cithrin's anxiety circled back to them, images of cracked seal and rotting leather spines dancing through her head like a nightmare that wouldn't fade.

"We could buy a fishing boat," Yardem said. "Sail it ourselves. Hug the coast."

"Fighting off pirates with our forceful personalities?" Marcus said. "Cabral is half rotten with free ships stealing the trade they can, and King Sephan isn't about to stop them."

"No good options," Yardem said.

"None. And weeks still before we can take the bad ones," Marcus said.

Cithrin put her plate on the ground and walked past Captain Wester. She took the topmost of the books, looked around the dim, gold-lit room, and found the short blade Yardem had used to carve cheese at midday. The blade was shining clean.

"What are you doing?" Marcus asked.

"I can't choose the right ship," Cithrin said, "or the right path, or a caravan to hide in. But I can see that the books aren't wet, so I'm doing that."

"We'll just have to seal them again," Marcus said, and Cithrin ignored him. The wax was as thick as her thumb, and came off in stubborn chunks. A layer of cloth beneath it gave way to a softer inner layer of wax, and then parchment wrapping. The book hidden inside it all could have been fresh from Magister Imaniel's desk. Cithrin opened it, and the pages hissed against each other. The familiar marks of Magister Imaniel's handwriting were like a memory from childhood, and Cithrin almost wept again seeing them. Her fingers traced sums and notations, balances, transactions, details of contract and return rate. Magister Imaniel's signature and the brown, cracked blood of his thumb. She let them wash over her, familiar and foreign at the same time. Here was the deposit the bank had taken from the bakers' guild, and there in blue ink, a record of the payments made as recompense, month by month, for the years they'd held the money. She turned the page. Here was the record of loss on shipping insurance from the year that the storms had come up from Lyoneia later than ever before. The sums shocked her. She hadn't guessed that the loss had been so profound. She closed the book, took her blade, and found another. Marcus and Yardem were still talking, but they could have been in another city for all it mattered to her.

The next book was older, and she followed the history of the bank in it, from the letters of foundation that began it through the years of transactions, almost until the day she'd left. The history of Vanai written in numbers and ciphered notes. And there, in red, a small notation of Cithrin bel Sarcour accepted as ward of the Medean bank until she reached legal age and took over the balance of her parents' deposits, less the costs of keeping her. There were as many words spent on a grain shipment or investment in a brewery. The death of her parents, the beginning of the only life she'd known, all on a single line.

She got another book.

Marcus stopped talking, ate his dinner, and curled up on the cot. The half moon rose. Cithrin traced the history of the bank like she was reading old letters sent from home. Wax and cloth and parchment mounded around her like wrapping paper. Growing in the back of her mind, almost forgotten in the fascination of old ink and dusty paper, was a sense of possibility. Not confidence—not yet—but its precursor.

It was only when Yardem woke her by taking the leather-bound book from her hand that she realized that—for the first time since Opal—she'd slept dreamless through the night.

Dawson

Rough, plank-board ladders and improvised stairways lined the sides of the Division, clinging to the ancient ruins like lichen to a stone. High above, the great bridges spanned the gap with stone and steel and dragon's jade: Silver Bridge, Autumn Bridge, Stone Bridge, and almost lost in the haze the Prisoner's Span hung with cages and straps. Lower, where the sides came close enough, rope lines swung and rotted in the air. Between them the history of the city lay bare, each stratum showing an age and empire on which the one above had been founded.

Dawson, wrapped in a simple brown cloak, could have passed for a scavenger from the midden at the Division's base or a smuggler making his way to the obscure underground passages that laced Camnipol's foundation. Vincen Coe might have been his conspirator or his son. The morning frost kept their footsteps slow. The smell of the rising air was nauseating—sewage, horse manure, rotting food, the bodies of animals and of men barely better than animals.

Dawson found the archway. Ancient, flaking stone shaped in classic form, an inscription eroded to illegibility but not yet washed away. Within, the darkness was absolute.

"I don't like this, my lord," the huntsman said.

"You don't need to," Dawson said, and walked proudly into the gloom.

Winter's hand still pressed on Camnipol, but its power was breaking. The underground was alive with tiny sounds: the chitter of the first insects of the coming spring, the sharp trickle of thaw streams, and the soft breath of the land itself preparing to wake itself again into green spring. It would be weeks yet, and then it would seem to come overnight. It occurred to Dawson as he paused in a wide, vaulted tile of an abandoned bathing chamber, how many things followed that same pattern. The seemingly endless stasis followed by a few small signs, and then sudden catastrophic change. He pulled the letter from his pocket and leaned back toward Coe to read it again in the torchlight. Canl Daskellin had written that one of the doorways would be marked with a square. Dawson squinted into the darkness. Perhaps Daskellin had a younger man's eyes...

"Here, my lord," Coe said, and Dawson grunted. Now that it was pointed out, the mark was clear enough. Dawson walked down the short, sloping hall that turned into a stairway.

"No guards yet," Dawson said.

"There are, sir," Coe said. "We've passed three. Two archers and one manning a deadfall."

"Well hidden, then."

"Yes, my lord."

"You don't sound reassured."

The huntsman didn't answer. The hall met a huge stone, its surface polished and glazed so well that the torchlight seemed to double. Dawson followed his shadow around a slow curve until an answering light appeared. Dragon's jade carved into unbreakable pillars held up a low ceiling. A dozen candles filled the dusty air with soft light. And there, sitting in a carved round, was Canl Daskellin with Dawson's old acquaintance Odderd Faskellan on his left and a pale Firstblood man Dawson didn't recognize on his right.

"Dawson!" Canl said. "I was beginning to worry."

"No need," Dawson said, waving Vincen Coe back toward the shadows. "I'm only pleased I was in the city. I'd hoped to spend part of the year in Osterling Fells."

"Next year," Odderd said. "God willing, we'll all be back to normal next year. Though with this latest news…"

"There's news, then?" Dawson said.

Canl Daskellin gestured to the seat across from him, and Dawson lowered himself into it. The pale man smiled politely.

"I don't think we know each other," Dawson said to the smile.

"Dawson Kalliam, Baron of Osterling Fells," Daskellin said with a grin of his own. "May I introduce the solution to our problems. This is Paerin Clark."

"The pleasure is mine, Baron Osterling," the pale man said. His voice had the slushy accent of Northcoast. Dawson felt the small hairs on his arm rise. The man had no title. He wasn't Antean. And yet he was here.

"What's the news," Dawson said. "And how does our new friend here enter into it?"

"He's married to the youngest daughter of Komme Medean," Odderd said. "He lives in Northcoast. Carse."

"I wasn't aware we had business with the Medean bank," Dawson said.

"Issandrian knows what we've been doing," Daskellin said. "Not only Vanai. The men we placed to stir trouble with the farmers, the move to strip Feldin Maas of his southern holdings. Everything."

Dawson waved the words away as if they were gnats. He was more concerned that this banker appeared to know it all as well. Issandrian would have discovered their traps and schemes eventually.

"He's petitioned King Simeon to sponsor games," Odderd said. "Issandrian and Klin and Maas, and half a dozen more besides. They're putting up the coin for it. Cleaning out the stadium. Hiring show fighters and horesemen. Borjan long archers. Cunning men. It's supposed to be a celebration for Prince Aster."

"It's a fighting force inside the walls of Camnipol," Canl Daskellin said.

"It's a bluff a child could see through," Dawson said. "If it came to insurrection, Issandrian would lose. He doesn't have the men or the money to back a war."

"*Ah*," the banker said.

Dawson lifted his chin like a forest animal scenting smoke. Canl Daskellin took a handful of folded paper from the seat beside him and held them out to Dawson. The paper was cheap, the handwriting plain and unadorned. Copies, then, of some more prestigious correspondence. Dawson squinted. The dim light set the words swimming, but with a little concentration he could make them out clearly enough. *I send the best wishes to you and your family* and so on. *Our mutual great-aunt, Ekarina Sakiallin, Baroness of the noble lands of Sirinae…*

"Sirinae," Dawson said. "That's in Asterilhold."

"Our friend Feldin Maas has family in the court," Odderd said. "Part of making peace after the Treaty of Astersan was a fashion for strategic marriages. It's three generations back now, but the ties are still there. Maas has been sending letters to a dozen of his cousins that we know of. There may be others we didn't intercept."

"They've gone mad," Dawson said. "If they think they can bring in Asterilhold against King Simeon—"

"That isn't the story," the banker said. His voice was cool

and dry as fresh paper, and Dawson was instinctively repulsed by it. "Maas has been telling of a conservative conspiracy of hidebound old men within the court pressuring King Simeon. He describes men who are willing to ally themselves with enemies of Antea for their own political gain."

"Idiocy."

"He suggests," the banker said, "that Maccia may have been invited to defend Vanai by someone who opposed Alan Klin, and he makes a plausible case. And so, in the face of others seeking foreign help to influence the throne, Maas has no option but to appeal for the aid of Asterilhold in defending the honor and legitimate rule of King Simeon and safeguarding the person and health of Prince Aster."

"We're the ones defending Simeon!" Dawson shouted.

"As you say," the banker said.

Canl Daskellin leaned forward. His eyes were bright.

"Things are starting, Dawson. If Issandrian's cabal has gotten the backing of Asterilhold to put an armed force in Camnipol—and, by God, I think they have—they aren't coming for Simeon. They're aiming at us."

"They've already tried to kill you once," Odderd said. "These men have no sense of bounds or honor. We can't afford to treat them as if they were gentlemen. We have to beat them to the blow."

Dawson lifted his hands, commanding silence. Anger and mistrust filled his head like bees. He pointed to the banker.

"What's Northcoast's interest in this?" he asked. Meaning, *Why are you here?* Daskellin frowned at his tone of voice, but the banker seemed to take no offense.

"I couldn't say. Lord Daskellin is Special Ambassador to Northcoast. I'm sure he would be in a better position to sound out the more influential opinions."

"But your bank's in Carse," Dawson said. It was almost an accusation.

"The holding company is, and we have a branch there," the banker said. "But all our branches account independently."

"What's that supposed to mean?" Dawson said.

"We aren't a company exclusively married to the interests of Northcoast," the banker said. "We have a close relationship with people in many courts—even Antea now that Vanai is under your protection—and a strong interest in peace throughout the northern kingdoms. Unfortunately, we have some very strict policies about lending in situations like this—"

"I wouldn't take your money if you left it in a sock on my doorstep."

"Kalliam!" Canl Daskellin said, but the banker continued on as if nothing had been said.

"—but in the cause of peace and stability, we would be pleased to act as intermediary if we were of use. As disinterested third parties, we might be able to approach people that you noble gentlemen found awkward."

"We don't need help."

"I understand," the banker said.

"Don't be an idiot," Daskellin said. "The Medean bank has branches in Narinisle and Herez. Elassae. If this comes to blades in the street, we'll need—"

"We shouldn't be talking about this," Dawson said. "We have guests."

The banker smiled and gave a brief nod. Dawson wished that etiquette allowed him to challenge a man of no status to a duel. The banker was nothing more than a trumped-up merchant. He should have been beneath Dawson's notice, but something about the man's studied placidity invited the drawing of blood. Canl Daskellin's brows were nearly a single knot, and Odderd was shifting his gaze between the others like a mouse at a catfight.

"I have known Paerin Clark and his family for years," Daskellin said, his voice tight and controlled. "I have absolute faith in his discretion."

"How sweet for you," Dawson said. "I met him today."

"Please, my lords," the banker said. "I came to make my position clear. I have done so. If Lord Kalliam should have a change of heart, the Medean bank's offer stands. If not, then surely no harm's done."

"We'll continue this another time," Dawson said, rising to his feet.

"Oh yes. We will," Daskellin said. Odderd said nothing, but the banker rose and bowed to Dawson as he left. Vincen Coe fell in behind him without a word. Dawson stalked up, following the winding paths that led through the roots of Camnipol.

When at length they reached the street, his legs ached and his rage had faded. Coe doused the torch in a snowbank, the pitch leaving a filthy smear on the white. Dawson had chosen to walk rather than take his carriage in part to show any of Issandrian's hired thugs that he didn't fear them, but also in the name of discretion. Leaving his own team sitting on the Division's edge waiting his reemergence from the underworld was as good as hanging a banner. Not that discretion seemed the first response from his cohorts. What had Daskellin been thinking?

And still, when he reached his mansion, his face numbed by the chill wind, he was so preoccupied that he didn't notice that a carriage not his own waited by the stables. The old Tralgu door slave flicked his ears nervously as Dawson approached.

"Welcome home, my lord," the slave said, his silver chain

clinking as he made a bow. "A visitor arrived an hour ago, my lord."

"Who?" Dawson said.

"Curtin Issandrian, my lord."

Dawson's heart went tight, his blood suddenly singing through his veins. The cold of the day and the frustration of the meeting fell away. He glanced at Vincen Coe, and the huntsman's expression mirrored his own shock.

"You let him *in?*"

The Tralgu slave bowed his head, an icon of fear and distress.

"The lady insisted, my lord."

Dawson drew his sword and took the front steps three at a time. If Issandrian had laid hands on Clara, this would be the shortest and bloodiest revolution in the history of the world. Dawson would burn Issandrian's bones in the square and piss on the fire. As he reached the atrium of the house, Coe was at his side.

"Find Clara," Dawson said. "Take her to her rooms, and kill anyone who comes in if they aren't of the household."

Coe nodded once and vanished into the hallways, swift and silent as a breeze. Dawson strode quietly through his own house, sword in hand. He rounded one corner to the gasp of a maid, her eyes wide at sight of the weapon and her master. His dogs found him when he entered the solarium and followed behind him, whining and growling.

He found Issandrian in the western sitting room, gazing into the fire grate. The man's unfashionably long hair spilled out over his shoulders like a lion's mane, the red-gold of it taking color from the flames. Issandrian noticed the sword and lifted his eyebrows, but made no other move.

"Where is my wife?" Dawson asked, and behind him his dogs growled.

"I couldn't say," Issandrian said. "I haven't seen her since she brought me here to await your return."

Dawson narrowed his eyes, his senses straining for some sign of duplicity. Issandrian glanced at the dogs baring their teeth, then up at Dawson. There was no fear in his expression.

"I can wait here a bit longer if you'd like to speak with her first."

"What do you want here?"

"The good of the kingdom," Issandrian said. "We're men of the world, Lord Kalliam. We both know where the path we're on leads."

"I don't know what you're talking about."

"Everyone says it. It's Issandrian's cabal against Kalliam's, with King Simeon flapping in between depending on which way the wind blows."

"No one talks about his majesty that way to me."

"May I stand, Lord Kalliam? Or does your honor call for you to set your dogs on an unarmed man?"

The weariness in Issandrian's voice gave Dawson pause. He sheathed his sword and gestured once to the dogs. They cringed back, quieting. Issandrian stood. He was a taller man than Dawson had remembered. Confident, at ease, and more regal than King Simeon. God help them all.

"May we at least talk of truce?" he asked.

"If you have something to say, say it," Dawson said.

"Very well. The world is changing, Lord Kalliam. Not just here. Hallskar is on the edge of calling their king down from his throne and electing a new one. Sarakal and Elassae have both given concessions to merchants and farmers. The power of nobility for its own sake is passing, and for Antea to be a part of the coming age, we must change as well."

"I've heard that song. I didn't like the tune."

"It doesn't matter whether we like it or not. It's happening. And we can act on it or else try to fence out the tide."

"So your farmer's council has all been a selfless action for the benefit of the crown, has it? Your own aggrandizement has nothing to do with it? Pull the other one, boy. It has bells on it."

"I can make it yours," Issandrian said. "If I gave sponsorship over the farmer's council to you, would you take it?"

Dawson shook his head.

"Why not?" Issandrian asked.

Dawson turned and pointed to the dogs sitting nervously behind him.

"Look at them, Issandrian. They're good animals, yes? Excellent in their ways. I've cared for each of them since they were pups. I see them fed. I give them shelter. Sometimes I let them rest on my couch and keep my feet warm. Should I dress them in my clothes and give them seats at my table?"

"Men aren't dogs," Issandrian said, crossing his arms.

"Of course they are. Three years ago a man working my land stole into his neighbor's house in the night, killed his neighbor, raped the wife, and beat the children. Now, would you have had me give the bastard a place on the judge's bench? A voice in his own punishment? Or should I nail his hands and cock to a log and throw him in the river?"

"That isn't the same thing."

"It is. Men, women, dogs, and kings. We all have our places. My place is in court, following the voice and law of the throne. A farmer's place is on a farm. If you tell a pig keeper he deserves a chair in court, you put the order of society itself in question, including my right to pass judgment on his actions. And once we've lost that, Lord Issandrian, we've lost everything."

"I think you're wrong," Issandrian said.

"You tried to have me killed in the street," Dawson said. "I don't have any concern to spare for what you think."

Issandrian pressed a palm to his eyes and nodded. He looked pained.

"That was Maas. It may not matter to you, but I didn't hear of it until it happened."

"I don't care."

The two men went quiet. In the grate, the fire murmured. The dogs shifted, uneasy but unsure what they were expected to do.

"Is there no way to bridge this?" Issandrian asked, but the hardness of his voice meant he knew the answer.

"Surrender your plans and intentions. Scatter your cabal. Give me Feldin Maas's head on a pike and his lands to my sons."

"No, then," Issandrian said with a smile.

"No."

"Will your honor permit me safe passage out of your house?"

"My honor requires it," Dawson said. "Unless you touched my wife."

"I came to talk," Issandrian said. "I never meant her harm."

Dawson stepped to the far side of the room and snapped his fingers, calling the dogs out of his enemy's path. Issandrian paused in the doorway.

"Believe what you will, I am loyal to the crown."

"And yet you're making friends in Asterilhold."

"And you're talking with Northcoast," he said, and then he was gone.

Dawson sat down. The leader of his pack came whining and pressing her head into his hand. He scratched her ears absently. When he was certain he'd given the man time enough to leave the house, he rose and walked to Clara's private rooms. She sat on the edge of her daybed, her hands knotted on her lap. Her eyes were wide and her face pale. Everything about her spoke of fear and tension.

"Where's Coe?" he said. "I sent him to—"

Clara raised an arm, gesturing behind him. Coe stood in the shadow behind the open door. The huntsman had a bared sword in one hand, a vicious curved dagger in the other. If Dawson had been an attacker, he'd never have known what killed him.

"Well done," he said. In the dimness, it was hard to tell whether Coe blushed. Dawson nodded to the doorway, and closed it behind the huntsman when he was gone.

"I am so sorry, dear," Clara said. "The footman brought word that Lord Issandrian was here, and I didn't even think. I just had them make him comfortable. I couldn't imagine leaving him to sit on the step like a delivery boy, and I thought if he needed to speak to you, then perhaps it would be best if he did. I never thought that he might have designs…"

"He didn't," Dawson said. "Not this time. If he comes back, though, don't let him in. Or any of Maas's people."

"I have to see Phelia if she comes. I can't simply pretend she doesn't exist."

"Not even her, love. After it's over. Not now."

Clara wiped her eyes with the back of her hand. The gesture was unladylike, unplanned, and broke Dawson's heart a little. He squeezed her knee, trying to impart some comfort.

"Has it gotten worse, then?" she asked.

"Issandrian's gathering soldiers. Cunning men. It may come to blood."

Clara took a long breath, the air curling slowly out her nostrils.

"Very well, then."

"Everyone claims to have Simeon's best interests, but God help us if someone should arrive who has the boldness to actually lead. Asterilhold and Northcoast are lining up to buy both sides, and either one would be as happy to see their puppet on the Severed Throne," Dawson said. He coughed. "We have to win this while it's still our war."

Geder

A riot?" Geder said, his heart sinking. "Why's there a riot?"

"People are going hungry, Lord Protector," Sir Gospey Allintot said. "The farmers have been taking all their grain to Newport."

Geder pressed a hand to his chin, determined to keep Sir Allintot from seeing that he was trembling. He'd been told, of course, something about farmers and grain shipments, but in the thousand different things that administering the city required, it hadn't stood out. Now angry voices roared one against the other until it sounded like a bonfire in the square beyond his windows. Someone was plotting against Vanai, an enemy out of the shadows weakening the fabric of the city. Maccia, perhaps, preparing to retake the city before Antea could solidify its claims. Or the exiled prince gathering allies throughout the countryside. Geder's thoughts whirled and skittered ahead of themselves, dry leaves driven by wind.

"Who's behind it?" he asked, forcing himself to sound calm.

Sir Allintot cleared his throat.

"I believe it's in reaction to your increasing the grain import tax, my lord," Allintot said. "The farmers make more coin for their grain, even though it means traveling farther, because the Newport tax rates are lower."

"So in order to make more money, they'll let Vanai starve?" Geder said. "That won't stand. We can send men out. Intercept the grain and bring it here."

Sir Allintot cleared his throat again. Either the man was getting sick, or he was struggling to hide laughter.

"All respect, my lord," Allintot said. "Even if we put all other things equal, riots are rarely solved by taking troops away from the city. Perhaps my lord might consider reducing the taxes to their previous level. Or, given the gravity of the city's supplies, slightly lower."

"And reduce the amount we have for the crown?" Geder said.

"Again, all respect, my lord. As long as no grain comes to Vanai, no grain taxes do either. The payments are already short of your stated marks."

The shouts from the square swelled. Geder jumped up from his seat and stalked to the window.

"God damn it. Why can't they be *quiet*?"

They swarmed at the steps leading up to the palace. Two or three hundred people, waving fists and stones and sticks. Two dozen men in Antean armor held firm, blades at the front, bows at the rear. Geder saw Jorey Kalliam pacing among the soldiers. The mob surged forward a few steps, then fell back.

"I'll talk to them," Geder said.

"My lord?"

"Tell them I'm coming out," Geder said. "I'll explain the problem, and tell them that I'll fix it."

"As you wish, my lord," Sir Allintot said, and bowed before he left the room.

Geder had the servants bring the black cloak he'd taken in lieu of taxes. The creak and smell of the leather left him feeling more confident, and the cut really was quite good. It occurred to him, as he descended the wide, polished wood stairs and walked across the wide hall, that he wore the cloak much the way he'd have worn a mask. Because it was well made and impressive, he hid in it, hoping people would see it and not him.

At his nod, two nervous Timzinae servant girls pulled the doors open, and Geder walked out. The soldiers guarding the palace doors seemed more exposed, now that he was standing behind them instead of looking down from above. The mob seemed larger. The crowd saw him, caught its breath, and screamed. Sticks and fists pumped in the air. Hundreds of faces looked up at him, mouths square and teeth showing. Geder swallowed and walked forward.

"What are you doing?" Jorey Kalliam said.

"It's all right," Geder said, and raised his hands, commanding silence. "Listen! Listen to me!"

The first stone seemed like a cunning man's trick. A dark spot against the sky, smaller than a bird, it rose from the back of the mob and seemed to hang in the air, motionless. It was only in the last few feet that the illusion broke and it sped toward Geder's face. The impact knocked him back, the world going quiet and distant for a moment, the daylight growing dusky at the edges of his vision. Then the air itself was roaring, the crowd surging forward. The voice that rose over the chaos was Jorey Kalliam's.

"Loose bows! Hold position!"

An arrow passed over Geder from the square, loose fletching buzzing. It struck the wall of the palace and shattered. Someone took his elbow and pulled him up the stairs. The left side of his face tingled, and he tasted blood.

"Get inside, and stay there," Jorey shouted. "Don't go near the windows."

"I won't," Geder said, and another stone sang past him. He hunched forward, running for the safety of walls around him. As soon as he was through the doors, the slaves closed them and dropped a wooden bar across a set of interior braces. Geder sat on the stairs, arms around his knees, as the shouts from the square became screams. Something loud happened, and a woman's voice rose in a shriek. He found he was rocking back and forth and made himself stop. His squire appeared at his side, a damp cloth in hand, to wash the blood off Geder's face.

After what seemed hours and was likely only minutes, the sounds of violence faded. When the silence had gone long enough, he gestured to the slaves. The doors were unbarred, and Geder peeked out. Only Antean soldiers stood in the square now. Five bodies lay at the foot of the palace stairs, their blood obscenely bright in the midday sun. The archers still held their places, arrow at the ready, but not yet drawn. Jorey Kalliam stood in the center of the square, half a dozen swordsmen about him. Geder could hear the snap and rhythm of his syllables without making out individual words. Geder turned away and walked back up to his private rooms. Someone had managed to loft a stone high enough to shatter one of the windows. The shards glittered in the sunlight.

It wasn't how things were supposed to go. He had been given the chance to make his name, and he was failing. He didn't even understand how he was failing, only that decisions he made spawned two more problems that were each twice as bad as the first. He knew that the soldiers didn't respect him. That the citizens of the city despised him. He knew too little to run a city with the complexity of Vanai by himself, and he didn't have enough allies to do it for him. He wanted Ternigan to call him home the way he had Klin. Being called to account—even to be condemned—would be better than staying here.

Except, of course, that he could already see the disappointment in his father's expression. Could already hear the falsely bluff consoling words. *You did your best, my boy. I'm still proud of you.* In his imagination, his father tried to protect Geder from the shame of failure. Anything would be better than that. Death at the hands of an angry rabble would be better. Geder's own humiliations ached, but he could endure them. To watch his father humiliated as well would be too much. There had to be a way. There *had* to.

A servant girl came in with a brush and dustpan and cleared away the broken glass. Geder barely looked at her. The air that seeped in through the broken pane was chilly, but he didn't call for anyone to repair the window. He had his leather cloak on. He was warm enough. And if he wasn't, it hardly mattered.

The light shifted along the wall, reddening as the sun completed its arc. A Firstblood man came in, hesitated, and then remade the fire in the grate. Geder's legs ached, but he didn't move. The same man returned a short time later with a sheet of leather that he tied over the broken window. The room grew darker.

It was unfair that Ternigan wouldn't pay the price of this. He was the one who'd put Geder in command without the guidance or loyal men to back him. If anyone deserved to be shamed over the state of things in Vanai it was the Lord Marshal. But of course, that would never happen. Because if Ternigan deserved blame for putting his faith in Geder, then King Simeon would deserve blame for naming Ternigan to command. No, the blame would be Geder's to eat, and Geder's alone.

Still, he couldn't imagine what Ternigan had been thinking. Everyone had been dumbfounded by the appointment. Even Geder himself had needed Jorey Kalliam's insight to find a plausible reason for the elevation. No one had thought the choice wise. The only two who'd had any faith in it at all were Geder and Lord Ternigan. They were the only two men who'd thought it possible, and even then...

Or perhaps not. What if *no one* had thought it possible? Not even from the start.

"Oh," Geder said to the empty room.

When he turned, his knees buckled. He had stood unmoving for too long. He limped to the couch nearest the fire, his mind turned the problem over of its own accord. How many times had he heard it said that Vanai was a small piece played in a much larger game? And he hadn't understood until now.

First point: as much as it stung to admit, Geder was in no sense equipped to manage the city.

Second point: Ternigan had put him in control of it.

Third: Ternigan was not a fool.

Therefore Ternigan—for whatever reasons and by whatever conflict of loyalties—*wanted* Vanai to fall into chaos. Geder was an acceptable sacrifice.

When he smiled, his injured lip split again. When he laughed, it bled.

Your Majesty, the letter began, *in my role as Protector of Vanai, I have been forced to conclude that the political environment within the greater court makes long-term control of the city impossible.*

Geder ran his eyes down the page again. He'd written half a dozen versions of the thing in the course of the night. Some had been angry screeds, others abject apologies. The form he'd finally adopted was modeled closely on a letter sent by Marras Toca to the king of Hallskar several centuries earlier. The full text was reproduced in one of his books, and the rhetoric of it was both moving and understated. Geder had changed enough to clear his conscience of any taint of plagiarism, and still the structure of the thing shone through. Geder sewed the letter, marked the exterior page, and pressed his seal of office into the purple wax. The essay with Marras Toca's letter rested on the table, and Geder paged through it again, his heart lighter than it had been in weeks. He found the passage he was looking for, and paused to underline the critical phrase.

… the destruction of Aastapal was done by Inys as a tactical gambit to keep it from Morade's control …

The notation in his own handwriting caught his eye. *Looking at ripples to know where the stone fell.*

Oh yes. Once he'd gone back to Camnipol, there would be time for that. Alan Klin might not realize that he'd lost his protectorate by betrayal. Geder, on the other hand, was perfectly aware of it, and he cast his grudges in iron. He would understand Ternigan's decision and all that lay behind it. But that would come later.

The night had been a trial. The long dark hours had been filled with his mind's constant drumbeat of how he had been used. How he had been created as a failure, and what the price of it would be. He had wept and he had raged. He'd read his books and the reports of his men and the history of Vanai. Briefly, he'd even slept.

"My lord," his squire said. "You called for me?"

"Yes," Geder said, rising to his feet. "There are three

things. First, take this letter and find the fastest rider we have. I want this in Camnipol as soon as it can be accomplished."

"Yes, my lord."

"Second, take that purse there. You know the scholar I've been working with? Buy all the books he has. Then bring them back here and pack them with my things. We'll be leaving Vanai, and I'll have them with me."

"Leaving, my lord?"

"Third, send word to my secretaries. I will meet with them in an hour. Any man who comes late, I'll have whipped. Tell them so. Whipped and salt poured on the wounds."

"Y-yes, my lord."

Geder smiled, and it hurt less now. His squire bobbed a quick bow and scurried out. Yawning and stretching, Geder left his rooms in the palace of the prince of Vanai for the last time. His step was light, his mood undiminished by a night without rest. The air smelled of the subtle promise of spring, and the thin light of morning spilled across the stones where the rioters had been the day before. At the far end of the square, some daring local had hung an effigy of Geder. The dummy had an immense belly, a black cloak that mirrored his, and an expression on the dried gourd of a head that was a masterwork of idiocy. A sign hung around the thing's neck: FEED US OR FREE US. Geder nodded at his other self, a brief and uncharitable salute.

His men sat in the same seats where he'd first addressed them. Many looked tousled from sleep. Jorey Kalliam was among them, his brow set in furrows. Gospey Allintot stood at the rear, his arms crossed and his chin held high. He likely thought he was going to be called to account for the previous day's riot. Geder stepped to the front of the former chapel. He didn't sit.

"My lords," he said sharply. "I apologize for the hour, but I thank you for coming. As Lord Protector, it is my duty and privilege to command you all in this, our final day in the city of Vanai."

He stood for a moment, letting the words sink in. Eyes brightened. Confusion softened the frowns and loosened the necks. Geder nodded.

"By nightfall, you will have your men outside the city gates and prepared for the march to Camnipol," Geder said. "I understand food is somewhat scarce, so be sure that gets packed before we pile on any last looting. This isn't a sack."

"Then what it is?" Alberith Maas said.

"Don't interrupt me again, Maas. I'm still in charge here. Sir Allintot, if you would be so good as to see that the canals are shut? We'll leave those beds dry, I think. And the street gates will need to be shut."

"Which street gates?"

"The iron ones at the street mouths," Geder said.

"Yes, sir. I know them. I meant which of them did you want shut."

"All of them. Lord Kalliam, I would have you guard the city gates. No one comes into the city, and no one besides ourselves leaves it. It is very important that no one escape."

"We're leaving?" Maas said.

"I have been forced to conclude," Geder said, "that the political environment within the greater court makes long-term control of the city impossible. You've all seen Sir Klin's best efforts, and what they came to. I've read the histories of Vanai. Do you all know how many times it's been Antean? Seven. The longest was for ten years during the reign of Queen Esteya the Third. The shortest was three days during the Interregnum. In every case, the city had been given away by treaty or sacrificed in pursuit of some other goal. Which is to say, Vanai has been lost to politics. Given the situation in Camnipol, we are in the path to do so again."

"What does *he* know about the situation in Camnipol?" someone muttered loud enough for Geder to hear, but not so loudly he couldn't pretend otherwise.

"My duty as Protector of Vanai is not to the city itself, but to Antea. If I thought our continued presence here would benefit the crown, I would stay, and so would all of you. But if the history books show anything, it's that this city has cost good and noble men their lifeblood with no lasting advantage to the Severed Throne, no matter who was seated there at the time. In my role as assigned me by Lord Ternigan in the name of King Simeon, I have determined that Vanai cannot be profitably held. I've written as much to King Simeon. The courier with my justification of these orders is already on the dragon's roads for Camnipol."

"So we just walk away home?" Maas said. There was outrage in his voice. "We hand it over to whichever of our enemies happens by?"

"Of course not," Geder said. "We burn it."

Vanai died at sundown.

If the people had known, if they had understood the threat, the little riot in the square before the palace would have been nothing. But despite the emptying of the canals, the wood and coal and oil spread through the streets and squares, and the arming of the gates, they couldn't imagine that they faced anything more than retaliation for a stone thrown at Geder's head. Likely some rioters would be caught and burned. They wouldn't be the first public executions that Vanai had seen. It was only when the Anteans marched through the gates that the city understood what was happening, and by then it was too late.

History had turned against Vanai. It was a city of narrow streets, of timber waterproofed with oils, of gates at every street mouth. It was smug, and certain that no lasting harm could come to it because none had before. It was the small piece in a much larger game.

Geder sat on a small dais that Sir Alan Klin had left behind. The seat was a leather sling, and a bit narrow for him, but more comfortable than his own field chair. The highest-ranked of his staff stood around him.

He'd rehearsed this moment in his mind. Once it was done, he would stand up, announce that he deemed Vanai no longer in need of protection, and give the order to march. It would be like something from the old epics. Around him, the officers fidgeted, glancing at him as if they weren't sure he really meant to go through with it.

A hundred yards before him, the gates of Vanai closed, glowing gold from the setting sun. Geder rose to his feet.

"Block the gates," he said.

The order went out, seeming to echo and grow as it passed from caller to caller. The sound would soon reach the southern gates as well. The engineers had been waiting, and they sprang into action. It took less than a minute for the great gates to be disabled. It wouldn't have been long work to force them open, but still longer than Vanai had remaining.

"Loose the fire arrows," Geder said, almost conversationally.

The order went out. Twenty archers lit their arrows and lifted their bows, the streaks of flame little more than fireflies in the light. Then again, and twice more. All around the city, archers wearing his colors would be doing the same as the order reached them. Geder sat down. In his imagination, it had all happened at once, but the sun slipped down below the horizon, the golden world fading to grey, and no particular sign of fire came. Geder was wondering whether he should have the archers try again when he saw the first trail of smoke rise. As he watched, it spread, but slowly. This might take longer than he'd thought.

The smoke thickened, and when the breeze turned toward him it was close and greasy. An answering tower of smoke rose in the south, the blackness rising so high in the air that it caught the last light of the sun, flaring red for a moment, and then dark again. Geder shifted in his seat. It was getting cold, but he didn't want to call for his jacket. He hadn't slept since the night before last, and he could feel the fatigue tugging at him. He forced himself to sit upright.

For a long time, nothing seemed to happen. Some smoke. The sound of distant voices. Geder didn't think that the fire, once started, could be easily put out, but perhaps. The smoke spread, widening its grasp on the night city. And then, as if coming to itself, fire claimed the city.

The screaming began, voices shrieking and wailing. He'd expected to hear something, of course, but he'd thought it would be like the riot that had disturbed him—God, had it only been the day before? This was a different beast. There was no anger in the sound, only hundreds of voices of raw animal panic. Geder saw movement from his own troops. Someone had slipped out of the city, and the swordsmen of Antea, true to their orders, hunted the refugees down. Geder touched his lip, worrying at the cut. He reminded himself of the effigy hung in the square. They'd started this. It wasn't his fault they were dying now.

Smoke billowed up from the streets now, lit from beneath and blocking out the moon. Flames crawled up the buildings nearest the wall and leapt up, leaving the city below and burning in the free air. Another sound, low and steady as an army on the march, came. Geder felt the ground shudder, and looked around for a landslide or an attack. For a moment, he imagined it was some last dragon, hidden under Vanai and disturbed into waking. But it was only the voice of the fire.

The gates shuddered, warping from the heat. A group of figures appeared on the wall, men and women trying to flee. In a moment as clear and sudden as a lightning strike, one in particular was silhouetted by the flames. Geder could tell that she was a woman, but not what race she was. She waved her arms, trying to communicate something. He had the sudden, powerful urge to send someone to her, to save her, but already she was gone. Some tendril of flame reached the near-empty granaries, and the stirred grain dust detonated like a thunderclap. Smoke rose whirling, a vortex of darkness that dwarfed the city. The wind that pushed past him was the draw of the flames. The roar was too loud to speak over.

Geder sat, eyes wide, as bits of ash rained down around him. The heat of the dying city pressed against his face like the desert sun. He'd imagined himself sitting there, watching until it was done. He hadn't understood that Vanai would burn for days.

He hadn't understood *anything*.

"Let's go," he said. No one heard him. "It's enough! Let's go!"

The order went out, and the army of Antea pulled back from the furnace. Geder abandoned the thought of his grand rhetorical gesture. Nothing he could say would measure up to the conflagration. He went back to his tent, wondering if they were camped too close. What if the fire broke through the walls? What if it came for him?

He waved his squire away and curled up on the cot. He was too tired to move, and the nightmare howl of the flames wouldn't stop. He stared at the top of his tent, seeing the small figure waving her arms and dying. Geder pressed his hand to his mouth, biting at the skin until it bled, trying to make the noise go away.

The smoke of ten thousand people rose into the sky.

CITHRIN

Word of the destruction of Vanai washed over Porte Oliva. In the Grand Market and at the port, in the taprooms and the wayhouses and the steps that led to the brick-and-glass labyrinth that was the governor's palace, detail piled upon detail as reports came in by ship and horse and raw speculation. The city had burned for three days. The Antean forces had barred the gate and slaughtered anyone who tried to escape. The canals had been drained so that there would be no water to slow the fire. The Anteans had poured barrels of lamp oil in the streets before they left. The heat had shattered stones. The smoke had carried the smell of burning as far as Maccia and turned the sunsets red. Charred bodies were still clogging the weirs at Newport.

Cithrin grabbed at each rumor like one of the ever-present beggars watching for dropped coins. At first, she hadn't believed it. Cities didn't die overnight. The streets and canals she'd known all her life couldn't become ruins just because someone said it, even if the man speaking was an Antean general. It was ridiculous. But with every retelling, every new voice that said the same things, her incredulity faded. Even if they were all only echoing one another, the weight of their combined belief pulled her along.

Vanai was dead.

"Are you all right?" Sandr asked.

Cithrin leaned forward, her legs swinging from the side of the actors' cart like a child sitting on too high a stool. Around them, the midday crowd shuffled. She watched a reed-thin Cinnae boy thread himself through the press of bodies, following the colorless thatch of his hair. The smell of the sea brine made the air feel cooler than it was. She didn't know how to answer, but she tried.

"I don't know. I think so. It's hard to live in the middle of all this," she said, nodding at the press of humanity around them, "and really feel the deaths. I mean, I know that Magister Imaniel is gone. And Cam must be too. All the boys who played in the streets are dead, and that makes me sad sometimes. But when I start thinking that it's *all* gone—the fresh market and the palaces and the flat barges and all of it—it gets...I don't know. Abstract?"

"That's a good word for it," Sandr said, nodding as if he knew what she meant.

"Nobody knows me now. I've lived my whole life in Vanai. It felt like everyone knew who I was. *What* I was. And now that they're all gone, there's nothing holding me to that anymore. Captain Wester, Yardem Hane, you, and Master Kit's company. You are the people in the world who know me best."

"It's hard," Sandr said, taking her hand.

No, that's the only good part, she thought. *When nobody knows what you are, you can be anything.*

"Sandr!" Master Kit called. "It's time."

"Yes, sir," Sandr said, jumping to his feet. He looked down at Cithrin and smiled gently, much the way he did when he took the stage. "You'll be here when it's done?"

Cithrin nodded. It wasn't as if she had someplace else to be. Besides which, Sandr's sudden change of heart was interesting.

She assumed that some more attractive girl had refused him, and he'd fallen back to court her while his confidence healed. He believed, after their moments beside the mill pond, that she was an easy conquest. Cithrin wondered whether she was. More than that, she wondered whether she'd like to be. She slipped off the cart and into the crowd.

Mikel was already there, halfheartedly pretending to be a local. He caught her eyes and grinned. She nodded back, then turned to watch Smit and Hornet lower the stage. When the chains had caught, Master Kit strode out onto the boards. He wasn't wearing his Orcus the Demon King robes anymore. With Opal gone, the story of Aleren Mankiller and the Sword of the Dragons had been set aside. Instead, a shimmering blue cape flowed from the shoulders of a matching tunic. Bright yellow ribbon gartered green hose, and the most ridiculous shoes seen by human eyes bobbled around his toes.

"Hell-*lo*!" Master Kit cried in comic falsetto. "I said, hello there! Yes, you, in that wonderful hat. Why don't you stop for a while. God knows you've nothing better to do. And you, there at the back. Come closer, you might see something you like. What? You might. And—"

Master Kit stopped, his face a mask of shock. Cithrin felt a thrill of fear, half turning to follow his gaze.

"Oh, not you, dear," Master Kit went on in the same false voice, his hand fluttering like a sparrow. "*You* keep right on going."

The crowd laughed. Cithrin and Mikel were meant to lead them, but there were already half a dozen others who had stopped to watch. The Bride's Curse was a comedic sex play with half a dozen costume changes that could be performed with only one woman. Master Kit had changed the traditional lines to match with the specifics of Porte Oliva: the rhymes appealing to the king had all been remade for a queen, and instead of the evil landlord being disguised as a Yemmu with a false shoulder and mouth tusks, Smit jumped onto the stage in a bead-woven sheep pelt as the world's least convincing Kurtadam. Cithrin laughed and clapped, not leading the crowd so much as adding to its flow.

When the end came and the players took their bows amid a modest shower of coin, she was almost surprised to find herself returned to her own life. Hiding in Porte Oliva, waiting for the next thieves to attack in the night.

And Vanai dead.

Sandr came out from the cart wiping the paint from his face with a damp rag. The smears at his eyes and mouth made him look younger than he was. Or perhaps they made him seem his age, when he usually passed himself as a worn coin.

"Went well," he said through a grin.

"It did," Cithrin agreed.

"Buy you that meal now, if you'd like," he said. Over his shoulder, Cithrin caught a glimpse of Cary scowling at them from the cart and imagined what she would see. Sandr, the leading man. Cithrin, the naïve second-choice girl. Or perhaps Sandr, member of the troupe, and Cithrin, the reason Opal was gone. The pinched lips and furrowed brow could have been disapproval of her or of Sandr. Cithrin didn't know which it was.

Find out, Magister Imaniel said from her memory or else his grave.

Cithrin lifted a hand only as high as her waist, barely a wave. Cary returned it, and then pointed at Sandr and tilted her head. *Really?* If she'd been angry about Opal, at most she would have smiled and waved. Surprised by relief, Cithrin shrugged. Cary rolled her eyes and went back into the cart.

"What?" Sandr said, looking over his shoulder. "Did I miss something?"

"Just Cary," Cithrin said. "You said something about a meal?"

The taproom nearest her rooms served plates of chicken and pickled carrots that they claimed went well with the dark beer. Sandr paid five extra coins for the privilege of a private table with a single bench, kept apart from the commons by a draped cloth too humble to be called a curtain. He slid onto the bench at her side, with a tankard of black beer and a wide mug of fortified wine for her. His leg settled easily beside hers, as if the touch were perfectly normal. Cithrin considered shifting to leave a few inches between them. Instead, she drank a generous mouthful of the wine, enjoying the bite of it. Sandr smiled and sipped at his own beer.

This was, she realized, a negotiation. He wanted to do some of the things he'd just finished mocking in the sex play, and he in turn was willing to offer up food and alcohol, attention and sympathy. And, whether he knew it or not, experience. Implicit exchange was something Magister Imaniel had talked about several times, and always with disdain. He'd liked the precision of measuring coin. Here, in the warmth of the taproom, the tastes of salted meat and fortified wine warming her blood, Cithrin wasn't sure she agreed. Surely imprecision had its place.

"I'm sorry about Vanai," Sandr said, using the same gambit he'd tried before the play.

Now what was the effect of saying that? Reminding her how badly she needed reassurance and the feeling of connection, she supposed. Making the things he offered seem valuable. Still, he'd made that point earlier. Stating it again was a mistake. Maybe if he'd interspersed it with other tactics. He could devalue her side of the exchange. If, for instance he'd criticized her dress or the cut of her hair, making it clear that lying down at her side wasn't likely worth so much. The danger there being that she might take offense and end the negotiation. Or pretend offense as a way of forcing him to raise his offer.

"Cithrin?" he said, and she shook herself.

"I'm sorry," she said. "My mind was elsewhere."

"The beer's good. Have you been here before?"

"I've meant to," she said. "Something's always come up."

"Want some?"

"All right," she said.

She'd expected him to pass his tankard to her, but instead he lifted his arm, calling over the server, and bought a tankard just for her. It was complex and thick, the alcohol lurking in a rich play of flavors. It didn't have the astringent cleanness of the fortified wine. How had Captain Wester put it? *Get her stupid drunk to get her knees apart.* Something like that.

It occurred to her that Sandr wasn't a man with a wide variety of strategies.

"I don't remember my parents," Cithrin said. "The bank raised me, bought my clothes and tutors."

"You must have loved them," Sandr said, playing the part of the consoler with his voice and pressing his thigh against hers with just a bit more fervor. Still, Cithrin considered the question.

Had she loved Magister Imaniel? She supposed so. She'd certainly loved Cam and wanted Besel. She'd wept for them all when the first news came. But she wasn't weeping now. The grief was still with her, but there was something else beside it. A terrible sense of possibility.

"I suppose I must," she said.

He took her hand, as if in sympathy. His brow furrowed and he leaned toward her.

"I'm so sorry, Cithrin," he said, and to her amazement, tears came to her eyes. That couldn't be right.

Sandr leaned forward, dabbing gently at her eyes with the cuff of his sleeve. Washing away the tears he had called forth. The stab of resentment at the little hypocrisy clarified many questions.

"Captain Wester!" she gasped, and Sandr dropped her hand like it had bit him. He glanced out from behind the almost-curtain.

"Where?" he said.

"He just stepped into the other room," Cithrin said. "Go, Sandr. Before he sees you!"

Sandr swallowed, nodded once, and slipped off the bench, heading for the alley door. Cithrin watched him go, then reached over and pulled his tankard to her as well. The chicken did go well with it after all. As she drank, her mind wandered. She wasn't angry at Sandr, but she couldn't bring herself to respect him. On another night, she might have let his scene play out, if only to see where it led. But it was increasingly clear that Master Kit intended to remain in Porte Oliva for some time. Since she wasn't sure when or how she'd depart the city, making that kind of connection was sure to complicate things. And then what if she got pregnant? Everything would fall apart then. Easier to stay out than to get out later. Still, she did wonder what it would have been like. Her mind shifted back to the mill pond, the snow against her skin, the weight of the boy upon her.

She finished the second beer and went back to the fortified wine. Alcohol was supposed to soften the mind, but she didn't feel soft at all. Or at least not in a way that left her unaware. She was more relaxed, certainly. The ever-present knot in her gut was looser, and she felt more at home in her skin. But her thinking was as clear as ever. Maybe clearer. She had the sense of huge thoughts shifting just beneath her awareness, her mind comparing and scheming with a speed and elegance that she couldn't quite keep up with herself. She ate some of the pickled carrots, finished the wine, and got another tankard of the beer.

When she stepped out the door, the sun had already set. Porte Oliva lounged in the grey twilight. Lanterns flickered and glowed. Men and women scurried through the streets, anxious to get home before twilight had entirely faded. The air was cold but not bitter. This wasn't a mild winter evening so much as a chilly springtime. She let herself drift down the street, her mind plucking at thoughts, turning them over, and dropping them again. How old Sandr seemed on the stage, and how young off it. The emptiness in her heart that was the death of Magister Imaniel and Cam, the almost vertiginous need to fill it, and her almost clinical detachment from her pain. The impending trip to Carse, smuggling wealth she hadn't stolen. The books of the bank records, sums and ciphers tracing history from the foundational document to the last rush of fleeing aristocracy. Opal's betrayal and Captain Wester's loyalty. She remembered something Master Kit had said about the shape of Wester's soul, and wondered what shape her own soul might take.

A Cinnae woman hurried past, her robes wrapped with pink-and-orange gauze, her face pale as the moon. A dog barked from the shadowed mouth of an alleyway. Three Kurtadam men walked past her, beads clicking and jingling in their pelts, said something she didn't understand, and then laughed together. She ignored them. The glow of her own windows shone just up ahead. If anyone were to attack her now, she'd only have to call out and Captain Wester and

Yardem Hane would come. It was a pleasant thought, and enough to make her feel safe whether she was or not.

She pulled herself up the stairs to the steady creaking of Captain Wester's pacing footsteps. She opened the door to his scowl.

"You've been out for quite a while," he said.

Cithrin shrugged.

"How much have you been drinking?"

Cithrin walked over to the cot and sat beside the Tralgu. Yardem smelled like open fields and damp dogs. She repressed the urge to scratch his wide back. Captain Wester was still looking at her, waiting for an answer.

"I don't recall exactly," she said. "I wasn't paying for most of it."

Wester hoisted an eyebrow.

"The thaw's almost come. We have to make a decision," she said, her words precise and unslurred.

"That's true," the captain said, crossing his arms. The failing daylight from the windows softened the lines of his scowl and the grey at his temples. He looked young. Cithrin remembered that Opal had found the man attractive and wondered whether she did. She'd lived with him for weeks. Months, counting the time on the road. She wondered for the first time whether his mouth would taste like Sandr's, then pulled her mind back to the moment, more than half repulsed by her own musings.

"No matter how we try to reach Carse," she said, "the danger is that someone will kill us and take the money."

"Old news," Captain Wester said.

"So we need to take the money ourselves," she said, understanding as she said it what she'd been considering all night. "We need to use it."

"Probably the wisest thing we could do," the captain said. "Take what we can carry and vanish."

"No," she said. "I mean take all of it."

The Tralgu at her side flicked a jingling ear. Captain Wester licked his lips and looked down.

"If we took all of it, we'd be in the same situation we are now," he said. "We'd still have to hide the money or protect it. Only we'd have your friends in Carse after our heads. That's not an improvement. We can talk about this when you're sober," he said.

"No, listen to me. We've been acting like smugglers. We aren't. You've always said we can't keep this much money quiet and we can't keep it safe. Opal proved that. So we shouldn't keep it quiet."

Wester and Yardem exchanged a silent glance, and the captain sighed. Cithrin stood and walked across to the unsealed books. Her feet were perfectly steady. Her hands didn't waver as she pulled out the black leather binding. She opened to the first pages and handed them to the captain.

"Documents of foundation," she said. "We write up a copy of our own, but for Porte Oliva instead of Vanai. We've got a hundred documents with Magister Imaniel's signature and thumb. We can pick some minor contract and use it to forge letters of foundation. File the documents with the governor, pay the fees and bribes, and then I can invest all of this."

"Invest it," the captain said as if she'd said *eat it*.

"The silk and tobacco and spices I can place on consignment. Even if they're stolen from the merchants, the bank would be paid. We can do the same with the jewelry or sell it outright for funds, and then make loans. Or buy into local businesses. We'll have to hold back some portion. Five hundredths, perhaps? But with the name of the Medean bank behind me, I could turn over nine-tenths of what we have in this room into papers of absolutely no value to anyone else before the trade ships come from Narinisle. What was left wouldn't be too tempting to guard."

"You are very, very drunk," Wester said. "The way you steal is you take something and then you leave."

"I'm not stealing it. I'm keeping it safe," Cithrin said. "This is how banks work. You never keep all the money there to be stolen by whoever finds a way to break your strongbox. You put it out into the world. If you take a loss or someone steals your working funds, you still have all your incomes and agreements. You can recover. And if it all goes wrong, what? We get thrown in prison?"

"Prison is bad," Yardem rumbled.

"Not as bad as killed and dropped in the sea," Cithrin said. "If you do what I say, the chances of keeping the money go up and the consequences of failure go down."

"You want," Captain Wester said, his voice tight, "to take a great deal of money that isn't yours and start your own branch of the bank that you're stealing the money *from*? They'll come for you."

"Of course they will," Cithrin said. "And when they do, I'll have what's theirs and more besides. If I've done it right."

Cithrin saw the disbelief in his face wavering on the border between amusement and outrage. She stamped her foot.

"Listen to me," she said. "Listen to my voice, Captain. *I can do this.*"

Marcus

B e careful," Marcus said.
    "I am being careful, sir."

"Well, be more careful."

Seven previous attempts lay on the floor between them: contracts and agreements between dead men over burned wealth, meaningless now. But, as Cithrin had said, each of them bore the signature and bloody thumbprint of Magister Imaniel of Vanai. The trick was to dip the parchment into the wax so that it covered the name and thumb, but nothing else. Then the page could be set in a wash of salt and rendered oil to loosen the ink. After a day in the bath, they could use a scrivener's stone to scrape away the ink, then a wash of urine to bleach away any remaining marks. In the end, they would have a blank page, ready to take whatever carefully practiced words Cithrin put on it, already signed and endorsed by the former head of the bank. A man, the story would have it, who foresaw the coming death of his city at Antean hands and concocted a scheme to refound his branch in Porte Oliva with Cithrin as his agent.

Provided they could put the wax in the right spot. Marcus leaned forward, fingers reaching toward the side of the document.

"If you just—"

"Sir?"

"Yardem?"

The Tralgu's ears sloped backward, set so close to his head that the earrings rested on his scalp.

"Go over there, sir."

"But I—"

"Go."

Marcus tapped at the air just before the parchment, grunted, and turned away. The boxes in the small rooms above the gambler's stall had been shifted and rearranged, making what had been one small room into two tiny ones. Outside, a warm spring wind hissed, rattling the shutters and making the world in general seem uneasy and restless. It had been a long time since Marcus had broken the thaw in a southern port, and the rich salt-stink of the bay reminded him of yesterday's fish. Cithrin sat on a stool, dressed in her carter's rough, with Cary squeezed in close beside her. Master Kit stood a few steps away, his arms crossed over his chest.

"That was better," Master Kit said, "but I think you've gone a little too far in the other direction. I don't want you to seem burdened. Instead of thinking of weight, imagine how you would move in a heavy wool cloak."

Cary put her hand to Cithrin's back.

"You're too tight here," Cary said. "Relax that and put the tension up *here*."

Cithrin frowned, tiny half moons appearing at the corners of her mouth.

"Like your breasts were too heavy," Cary said.

"Oh," Cithrin said, brightening. "Right."

She rose from her stool, took a step toward Master Kit, turned, and sat back down. Marcus couldn't have said what had changed in the way the girl moved, only that it was different. Older. Master Kit and Cary smiled at each other.

"Progress," Master Kit said. "Unquestionable progress."

"I think we're ready to walk down to the square," Cary said.

"With my blessing," Master Kit said, stepping back until he was almost pressed to Marcus's belly. The two women made their way across the thin strip of floor to the head of the stairway, hand in hand.

"Lower in the hips," Master Kit said. "Sink into them. Don't walk from your ankles."

The creak of boards descended until the pair were out in the street and gone. The wind gusted up the stairway, and the door at the bottom slammed shut. Marcus blew out his breath and sat on the newly vacant stool.

"I think she's quite good," Master Kit said. "Not much natural sense of her own body, but no particular fear of it either, and I find that's half the work."

"That's good," Marcus said.

"It seems the cuts on her thumbs are scarring nicely. I expect she'll have a good callus when that's through. Like she's been signing contracts for years. Did you put lye in the wounds?"

"Ash and honey," Marcus said. "Just as good, and it doesn't tend to go septic."

"Fair point. I thought that calling her three-quarters Cinnae was a good choice. If she's nearer full-blood, the First-blood thickness may read more as years than parentage."

"I've always thought Cinnae look to be about twelve anyway," Marcus said. "Terrible in a fight. No weight behind the blows."

Master Kit leaned a shoulder against the wall. His dark eyes flitted across Marcus as if the actor were reading a book.

"And how are you, Captain?"

"I hate this," Marcus said. "I hate this plan. I hate that we're forging documents. I hate that Cithrin pulled you and yours into it. There's nothing about the entire scheme I don't hate."

"And yet it seems you've chosen to come along."

"I don't have a better idea," Marcus said. "Except fill our pockets and walk away. That's still got some charm."

"So why don't you do that? The boxes are here. I'd say you've more than earned your pay."

Marcus let out a mirthless chuckle and leaned forward, elbows on his knees. From the far side of the room, Yardem made a satisfied grunt. The wax dip had worked this time.

"There are going to be consequences," Marcus said. "She can't just say it's all hers now and make it true. It's like walking into Cabral and casually announcing that you're the new mayor of Upurt Marion, and all the port taxes go to you now. And what's it going to upset? We don't know. By the end of the season, every trading house and royal court is going to have a theory of what exactly Komme Medean is signaling by investing in Porte Oliva. It's going to mean something about the relationship of Birancour and Cabral, and whether the freight from Qart-hadath is landing here or there. Why isn't there a branch here already? Is it because the queen warned them off? We might be violating half a dozen treaties and agreements right now, and we wouldn't know it."

"I agree with all of that," Master Kit said. "The risk seems real."

"We're about to be the bold, unexpected move on the part of a bank with a great deal of money and influence, and don't think for a moment that they'll appreciate our putting our hand to the tiller."

"And that's why you dislike the plan?"

"Yes," Marcus said.

Master Kit looked down. The wind stilled, then gusted again, pressing against the little rooms and stirring the air.

"Why do you dislike this plan, Captain?" the actor said.

He felt a stab of annoyance, and then the cool, almost sick feeling of the right answer swimming into his mind. He scratched his leg, feeling the tooth of the cloth against his fingertips. His hands seemed older than they should. When he thought of them, they still looked like they had when he'd first been on campaign. Strong, smooth, capable. Now there was as much scar to them as skin. The nail of his right thumb had been cut half off once, and it hadn't grown back quite right. The knuckles were larger than they had been. The calluses had more yellow to them. He turned them over, considering his palms as well. If he looked closely, he could still make out the dots of white where a dog had bitten him once, a lifetime ago.

"She knows the risks, but she doesn't understand them," Marcus said. "I can say everything to her I just said to you, and she'll answer me back. Argument for argument. She'll say the regained capital justifies the decision. That the holding company isn't liable for her, nor are the other branches, so anything they make back is a step above where they were when the money was simply lost."

"And yet," Master Kit said.

"I know how to protect her from thugs and raiders. I know how to fight pirates. I don't know how to protect her from herself, and hand to God, that girl is the worst danger she'll ever face."

"It can be hard, can't it? Losing control," Master Kit said.

"I don't control her," Marcus said.

"I think you do, but I'm open to being proven wrong.

What are three decisions she's made before this? In the time you've known her, I mean."

Yardem Hane loomed up behind the actor, wiping oil from his fingers onto a bit of grey cloth. For a moment, Marcus thought it might offer distraction, but the Tralgu's passive expression told him that he'd come to listen to the conversation, not to end it.

"She got that dress of hers," Marcus said. "And she chose to go to your performances."

"Two, then?" Master Kit said.

"She picked the fish for dinner," Marcus said.

"And how would you compare that with other contracts you've had?" Master Kit asked. "I don't believe you have thought of Cithrin as your employer so much as the little girl who'd swum out near the riptide. Has she paid you?"

"She hasn't," the Tralgu rumbled.

"You can stay out of this," Marcus said. "She couldn't. She didn't have any money of her own. All of this belongs to someone."

"And now," Master Kit said, "it seems she might be able to offer gold. And make decisions of greater weight than whether to have fish or poultry. Or what dress to buy. If this scheme of hers works, she'll be choosing where to live, how and whether to protect herself, and all the other thousand things that come with her trade. And I suspect you'll be here as well, at her side and protecting her. But only as her hired captain."

"Which isn't what I've been doing all along?" Marcus said.

"Which isn't what you've been doing," Master Kit said. "If you had been, you'd have asked Cithrin before you killed Opal."

"She'd have told me not to."

"And I think that's why you didn't ask. And why you dread the time when you have to ask, and you have to defer to her judgment even if you think she's wrong."

"She's a little girl," Marcus said.

"All women were little girls once," Master Kit said. "Cithrin. Cary. The queen of Birancour. Even Opal."

Marcus said something obscene under his breath. Outside in the street, the gambler's man called out. Great fortune could be theirs. Odds offered on any fair wager.

"I am sorry about Opal," Marcus said.

"I know you are," Master Kit said. "I am too. I knew her for a very long time, and I enjoyed her company for more than half of that. But she was who she was, and she made her choices."

"You were her lover, weren't you?" Marcus said.

"Not recently."

"And she was a part of your company. She traveled with you. She was one of your people."

"She was."

"And you let me kill her," Marcus said.

"I did," Master Kit said. "I believe there is a dignity in consequences, Captain. I think there's a kind of truth in them, and I try to cultivate a profound respect for truth."

"Meaning this is Cithrin's mistake to make."

"If that's what you heard me say."

Yardem flicked an ear, his earrings jingling against each other. Marcus knew what the Tralgu was thinking. *She's not your daughter.* Marcus set his foot against the wall of boxes. The wealth of a city that didn't exist anymore. The gems and trinkets, silk and spices traded to let the lucky escape the flames. All of it together wouldn't buy back one of the dead. Not even for a day.

So what was the point of it?

"Her plan isn't bad," Marcus said. "But I have the right to hate it."

"I can respect that position," Master Kit said with a grin. "Shall we prepare the oil bath for the future foundational documents of the Medean bank in Porte Oliva before the women come back?"

Marcus sighed and rose.

When the morning came, Marcus walked beside her. The mornings were still cold, but not so much that he could see his breath. Men and women of the three predominant races of the city passed one another as if the differences in their eyes and builds and pelts were of no particular concern. The morning mist drifted through the great square, greying the dragon's jade pavement. The condemned of the city shivered in the cold where all could see. Two Firstblood men hung as murderers. A Cinnae woman sat in the stocks with chains around her ankles as a recalcitrant debtor. A Kurtadam man hung by his knees and barely able to draw breath. Smuggling. Marcus could feel Cithrin pause. He wondered what the penalty would be for what they were about to do. It seemed unlikely to have precedent in the judges' tables.

The wide copper-and-oak doors of the governor's palace were already open, a stream of humanity pouring in and out from the center of authority. Cithrin lifted her chin. Smit had painted her face before they left. Faint, greyish lines around her eyes. Rose-grey blush coloring her cheeks. She wore a black dress that flattered her hips, but the way a matron might be flattered. Not a girl fresh from her father's home. She could have been thirty. She could have been fifteen. She could have been anything.

"Come with me," she said.

"Don't walk from your ankles," he said, and she slowed, taking the brickwork steps one at a time.

Within the palaces, the sunlight filtered through great walls of colored glass. Red and green and gold spilled across the floors, the twinned stairways. It mottled the skins of the people walking through, leaving Marcus with the sense of being in some enchanted grotto from a children's song, where all the fish had been changed to minor political officials. Cithrin took a long, shuddering breath. For a moment, he thought she would leave. Turn on her heel, flee, and leave the whole mad folly behind. Instead, she stepped forward and put a hand on the arm of a passing Kurtadam woman.

"Forgive me," Cithrin said. "Where would I find the Prefect of Trades?"

"Up the stairs, ma'am," the Kurtadam said with a soft southland lisp. "He'll be a Cinnae like yourself. Green felt table, ma'am."

"My thanks," Cithrin said, and turned toward the stairs. The Kurtadam woman's gaze stayed on Marcus, and he nodded as they passed. As a bodyguard, he felt out of place. There were a few queensmen here, scattered among the crowd, but no other private guards that he could see. He wondered if the real Medean bank would have brought him along or left him outside.

At the top of the stair, Cithrin paused, and he did as well. The prefectures were set haphazardly about the room like a huge child had taken up the tables and scattered them. There were no aisles, no rows. Each table stood at an angle to the ones around it, and if there was a system to the chaos, Marcus couldn't see it. Cithrin nodded to herself, gestured that he should stay close, and waded into the mess. A third of the way across, she came to a table covered with green felt where a Cinnae man in a brown tunic sat paging through stacks of parchment. A small weighing scale perched beside him, a row of weights behind it like soldiers at attention.

"Help you?" he said.

"I've come to submit letters of foundation," Cithrin said. Marcus felt his heart speeding up, like the moments before a battle. He crossed his arms and scowled.

"What class of trade, ma'am?"

"Banking," Cithrin said, as if she were doing something perfectly normal. The Prefect of Trades looked up as if seeing her for the first time.

"If you mean a gambling house—"

"No," Cithrin said. "A branch house. The holding company is in Carse. I have the papers, if you'd like."

She held them out. Marcus was certain he caught a whiff of old urine, that the section of the page that the wax had protected showed three shades darker than the rest. The prefect would laugh, call the queensmen, end the game here before it began.

The Cinnae man took the parchment as if it were spun glass. He frowned, his gaze skipping over the words. He stopped and looked up at Cithrin. His pale face flushed.

"The...the *Medean* bank?" he said. Marcus saw the conversations around them shudder and stop. More eyes were turning their way. The prefect swallowed. "Will this be a restricted license or free?"

"I believe the letter calls for free," Cithrin said.

"So it does. So it does. A full and unencumbered branch of the Medean bank."

"Is that a problem?"

"No," the man said, and fumbled, reading for her name on the papers. "No, Mistress bel Sarcour, only I hadn't been told to expect it. If the governor knew, he'd have been here."

"Not called for," Cithrin said. "Would I pay the fees to you?"

"Yes," the prefect said. "Yes, that would be fine. Let me just..."

For what felt like a day and likely took less than half an hour, Cithrin fenced with the bureaucrat. Payment was delivered from the bank, assayed, accepted, and receipts issued. The man scribbled a note on a sheet of pink onionskin, pressed an inked signet on the page, signed, and had Cithrin put her name over his signature. Then he offered her a small silver blade. As if she had done it a thousand times before Cithrin cut her thumb and pressed her print onto the page. The prefect did likewise.

And it was done. Cithrin took the onionskin, folded it, and slipped it in the purse that hung from her belt. Marcus followed her back down the stairs and out to the square. The sun had burned off the mist now, and the sounds of human traffic were the same low roar he'd become accustomed to.

"We're a bank," Cithrin said.

Marcus nodded. He would have felt better if there had been someone to fight. Or at least threaten. The anxiety of what they'd just done wanted some release. Cithrin took a handful of coins from her purse and held them out to him.

"Here," she said. "That's to hire on more guards. Now that it's my money, we might as well spend it. I'm thinking a dozen men, but use your best judgment. We'll want day and night guards, and then a few to accompany goods when we transfer them. I didn't haul these silks all the way from the Free Cities to have some back-alley thief take them now. I've got my eye on a couple of places the bank might operate from that give a better impression than squatting over a gambling shop."

Marcus looked at the coins. They were the first she'd ever paid him, and so what she'd just said was her first true order. The warmth in his chest was as surprising as it was powerful.

However it unfurled from this, whatever the consequences, the girl had done what damn few would have had the nerve for. This from the half-idiot carter boy he'd met in Vanai last autumn.

He was proud of her.

"Is there a problem?" Cithrin asked, real concern in her voice.

"No, ma'am," Marcus said.

Dawson

Issandrian's parade began at the edge of the city, snaked through the low market, then north along the broad king's road, past the gates of the Kingspire, and then east to the stadium. The broad streets teemed with the subjects of King Simeon, sworn loyalists of the Severed Throne, all standing on their toes to catch a glimpse of the slave races arrived to turn Antea into the puppet of Asterilhold. The roar of the assembled voices was like the surf, and the smell of their bodies threatened to overwhelm the gentle scents of springtime. Some follower of Issandrian's cabal had paid the rabble to carry banners and signs celebrating the games and Prince Aster. From where Dawson sat, he saw one—beautiful blue-dyed cloth with the prince's name in letters of silver—held aloft on poles, but with the wrong side up. It was Issandrian's revolt in a nutshell: the words of nobility hefted by men who couldn't read them.

The noble houses had their viewing platforms set in order and position according to the status of each family's blood. The place each man stood told where he put his allegiance. The state of the court as a whole could be read in a glance, and it wasn't a pleasant sight. Banner colors from a dozen houses fluttered about king and prince, and more of them belonged to Issandrian's cabal than not. Even Feldin Maas's grey and green. King Simeon sat high above it all, dressed in velvet and black mink, and managed to smile despite what was before him.

A column of Jasuru archers marched through the streets, the bronze scales of their skins oiled and glittering like metal in the sun. They carried the stripped-hide banners of Borja. Dawson made a rough count. Two dozen, say. He noted it down as the archers paused before the royal stand and saluted King Simeon and his son. Prince Aster returned the gesture with the same wide grin that he had each company before and would each one still to come.

"Issandrian's a cruel bastard," Dawson said. "If you've come to steal the boy's place, you should have the dignity not to put ribbons on it."

"For God's sake, Kalliam, don't say that sort of thing where people might hear you," Odderd Faskellan said. Behind them, Canl Daskellin chuckled.

On the road, five Yemmu lumbered. Their jaw tusks were dyed improbable colors of green and blue, and they towered over the watching crowd of Firstbloods. They didn't seem to have armor or weapons apart from the freakish size of their race. The five stopped before the king and made their salute. Prince Aster returned it, and one of the Yemmu men lifted his voice in a rolling, barbaric call. The others joined in, one voice layering over the other until the sounds seemed to braid. A soft breeze tugged at Dawson's cloak, and the trees that lined the street bobbed and shuddered. The air called in from all directions. The voices deepened, and the Yemmu at the center of the pack lifted a great, meaty fist. They were whipped by the tiny whirlwind.

Cunning men, then. Dawson made a note.

"Do you think the blow will come before the games commence?" Daskellin asked as if wondering aloud about the chance of rain.

"There doesn't have to be a blow, does there?" Odderd asked.

"More likely during," Dawson said. "But anything's possible."

"Reconsider Paerin Clark's offer," Daskellin said.

"I will not," Dawson said.

"We have to. Or aren't you seeing the same display I am? If we're standing against this, we need allies. And, frankly, gold. Do you have a way to get them? Because as it happens, I *do*."

A troop of swordsmen marched past. Fifty of them, all in the bright-burnished armor of Elassae, and evenly divided between black-scaled Timzinae and wide-eyed Southling. Cockroaches and night-cats. Races created in slavery to serve their dragon masters, marching into the center of First-blood power.

"If we can't win as Anteans, we deserve to lose," Dawson said.

The shocked silence behind him meant he'd gone too far. He noted the swordsmen.

"I began this because I believed you were right, old friend," Daskellin said. "I didn't say I'd crawl into your grave."

"Something—" Odderd began, but Dawson ignored him.

"If we win this by putting ourselves out to bid, we're no better than Maas or Issandrian or Klin. So yes, Canl, I will go to my grave for Antea. And with one loyalty. Not so many hundredths to the throne and so many on a green table in Northcoast."

Daskellin's face went still as coal.

"You're talking out of fear," he said, "and so I'll excuse—"

"Both of you, shut up!" Odderd snapped. "Something's happening."

Dawson followed the man's gaze. On the royal platform, an older woman in the colors of the Kingspire bent her knee before King Simeon. A youth was at her side, leather-armored and still dusty from the road. Prince Aster was looking at his father, the parade forgotten. King Simeon's mouth moved, and even at distance, Dawson recognized shock in his expression.

"Who's the boy?" Canl Daskellin said, almost to himself. "Who brought him news?"

Footsteps came from the wooden stairs behind them, and Vincen Coe appeared. The huntsman bowed to the two other men, but his eyes were on Dawson.

"Your lady wife sent me, lord. You're needed at home."

"What's happened?" Dawson said.

"Your son's returned," Coe said. "There's news from Vanai."

He *what*?" Dawson said.

"He burned it," Jorey said, leaning forward on the bench and scratching a dog between its ears. "Poured oil in the streets, closed the gates, and burned it down."

The year that had passed since Dawson had seen his youngest son had changed the boy. Sitting in the sunroom, Jorey looked more than a year older. His cheekbones had the thin look that came with time on campaign, and the smile that had always lurked just behind whatever expression he wore was gone. Exhaustion pulled at the boy's shoulders, and he smelled of horse sweat and unwashed soldier. It struck Dawson like a detail from a dream that Jorey and Coe could have passed for cousins. Dawson rose and the floor tilted oddly beneath him. He walked to the windows and looked out at the gardens. Snow still haunted the shadows, and the first press of green was softening the bark of the trees. At the back, cherry trees bloomed white and pink.

Geder Palliako burned Vanai.

"He didn't even have us loot it," Jorey said. "There wasn't time, really. He sent out a courier the day before. I've killed horses trying to beat him here."

"You nearly did," Dawson heard himself say.

"Does he know that you were the one who put Geder in place?"

It took Dawson almost a breath to understand the question, and by then his mind was on to questions of its own.

"Why did Palliako do it?" Dawson said. "Was he trying to undermine me?"

Jorey was silent for a long moment, looking into the dumb, bright eyes of the dog before him as if they were in some private conversation. When at last he spoke, his words were tentative.

"I don't think so," Jorey said. "Things were going poorly. He made some bad decisions, and they were bearing fruit. He knew that no one took him seriously."

"He put one of the Free Cities to the torch because he was embarrassed?"

"Humiliated," Jorey said. "Because he was humiliated. And because it's different when it isn't before you."

One of the dogs groaned long and soft. A bluebird fluttered onto a branch, peered in at the two men, and flew off again. Dawson put his fingers to the cold pane of the sunroom's glass, the heat of his flesh fogging the glass. His mind darted one way and then another. The stream of show fighters and mercenaries coming to Camnipol, paid by Issandrian with coin borrowed from Asterilhold. The bland, implacable expression of Paerin Clark, banker of Northcoast. Canl Daskellin's anger. And now, the burned city.

Too many things were moving, all in different directions.

"This changes everything," he said.

"He was different afterward," Jorey said as if his father hadn't spoken. "He was always apart from the rest of us, but before it was that he was a buffoon. Everyone laughed at him. They mocked him to his face, and more than half the time he didn't even notice it. But after, no one laughed anymore. Not even him."

The boy's eyes were toward the window, but he was seeing something else. Something distant, but more real the than the room, the glass, the spring trees in the garden. There was pain in that emptiness, and it was one he recognized. Dawson put aside the chaos. His son needed him, and so however much it howled for his attention, the world would wait.

Dawson sat. Jorey looked at him, and then away.

"Tell me," Dawson said.

Jorey smiled, but it didn't reach his eyes. He shook his head.

"I've been to war," Dawson said. "I've seen men die. What you're carrying now, I've carried as well, and it will haunt you as long as you hold it. So tell me."

"You didn't do what we've done, Father."

"I've killed men."

"We killed *children*," Jorey said. "We killed women. Old men who had nothing more to do with the campaign than to live in Vanai. And we killed them. We took away the water and lit them on fire. When they tried to come over the walls, we cut them down."

His voice was trembling now, his eyes horror-wide but tearless.

"We did an evil thing, Father."

"What did you think war is?" Dawson said. "We're men,

Jorey. Not boys swinging sticks at each other and pronouncing the evil wizard's defeat. We do what duty and honor demand, and often what we do is terrible. I was hardly older than you are now for the siege of Anninfort. We starved them. It wasn't fire, but it was a slow, painful death for thousands. And the weak die first. Children. Old men. The plague in the city? We put it there. Lord Ergillian sent riders out to find the sick from all around the countryside, and who we found, we named emissary and sent into the city. They were killed, but not before the illness spread. Every day, women came to the gates with babies in their arms, begging us to take their children from them. Usually we ignored them. Sometimes we took the babes and killed them there, just out of their mother's reach."

Jorey's face had gone pale. Dawson leaned forward, his hand on the boy's knee as he had since the child had been old enough to sit. Dawson felt a moment's sorrow that that thin-limbed boy was gone, and this moment—this conversation so like one he had had with his own father once—was part of that child's passage out of the world. The child had to go and make way for the man. It gave meaning to the loss, and made it bearable. That was the most Dawson could offer.

"Anninfort rebelled against the throne," he said, "and so it had to fall. And in order that it fall, it had to know despair. The ones they brought were on the edge of starvation. They wouldn't have lived. If the children we killed—the children *I* killed—brought the end a week sooner than it would have come otherwise, then I did the right thing. And I suffered then as you are suffering now."

"I didn't know that," Jorey said.

"I didn't tell you. Men don't put their burdens on their

children. I didn't tell your mother. It isn't hers to bear. Do you understand what I'm saying?"

"Vanai was different. There was no need for it."

Dawson opened his mouth to say something—hopefully something wise and comforting—but he felt the thoughts come into place with an almost physical click. Vanai. Issandrian. The armed mercenaries riding to Camnipol under the thin claim of honoring Prince Aster. The occupying force returning from the south, Geder Palliako at its head.

"Ah," Dawson said.

"Father?"

"Where is Palliako? Is he here?"

"No. With the men. A week behind me, perhaps?"

"Too far. We need him back sooner than that."

Dawson was on his feet again. He threw open the door, shouting for Coe. The huntsman might have been waiting for him. The first instructions were simple enough: find the others. Not only Canl Daskellin, but all the half dozen men who'd thrown their lots with him. Time was short, and victory uncertain. Coe didn't question, only saluted and vanished. When he turned back, Jorey looked bewildered.

Dawson raised his hand, stopping the questions before they came.

"I need one last favor of you before you rest, my boy. I'm sorry to ask, but I believe the fate of the throne rests on it."

"Anything."

"Bring me Geder Palliako. And quickly."

"I will."

"And Jorey? Vanai's death may have saved us."

Hardly an hour passed before Dawson's guests arrived. In addition to Odderd and Daskellin, the Earl of Rivermarch and Baron Nurring came. The others weren't at home, and

Coe had gone back out searching for them. This, however, was enough. Five men, all commanding the loyalty of high families and strategic lands, sat or stood or, in Canl Daskellin's case, paced restlessly around the back wall. They still wore the brocade and embroidered hats they'd sported at Issandrian's parade. Clara had brought in two servant girls bearing a tray of water flavored with cucumbers and rounds of twice-baked cheeses that still stood untouched by the wall.

In the time between the courier's arrival at Simeon's side and now, a dozen rumors had already spread. Dawson could see the uncertainty on the faces before him, and he could feel it on the breeze. His own sense of urgency was like a live thing crawling on his back. If this were to be done, it had to be done quickly, before the court had time to decide what the news meant. Before Simeon had the time.

Like a priest before his congregation, Dawson lifted his hands.

"The slaughter of—" he began, then stopped. "The *sacrifice* of Vanai has come like a torch in our darkest hour. And the salvation of the Severed Throne is at hand."

The silence was profound.

"You've lost your mind," Daskellin said.

"Let him talk," the Earl of Rivermarch said. Dawson nodded his gratitude.

"Consider this. Geder Palliako is known to have been at odds with Sir Alan Klin, one of Issandrian's closest allies, almost from the beginning. He managed to supplant Klin as protector of Vanai—"

"*He* managed?" Daskellin said.

"—and rather than use his position to gain wealth or play court politics, he made a decision. A brave and principled decision."

"Geder Palliako," Daskellin said, running a hand through

his hair, "is a buffoon we lifted up in order to embarrass Issandrian by making the occupation of Vanai a bog. He's an untried youth whose entire military experience has been taking an arrow in the leg and falling off his horse. Now he also appears to be a bloodthirsty tyrant in the mix. By tonight, Issandrian will have a dozen men who'll swear that his appointment was our doing, and it's almost certain that one of those will be Lord Ternigan. We won't be able to deny it."

Dawson could see the unease in the eyes of the other men, the slope of their shoulders, the angles at which they held their heads. If he answered rage with rage, it would end here with the two of them snapping at each other like pit dogs and the confidence of the cabal broken. Dawson smiled, and Daskellin spat into the ashes of the fire grate.

"Deny it?" Dawson said. "I'll sit at Palliako's side and be proud. Or did all of you see some different parade than I saw today? Has is not occurred to anyone else that several hundred loyal Anteans under Palliako's command are marching to Camnipol as we speak?"

"I don't understand," Odderd said.

"Here is what we say," Dawson said. "When Palliako discovered that Issandrian was bringing an armed force into Camnipol, he chose to bring his troops to the defense of the throne. Rather than abandon Vanai to our enemies, he took action that would show the steel of his intent. He didn't scrape the city of every last bit of silver. He didn't trade it away for concessions on tariffs. He burned it like a warrior of old. Like the dragons. What other man in all of Antea is so fierce and pure of intention? Who else would have done what he did?"

"But the king gave permission to hold these games. And this army coming to save us? Half of the men are Issandrian's, and the others disdain Palliako at best," Daskellin said. "This is a fairy story."

"They don't disdain him. They *fear* him. And if we all say it loud enough and often enough Issandrian will fear him too," Dawson said. "And since our lives may depend on it, I'd suggest we all practice in chorus."

"So this is what desperation looks like," Daskellin said. Dawson ignored him.

"If Issandrian moves against us, it will show that Palliako was justified. If he doesn't, it will be because Palliako cowed him. Either way, Issandrian loses some part of his grip on the king. And we do it without selling ourselves to Northcoast and the Medean bank. This is a windfall, my lords. We'd be idiots to turn it away. But we must go tell our version of it now. Today. When the court goes to bed tonight, it's our story they have to whisper to their pillows. Wait until opinion is set, and it will be a hundred times harder to change."

"And if Issandrian turns his plot against this Palliako boy?" Barron Nurring said.

"Then the blade meant for your belly may be stuck in his instead," Dawson said. "Now. Tell me you wouldn't prefer that."

Geder

Geder's thighs were chapped and weeping. His back ached. The spring breeze that blew down from the heights smelled of snow and ice. Around him, the remnants of the Vanai campaign rode or marched. They sang no songs, and no one spoke to Geder apart from the bare necessary business of moving the few hundred men, carts, and horses the last few days' journey. Even in his tiny rooms in Vanai with only his lamp-eyed squire for company and Alan Klin's worst duties to fill his day, Geder hadn't felt the full power of being isolated within a crowd.

He could feel the attention of the men on him, the condemnation. No one said a word, of course. Not one among them all stood up and told Geder to his face that he was a monster. That what he'd done was worse than crime. There wasn't any need, because of course Geder knew. In all the long days and cold nights since he'd turned back to the north and home, the roar of the flames hadn't left his ears. His dreams had all been of men and women silhouetted against the fire. He'd been ordered to protect Vanai, and instead he'd done this. If King Simeon ordered him cut down on the throne room floor, it would only be justice.

He had tried to distract himself with his books, but even the legends of the Righteous Servant couldn't pull him away from the constant, gnawing question: what would the king's

THE DRAGON'S PATH   319

judgment be? On his best days, Geder imagined King Simeon stepping down from the Severed Throne itself to put a royal hand on Geder's weeping eyes and absolving him. On his worst, the king sent him back to Vanai to be staked to the ground among the dead and eaten by the same crows that had gorged themselves on their bodies.

Between those extremes, Geder's mind found room for a nearly infinite variety of bleak imaginings. And as the mountains and valleys grew familiar, the dragon's road shifting between hills that he'd known a hundred times before, Geder found that each new scenario of his death and humiliation left him with a grim hope. Would he be set afire himself? That would be just. Would he be put in a public gaol and pelted with shit and dead animals? It would be what he deserved. Anything—*anything*—would be better than this grinding and silent regret.

The great promontory on which Camnipol sat appeared at the horizon, the dark stone blued by air and distance. The Kingspire itself was hardly more than a sliver of light. A lone horseman could make the ride in a couple of days. The full company might need as long as five. The king's cunning men could probably see them already. Geder's gaze kept drifting up to the great city, caught by longing and dread. With every mile, the fear grew stronger and the other traffic upon the road thicker.

The farmlands surrounding the capital city were among the best in the world, dark soil irrigated by the river and still rich from battles fought there a thousand years before. Even in the starving season just after the thaw, the land smelled of growth and the promise of food. Goatherds drove their flocks down the dragon's road from the low winter pastures toward the mountains in the west. Farmers led oxen to the fields ripe for tilling and planting. Tax collectors rode with their petty entourages of sword-and-bows, scraping what could be had of the small towns before their rent contracts expired. It was a rare thing to see a lone man on a good horse, and so Geder knew that the grey stallion coming south was meant for him. It was only when the horse drew up and he saw the rider was Jorey Kalliam that his anxiety broke and his breath came easily.

He turned his own mount off the dragon's jade and into the roadside muck, letting the column move forward without him. Jorey pulled his horse so close that the beasts could have slapped each other's faces with their tails, and Geder's knee nearly touched Jorey's saddle. Exhaustion greyed Jorey's face, but his eyes were bright and sharp as a hunting bird.

"What's the news?" Geder asked.

"You need to come ahead," Jorey said. "Quickly."

"The king?" Geder asked and Jorey shook his head.

"My father," he said. "He wants you there as soon as you can."

Geder licked his lips and looked up at the carts passing slowly by them. Some of the carters and swordsmen pretended not to notice the two of them, others stared openly. Ever since they'd left the corpse of Vanai, Camnipol was the goal he'd held before him, an end to his struggles. Now that the time had arrived, he wanted to delay it just a little more.

"I don't think it would be wise," Geder said. "There's no one to leave in command, and if I'm—"

"Give it to Broot," Jorey said. "He's not particularly bright, but he's competent enough to lead a column down a road. Just tell him to make camp outside the eastern gate and wait for word. *Don't* let him order the disband."

"It's... There's morale to think of," Geder said. "I don't want the men to feel I've abandoned them."

Jorey's expression was eloquent. Geder hung his head, the blush glowing from his cheeks.

"I'll find Broot," he said.

"And bring your best clothes," Jorey said.

While he gave Broot the instructions Jorey had given him, Geder also changed for a bay gelding who had been at rest trot for the morning. When Geder left his first command behind, it was on a young, fast horse with Jorey Kalliam at his side. The city was much too far to make at a gallop, but Geder couldn't help himself. For a few minutes, he let the animal beneath him press itself against the wind, glorying in the illusion of freedom if not the fact.

They stopped for camp at a black-roofed shack where a muddy path met the dragon's road, both of them too exhausted to do more than see to their horses. Geder collapsed into a dreamless sleep and woke in the morning to find Jorey cinching the girth on the gelding. They had taken to the road almost before Geder had cleared the grogginess from his head.

Before them, Camnipol rose.

The approach from the south was the steepest, the green band of dragon's jade tracing its way up the stone of the promontory like a bit of child's ribbon dropped to the ground. Time and weather had eaten away the stone itself, leaving stretches of a hundred feet or more where the road curved out into the empty air with nothing but caution to hold travelers to the path. The biting spring wind didn't come from any of the four points of the compass, but only down from the city or up from the plain below. The caves and shacks that clung to the face of the stone often needed rough wooden bridges to reach the road itself. The constant ache in Geder's legs distracted him, and the bulk of stone and rough brush obscured his view, so that until they were nearly at the last turn he didn't notice the Kingspire growing larger, the walls of the city gaining bulk. Instead, the great, shining arches and grand towers seemed to appear from nothing, a city built of dreams.

The southern gate was narrow, hardly more than a slit in the high grey stone with doors of worked bronze and dragon's jade that slid aside to allow passage. Just outside the doors, a dozen men in enameled plate sat on warhorses with barding that matched their riders.

As Geder and Jorey drew near, the men drew their swords. The blades flashed in the afternoon sun, and Geder's heart thudded in his chest like a fox in a trap. Here was the moment he'd been anticipating and dreading. Jorey nodded him forward with a smile that Geder couldn't quite interpret. It didn't matter. Geder swallowed his fear and rode trembling to his surrender wishing he'd remembered to put on his good leather cloak.

A single figure strode out of the shadows where the road passed through the wall. Though he wasn't mounted, the man commanded the attention of all those assembled. He was Firstblood, and older. His temples were grey, his face sharp and intelligent. The way he held himself gave the impression of being taller than the horsemen. Geder encouraged his gelding forward. Up close, there was no mistaking Jorey's father. Their eyes were the same shape, and the set of their jaws. He looked down at Dawson Kalliam.

"Sir Palliako," the elder Kalliam said.

Geder nodded.

"It is my honor to welcome you to the Undying City," Dawson Kalliam said. And then, sharply, "Honors!"

The horsemen lifted their swords in salute. Geder squinted at them. He'd never seen someone of noble blood called to the king's justice, but this wasn't how he'd expected it to be. From nowhere, voices rose together in a long, celebratory cry. And strangest of all, snowflakes began skirling down from the broad blue sky.

No. Not snowflakes. Flower petals. Geder looked up, and from at the top of the walls, hundreds of people looked back. Geder lifted an uncertain hand, and the crowd above him roared.

"Coe will see to your mount," Dawson said. "We have a litter waiting."

It took a moment to understand, but then Geder slid to the ground, letting Jorey's father lead him into the twilight break between the city walls. He didn't think to ask who Coe might be.

The litter was ornate, bearing the crest and colors of House Kalliam, but with a blaze of cloth on either side in the grey and blue of Palliako. It had two velvet-upholstered chairs facing each other, and eight Tralgu squatted by the poles. Dawson took the seat that faced backward. Geder pushed a lock of greasy hair back from his eyes. His legs were trembling from the ride. The arrow slits and murder holes all through the city wall were crowded with smiling eyes.

"I don't understand," Geder said.

"A few of my friends and I have sponsored your revel. They're traditional for a leader returning from military victory."

Geder turned around slowly. Something heavy seemed to have taken root in his belly, and the high stone rising above him tilted a little, like a young tree in a high wind. His mouth was dry.

"Victory?" he said.

"The sacrifice of Vanai," Dawson said. "Bold and commanding. It was a braver decision than this kingdom has seen in a generation, and there are those of us who would see that fierceness return to Antea."

In Geder's mind, a woman crawled up over the walls of the dead city, flames leaping behind the darkness of her body. In his memory, she fell. The roar of the flames filled his ears again as if it had followed him, and his vision narrowed. That was a *victory*? Wide Tralgu hands took his shoulder and guided him into his seat. He stared dumbly at Dawson as the litter shifted under them, and they rose.

The southern gate opened into a rough square. Geder had been there before, and knew what the chaos of beggars, merchants, and guards, oxen and carts and feral dogs looked like. This was like walking into the Camnipol dreamed by a boy who had only heard its glories described. Three hundred people at the least stood behind another honor guard, waving banners of House Palliako. A platform stood to the right with men in embroidered cloaks and cloth-of-gold tunics. There was the Baron of Watermarch. Beside him, a young man in the colors of House Skestinin. Not the lord himself, but perhaps his eldest son. Perhaps half a dozen more whom Geder's reeling mind half recognized before the litter moved on. And then, at the end, his head held high and tears streaming down his cheeks, Geder saw his father's face, and he saw the pride in it.

The crowd followed, cheering and tossing handfuls of flowers and paper-wrapped candies. The sound of them overwhelmed any hope of conversation, so he could only stare at Lord Kalliam in amazement.

At a meeting of half a dozen streets, the litter hesitated. Near the Kingspire, the buildings grew three and four stories high and people hung out of every window, watching him pass. A girl high and to his left pitched out a fistful of bright-colored ribbon, the threads dancing in the air as they fell. Geder waved to her, and something veritiginous and sweet washed through him.

Despite what he'd done, he was a hero. *Because* of what he'd done. It was more than relief; it was reprieve, forgiveness, and absolution. He lifted his arms, drinking in the adulation like a starving man. If it was a dream, he'd rather die than wake from it.

It was a difficult decision," Geder said, leaning across the table and talking loud. "To raze a city like that is a terrible thing. I didn't choose that path lightly."

"Absolutely not," the second son of the Baron of Nurring said, hardly slurring his words at all. "But that's the point, isn't it? Where's the valor in doing the easy thing? There isn't any. But to face the dilemma. Take action."

"Definitive action," Geder said.

"Exactly," the boy replied. "Definitive action."

The revel grounds connected to Dawson Kalliam's mansion. It wasn't as grand as the ballrooms and gardens on an actual holding, but it was near. And to have so much room inside the walls of the Undying City said more than three times the space in the countryside. Candles glowed up and down the high-domed walls, and blown glass lanterns hung from threads too thin to see in the dusk. Wall-wide doors opened to fresh gardens that still smelled of turned earth and early flowers. The feast and dance had run their course. Half a dozen highborn men had taken to the dais to proclaim the virtues of Geder's actions in the Free Cities.

There had been none of the weakness, timidity, and

corruption that had poisoned the generals of Antea for too long now, they said. Geder Palliako had shown his mettle not only to the Free Cities, not only to the world. He had shown it to his own countrymen. Through his actions, he had reminded them all what purity could accomplish. Even the king had sent a messenger with a written notice recognizing Geder's return to Camnipol.

The applause had been intoxicating. The respect and admiration of men who hadn't so much as nodded to him in any of his times at court. Then the dance. Geder generally avoided that particular court pastime, but Dawson Kalliam's wife Clara had insisted that that he accompany her around the garden yard at least once, and by the time he'd made the circuit, he felt almost surefooted. He'd made another few rounds with a few younger, unattached women before his thighs and ankles began to protest sharply enough to stop him. Jorey had brought his leather cloak, and as the day cooled toward night and the wine and beer flowed a bit more freely, Geder was glad of it.

"The mark of a real leader," Geder said, and then lost the thread. "The mark of a leader..."

"I hope you'll excuse me," his father said. "Geder, my boy?"

Geder rose to his feet and his drinking companion nodded his respect and turned away, his steps generally steady.

"It's getting late for an old man," Lerer Palliako said, "but I couldn't go without seeing you. You have exceeded anything I could have hoped. I haven't seen people talking about our family in terms like this since...Well, ever, I suppose."

"Let me go with you," Geder said.

"No no no. It's your night. Enjoy it."

"I'd enjoy talking with you," Geder said, and his father's eyes softened.

"Well, then."

Together, Geder and his father found Lady Kalliam and offered their profound thanks. Somehow the conversation turned until they were accepting her kind words, and they left with the feeling that the night had been an intimate affair with old friends they'd rarely seen. She insisted that they take the litter that had carried Geder through the streets earlier. Walking through the darkened streets wasn't safe, and even if it had been, it wouldn't do. Jorey appeared as they were about to take their last leave and offered Geder his hand. Geder almost wept, taking it.

As the Tralgu slaves hauled them through the night-dark streets, Geder looked at the stars scattered across the sky. Away from the gleeful crowd, the elation of relief cooled a degree. He was surprised to find that some part of the dread was still there, not sharp anymore, not strong, but present. Not even fear, but the as yet unbroken habit of fear.

His father cleared his throat.

"You're on the rise, my boy. You're very much on the rise."

"I don't know about that," Geder said.

"Oh, no. No, I heard those men tonight. You've caught the court at a delicate time. You're in very real danger of becoming a symbol of something." His father's intonation was merry, but there was something in the way he held his shoulders that made Geder think of a man bracing for a blow.

"I'm not a court pigeon," Geder said. "I'll be pleased to come home and work through some of the books that I found down there. You'd like some of them. I've started a translation of an essay about the last dragons that claims to date from only a few hundred years after Morade fell. You'd like it."

"I'm sure I would," Lerer said.

The Tralgu in the lead grunted expressively and the litter spun elegantly around a tight turn, dipping just a degree to counterbalance the shift.

"I saw Sir Klin didn't attend tonight," Lerer said.

"I wouldn't have expected him," Geder said. For a moment, he was on a frozen mill pond again, discovering the fortune that would have saved Klin's protectorate. "I imagine he's feeling a bit chagrined after all. Vanai was his, and he got called back on a leash. It must embarrass him, seeing me greeted with all this."

"It must. Indeed it must. Lord Ternigan didn't come either."

"He may have been called for elsewhere," Geder said.

"That's it. I'm sure that's it."

In the dark streets, a dog yapped and complained. The breeze that felt cool in the crowded ballrooms and gardens was chill now.

"Court events usually don't have everyone appear," Geder said. "I wasn't even expecting this much."

"Of course not. And it was quite a thing, wasn't it?"

"Yes."

They lapsed into silence. Geder's back ached. Between riding and dancing, he expected to feel half crippled in the morning.

"Geder?"

Geder grunted.

"Be careful with these men. They aren't always what they seem. Even when they take your side, it's best to spare an eye for them."

"I will," Geder said.

"And don't forget who you are. Whoever they want you to be, don't forget who you really are."

"I won't."

"Good," Lerer Palliako said. He was hardly more than a shadow against a shadow, except that the starlight caught his eyes. "That's my good boy."

Marcus

Marcus leaned low, arms to his sides. The pommel of the blackwood sword in his hand was slick with sweat. The Firstblood boy shifting on the far side of the pit wore a pair of fighter's trousers and a serious expression. Marcus waited. The boy licked his lips and hefted his sword.

"No hurry," Marcus said.

The air of the gymnasium was hot, close, and damp. The grunts and shouts of the other fighters struggled over the rush of water in the pipes that fed baths. At least a dozen men stood around the edges of the pit. Most were Kurtadam or Firstblood, though a pair of Timzinae held themselves a little apart. And Yardem Hane, panting and sweat-soaked. No Cinnae had come.

Marcus saw the boy's weight shift, committing to the attack. The boy held his sword to the side, eastern-style, so he had some training. Marcus blocked, chalk dust rising from the blackwood blade, and moved to the boy's left. The boy turned, and Marcus brought his sword down overhand. The boy blocked so aggressively that both swords bounced back. Marcus shifted the blade to his left hand and struck again, low this time, watching the boy's stance.

Avoiding both of Marcus's blows emboldened him. The boy took a firmer grip, feinted clumsily to the right, and darted left. Marcus blocked the attack casually, pulling his blade through the thick air to slap hard across the boy's chest. Marcus watched his opponent stumble back. The chalked practice sword left a line from the boy's lowest rib up to his collarbone.

"Who's next?" he called.

"That's the last, sir," Yardem said.

"Thank you, Captain Wester, sir," the boy said. The skin where Marcus had struck was red and rising. He felt a passing chagrin. He hadn't meant to hurt him.

"Thank you, son. You did well," Marcus said, and the boy grinned.

Marcus put his hands on the side of the pit and pulled himself up. He ached from shoulder to foot, and the pain felt good. Yardem tossed him a wad of the threadbare cloth, and Marcus wiped the sweat off his face and neck. This was the third collection of men they'd tried as new additions to the company. As with the others, it had been a mixed lot. Some had come because they were desperate and had no skills apart from a willingness to cause pain. Others because, by doing it, they could say they'd been in the pit against Marcus Wester. And a few—no more than a handful— because it was the work they knew and they happened to be at loose ends when Marcus had put out his call.

One of the latter was a stout Kurtadam with a gray-gold pelt and a Cabral acent. Marcus met Yardem's gaze and pointed his chin toward the candidate. Yardem nodded once.

"You," Marcus said. "What was your name again, friend?"

"Ahariel," the Kurtadam said. "Ahariel Akkabrian."

"You know how to fight. What put you in Porte Oliva?"

"Took contract with a company out of Narinisle. Mostly garrison work, but the commander started bunking with the footmen. Got to be about gossip and hurt feelings, I had to get out. I was thinking of the Free Cities. Figure they'll be jumpy for years with what happened to Vanai and all. But I heard you were looking."

"It won't be garrison work," Marcus said.

The Kurtadam shrugged.

"I figured you have your pick of work. Wodford and Gradis and all. If it was good enough to hold you, it'd be enough for a sword-and-bow like me."

"You're an optimist," Marcus said. "But we'd be pleased to have you if the terms suffice."

"Wouldn't waste your time if they didn't," Ahariel said.

"Report in the morning, then. We'll put you on the duty roster."

Ahariel saluted, turned, and walked away.

"I like him," Marcus said. "Doesn't talk much."

"Fit right in, sir," Yardem said.

"Feels good, having a real company again."

"Does."

Marcus dropped the scrap of cloth onto the edge of the pit.

"Is it time?" he asked.

"We should go soon," Yardem said.

The early summer streets of Porte Oliva were hot and crowded. Beggars haunted the corners, and the press of bodies in the streets seemed to add as much heat as the wide, golden coastal sun. The air smelled of the ocean, of honey and hot oil and cumin. The clothes also changed. No jackets, no cloaks. Cinnae men and women strode through the street in diaphanous robes that made their thin bodies seem to shift and bend like shadows or spirits. The Kurtadam shaved themselves until there was hardly enough fur to tie beads onto and wore loincloths and halters barely sufficient to protect the most basic modesty. It was the Firstblood, though, that kept Marcus's attention. Men and women split out of their winter cocoons into bright colors, green and yellow and pink. Tunics were cut down the sides to let air and covert glances skid across bare skin. Every day had the feeling of festival about it.

Marcus didn't like it.

It reminded him too much of a time when he'd been young and unable to distinguish lust from affection, and memories of that time always led to the times that came after. Meeting a blue-eyed girl named Alys, wooing her with brave tales and pale flowers. The nights of longing, and then one moonlit night at the end of springtime, a shared apple, a kiss beside a waterfall, and the end of longing. His perfect woman. In a just world, she'd be with him still.

Meriam would have been old enough now to suffer the same stirrings and confusions of the flesh, and he would have been as powerless to force wisdom upon her as his father had been with him. But no. By now she'd have been old enough to have married young and imprudently. Another season, and Marcus might have been tickling a grandson under the chin. Being reminded of all those unlived moments was what he disliked about the city. But it was also what he disliked about the world. So long as there was work that needed doing, he could put it all aside.

The question of where to put the permanent home of the new bank had been easily solved when Cithrin spoke to the daughter of the gambler whose stall they slept above. She'd been hoping to talk her father into leaving the trade for years, and had very nearly succeeded. The lower floor was wide enough to support a small barracks, and the basement had an iron strongbox set in stone and countersunk deep into the earth. And so now, where the gambler's stall had once been, the Medean bank of Porte Oliva now lived in modest elegance. The day that the old gambler had signed the contracts, Cithrin announced the change by having the walls repainted in the brightest white she could find. Where the caller had stood, chanting his litany of wagers and odds, a wide tin pot filled with black soil had the thin green stalks and broad sloping leaves of half a dozen tulips still only threatening to bloom.

"Straight to her?" Yardem asked, gesturing at the private stair that led to the rooms that were now exclusively Cithrin's. Marcus shook his head.

"When we're ready to go," he said.

Once, the thick wooden door had opened onto a common area with a high counter on one end. The counter was gone now, and the chalk marks on the slate weren't offered odds, but the names of Marcus's new guards and their duty rotations. All four were waiting now where the gambler's clients had been, looking out the narrow, barred windows and making crude jokes about the people passing by on the street. When Marcus entered, the laughter stopped, and the new guards—two Firstblood men, a Kurtadam woman, and a Timzinae boy Marcus had taken on a hunch—stood to attention. He'd need more. Overhead, the boards creaked where Cithrin was pacing.

"Bag ready?"

"Yes, Captain Wester, sir," the Kurtadam woman said.

Marcus nodded at her, his mind suddenly an embarrassing blank. She had broad shoulders and hips, and arms as thick as her legs. Her pelt was a glossy black, darker even than the Timzinae boy's scales. And her name was...Edir? Edem?

"Enen," Yardem said. "You carry the coin. Barth and Corisen Mout take forward and back. Captain and I will take flanks."

"And me?" the Timzinae boy asked. The nictatating membranes of his eyes opened and closed in a fast nervous tic. He was easy enough. Whatever his name was, everyone called him Roach.

"You'll stay here and wake the others if anything interesting happens," Marcus said. Roach deflated a bit, so Marcus went on. "If anyone's going to make a play for the strongbox, they'll do it when most of us are away. Keep the door barred, and your ears sharp. You're going to be in more danger than we are."

Roach saluted sharply. Enen stifled a smile. The two Firstblood men went to the weapons chest and started arraying the most vicious weapons that the queensmen would let them carry through the streets. Marcus turned and went back out toward the private stairway, Yardem at his side.

"I'm never going to remember all these names," Marcus said.

"You always say that, sir."

"I do?"

"Yes."

"Hm. Good to know."

The rooms that had seemed so small and cramped when it had been just him, Yardem, Cithrin, and the piled wealth of Vanai had become a respectable private residence for the new head of the Medean bank. It was little more than a room in the back with her bed and desk and a meeting room at the front with a small privacy closet to the side, but Cithrin had put together a hundred small touches that transformed it: fine strips of cloth that hung over the windows, a small religious icon nestled in a corner, the short lacquered table presently covered with old shipping records and copied bills of lading. Taken together, they gave the impression of the home of a woman twice her age. It was as much a costume as anything Master Kit and his players sported, and one that Cithrin wore well.

"I need someone from the Port Registry who'll talk to me," Cithrin said instead of hello. "The trade ships from Narinisle should be coming, and I need to know better how that works. It looks like half the trade in the city happens when those ships come in."

"I'll see what I can find," Yardem said.

"Where to today?" Marcus asked.

"A brewer's just outside the wall," Cithrin said. "I met her at the taproom. Her guild's letting her replace her vats, but she doesn't have the coin to afford it."

"So we're loaning it to her."

"Actually, she's not permitted to accept loans at interest," Cithrin said, pulling a light beaded shawl across her shoulders and arranging it the way Master Kit had taught her. "Guild rules. But she is permitted to take money from business partners. So we're buying part of her business."

"Ah," Marcus said.

"If she comes short, we're in a position to take her shop in hand. If I cultivate a relationship with a cooper and a few taphouses, I can arrange the kind of mutual support that makes everyone very happy for a very long time."

"Long time," Marcus said, tasting the words.

"And anyway, breweries are always good investments," Cithrin said. "Magister Imaniel always said so. There's never going to be an off market for ale."

Cithrin looked around the room, pursed her lips, and nodded more to herself than to them. Together, they walked back down the stairway, Cithrin stopping to secure the door behind them. In the street, a half dozen children were playing a game that involved kicking an old wineskin and screaming. Cithrin turned toward the entrance, almost bumping against a Kurtadam man. Marcus silently added the construction of an interior door to his list of things that ought to be done. Having to walk outside to go from one set of rooms to the other had been pleasant enough when they were hiding. Now it was just an unnecessary risk.

The Firstblood men, Corisen Mout and Barth, were laughing with each other but sobered as the three of them came in. Enen was ready, a small leather bag strapped across her shoulders, her hands free and ready. She wore a curved dagger and a weighted baton on her hips. When they walked out to the street, the six of them fell into an easy formation. Despite the close, crowded streets, their path was always clear, the citizens of Porte Oliva standing aside to let them pass. Curious gazes followed them, but only a few especially bold beggars attempted the approach, and they tried for Cithrin. No one came near Enen and her burden of coin. They moved north, through the great wall, and to the spill-over buildings of the city beyond it. The press of bodies was more than Marcus liked. The smells of sewer and sweat were thicker here, the streets both more crowded and wider than behind the wall in Porte Oliva's center.

The brewer's, when they reached it, was a two-story shop built around a narrow courtyard with its own well. Wide doors stood open to the yard, the vats and barrels squatting in the yeast-stinking shadows. The brewer, a Cinnae woman so thick about the body and face she could almost have passed for Firstblood, came out to meet them, grinning like they were family.

"Magistra Cithrin! Come in, come in!"

Marcus watched as Cithrin and the brewer kissed one another's cheeks. He nodded to Enen, and she shrugged off the bag of coins and presented it to the girl as if Cithrin were what she appeared to be. None of the new guards thought the bank was anything different than it claimed. There was no reason that they should.

Cithrin took the bag and gestured to Marcus that he and the others should stay in the yard. He nodded once, and Cithrin and the brewer took one another by the hand and walked into the dim recesses of the brewery, talking like old friends. A Cinnae boy no older than Roach came out wearing a thin leather apron and bearing mugs of fresh ale. It was sweeter than Marcus liked, but with an almost bready aftertaste that he could learn to enjoy. Marcus let the three new guards settle themselves on the stone wall of the well before he met Yardem's eyes and glanced across the yard. The Tralgu drank down his ale, belched, and ambled along at Marcus's side.

"Decent ale," Marcus said.

"Is."

"What do you think of this scheme of hers?"

Yardem's ears flicked back, then forward again, considering. Marcus knew that just by asking he'd changed the Tralgu's answer. What Yardem thought about a scheme that Marcus hadn't questioned was a different thing.

"Seems to be working," Yardem said. "Still more jewelry than I'd like in the basement, but we've got enough swords to scare off stray knives. I don't know much about it, but it seems she's likely to earn back the money she's spending or near to it."

"So that when the big men from Carse swoop down here, they'll find it all more or less intact," Marcus said. "She can hand it over to them, wash her hands, and there's no harm done."

"That's the plan," Yardem said carefully.

"Do you see her handing it back to them?"

Yardem stretched his long, thick arms, turning to look at

the open brewery as if he were bored and it was in the way. Marcus waited in silence, hoping that the Tralgu would disagree and expecting that he wouldn't.

"She's going to try to keep it," Yardem said.

"She doesn't know she's thinking about it, but yes," Marcus said. "She's good at this. Maybe very good. And she's not the kind of girl who stops when she likes something too much."

Yardem nodded slowly.

"How's she going to do it?" he asked.

Marcus sipped his ale, washing his mouth with it, then spat it onto the courtyard stones. A dozen pigeons lifted off from the rooftop, spinning across the wide blue overhead.

"I don't understand half of what she's doing now," he said. "Do you?"

"No."

"I don't know what she'll try. Likely she doesn't either. But when she sees it, she's going to reach for it. Whether it's a good idea or not."

Geder

The days that followed Geder's return to Camnipol flowed around him like river water around a stone. Gatherings at the houses of the highest families in Antea filled his days, celebrations for his own victory in Vanai and for the coming anniversary of Prince Aster's naming took the nights. Almost the day after his unexpected revel, he began seeing black leather cloaks the image of his own appearing among the brightly dyed fashions of the court. Men who had never bothered to cultivate a connection to House Palliako had begun calling on him. If his father seemed put off by the attention, that was understandable. Changes that came suddenly could feel catastrophic even when they were changes for the better.

The only things that would have made the ripening spring better would have been rooms within the city itself instead of night after night of heading out before the city gates closed and sleeping in his campaign tent and for the nightmares to stop.

"I don't understand why I shouldn't order the disband," Geder said, spreading a spoonful of apple butter over his morning bread. "If I don't do it soon, Lord Ternigan's sure to."

"He doesn't dare," Canl Daskellin, Baron of Watermarch,

said. "Not until all the foreign swords and bows are safely out of Camnipol."

"It's a disgrace," Marrisin Oesteroth, Earl of Magrifell, said, nodding. "Armed rabble in the streets of Camnipol. And hardly even a Firstblood among them. I don't know what Curtin Issandrian was thinking, bringing the slave races. Next he'll be honoring Price Aster with pigs and monkeys."

Around them, the lesser gardens of House Daskellin glowed in the late morning sun. The golden blossoms of daffodils nodded in the breeze. To the east, the reconstructed stadium loomed, stories tall and painted white and red. The games for the prince were to start the next day, but the preliminary spectacles had been running for days—bear baiting, show fights, archery competition. And with them, a growing tension that reminded Geder of the still, heavy heat of the clear summer day before a storm night.

"Did you smell those Yemmu cunning men?" Odderd Faskellan, Viscount of Escheric and Warden of the White Tower, asked with a snort. "The stink coming off them made my eyes water from the platform. And the Southlings."

The plain-faced man at Geder's side—Paerin Clark, he was called, and with no other title given—drank from his cup as if to hide his expression, but the others around them nodded and grunted their agreement and disapproval.

"They fuck their own sisters," Marrisin Oesteroth said and took a drink of cider. "It's not their fault that they do. Dragons made them that way. Keep their bloodlines true, just like hunting dogs."

"Really?" Geder asked. "I read an essay that said that was a myth started by the Idikki Fellowship after the second expulsion. Like Tralgu eating babies, or Dartinae poisoning wells."

"You're assuming Tralgu don't eat babies," Marrisin Oesteroth said with a laugh, and the others joined in. Including
Geder.

The conversation turned to other matters of court: the
increasing unrest in Sarakal, the foundering movement to
create a farmer's council, rumors of a second war of succession in Northcoast. Geder listened more than he spoke, but
when he did, the men seemed to listen to him. That alone
was as intoxicating as the cider. When the last of the food
was carried away by the servants, Geder took his leave.
There would be another gathering like this tomorrow, and
another the day after that. And an informal ball that night,
scheduled opposite a feast for King Simeon hosted by Sir
Feldin Maas. Geder knew because Alberith Maas had asked
grudging permission to attend the feast. Geder had allowed
it. The court might be divided, but he assumed it always
was. Given the number and quality of people at the gatherings he'd attended, he felt fairly sure that the half that had
lifted him up into their number was both larger and more
powerful. He could afford to be magnanimous.

The sun shone in the late morning sky, the warmth soaking into Geder's cloak and leaving his body feeling soft and
comfortable. He strolled through the black-cobbled streets,
feeling almost as sure of himself as he had during his first
days in Vanai. The lowborn man with a long dirty beard
saw him coming and scuttled out of his way. A young
woman with a beautiful tea-and-milk complexion smiled at
him from her slave-drawn carriage. Geder smiled back and
watched her turn to watch him as she was borne away. His
jaw ached pleasantly from grinning.

The eastern gate of the city was wider than the southern,
built beneath a great archway of worked stone that reached
almost as high as the Kingspire itself. Horses' hooves and

carriage wheels clattered against the voices of small merchants. The air stank of manure, animals soiling the streets as quickly as prisoners of the petty court could scrape it up. Callers walked under rough wooden signs, announcing whatever news they were paid to repeat: a particular butcher had been soaking his meat in water and selling it by weight, an outbreak of the pox had been traced to a brothel in tanner's row, a boy had been lost and a reward posted for his return. It was the gossip of any great city, and Geder enjoyed the sound of it without paying attention to the meaning of the words. Every syllable had been paid for, and it was safe to assume most were lies. Geder paused at a stand where a crag-faced Tralgu with a missing leg sold treats of candied lavender and honey stones. When Geder tossed him a coin, the scowling Tralgu caught it overhand, snatching it out of the air.

Outside the walls of Camnipol, the northern plains spread out to the horizon, the green of grass and scrub, but treeless. Anything big enough to burn as firewood had been stripped off the land generations before. What hills there were rose in gentle swells like waves on a calm sea. The camp was scattered just to the east in the shadow of the city. At Jorey Kalliam's suggestion, Geder had given orders to keep it in order as a military group rather than letting the casual disorder of being home run its course. Despite sitting at Camnipol's side, the camp had its perimeter, its sentries, its cookfires, and its acting commander. Fallon Broot, Baron of Suderling Heights, rolled toward him as he reentered the camp.

"What news?" Broot asked. "Word yet from Ternigan?"

"Not yet," Geder said.

"All respect to the man, but there won't be a good seat left in the stadium if he waits much longer."

"We could appeal to King Simeon," Geder said.

"Or you could give the order yourself," Broot said, his deep-drooping mustache twitching.

"Wouldn't presume," Geder said.

Broot laughed once, almost a bark.

"Camp's yours, then. I'll retire, get a bit of rest. Maas is putting on a feast tonight, and it's my turn for leave."

"There's also an informal ball," Geder said with as much nonchalance as he could muster.

"No one wants to see me dance," Broot said. As he walked away, Geder wondered which event the tea-and-milk girl would attend.

In his tent, his squire had cleaned away all the remnants of sleep, but left his books and the tools of translation where they were. Geder sat down at his field desk, picked up the cracked leather of the multiform essay he'd been wrestling with, and searched through the delicate, ancient pages until he found where he'd left off.

It was the discovery of these weapons in the Sinir mountains that allowed the allied forces of Hallskar and Sarakal to limit the interference of Borja, and eventually reclaim the lands ceded under the agreements five generations before. Despite this, there has been no concerted effort, either among the elected Hallskari kings or the traditional families of Sarakal, to explore further caches. The commonly held explanation for this unimaginable oversight was a superstitious fear of something within the valley. The unnamed scribe of Atian Abbey suggests that this might have been a pod of hibernating dragons placed by Drakis Stormcrow or the Dragon Morade's righteous servant, but it seems most likely that it was instead that the plague season that followed the end of the Borjan expansion made all such exploration impossible, and the mountains themselves limited any expedition to the summer months, and foot traffic. This alone should justify a longer and more systematic examination of the footwear of ancient Hallskar, which I shall undertake in my next section.

Sinir mountains. *Sinir*. The word seemed very familiar, but he couldn't quite recall where he'd seen it before. It was recently, though. It was something to do with the Righteous Servant, though. He was sure of that.

The legend that had begun as a pet project had grown to be something more interesting. In the dark hours of the morning after his dreams woke him, Geder would sit with his books, marking each reference and considering the finer points of his translations until the voice of the fire faded from his mind and he could sleep again.

His understanding of the weapon was far from clear, except that it had played a part in the final war of the dragons and involved a magic that separated truth and lies definitively. There were two comments about corruption or infection of blood, but what exactly that meant wasn't clear. It might have been a reference to the rites and spells that Morade had worked in order to bring the Righteous Servant into being, or a description of its function, or a story put out by those who opposed Morade and who had outlived their enemy.

The location associated with the weapon's use was unquestionably in the eastern mountains and wastes that bordered Hallskar, Borja, the Keshet, and Pût. Granted, that left a huge swath of land, much of it near impenetrable. But by dating the references and consulting where the national and tribal borders had shifted through the ages, Geder thought he might be able to make a case as to the particular range associated with it. So, for instance, one book placed the Righteous Servant as east of the Keshet, but using an antiquated name. Another called it east of Borja, using a slightly more recent term. By comparing how the border between the two had changed in the intervening centuries, Geder could speculate a range no larger than four days' ride from north to south. And now if there were a range within that called Indische, he might be able to put a finger on it.

For the first time in his life, he'd begun the outline of a speculative essay of his own on the subject. It seemed unlikely that the section on ancient Hallskari footwear was likely to be useful, but he wouldn't know until he tried it, so with a deep sigh, Geder leaned on his elbows and began reading. The text wasn't particularly well written, but he still found himself being drawn into the subject. The change in toe bridges as a guide to the racial makeup of the royal court was actually fascinating, given that at least six centuries of historical records had been systematically wiped out during the reign of Thiriskii-adan. The suggestion that there had been a period where Hallskar was ruled by the lamp-eyed Dartinae rather than Haavirkin was enough to raise Geder's eyebrows. He found himself so caught up in the text that he didn't notice the shouting until his squire burst into the tent.

"My lord," the old Dartinae said. "In the city. Something's happened."

Geder looked up, and for a moment his mind kept along its track, judging what his squire might have looked like in the regal leather and gold of Hallskar. The din of voices and crashing metal worked its way into his awareness, and fear hit his blood like winter. Geder leapt up from his desk and ran out of the tent. His imagination already had smoke rising from the walls of Camnipol, the fire of Vanai already roaring his name. Daved Broot, son of Fallon, was running across the plain. Blood soaked his tunic scarlet.

"Someone help that man!" Geder screamed, his voice high and tight. "He's hurt! Someone help him!"

But men were already streaming toward the wounded boy. Geder looked around, trying to find the battle. There was no smoke. No fire. But men were screaming, and nearby. Six men had reached Daved Broot, linked hands under him, and were carrying him back into camp, their arms as a gurney. Geder hurried to meet them. When the wounded man saw him, he reached out.

"Lord Palliako!"

"I'm here," Geder said. The bearers paused.

"The gladiators. They're taking the gate."

"What?"

"The gladiators from the stadium. They're at the gate. They're trying to close it."

It's a riot, Geder thought. *It's a riot in the streets of Camnipol.*

And then, a moment later: *No. A coup.*

"Get him to the cunning man," Geder ordered the bearers. "And then get your blades. Call the formation! Formation!"

First in confusion, and then in disbelief and fear, the camp came to order. Geder's squire scurried up with sword and armor in hand. Geder took the blade, then gave it back and reached for the armor.

"No time for that," Fallon Broot said, appearing at his side. The man's face was a storm cloud. "If they close the gates, we'll be useless. Speed now, safety in hell."

Geder swallowed. His knees were actually shaking. He heard himself calling the attack as if someone else were doing it, and then, sword in hand, he and Broot and a dozen of the veterans of Vanai were running across the grass field toward the eastern gate. Geder's black leather cloak flapped about him like bat's wings. His sword felt heavy and awkward, and when he reached the gates his breath was short and painful. And under the great eastern arch of the city, the gates were beginning to close.

"To me!" Geder shouted, and pushed himself forward. "Vanai to me!"

He and his men burst through the narrowing space between the gates like a handful of dried peas thrown against a window, first the fastest, then one or two more together, and then all of them in a lump. The square Geder had strolled through not two hours before was changed past recognition. Where there had been carts and carriages, bodies lay in the street. From the overturned table of honey stones and candied lavender, a line of Jasuru archers stood, their scales glittering gold. They loosed arrows, and the man to Geder's left fell down screaming.

"Attack!" Geder shrilled. "Stop them! Attack!"

Geder's men charged, heads down and voices raised. The archers fell back, and from the right, a group of Yemmu in banded steel and leather with huge two-handed swords lumbered toward them. With jaw tusks painted the color of blood, they were like something out of a nightmare. One raised his wide head and howled. There were words in the cry. Geder turned toward the retreating archers, then the advancing swordsmen, and back again.

A wide blade a yard long whirred toward him, and he danced back. The Yemmu was almost half again as tall as a Firstblood man, wide as a cart across the shoulders. Geder lifted his own blade in both hands, and the Yemmu grinned. With a groan, the Yemmu pulled his sword through the air, forcing Geder back again. To the left, a huge blade caught a gap in the armor of one of the Vanai men, spraying hot blood across Geder's chest and face. Somewhere behind him, someone shrieked.

Geder's opponent lifted his sword, preparing to bring it down like an axe. Geder raised his own blade, knowing as he did that he couldn't even deflect the coming blow. Someone ran by him, slamming into the Yemmu soldier and making him stumble.

"Now, Geder!" Jorey shouted. "Cut him!"

Geder scuttled forward, swinging with his blade. The cut wasn't deep, but it got through the leather armor. The Yemmu shouted, and Jorey jumped back. Geder swung again. He was trying for the thing's belly where the armor was thin to let it twist, but the blow went low, dropping toward the thing's thigh. The Yemmu put out its huge grey hand and shoved Geder back, but Jorey Kalliam's blade cut down, drawing a gout of blood from its wrist. It howled, dropping its sword and grabbing at the wound to stanch the flow. Geder rushed in, hewing two, three, four, times at the Yemmu fighter's knee like he was trying to cut down a sapling.

The Yemmu stumbled and fell, lifting its arms in surrender. Geder spun around.

The gates had stopped, neither fully open nor closed, and more of the Vanai soldiers were pouring through the gap. The Jasuru archers were nowhere to be seen, and four of the Yemmu had fallen, with half a dozen more locked in battle against a rising tide of Antean swords. Jorey Kalliam was bent over, breathing hard. Blood trickled from his mouth and stained his teeth, but he was smiling.

"Didn't know what they were starting when they crossed us," Jorey said through a foam of his own blood and saliva. Geder grinned.

*   *   *

Well," Lerer Palliako said, leaning against the parapet of his balcony. "Well, well, well."

"They actually took the southern gate," Geder said. "Closed it and jammed the mechanism. We still can't open it."

Geder shrugged. The twilight was fading and stars coming out. The feasts and balls were all canceled by order of the throne. Blades and blood in the streets of Camnipol had the king's guard patrolling the streets. King Simeon himself had gathered a select group of nobles in the Kingspire, and set a dusk-to-dawn curfew that meant anyone found in the darkened streets would be slaughtered without question or warning. The houses were being closed and barred, and a fire watch set on the walls of the city. The stadium that had been remade to house Prince Aster's celebratory games instead had a dozen gladiators hung from makeshift gallows. Twice that number had been bound and dropped off bridges, their bodies unburied at the bottom of the Division.

The city's shock and fear seemed to change the air itself. Everything seemed fragile, poised at some great catastrophe. Geder knew he should have been frightened too, but he was exhilarated. An armed revolt in the capital city, and he'd put it down. If he'd been celebrated for the burning of Vanai, he could hardly imagine the glory that would rain down on him now. He was half drunk with the idea of it.

"I also hear Lord Ternigan has ordered the disband," his father said.

"The men were all desperate to defend their houses and families. If Lord Ternigan hadn't, I likely would have."

His father shook his head and sighed. From the window, they could see the Kingspire at the city's edge, towering above Camnipol and therefore the world. Lights glittered in the windows like stars or the cookfires of an army. Lerer Palliako cracked his knuckles.

"Bad times," he said. "Very bad times."

"It won't go on," Geder said. "This ends it. There aren't any more of the gladiators, and if there are, they'll be hunted down. The city's saved."

"There's whoever suborned them," his father said. "Whoever arranged the attack. And the names I can put on that list are too powerful to die on a rope. I never spent time at court when I was a young man. I never made the connections and alliances. I wonder now if I should have. But it's too late, I suppose."

"Father," Geder said, but Lerer coughed and held up a hand.

"The disband's been called, son. You can go anywhere you'd like. Do anything. It might be wise if you were out of Camnipol for a time. Until this is all settled out."

Unease cut through Geder's euphoria for the first time since the fighting stopped. He looked around the night-soaked buildings and streets. Surely his father was jumping at shadows. There was nothing to be afraid of. They'd won. The coup had been stopped.

This coup. *This* time.

"I suppose there's no harm in going home now," Geder said. "I have an essay I'm thinking about that I think you'd find interesting. I'm tracking geographic references by time and comparing them with contemporary maps to—"

"Not Rivenhalm," Lerer said.

Geder's words trailed off.

"You should leave Antea," his father said. "You're too much a part of politics we don't fully understand. First Vanai, and now this? For the season at least, you should go where they can't reach you. Take a few servants. I'll give you the money. You can find someplace quiet and out of the way. By autumn, perhaps, we'll know better where things stand."

"All right," Geder said. He felt very small.

"And son? Don't tell anybody where you're going."

Dawson

Simeon paced before them all. The king's face was a mixture of hesitation and determination that Dawson had seen on hunting dogs unsure of how to get down a slope, aware that once they began there would be no stopping. Whatever counsel his old friend had taken in the long night, it hadn't been with him. On the other hand, he was certain it hadn't been with Curtin Issandrian either.

The audience chamber they sat in now wasn't the usual. There were no tapestries or soft velvet cushions, the walls were bare brick. There were no rugs or cushions to support the bent knees of Simeon's subjects. The king's guard stood along the walls with swords and armor that could not be mistaken for merely decorative. Prince Aster sat on a silver throne behind his father. It was clear the boy had been crying.

Curtin Issandrian knelt across the aisle from Dawson, his face drawn and pale. Alan Klin was at his side. Canl Daskellin and Feldin Maas had both managed to avoid attention. Odderd Faskellin was dead of an arrow to the throat, and his killer already feeding the gallows flies. Geder Palliako, by all rights the hero of the hour for holding the southern gate, had already left the city. Dawson was alone.

Behind and above the three of them, the viewing galleries were packed. Every man of nobility sat on low, uncomfortable stools behind the length of woven rope that pretended to separate them from the formal audience. The women stood in the upper gallery, including, somewhere amid the press, Clara. The highest gallery was customarily reserved for the most honored lowborn subjects of the king and ambassadors from foreign courts. Today, it stood empty.

The king stopped pacing, and Dawson didn't lift his head.

"This ends today," Simeon said, his voice ringing out to the farthest corners of the chamber. "It ends now."

"Yes, Your Majesty," Dawson said, his voice carefully humble. A moment later, Issandrian and Klin echoed him.

"Antea will not follow the dragon's path while I sit on the Severed Throne," Simeon went on. "These petty intrigues and political games will *not* bring confusion and strife to the empire at the heart of the world. I swear my life to it, and as your lord, I expect and demand the same of each of you."

This time when Dawson said, *Yes, Your Majesty,* Issandrian's cabal spoke with him.

"Noble blood has been spilled on the streets of Camnipol. Foreign swords have been drawn on our streets," the king went on. "It no longer matters whether the motives behind it were pure. There must be a reckoning."

In the corner of his vision, Dawson thought he saw Alan Klin grow even more ashen.

"Do you have any statements before I pass judgment?" the king asked. "Lord Kalliam?"

"No, Your Majesty," Dawson said. "I abide in loyalty to you and to the Severed Throne."

"Lord Issandrian?"

"Your Majesty," Curtin Issandrian said. His voice was shaking. "I wish to draw only two things to your attention. First, I beg that you consider that the violence yesterday may not have been the intention or plan of any man present. But if Your Majesty is adamant that punishment must be meted out, I ask that you spare my compatriot. The games for Prince Aster were my project, and mine alone. I would not have innocent men suffer simply because they know me."

It was a pretty speech, Dawson thought. But ill-advised.

"My Lord Issandrian forgets that this is not the first violence that your disagreements with House Kalliam have spawned. If you would like to offer yourself up to be made an example of, I will consider it, but don't think that anyone will find safety behind your skirts."

"Majesty," Issandrian said.

In the silence that followed, Dawson closed his eyes. His leg ached where his weight ground bone and skin into the stone floor, but he wouldn't shift. Fidgeting would be beneath the dignity of the occasion.

"Dawson Kalliam, Baron of Osterling Fells," King Simeon said. "I am doubling the duties owed by your holdings for the next five years. You are to absent yourself from the court and Camnipol for not less than half a year, nor are you permitted to raise soldiers or hire mercenaries without the express permission of the throne."

Dawson didn't speak, but deepened his bow. His heart was beating faster now, and he was careful not to show his anxiety.

"Curtin Issandrian, Baron of Corsa," the king went on. "I reclaim all lands previously held by you south of the river Andriann, and dismiss you from your positions as Warden of Estinport and Protector of the East. I am doubling the duties owed by your holdings for the next five years, and you are to absent yourself from the court and Camnipol for not less than half a year, nor are you permitted to raise soldiers or mercenaries without the express permission of the throne."

Dawson closed his eyes. He had to force himself not to shake his head. The disappointment sank in his belly like he'd swallowed a stone. The judgment against Klin would necessarily be equal or less. And indeed, King Simeon sent him into the same exile, increased his obligations, and stripped him of minor titles. Feldin Maas, wherever he was hiding, escaped without even that much.

When he called them to stand, Dawson looked up at his old friend. His king. Simeon's face was flushed, his breath fast, his face still set in a furious scowl. Behind him, Price Aster's chin was lifted as if in defiance. For a moment, Simeon looked into Dawson's eyes. If there was a flicker in the king's apparent outrage, it was the only acknowledgment Dawson would get. The king's guard stood aside, and Simeon strode out, Aster following, and the galleries burst into a thunderous clamor of voices. Dawson looked across the aisle to where Issandrian and Klin huddled in conversation of their own. Klin looked stunned. Issandrian seemed sad, and Dawson wondered whether it was for the same reason he was.

"Lord Kalliam, sir?"

The captain of the king's guard was a tall man, broad across the shoulders, with a pug face and apologetic, watery eyes. Dawson nodded to him.

"I'll have to ask you to be outside the gates by sundown, my lord," the man said.

"Is my household bound?"

"No, my lord. They can stay if they please."

Dawson scratched at his aching knee. The captain stood for a moment in silent respect, then moved to Issandrian's cabal to deliver, Dawson assumed, the same warning. He turned and walked out. The outer hall was black marble and worked silver. The midday sun glared through tall, unshuttered windows. Clara was there already, waiting for him with Vincen Coe behind her like her shadow. Jorey appeared at the hallway's end walking toward them quickly. His boots rang on the stone floor.

"I thought that went quite well," Clara said.

Dawson shook his head once.

"It was a travesty, dear," he said. "It was the end of the empire."

The carriage awaited them on the street, the team of horses snorting and impatient, as if the animals felt the changes in the city itself. A hundred others like it crowded the narrow streets, waiting for the assembled nobility of Antea to trickle out from the Kingspire. All of them made way for House Kalliam. A swift return to his home was the traditional last respect given an exile.

The rough cobbles rattled the carriage wheels. No one tried to speak. Dawson watched out the side window as the Kingspire vanished around a corner. They passed through the great square and into the streets of the city. Pigeons rose in great flocks, circled, and returned to earth. Then the Silver Bridge, and the great drop of the Division. Smoke rose from the forges and ovens.

A day ago, noble blood had spilled in these streets. Today, it looked the same as it always had, except to the few like himself who knew better.

At his private mansion, the servants brought out the steps as they always did. Dawson waved away the offered hands. The old Tralgu door servant greeted him solemnly. Within, the servants of the household were preparing the house. Tapestries were being taken down, furnishings draped against dust. His houndsman already had the dogs in their traveling cages; the animals whimpered their confusion and distress. Dawson knelt by them, pressing his hand against the bars to let the dogs smell him and lick at his fingers.

"I can stay on," Jorey said.

"Do that," Dawson said. "I won't have time to put everything to rights before I leave."

"Some of the servants have to stay, dear," Clara said. "The gardens won't survive without the gardeners to look after them. And the fountain in the rose court still needs repair."

In the cage, the dog looked up at Dawson. Its huge brown eyes were soft and frightened. He reached through a finger and stroked its muzzle. A jaw strong enough to sever a fox's spine with a bite leaned gently into him.

"Do what's best, Clara," he said. "I trust you."

"Lord Kalliam?"

Vincen Coe gave a huntsman's salute. Dawson brought himself to nod.

"Lord Daskellin's come, my lord," Coe said. "He's in the western sitting room."

Dawson drew himself to his feet. The dog whined as he walked away from it. There was nothing he could do. He had no more comfort to offer. In the sitting room, Canl Daskellin stood at the window, his hands clasped behind his back like a general overseeing the field of battle. His pipe smoke was sweet enough to cloy.

"Canl," Dawson said. "If there's anything you want of me, it had best be something quick. I don't have time for a hand at cards."

"I came to offer my sympathies and congratulations."

"Congratulations? For what?"

"We've won," Daskellin said, turning away from the window and striding into the room. "You played your hand brilliantly. You lured Issandrian into a thrust he couldn't follow through, then cut his conspiracy down. Now he's in disgrace. His inner circle is exiled. Stripped of lands and titles. There's no saying who will take Prince Aster as ward, but it won't be any of them. There won't be a farmer's council in our lifetimes. I'm sorry it came at a price to you, but I swear that your name will be praised as a hero while you're gone."

"What good's winning battles when the war's lost?" Dawson said. "Did you actually come here to celebrate, Daskellin? Or is this how you gloat?"

"Gloat?"

"Odderd Faskellin was a rabbit and a coward, but he had high blood. He *died* yesterday. In Camnipol, and by foreign hands. That hasn't happened in centuries. And how did Simeon reply? Increased taxes. Petty exile. A few minor lands and titles shuffled about."

Daskellin leaned against the wall, his arms crossed. Grey smoke spilled from his lips and nostrils.

"What would you have had him do?"

"Slaughter them all himself. Bind them, take sword in hand, and take their heads with his own hand," Dawson said.

"It sounds like you're missing Palliako already," Canl said dryly. Dawson ignored him.

"An armed company in the streets? It's treason against the throne, and to answer it with less than death is one step short of open surrender. He made himself a mask of fierceness, and all it did was point out how frightened he is. You should have seen it. Simeon strutting and raging and calling for an ending. It was like watching a shepherd boy trying to shout down wolves."

"Frightened? Of whom?"

"The power backing Issandrian. He's afraid of Asteril-hold," Dawson said, and then pointed an accusing finger at Daskellin himself. "And he's afraid of Northcoast."

The imitation of a smile bent Daskellin's lips and he took his pipe from his mouth.

"I am not Northcoast, old friend," he said. "And if consideration of the reactions of the other courts and kingdoms brought King Simeon to a place of greater mercy, that's wisdom on his part."

"That's permission for every landholder in the kingdom to spread his loyalty as widely as he can," Dawson said. "As long as answering to a duchess in Asterilhold or a bank in Northcoast makes us safer than standing by Antea, Simeon won't have a court of his own. He wants to keep the kingdom off the dragon's path so badly that he's walking down it."

Daskellin knelt by the fire grate, knocking the bowl of his pipe against the soot-stained brick. A rain of ashes fell from it.

"We disagree," he said, "but there can be room for a little differences between allies. You're right, of course, that even with Issandrian's cabal hobbled, the danger to the kingdom hasn't entirely passed. Whether you believe me or not, I'd thought to reassure you that I would keep working during your exile."

"By selling us to the Medean bank?"

"By seeing that King Simeon has the support and loyalty he needs."

"Spoken like a diplomat," Dawson said.

Daskellin bristled, and then as Dawson watched, gathered his temper in. He tucked his pipe into his belt and stood. The smell of old smoke still hung in the room.

"It's a dark day for you," Canl said, "so I'm going to take

that for what you said and ignore what you meant by it. Whatever you think, I didn't come to gloat."

The two stood for a moment, the silence between them stretching. Canl Daskellin made a rueful half-smile, then walked out, putting a hand on Dawson's shoulder as he passed. Dawson listened to the footsteps draw away, drowning in the noise of his household being uprooted. He stood a moment longer, looking out the window without seeing the early summer trees beyond it. Without hearing the birds or the servants or the whining of dogs.

He turned away.

Dawson left in a single open carriage. He sat on the forward seat, looking back toward the city, Clara sat at his side. Vincen Coe on the bench beside the teamster. Carts with his belongings would come more slowly, but they would come. The path to Osterling Fells would carry them over the dragon's roads for half a day, and the dragon's jade under their wheels was smoother than the streets of Camnipol.

"There isn't any chance of coming upon them, is there?" Clara asked.

"Who?"

"One of them," Clara said. "Lord Issandrian or Lord Klin. Or Lord Maas. It would by entirely too awkward, I think. I mean really, what does one say? I can't see inviting them to share a meal, but it would be rude not to. Do you think we should tell the driver to keep distance if he sees another carriage? If we can pretend not to have realized who they are, we can all keep to form. Unless it's Maas. Phelia must be in ruins over this."

Despite everything, Dawson smiled. He took his wife's hand in his. Her fingers were thicker than when he'd first known her. His own, rougher. Time had changed them both in some ways, and in some ways left them untouched. From the first day of their marriage, before even, he'd known she saw a different world than he did. It was part of what he loved in her.

"I'm sure we won't," he said. "Issandrian and Klin won't be taking this road, and there's no reason for Maas to leave court. Not now."

Clara sighed and leaned her head on his shoulder.

"My poor man," she said.

He craned his neck a bit, kissing the hair just above her ear, then put his arm around her shoulders.

"It won't be so bad," he said, trying to sound as if he believed it. "I missed the winter in Osterling Fells. This can make up for it. We'll summer at home, run back to Camnipol for the closing of court, and then turn back for the winter."

"Can we?" Clara said. "We could stay through the winter if you'd rather. We don't have to make two trips."

"No, love," he said. "It's not just to see the autumn pageant. I'll want to see how things have played in court before winter anyway. It only seems like I'm indulging you. I'm really a selfish boor."

Clara chuckled. A few miles later, she began snoring gently. Coe, noticing, handed down a wool blanket in silence, and Dawson covered Clara without rousing her. The sun sank behind them, reddening. Shadows spilled across the landscape, and the trilling, shrill birds of evening announced themselves.

Dawson was leaving the field of battle, but the fight would go on without him. Issandrian, Maas, Klin. They weren't killed, nor had they acted alone. Maas and his allies in court would do everything in their power to see their names raised again to respectability. Daskellin would doubtless take the helm of Dawson's own group, or at least that part of it that could stomach the bland little banker from Northcoast. Simeon would dance between the blades and tell himself there was a place at the middle where everything could balance, that peace could be kept if he only never made a stand.

A weak king might survive if he had a loyal court, but in casting Dawson out, Simeon had exiled the only man who had truly championed him. Nothing good could come now. The court was being led through an idiot's dance, made up of men with their own agendas. Shortsighted, self-serving idiots.

It would take a miracle to redeem King Simeon now. The best hope of the kingdom was that Prince Aster be sent as ward of a family that could show him what kingship was better than the king himself. Dawson indulged himself for a moment in the fantasy of taking the prince under his own wing and teaching him what Simeon could not. Clara murmured in her sleep, pulling the blanket more tightly around her.

The sun dipped down to the horizon, the walls and towers of Camnipol obscured by the power of its fire. For a moment, Dawson imagined the light came from a great conflagration. Not the sunset, but Camnipol burning. It had the weight of prophecy.

Shortsighted, self-serving idiots. A burning city.

Dawson wondered, almost idly, where Geder Palliako had gotten to.

Cithrin

Coffee houses had always had a place in the business of business. In the cold ports of Stollbourne and Rukkyupal, merchants and sea captains hunched over the tiled tables and warmed mittened hands with steaming cups as they watched the winter sun set at midday. Beside the wide, moonlit waters of the Miwaji, the nomadic Southling pods sipped cups of something hardly thinner than mud and declaimed poetry between haggling over fortunes in silver and spice. All through the world that the dragons had left behind, trade and coffee went together.

Or at least that was the way Magister Imaniel had told it. Cithrin had never been outside Vanai, and the bank there had been its own small building. Still, when the time came, Cithrin chose a small café with a private back room and rough wooden tables on the street. It was across the square from the Grand Market, so she would be near the rough-and-tumble of the city's trade without having to do her business in one of the shifting stalls. The owner of the café — Maestro Asanpur — was an ancient Cinnae man with one milky eye and a touch at making fresh coffee that bordered on magical. He had been very happy to accept a bit of rent that gave Cithrin rights to the privacy of his back room. If the day was cloudy, she could sit in the common room, sip her coffee, and listen to gossip. If the sun came out, she could take one of the white-painted street tables and watch the traffic through the Grand Market.

Ideally, Maestro Asanpur's café would become known as a center of banking and business in the city. The better it was known, the more people would come to it, and with them more news and gossip and speculation. Cithrin knew that her own presence was a good beginning, but she likely didn't have enough time to let things take their course. Sooner rather than later, the legitimate Medean bank would come to investigate their new branch, and when that happened, she wanted it to be wildly prosperous.

Which, in the short term, meant a little harmless dishonesty.

Cithrin saw the reaction to Cary's arrival before she saw the woman herself. Gazes shifted through the square like wind passing over a field of grass, then away, and then, more covertly, back again. Cithrin drank her coffee and pretended not to notice as the mysterious woman walked across the square toward the great kiosks where the queensmen who administered the Grand Market stood. Cary had chosen the longest approach possible, and it gave Cithrin time to admire the costume. The cut was Elassean, but the silk wrapping and the beaded veil spoke of Lyoneia. The jewels that adorned her came from Cithrin's own stock, and would have sold for enough to buy the café twice over. Taken together, the design spoke of all the trade of the Inner Sea with an authenticity that came from Master Kit's travels there. It wasn't a look often seen in Birancour, and the combination of exoticism and wealth drew attention better than a song. Hornet and Smit walked behind her in boiled leather with the swagger they'd learned on the caravan, indistinguishable from real fighters.

Cary reached the kiosk and spoke with one of the

queensmen. They were much too far to hear, but the queens-man's posture was clear enough. He gestured across the square toward Cithrin and the café. Cary bowed her thanks and turned, taking the walk slowly. When she came close enough to speak with, Cithrin rose.

"Enough?" Cary asked.

"Perfect," Cithrin said. "Come this way."

She led the actors through the common room, the wooden floors creaking under their weight. The interior of the café was a series of small rooms set off by low archways. The windows had carved wooden shutters that scented the breeze with cedar. A young Kurtadam girl sat in the back gently playing a bottle harp, the soft notes murmuring through the air. In one of the rooms, an old Firstblood man talking ani-matedly with a wide-eyed Southling stopped to stare at Cary and her guards. Cithrin caught Maestro Asanpur's eye and held up two fingers. The old man nodded and set to grind-ing the beans for two small cups. Cithrin meant for anyone paying attention to know that the exotically dressed woman was someone the Medean bank honored. They moved on to the privacy of her hired room.

"So this is all?" Smit said after the door closed behind them, groaning on its leather hinge. "I thought there'd be more to it."

Cithrin sat at the small table. There was enough room for the others, but rather than sit, Hornet went to the thin win-dow, peering out through the blue-and-gold glass to the alley beyond. As Cary started plucking off the borrowed jewelry, Cithrin pulled the iron lockbox out from under her chair, sliding it on a small red carpet to keep from scarring the floor.

"I don't need very much here," Cithrin said. "A record

book, a little spare coin. It's not as if I'll be handing out large sums every day."

"Wasn't that the point, though?" Cary said, handing across a bracelet studded with emeralds and garnets. "To get rid of all that stuff?"

"Not by handing it out like candy," Cithrin said. "There are only so many good investments to make in a city. It takes effort finding which ones are worth having. This is where I talk with people. Negotiate agreements, sign contracts. It's all arranged here, but I don't want to have all the guards standing around intimidating people."

"Why not?" Hornet said. "I would."

"Better to put them at ease, I expect," Cary said, and a soft knock came at the door. Smit opened it to Maestro Asanpur carrying a tray with two small bone-colored cups. Cithrin unlocked the iron box. As Maestro Asanpur presented the coffee to Cary, Cithrin folded the jewelry into soft cloth and put it into the box beside the red leather record book and her purse of small coin. The lock was crude but solid, the key reassuringly heavy on its leather necklace. Cithrin tucked the key away. Cary sipped the coffee and made a small, appreciative sound.

"Another advantage of the site," Cithrin said.

"We can't stay," Hornet said. "Master Kit's bent on having the Tragedy of Four Winds ready to put on before the trade ships from Narinisle come."

"Are you going to try to sponsor one?" Cary asked.

"A ship or a tragedy?" Cithrin asked dryly.

"Either one."

"Neither," she said.

In truth, the trade ships from Narinisle had been very much on Cithrin's mind.

The great wealth in the world lay in the patterns of commerce. The Keshet and Pût might have olive trees and wine enough for every city in the world, but no mines there produced gold and the iron was in rough, roadless terrain and difficult to reach. Lyoneia grew fabulous woods and spices, but struggled to grow enough grain to feed its people. Far Syramys with its silks and dyes, magic and tobacco, promised the rarest goods in the world, but the blue-water trade to reach them was so uncertain that more fortunes were lost than made in going there. Everywhere, there was imbalance, and the surest path to profit was to be between something valuable and someone who valued it.

On land, that meant control of the dragon's roads. No merely human assembly of stone and mortar could match the permanence of dragon's jade. All the great cities grew where they did because of the arrangements of paths made when humanity was a single race and the masters of the world flew on great scaled wings. Dragons themselves had rarely if ever lowered themselves to travel the roads. They were the servants' stairs of the fallen empire, and they determined the flow of money for all land trade.

The trackless sea, however, could be remade.

Each autumn, ships in the south loaded themselves with wheat and oil, wine and pepper and sugar, and, paid with gold adventurous or desperate enough, made the trek to the north. Northcoast, Hallskar, Asterilhold, and even the northern coast of Antea would buy the goods, often for less than the same items that had traveled overland. The trade ships might take on some cargo in those ports—salt cod from Hallskar, iron and steel from Asterilhold and Northcoast—but most would take their money and hurry to the open ports of Narinisle to wait for the blue-water trade from Far Syramys. This was the great gamble.

Accidents of wind and current made the island nation of Narinisle the easiest end port for ships from Far Syramys, and if a trade ship could exchange its cargo and money for a load freshly arrived from those distant lands, an investor might triple her money. If not, she risked seeing her trade ship return from Narinisle with only what could be bought from the local markets, making a much smaller profit, assuming prices went with her. Or the ship could be lost to pirates, or it might sink and everything either lost entirely or ransomed back at exorbitant rates and glacial slowness from the Drowned.

And when the ships returned to their southern ports and the fortunes of those who had sponsored them rose or fell, the sponsorship of this fleet of gold and spice that sailed together without alliance and answered to no single flag reshuffled. A house that had placed its wager on a single ship and did well might make enough to hire half a dozen the next year. Someone whose ship had been lost would scramble to find ways to survive in their new, lessened circumstances. If they had been wise and insured their investment, they might gain back enough to try again by appealing to someone like Cithrin.

The ships would already have left Narinisle. Soon, the seven that had set out the year before from Porte Oliva would return, and not long after that, someone would come to her and ask that the bank insure them to sponsor a ship for the next year's work. Without knowing which captains were best, without knowing which families were best positioned to buy a good outgoing cargo, she would be left with little better than instinct. If she took all those who came to ask, she'd be sure to take too many bad risks. If she took no one, there would be no chance for her bank to prosper and nothing to show the holding company when they came. This was the species of risk that her life was built on now.

Betting on pit dogs seemed more certain.

"A few insurance contracts, maybe," Cithrin said, as much to herself as to Cary and the others. "Part sponsorship in a few years, if things go well."

"Insurance. Sponsorship. What's the difference?" Smit asked.

Cithrin shook her head. It was like he'd asked the difference between an apple and a fish; she didn't know where to start.

"Cithrin forgets that we didn't all grow up in a counting house," Cary said and drank down the last of her coffee. "But we should go."

"Let me know when the new play's ready," Cithrin said. "I'd like to watch it."

"See?" Smit said. "I told you we'd have a patron."

They left through the alley, transformed from mysterious woman of business and her guards back to seafront players. Cithrin watched them go through her thin window, the glass distorting them as they went. A patron. It was true she wouldn't be able to go and lead the crowd with Cary and Mikel anymore. She probably wouldn't be able to go out to a taproom with Sandr. Cithrin bel Sarcour, head of the Medean bank of Porte Oliva, drinking with a common actor? It would be terrible for the bank's reputation and her own.

The loneliness that came with the thought had little to do with Sandr.

When, an hour later, Captain Wester arrived, Cithrin was out on the street, sitting at the same table where Cary had found her. He nodded his greeting and sat across from her. The sunlight brought out the grey in his hair, but it also brightened his eyes. He handed a sheet of parchment across to her. She looked over the words and figures, nodding to herself as she did. The receipt looked fine.

"How did it go?" she asked.

"No problems," he said. "The tobacco's at the seller's stall. He argued over a few of the leaves, but I told him he either took all of it or none."

"He shouldn't have done that," Cithrin said. "He should be negotiating with me."

"I may have mentioned something like that. He accepted the delivery. The pepper and cardamom goes out tomorrow. Yardem and a couple of the new men will take that."

"A start," Cithrin said.

"Any word from Carse?" Marcus asked. The question sounded almost casual.

"I've sent a dispatch," Cithrin said. "I used Magister Imaniel's old cipher, and a slow courier, but I expect they'll have it by now."

"And you said what?"

"That the branch had placed its letters of foundation and was beginning trade as Magister Imaniel and I had planned," Cithrin said.

"Not telling them the truth of it, then."

"Letters go astray. Couriers take extra payment to unsew and copy them. I don't expect anyone to intercept it, but if they do, it will look exactly like what it's supposed to be."

Marcus nodded slowly, squinting up into the sun.

"Any reason you picked a *slow* courier?"

"I want time to put things in order before they come," she said.

"I see. There's something we should—"

A deeper shadow than the cloud's fell over the table. Lost in her conversation, she hadn't seen the man approach, and so now he seemed to have sprouted out of the pavement. Taller than Captain Wester, but not so tall as Yardem Hane, he wore a wool tunic and leggings, a blue-dyed cloak several layers thick against the spring cold, and a bronze chain of office. For the most part his features were Firstblood, but slight and fair enough that he might have had a grandfather among the Cinnae.

"Forgive me," he said, his voice scrupulously polite. "Am I addressing Cithrin bel Sarcour?"

"You are," Cithrin said.

"Governor Siden sent me," the man said.

Fear punched the breath out of her. They'd discovered the forgery. They were sending the guard. She cleared her throat and smiled.

"Is there a problem?" she asked.

"Not at all," the messenger said, and produced a small letter, the smooth paper neatly folded and the sides sewn and sealed. "But he did suggest I wait in the event that you wished to reply."

Cithrin held the paper, uncertain where to look — it, the man, the captain. After what seemed entirely too long, she shook herself.

"If you'll let Maestro Asanpur know you've come on my business, he'll see you in comfort."

"You are very kind, Magistra."

Cithrin waited until the man disappeared into the café before she pulled the thread. It cut through the paper with a rattle. Trembling a little, she pressed the opened page onto the table. The script was beautifully shaped, the work of a professional scribe. *To Magistra Cithrin bel Sarcour, voice and agent of the Medean bank in Porte Oliva, I, Idderrigo Bellind Siden, Prime Governor of Porte Oliva by special commission of Her Royal Highness* and on and on and on. Her fingertips slid down the page. *I request your private attention as a voice of trade and a citizen of Porte Oliva concerning certain matters central to the health and vigor of the city* and on and on and on. And then, near the bottom of the first page, she stopped.

The solicitation and arrangement of joint civic security as concerns the safe conduct of maritime trade in the coming year...

"Good God," she said.

"What is it?" Captain Wester said. His voice was low and steady. He sounded ready for her to say they had to kill the messenger and flee the city. Cithrin swallowed to loosen her throat.

"If I am reading this correctly," she said, "the governor is asking us to propose a joint venture with the city to escort the trade ships from Narinisle."

"Ah," Wester said. And then, "You know I don't understand what you just said, yes?"

"He's putting together a fleet. Fighting ships to see the traders safely up and back. And he's looking for someone with the purse to fund it."

"Meaning us?"

"No," she said, her mind running through the implications with an eerie and cool precision. "He'll want several parties to make proposals, but he's inviting us into the fight. He's asking the Medean bank to make a proposal to underwrite a single-city fleet."

The captain grunted as if he understood. Cithrin was already miles ahead of him and running fast. If Porte Oliva could make itself a more attractive port than the Free Cities, more ships would contract from here. Insurance rates would drop, as the trade seemed less risky. That would hurt anyone who had been trading on insurance alone. And Maccia would hate it, and Cabral would take it poorly if the escort went that far. She wondered what the chances were of direct retaliation against the escort ships.

"Is that the kind of thing we'd be likely to do?" Wester asked from some other part of the world.

"If we took the commission and did the thing well, we'd have connections all through the south and a thumb on the Inner Sea. We'd have something to give the holding company more valuable than a cartload of gold," Cithrin said. "They *couldn't* object to what we've done."

"So it is something we might take on, then."

The knot in Cithrin's belly was still there, but something about it changed. She found herself smiling. Grinning.

"Win this," she said, holding up the pages, "and we win *everything.*"

The meeting at the governor's palace pretended to be nothing. A half dozen men and women sat in a garden courtyard. Queensmen poured out scented water and spiced wine. The governor was a small man, thick-bellied and balding. He treated all his guests with grace and kindness, and as such was practically useless as a guide to who among the assemblage were important. She had hoped to follow his cues, paying attention to the people with whom he spent the most time. Instead, she was left to wonder.

There was an older Kurtadam man, his pelt graying across the face, throat, and back, who represented a chartered collaboration of the shipwrights' guild and two local merchant houses. A Cinnae man with slightly too much rouge on his cheeks turned out to be the owner of a mercenary company large enough to rent itself to kings. Sitting alone under the spreading fronds of a palm tree, a Tralgu woman drank water and ate shrimp, listening to everything said with a concentration that left Cithrin unnerved. All of them had agendas and histories, interests and weaknesses. Magister Imaniel would have been able to glance across the room and draw conclusions. Or at least educated guesses. Cithrin, on the other hand, was still a year too young to claim her inheritance. The wine was excellent. The conversation friendly and convivial. She felt like she was swimming in a warm ocean, waiting for something to come up from the depths, take her by the leg, and draw her down to the cold.

It didn't help untie her knots that everyone seemed to view her with curiosity. The voice and agent of the Medean bank, newly arrived in the city, and throwing off everyone's plans. None of them, Cithrin told herself, had expected her to be a player in this game. She was badly behind in understanding the politics at play in the courtyard with its brightly colored finches and sun-warmed flagstones, but she had mysteries of her own. The longer she remained a cipher to them, the more she could make sense of the game. She handed her empty glass to one of the queensmen and took another. Wine kept the fear at bay.

"Magistra bel Sarcour," the governor said, appearing at her elbow. "You were in Vanai, yes? Before the Antean aggression."

"Just before," Cithrin said.

"Lucky you got out," the Tralgu woman said. Her voice was as low as Yardem Hane's, but it didn't have the same warmth.

"I am," Cithrin said, keeping her tone neutral and polite.

"What do you make of the fate of the city?" the governor asked. Cithrin had anticipated the question, and she had her answer at the ready.

"Antea has a long history of military interference in the Free Cities," Cithrin said. "Magister Imaniel and I were expecting the occupation a season earlier than it came. That the Anteans didn't intend to hold the city was only clear in the last few weeks before they arrived."

"You think they always intended to destroy Vanai?" a man behind the governor said. He had the features of a Firstblood, but golden skin with a roughness to it that reminded Cithrin of a Jasuru. His eyes were a shocking green. His name was Qahuar Em, and he spoke for a group part trading association and part nomadic tribe from the north reaches of Lyoneia. From his appearance, she guessed he was half Jasuru, though Cithrin hadn't known that was possible.

"We had a strong suspicion," she said to him.

"But why would the Severed Throne do such a thing?" the governor asked.

"Because they're a bloodthirsty bunch of unmodified northern savages," the Tralgu woman said. "Barely better than monkeys."

"The story I'd heard was that the burning was unexpected, even by King Simeon," the Cinnae mercenary said. "The local commander took the action as some sort of political theater piece."

"Doesn't argue against my monkeys-with-swords thesis," the Tralgu woman said, and the governor chuckled.

"I'm not surprised that there's more than one interpretation," Cithrin said. "Still, you'll forgive me if I'm pleased that I followed the information that we had."

"I heard that Komme Medean was moving his interests to the north, and Antea in particular," the graying Kurtadam said. "Damned odd seeing him take an aggressive position in the south."

Cithrin felt a flutter of concern. If the bank were involving itself in the northern countries—Antea, Asterilhold, Northcoast, Hallskar, and Sarakal—she might well have stepped on toes by founding a branch at the far end of the continent.

It wasn't something she was ready to address, so the conversation had to be moved away from the issue and quickly. She smiled the way she imagined Magister Imaniel might have.

"Is there really such a thing as purely northern interests?" she asked. "Narinisle is in the north, and it seems to concern all of us."

The air in the courtyard seemed to still. She'd pulled the hidden meaning of all their banter and laid it on the table. She wondered whether she'd just been rude, so she smiled and sipped her wine, acting as if it had been intentional. Qahuar the half-Jasuru smiled at her, nodding as if she'd won a point in a game.

"Narinisle may be in the north," the graying Kurtadam said, "but the problems are all in the south, aren't they? King Sephan and his unofficial pirate fleet."

"I agree," the Cinnae mercenary captain said. "The only way that trade can be made safe is if Cabral agrees that it is. And that can't be done on the water alone."

The Tralgu woman grunted and put down the shrimp that she'd been eating.

"You aren't going to go on about putting a land force together to protect ships again, are you?" she said. "Porte Oliva starts a land war with Cabral, and the queen'll burn us down as an apology to King Sephan faster than the Anteans lit Vanai. We're a city, not a kingdom."

"Done right, you don't have to use it," the Cinnae said, bristling. "And it isn't an invasion force. But the escort that protects trade ships needs to be able to put swords onto land. The pirate problem can't be solved if they can run into a cove someplace and declare themselves safe."

Cithrin sat on a high stool, cocked her head, and listened as the façade of politeness began to crack. Like an artist putting a mosaic together one chip at time, she began to make out the shape of divisions and arguments in the group around her.

The chartered collaboration between the shipwrights and the merchant houses was pressing for a limited escort restricted in its range to within a few days' sail from Porte Oliva. Protect the neighborhood, their argument went, and the trade ships will come of their own accord. It would cost less, and so the offsetting tariffs could be small. Listening to the Cinnae man and Tralgu woman press, Cithrin was fairly certain the merchant houses in question traded in insurance. The limited escort still left a great territory of water unsafe, the chance of piracy and loss high, and so the return on insurance wouldn't go down.

The Cinnae man, on the other hand, was a militarist, because what he brought to the table was a military force. If the others could be made to agree that only a massive force of arms—and especially the sword-and-bows of a mercenary company—would ensure that piracy end, he would be in the best position to provide it. Naturally, none of the others agreed.

The Tralgu woman's argument centered on a treaty between Birancour and Herez that Cithrin didn't recognize. She would need to find a copy to understand how it applied, but simply knowing what she didn't know felt like a little victory.

As the wrangle went on, her smiles felt less and less forced. Her mind danced through each phrase her enemies used, drew connections, set up speculations that she would research once the evening was done. The governor kindly, gently kept the tone from escalating to blows, but stopped short of making peace. This was what he'd brought them here for. This was how he worked. Cithrin held that information as well.

After her third glass of wine, she felt certain enough to put her own argument out.

"Forgive me," she said, "but it seems that we've all become somewhat fixed on piracy as the only problem. But there are other things that can happen to a trade ship. If I understand correctly, three ships were lost in a storm five years ago."

"No," the Tralgu woman snapped.

"Those sank off Northcoast," the Kurtadam said. "They never got as far as Narinisle."

"And yet the investment in them was just as lost," Cithrin said. "Is the question we're considering how to protect trade? Or is it only how to make pirates a lesser risk than storms? It seems to me that an escort ship should be able to answer any number of crises."

"You can't have an escort that follows the ships every where and answers every problem," the Cinnae man said.

"The initial cost would be high," Cithrin said, as if that were the objection he'd raised. "It would require a commitment from Porte Oliva long enough to ensure a reasonable expectation of return. And likely some understanding with ports in the north."

She said it all as if it were idle speculation; a chat among friends. They all knew what she'd just said.

The Medean bank would protect trade ships from Porte Oliva as far as they wished to go and all the way home again. She had enough money that she could pour gold into the project and not see a return for years. And the bank, with its holding company in Carse, had connections throughout the northern countries. If it was a grander vision than she'd meant to bring to the table, that was fine. The others could compare how many soldiers they had, how cheaply they could do something small, how treaties and trade agreements could be brought to bear. Cithrin could say, *I am the biggest dog in this pit. I can do what you cannot.*

She liked the feel of it.

The courtyard was silent for a moment, then as the Kurtadam drew in an angry breath, the half-Jasuru with the green eyes spoke.

"She's right," he said.

Qahuar Em was sitting at the governor's side. In the light that spilled down from the saturated blue sky, his skin had taken an almost bronze tone, like a statue brought to life. When he smiled, she saw that his teeth, white as a Firstblood's, had the hint of Jasuru points to them.

"You're joking," the Kurtadam said, sounding deflated.

"You could do it by halves," he said, his gaze shifting to the Kurtadam for a moment before shifting back to Cithrin. "But what would stop Daun from doing the same? Or Upurt Marion? Newport or Maccia? You could make Porte Oliva a little bit safer, and be more popular as a place to trade for a few years while other cities followed your example. Or you could move decisively, dominate trade in the region, and capture the trade route for a generation. It just depends what your goals are, I suppose."

Cithrin found herself smiling at him even as it occurred to her that he'd spoken even less than she had. She'd need to watch him, she thought. And as if he'd read her mind, he grinned.

The conversation went on for another hour, but the wind had shifted. The Kurtadam restricted himself to petulant asides, the mercenary reframed the military aspect as part of a wider strategy, and the Tralgu lapsed back into silence. The undercurrent of anger and suspicion was palpable, and the governor seemed quite pleased with the entire proceeding. When Cithrin left, her beaded shawl wrapped around her shoulders, it was hard to remember to step like a woman twice her age. She wanted to walk from the ankle.

She waited on the steps looking out across the square toward the great marble temple, pretending a piety she didn't feel. The sun sank lower in the west, shining into the temple's face and making the stone glow. The moon, already risen, hung in the cloudless indigo of the sky, a half circle of white and a half of darkness. Between the beauty of city and heaven and the perhaps slightly too much wine she'd drunk, she nearly missed her quarry when he walked by.

"Excuse me," she said.

The half-Jasuru turned, looking back over his shoulder as if he didn't know her.

"You're called Qahuar?" she said.

He corrected her pronunciation gently. Standing on the step below hers, their heads were even.

"I wanted to thank you for supporting me in there," she said.

He grinned. His face was broader than it had seemed in the courtyard. His skin less rough, his eyes softer. It struck her that he was roughly the age she pretended to be.

"I was going to say the same of you," he said. "Between us, I think we'll shake loose the smaller players. I admit, I hadn't been expecting to compete against the Medean bank."

"I hadn't expected to be competing at all," she said. "Still, it's flattering of the governor to think of me."

"He's using you to get better terms from me," Qahuar said. And then, seeing her reaction, "I don't mind. If it goes poorly, he'll be using me to get better terms from you. One doesn't reach his position by being sentimental."

"Still," Cithrin said.

"Still," Qahuar said, as if agreeing.

They stood silently for a moment. His expression shifted, as if seeing her for the first time. As if she confused him. No. Not confused. Intrigued. The angle of his smile changed, and Cithrin felt a warmth in her own expression. She found herself particularly pleased that the man was her rival.

"You've made the game more interesting, Magistra. I hope to see you again soon."

"I think you should," Cithrin said.

Geder

In the rolling flint hills where Sarakal gave way in no
clearly marked fashion to the Keshet, the term *prince* had
a different meaning than Geder was accustomed to. A man
might call himself a prince if he controlled a certain amount
of land, or commanded a force of soldiers, or had been son
or nephew to a prince. Even race had little impact. The
princes of the Keshet might be Yemmu or Tralgu or Jasuru,
and there was apparently no formal barrier to other races,
though in practice no others were.

Firstblood were especially absent from the wide, arid
plains, and Geder found that his small group — himself, his
squire, and four men of his father's service — quickly became
an object of curiosity in the towns and villages east of Sarakal. The Firstblood prince, they called him, and when Geder
tried to correct them, confusion followed. Translating his
rank into the terms of the Keshet was a pointless and probably impossible task, and so when the traveling court of
Prince Kupe rol Behur extended Geder its hospitality, he
found it easiest to pretend he was more or less an equal to
the gold-scaled Jasuru lord.

"I don't understand, Prince Geder. You've left your land
and your people searching for something, but you don't
know what or where it is. You have no claim to it, nor any

idea whether claim could be made. What profit do you hope to make?"

"Well, it isn't that kind of project," Geder said, reaching for another of the small, dark sausages from their communal plate.

When Geder had seen the dust plume from the traveling court rising above the horizon like smoke from a great fire, he'd expected it to be like being on campaign. He'd imagined the tents to be something like the kind he'd slept in to and from Vanai, that he slept in now in his quiet exile. He had misunderstood. He hadn't ridden into a camp—not even a grand and luxurious one. It was a township of wood-framed buildings with a temple dedicated to a twinned god Geder hadn't heard of and a square for the prince's feast. Weeds and scrub in the streets showed that it had not been there the day before. Geder assumed it wouldn't be there tomorrow. Like something from a legend, it was a city that existed for a single night, and then vanished with the dew. Torches smoked and fluttered in the breeze. The stars glowed down. The summer heat rose from the ground, radiating up into the sky.

Geder popped the sausage into his mouth. It tasted salty and rich, with an almost occult aftertaste of sugar and smoke. He'd never eaten anything like it before, and if it had been made of lizard eyes and bird feet, he'd have eaten them anyway. They tasted that good. Of the sixteen communal plates that the slaves carried around the table, this was his favorite. Although the green leaves with red spots and oil was a close second.

"I'm not looking," he said through his full mouth, "for something that will get me gold."

"Honor, then."

Geder smiled ruefully.

"Speculative essay isn't something that gives a man great honor. At least not among my people. No, I'm going because I've heard about a thing that existed a long time ago, and I wanted to see what I could find out about it. Write down what I've learned and what I suspect, so that someday someone can read it and add what they know."

And, he thought, *stay away from the turmoil in Camnipol and find a corner at the farthest edge of the world where the trouble's least likely to reach me.*

"And then?"

Geder shrugged.

"That's all," he said. "What more would there be?"

The Jasuru prince frowned, drank from a mug either cast in the shape of a massive skull or else made from one, and then grinned, pointing a long worked-silver talon at him.

"You're a holy man," the prince said.

"No. God no. Not me."

"A cunning man, then. A philosopher."

Geder was about to protest this too, but then caught himself.

"Maybe a philosopher," he said.

"A man, his mount, and the horizon. I should have seen it. This project is a spiritual matter."

The prince lifted his massive arm, barked something that sounded like an order. The hundred men and women at the long tables—knights or only sword-and-bows, Geder couldn't be sure—raised a shout, laughing and sneering and pushing one another. A few long moments later, a pair of guards appeared at the edge of the square, each with an iron chain in his hand. The chains led back into the darkness, slack in a way that left Geder thinking they were mostly ceremonial.

The woman who came into the light at the end of the

chains looked ancient. The broadness of her forehead and the swirling black designs on her skin marked her as a Haavirkin even before she lifted her long, three-fingered hand in salute. Geder had met Haavirkin before when the elected king of Hallskar sent ambassadors to court, but he'd never seen one as old or with the same sense of utter dignity.

The guards walked before the woman as she approached the prince. Geder couldn't tell from the noise of the crowd whether they were mocking her or celebrating her presence. Her eyes swept over Geder, sizing him up.

"This is my seer," the prince said to him. And then to the woman, "This man is our guest. His travels the Keshet on a spiritual matter."

"He does," the woman agreed.

The prince grinned like she'd given him a present. He put his hand on Geder's arm in an oddly intimate gesture.

"She is yours for tonight," the prince said. Geder frowned. He hoped that this wasn't a question of having a bed servant, though he had heard stories about that kind of thing from old stories about the Keshet. He coughed and tried to think of a way clear, but the seer only lifted her hand. Another servant hurried forward with a wooden stool, and the Haavirkin sat on it, staring at Geder's face.

"Hello," Geder said to her, his voice uncertain.

"I know you," she said, then turned and spat on the ground. "When I was a girl, I had a dream about you."

"Um," Geder said. "Really?"

"She is very good," the prince said. "Very *wise*."

"My uncle had an illness," the seer said, "only it had no signs. No fever, no weakness, nothing, so there was nothing we knew to cure."

"But then how can you say he was sick?"

"It was a dream," the seer said patiently. "He ate bitter

herbs to cure himself, and afterward the water he drank tasted sweet. But there wasn't anything in it but water. The sweet was in him, and it wasn't sweet really. Only that it wasn't bitter. It didn't have the power to cure anything."

The seer took his hand, her long fingers exploring the joints of his fingers as if she were searching for something. She lifted his palm to her nose and sniffed at it. Geder's skin crawled, and he tried to pull away.

"You will see her thrice," she said, "and you will be different people each time. And each time, she will give you what you want. You have already seen her once."

The seer lifted her eyebrows, as if to say, *Do you understand?*

That was supposed to be about me? Geder thought.

"Thank you," Geder said, and she nodded as much to herself as to anyone else. The dancing torchlight made the black marks on her skin seem to shift with a motion of their own.

"That's all?" the Jasuru prince said.

"That is all that I have for him," the seer said mildly. She rose to her feet, the chains leading from her neck jingling. "You and I will speak, but later."

She made her obeisance, turned, and walked back out through the low scrub and dust, the wooden tables of Keshet warriors and shadows. The chain bearers followed her as if she were leading them. The silence was broken only by the sound of the chain and the mutter of fire from the torches. Geder thought he saw surprise, even shock, on the faces of the knights, but he didn't understand it. Something had just happened, but he couldn't say what.

The prince scratched at the scales along his jaw and neck like a Firstblood stroking a beard. He grinned, sharp dark teeth like a wall.

"Eat! Sing!" he called, and the knights' voices and clamor rose again as they had before. Geder took another sausage and wondered what he'd just missed.

The feast left Geder's stomach unsettled. He lay in his tent listening to the soft summer wind moving through the desert, and failing to will himself to sleep. He heard his squire's soft snores, smelled the fine Keshet dust that seemed to get into everything, and tasted the spiced meats from the feast, the pleasure of them long since gone. Moonlight pressed in at the edges of the tent, turning the darkness silver. He felt restless and torpid at the same time.

The sweet was in him, and it wasn't sweet really. Only that it wasn't bitter. It didn't have the power to cure anything.

Of all the seer's ramblings, those were the words that gnawed at him, as troubling as the spices. It seemed to him now that the Haavirkin woman had been talking about Vanai and Camnipol. If he thought about it, he could still feel the scar healing in his leg where the bolt had struck him. In exactly the same way, the smallest shift of his attention could remind him of the black knot in his chest that had bent him down on the long ride back from Vanai. He couldn't quite recall the shape of his dead mother's face, but the silhouette of the woman against the flames towering above Vanai was as clear to him as the tent around him now. Clearer.

The celebrations and revels that had greeted him in Camnipol should have washed that away, and for a time they had. But not forever. It had been sweet—he'd thought at the time that it was—but maybe it hadn't been. Certainly it had felt glorious when it was going on. He'd risen in the court. He'd saved the city from the mercenary insurrection. And yet here he was, in exile again, fleeing from political games he didn't understand. And as unpleasant as the unease in his belly might be, it was still better than the nightmares of fire.

In truth, what had happened in Vanai wasn't his fault. He had been used. The lost sleep, the constant dread, even the suspicion that during all his revels and celebrations Alan Klin and his friends had been laughing down their sleeves at him. They were the scars he bore.

He turned the thought over in his mind. The court games that soaked the Kingspire and Camnipol weren't anything he'd ever chosen to put himself into. The relief he'd felt coming back from Vanai to adulation and approval were hollow to him now, and at the same time, he wanted it back. It had let him forget the voice of the flames for a little while. But like the Haavirkin seer's dreamed water, the sweetness hadn't been sweet, just relief from the bitterness. And it hadn't cured anything.

If he only understood what had happened, if he could see through the games and the players, he'd know who was really to blame. And who his own friends really were.

He shifted to his side, pulling his blankets with him. They smelled of dust and sweat. The night was too warm to justify them, but he found the cloth comforting. He sighed and his belly gumbled. The Haavirkin seer had been right in her way. Maybe she was as wise at the prince said. Geder considered finding her in the morning, asking her more questions. Even if it were all superstition and nonsense, it would give him something to think about in the long, isolated nights in the desert.

He didn't notice that he was falling asleep until he woke. Sunlight glowed the fresh yellow of wildflowers, and the brief dew made the world smell cooler than it was. He pulled on his hose and a tunic. It was rougher wear than he'd had last night, but he wasn't going to a princely feast. And after all, this was the Keshet. Standards were likely different. The wooden buildings still stood, and Geder marched out toward them, his gaze shifting, looking for the sentries. He didn't see them.

He didn't see anyone.

When he reached the structures, the great open square where he'd dined less than a day before, they were deserted. When he called out, no one answered. It would have been like a children's song where they'd all been ghosts, except he could follow the footprints and smell the horse droppings and see the not-quite-dead coals still lurking white and red in the firepit. The horses were gone, the men and women, but the wagons remained. The heavy winches that the prince's servants used to construct their sudden towns were still where they had been. He even found the long chains that the seer had worn, wrapped around a bronze spool and dropped in the dust.

He went back to his own camp, where his squire was just putting down a meal of stewed oats and watered cider. Geder sat at his field table, looking at the tin bowl, then up at the abandoned camp.

"They left in the middle of the night," Geder said. "Took what they could carry without making noise and slipped away in the darkness."

"Perhaps the prince was robbed and murdered by his men," his squire said. "Things like that happen in the Keshet."

"Lucky we weren't caught up in it," Geder said. His oats were honey-sweet. His cider had a bite to it, despite the water. His squire stood quietly by while Geder ate and the other servants struck camp. The sun was hardly two handspans above the horizon when Geder finished. He wanted to be away, back on his own path, and the eerily silent camp left well behind.

He did wonder, though, what else the Haavirkin had seen, and what she had told her prince after the foreign guest had left.

Marcus

I would prefer to give it to Magistra bel Sarcour directly," the man said. "No disrespect, sir, but my contracts don't have your thumb on them."

He was a smallish man, the top of his head coming no higher than Marcus's shoulder, and his clothes smelled like his shop: sandalwood, pepper, cumin, and fennel. His face was narrow as a fox, and his smile looked practiced. The lower rooms of the Medean bank of Porte Oliva had Marcus, Yardem, Ahariel the stout Kurtadam, and the ever-present Roach. The weight of their blades alone was likely as much as the spicer, and yet the man's disdain for them radiated like heat from a fire.

"But since she isn't here," Marcus said, "I'm what you've got to work with."

The spicer's eyebrows rose and his tiny little lips pressed thin. Yardem coughed, and Marcus felt a stab of chagrin. The Tralgu was right.

"However," Marcus went on, "if you'll accept our hospitality for a few minutes, sir, I'll do my best to find her."

"That's better," the man said. "Perhaps a cup of tea while I wait?"

I could kill you with my hands, Marcus thought, and it was enough to evoke the smile that etiquette called for.

"Roach?" Marcus said. "If you could see our guest is comfortable?"

"Yes, Captain," the little Timzinae said, jumping up. "If you'll come this way, sir?"

Marcus stepped out the door and onto the street, Yardem following him as close as a shadow. The evening sun was still high in the western sky. The pot of tulips in front of the bank was in full, brilliant bloom, the flowers sporting bright red petals veined with white.

"You take the Grand Market," Yardem said, "I'll check the taproom."

Marcus shook his head and spat on the paving stones.

"If you'd rather find her, I can go to the Grand Market," Yardem said.

"Stay here," Marcus said. "I'll be right back."

Marcus walked down the street. Sweat pooled between his shoulder blades and down his spine. A yellow-faced dog looked up at him from the shadow of an alleyway, panting and too hot to bark. The streets were emptier now than they would be after sunset, the light driving people to shelter more effectively than darkness. Even the voices of the beggars and street sellers seemed overcooked and limp.

The taproom was cool by comparison. The candles were unlit to keep from adding even that little extra heat to the darkness, and so despite the brightness of the street, the tables of the common room were dim. Marcus squinted, willing his eyes sharper. There were a dozen people there of several races, but none of them was her. From the back, Cithrin laughed. Marcus threaded his way across the common room, following the familiar tones of her voice to the draped cloth that kept the private tables private.

"...would have the effect of rewarding the most reliable debtors."

"Only until they start becoming unreliable," a man's voice said speaking more softly. "Your system encourages debtors to extend, and if that goes on long enough, you change good risks to bad."

"Magistra," Marcus said. "If you have a moment?"

Cithrin pulled aside the cloth. As Marcus had expected, the half-Jasuru man was with her. Qahuar Em. The competition. A plate of cheese and pickled carrots sat on the table between them alongside a wine bottle well on its way to empty. Cithrin's dress of embroidered linen flattered her figure, and her hair, which had been pulled back, was spilling in casual disarray down her shoulder.

"Captain?"

Marcus nodded toward the alley door. Profound annoyance flashed across Cithrin's face.

"I could step out," Qahuar Em offered.

"No. I'll be right back," Cithrin said. Marcus followed her out. The alley stank of spoiled food and piss. Cithrin folded her arms.

"The spicer's come with the commissions for the week," Marcus said. "He won't give over to anyone but you."

Cithrin's frown drew lines at the corners of her mouth and between her brow. Her fingers tapped gently against her arms.

"He wants to talk about something else," she said.

"And not with your hired swords," Marcus said. "That's my assumption."

The girl nodded, attention shifting inward.

It was moments like this, when she forgot herself, that she changed. The false maturity that Master Kit and the players had trained her into was convincing, but it wasn't Cithrin.

And the giddy young woman who shifted between overconfidence and insecurity wasn't her either. With her face smooth, her mind moving in its own silence, she gave a hint of the woman that was in her. The woman she was becoming. Marcus looked away from her, down the alley, and told himself that by doing it he was giving her privacy.

"I should see him," Cithrin said. "He's at the house?"

"Roach and Yardem are with him."

"I should hurry, then," she said, humor warming the words.

"I can give Qahuar your regrets—"

"No, tell him I'll be right back. I don't want him to leave without me."

Marcus hesitated, then nodded. Cithrin walked off down the alleyway, careful where she stepped, until she reached the corner, turned into the street, and disappeared. Marcus stood in the reeking shadows for a long moment, then ducked back inside. The half-Jasuru was still sitting at the table, chewing a pickled carrot and looking thoughtful. At a guess, the man was a few years younger than Marcus, though the Jasuru blood made it hard to be sure. The vesitigial scales of his skin and the vibrant green eyes reminded Marcus of a lizard.

"The magistra's called away for a few minutes. Small business," Marcus said. "She said she'd be right back."

"Of course," Qahuar Em said, then gestured toward the seat where Cithrin had been. "Would you like to wait with me, Captain Wester?"

The wise choice would be to walk away. Marcus nodded his thanks and sat.

"You're the actual Marcus Wester?" the man asked, motioning to the servant boy for a mug of ale.

"Someone had to be," Marcus said.

"I'm honored. I hope you don't mind my saying, I'm surprised to see a man of your fame doing guard work, even for the Medean bank."

"I'm well enough known among a certain group of people," Marcus said. "Just walking down the streets, I could be anyone."

"Still, after Wodford and Gradis, I'd have thought you could command any price you asked as the head of a mercenary company."

"I don't work for kings," Marcus said as the servant boy set the mug onto the table before him. "It narrows my options. Since we're on good terms, you and I...?"

Qahuar nodded him on.

"I didn't know you could mix Firstblood and Jasuru," Marcus said. "You're the first I've seen."

The man spread his hands. *And yet here I am.*

"We're more common in Lyoneia. And there's some work people would rather give a man who has no family."

"Ah," Marcus said. "You're a mule, then? No children."

"My blessing and my curse."

"I knew some men like that in the north. You get it with Cinnae and Dartinae mixes too. Knew some men who just claimed it too. Made them more popular with the women. Safe."

"There are consolations," Qahuar said, smiling.

Marcus imagined himself reaching across the table and breaking the man's neck. It would be difficult. Jasuru were strong bastards, and fast besides. He took a long drink of his ale. It tasted of the brewery Cithrin had bought into. Clearly she'd arranged a deal with the taphouse. Qahuar cocked his head, smiling politely with his sharp-tipped teeth.

She's half your age, Marcus thought. *She's still a* child. But he couldn't say that either.

"How are you finding life in Porte Oliva?" Marcus said instead.

"I like it here. I miss being with my clan, but if I can bring them work ... Well, it's worth the price."

"Must be an impressive clan to go against the Medean bank. Not many would do that."

"I think of it more as the Medean bank going against us. It'll be a good fight. Magistra Cithrin is an impressive woman."

"I've always thought so," Marcus said.

"Have you worked with her for a long time?"

"We met in Vanai," Marcus said. "Came out here with her."

"She's a good employer?"

"I've got no complaints."

"There was talk about you, you know. A simple branch bank, even one with a holding company like the Medean, with Marcus Wester guarding their house? People have read that as a sign that Magistra Cithrin favors a broader, more military strategy."

"What do you think?" Marcus asked, keeping voice neutral.

"What do I think?" Qahuar said, leaning back against the wall. His brow was furrowed as if he were considering his own thoughts for the first time. He lifted a finger. "I think you have chosen this work because you aren't interested in fielding a private army. And so I think the magistra isn't either."

"Interesting thought."

"You're a valuable man, Captain Wester. Many people know it."

Marcus laughed.

"Are you trying to bribe me?" he asked. "You are, aren't you? You're asking whether I can be bought?"

"Can you?" Qahuar Em asked without the slightest hint of shame in his voice.

"There's not enough gold in the world," Marcus said.

"I understand and respect that. But you understand that my duty to my clan required me to ask."

Marcus finished the last of his ale in a gulp and stood up.

"We have any more business, sir?"

Qahuar shook his head.

"Truly, I am honored to have met you, Captain Wester. I respect you and I respect your employer."

"Good to know," Marcus said, and then walked back out through the common room to wait for Cithrin on the street, and the heat be damned. When she came, hurrying down the street like a girl her own age, Marcus stepped out. Sweat beaded her skin and smudged the paints that she'd put to her eyes and lips.

"It's taken care of," Cithrin said. "It's good you came for me. That man's a pretentious ass, but he's going to be very useful."

"Your suitor in there tried to bribe me," Marcus said.

Cithrin paused, and he could see the chagrin in her eyes for less than a heartbeat, and then the mask fell back in place. She became neither the girl nor the woman-still-to-be but the false sophisticate that Master Kit had fashioned. It was the Cithrin that Marcus liked least.

"Of course he did," she said. "I wouldn't have expected any less. Captain, I may not be returning to the house tonight. If I'm not there in the morning, don't be alarmed. I'll send word."

She might as well have thrown a brick at his head. *He's your enemy* and *I forbid you to sleep with that man* and *Please don't do this* crowded each other out. All he could manage was a nod. Cithrin must have seen something of it in his eyes, because she put her hand on his arm and squeezed gently before she went back inside.

Marcus walked back down the street toward the house, then stopped, turned, and headed for the port instead. The sun, lazing down toward the horizon, pressed on his right cheek like a hand. Near the port, the traffic on the streets thickened. Someone had started putting up streamers of thread, the knots hung from windows and trees, the trailing ends blowing in the breeze like the tentacles of a jellyfish. The street puppeteers were staking out corners and public squares, sitting at them even when they weren't performing. The ships from Narinisle might not arrive for weeks, but the celebration was already being prepared.

The smell of the port itself was brine and fish guts. Marcus threaded his way past sailors and longshoremen, beggars and queensmen, to the wide square just past the final dock. Two taphouses and a public bath pressed for attention at the edges of the square, bright cloth banners and bored-looking women in too little cloth. At the farthest edge, a crowd stood enthralled around a theater cart. Master Kit wore a flowing robe of scarlet and gold and a wire-worked crown. He held Sandr's unmoving body in his arms, a thin trickle of red-tinted water dripping down the boy's flank.

"How? How have I let this be? Oh Errison, Errison my son! My only son!" Master Kit called out, his voice breaking carefully so that all the words were still clear, and then slipped gracefully into verse. "I swear, dear boy, and heed this call! By dragon's blood and bones of God, Alysor house shall *fall*!"

Kit froze then, and a moment later, applause rang out. Marcus shifted forward through the crowd as Cary and Smit took the stage, Smit in a mockup of steel armor made from felt and tin and Cary in a tight black dress that had clearly been cut for Opal. Marcus watched through the long final act as the ancient rivalry between noble houses slaughtered first the guilty and then the innocent, mothers killing their daughters, fathers falling to poisons meant for their sons, and the world in general crashing in until at last Master Kit stood alone, all the other players lying at his feet, and wept. By the time the company rose, grinning to take their bows and gather the coins thrown to them, Marcus's mind was almost back in order.

As the company broke down the stage, Marcus walked to the back. Master Kit had changed back to his more customary clothes and was leaning against the seawall and wiping his face with a soft cloth. He smiled when he saw Marcus.

"Captain! Good to see you. What did you think of the show?"

"Convinced me," he said.

"I'm glad to hear it. Hornet! Watch the line there. No, the one you're standing on!"

Hornet danced to the side, and Master Kit shook his head.

"Some days I'm amazed that boy hasn't broken his leg getting up from his bedroll," Kit said.

"Cary's getting better."

"I think she's more comfortable now. By the end of the season I expect she'll have all Opal's old roles in place. I'm still hoping to find a girl to replace Cary, though. I can put Smit in fancy dress and high voice, but I'm afraid it gives the tragic scenes a somewhat lighter tone."

"Any luck?"

"Some," Kit said. "I've talked with a couple of girls who might be good. One's more talented, but she lies. I find that being a good companion on the road is more important than being a good player on the stage. Theater craft is something

I think I can teach. How to be a decent person seems to be a harder thing."

Marcus sat, his back to the wall. In the west, the sun had fallen behind the roofs, but the clouds overhead still glowed gold and orange. Kit took a last swipe at his eyes and tucked the cloth into his belt.

"There's a tavern just the other side of the wall," Master Kit said. "We're staying in the back free of charge every night we play one of the comedies. We're on our way back there now, if you'd care to join us."

"I'll think about it."

Master Kit folded his arms. Concern showed in his eyes.

"Captain? All's well with the bank, I hope? Everything I've heard suggests that our girl is doing quite well."

"People keep bringing her money," Marcus said.

"That's what we'd hoped for, isn't it?"

"Is."

"And yet?"

Marcus squinted toward the bathhouse. Two Kurtadam men were shouting at each other, gesticulating toward the house, their words running over each other. A gangly Tralgu girl ambled by, watching them.

"I need a favor," Marcus said.

"What did you have in mind?"

"I'd like you to tell me again how this is her mistake to make. And that I shouldn't be trying to strap padding to every sharp edge she runs at."

"Ah," Master Kit said.

"She's playing at higher stakes than she knows," Marcus said, "and against people who have decades of experience. And..."

"And?"

Marcus ran his hand through his hair.

"She's wrapped herself in it. She doesn't have any idea how much of herself she's putting into this scheme. When it falls out from under her...I want to stop it now. Before she gets hurt."

"I hear you saying that you want to protect her."

"I don't," Marcus said. And then a moment later, "I do. And I have a poor record protecting women. So I want you to tell me that I shouldn't be trying to."

"Why not take this to Yardem? He knows you better than I do, I expect."

"I know what he's going to say. I even know the tone of voice he's going to say it in. No point going through those motions."

"But you think you'd believe me?"

"You're persuasive."

Master Kit chuckled and squatted down beside him. Cary shouted, and the actor hauled the stage up on its hinges, the wooden planks transforming from floorboards to the side of a tall cart. Sandr went to harness the mules. The salt breeze stilled for a moment, then shifted, cool against Marcus's cheek. The clouds greyed, losing the sunlight. It wouldn't be long before the taverns and brothels and bathhouses all hung out their colored lanterns, trying to draw coins and customers the way they drew moths. The queensmen would be out. And Cithrin. Marcus tried not to think what Cithrin would be doing.

Slowly, he laid out everything to the actor. Cithrin's business plans, her ambitions for the bank and the escort fleet, her courting a relationship with her half-Jasuru rival. Master Kit listened carefully, and when Marcus ran out of words, he pursed his lips and looked up at the darkening sky.

"I'll say this, Captain, because it's true. I believe that Cithrin has all the tools and talents she needs to make this work. If she pays attention, uses her best judgment, and gets only a little bit lucky, she can do this."

"*Can* is a lovely thing. Do you think she *will*?"

Master Kit was silent for four long breaths together. When he spoke, his tone was melancholy.

"Probably not."

Cithrin

Cithrin lay in the darkness. Qahuar lay beside her, the slow deep rhythm of his breath barely audible under the chorus of crickets singing outside the window. The bedding beneath her, around her, was softer than skin and still damp with sweat.

She'd thought that the first time was supposed to hurt, but it hadn't. She wondered how many of the other things she'd heard about sex were wrong. If she'd been raised by a mother, there might have been someone to ask. Still, for someone who hadn't had any clear idea what she was doing, the experiment seemed to have been a success. Qahuar had been drunk enough to abandon his discretion, and she'd followed his lead. A few kisses, a few caresses, and then he'd lifted off her dress, laid her back on his bed, and she'd had to do very little from there. The business of thrusting and grunting had been intimate and absurd, but she found herself thinking of him a bit more fondly afterward. Perhaps the bond that sex made grew from that combination of shared indulgence and indignity.

Still, she was pleased that he was asleep. She was sober now, and between the excitement of the evening and her present sobriety, she had no illusions that rest would come to her. If he'd been awake, trying to maintain a conversation or play the host, it would only have been awkward. Better that he should snore and embrace his pillow and leave her free to think.

If the spring shipping had gone quickly, if the blue-water trade was a bit early, if a hundred things that neither she nor anyone in the city had any way of knowing had happened, the first ships from Narinisle might arrive tomorrow. Or it might be weeks, as much as a month, before the traders knew what their fortunes were. The reports of the captains would carry the last information she needed—the activity of the pirates, the state of the northern ports, the possibility of civil war in Northcoast or of further military action from Antea. The governor would be expecting her proposal shortly after that.

She imagined the auditor arriving. Maybe Komme Medean himself. She would greet him with a smile and lead him up to her rooms. Or perhaps it would be at the café. That would be even better. The milk-eyed Maestro Asanpur would lead him back into the private room, and she would rise from her table to greet him. She'd have the books ready, the accounting made. She imagined him as an old man with fierce eyes and wide hands.

He would look over her statements, her contracts, and his expression would soften. The confusion and rage would wash away, leaving admiration behind. Had she really done so well with the bank's money? Had she really saved it all, and more besides? In the darkness, she practiced raising her eyebrow just so.

"It was nothing," she said, softly but aloud.

She would take the box from beneath her chair with her annual report and her contribution to the holding company. He would look it over, nodding. And then, when everything had been made whole, only then would she bring out the agreement with the governor of Porte Oliva, and hand over the keys to the southern trade. She imagined his hands trembling as he saw the brilliance of all she'd done. A half-breed girl with no parents, and she had managed this. *But only,* she'd say, *only if my branch is accepted.*

"The Porte Oliva bank is *mine,*" she said, and then in the low, rough voice of her imaginary auditor, "Of course, Magistra."

She grinned. It was a pretty thought. And truly, why not? She'd been the one who kept the wealth of Vanai from being captured by the city's prince or the Anteans. She'd been the one to protect it. Once she'd proven that she could manage the bank, why wouldn't the holding company leave her in place? She'd have earned her bank and the life that went with it. The auditor would see that. Komme Medean would see it. She could do this.

Some tiny, invisible insect crawled over her hand and she brushed it away. Her rival and lover muttered something, shifting. She smiled at his sleeping back, the rough texture of his skin. She would be almost sorry to beat him out. But only almost.

As if from a previous life, Yardem Hane's landslide of a voice spoke in her memory. *There's no such thing as a woman's natural weapon.* She saw now that it wasn't true.

When she slipped out of bed, he didn't stir. In the darkness, her clothes were lost somewhere in a tangle on the brickwork floor. She didn't want to risk waking him, so when she found the tunic he'd tossed aside, she pulled it over her head. It reached as far as her thighs. Close enough. She trotted to the corner of the room, her fingers brushing the floor until she found it: a leather thong and brass key that Qahuar Em always wore next to his skin.

Well. Almost always.

The bricks were cool against the soles of her feet, and the

sound of her footsteps was as near to silence as made no distinction. The compound was near the port, the rooms small and close, but arrayed around a small courtyard garden. The four servants were full-blooded Jasuru, and of them, only the door slave stayed in his place through the night. Qahuar Em might be the voice of a great Lyoneian clan, but space was expensive in Porte Oliva, and having a more lavish home than the local nobles was a kind of boasting that would serve him poorly. Cithrin turned a corner in the darkness and counted three doors on her left. The third was oak bound in iron. She found the keyhole and carefully put the stolen key in. When she turned it, the clack of the mechanism sounded as loud as a shout. Her heart raced, but no one raised the alarm. She opened the door and slipped into Qahuar's private office.

The shutters were closed and barred, but once she'd undone them, the light of the quarter moon was enough to make out the general shapes of things. There was a writing desk. A strongbox bolted to the floor. A latticework holder, filled with scrolls and folded letters. A hooded lantern with rings of carved flint and worked steel on a string. Cithrin struck sparks to the wick, then quickly closed and barred the shutters. What had been shadows and silhouettes sprang to life in shades of dim orange and grey. The strongbox was locked, and the key to the office wouldn't fit it. The writing desk was bare apart from a thumb-sized bottle of green ink and a metal stylus. She went to the scrolls and letters, moving quickly, methodically from one to the next, being sure to keep each stack in order and put them back precisely as they were.

She was aware of the anxiety pressing at her gut and the rapid beat of her heart, and she pushed it all aside. She would let herself feel again later, when there was time. A letter from the governor thanking Qahuar for his gift. The chocolate had been exquisite, and the governor's wife especially extended her gratitude. Cithrin put the letter back. An unfurled scroll listed the names and relationships of several dozen people, none of whom meant anything to her. She put it back.

Outside the shuttered window, a salt thrush sang. Cithrin ran her fingers through her hair. Something in this had to be of use. Somewhere in the papers, Qahuar would have said something that told something of what his offer to the governor would be. She reached for another letter, and her arm brushed the lantern. Glass and metal shifted, teetered, and she grabbed it. A second more and it would have fallen. Shattered. Lit the room on fire. Cithrin put it carefully in the middle of the writing desk and went back to her search with trembling hands.

Hours seemed to pass before she found it. A long scroll of fine cotton. The lines of cipher were spaced widely enough that Qahuar had been able to write the message beneath them. Cithrin ran her fingertips along his words. It had been written by an elder of the clan, and it was everything Cithrin had hoped to discover. They could commit fifteen ships to the effort. Each would be manned with a full crew of two dozen sailors. She kept on reading, her fingers making a soft hushing against the cloth. In compensation, they would ask sixteen hundredths of every transaction in each port for ships accompanied and protected, or nineteen if they asked the clan to guarantee. The elder estimated the initial outlay at two thousand silver, with a profit to the clan of five hundred in a season. The agreement would have to be for a full decade.

Magister Imaniel had often talked about the tools of memory. Ink was best, but writing the figures down and sneaking them out of the house was a risk she didn't have to take. Fifteen ships of two dozen men.

"At the age of fifteen, she'd had two dozen men," Cithrin said to herself.

Sixteen hundredths without guarantee, or nineteen with. So the guarantee was worth three.

"Sixteen for the company, and three more for love."

Two thousand to begin, with an estimated profit of five hundred each year of a ten-year agreement.

"She gave two thousand kisses, took five hundred back, and died alone ten years after that."

There were more details in the scroll—the specifications of the ships, the names of individual captains, the routes the trade would be encouraged to take—and she read as much of it as she could, but at the base, she had what she needed.

She put the scroll back where it had been, then put the lantern in its place and blew the flame out. Used to the light as she'd become, the darkness seemed absolute. The smell of spent wick was acrid and sharp. She closed her eyes and, tracing fingers along the wall, found her way to the door. She slipped into the corridor, turned the lock, and, almost skipping, went back to Qahuar's sleeping chamber. She put the key in the corner where she'd found it, stripped off the tunic, and slipped quickly back into bed.

Qahuar murmured and reached out an arm to drape over her belly.

"You're cold," he said, the words thick.

"I'll be warm soon," she said, and felt his smile as much as she saw it. He nuzzled against her, and she tried to let herself relax into him. She closed her eyes and repeated her rhyme in the privacy of her mind.

At the age of fifteen, she'd had two dozen men, sixteen for company and three more for love. She gave two thousand kisses, took five hundred back, and died alone ten years after that.

Well, you look exhausted," Captain Wester said, leaning against the wall beside the pot of tulips where the old gambler's caller used to stand. "I was starting to think we'd have to put together a raiding party, take you back by force."

"I told you I wouldn't be back," Cithrin said, walking past him toward her private entrance. He followed her as if she'd invited him.

"You're supposed to be meeting with that woman from the needlemakers' guild at midday. She's likely on her way to that coffee house right now. Unless you're planing to wear that same dress—"

"I can't see her," Cithrin said, walking up the stairs. She heard his footsteps falter, then hurry to catch up. When he spoke, his voice was careful and polite. It sounded like he was talking from half a mile away.

"Do you want to give her a reason?"

"Send someone. Tell her I'm ill."

"All right."

Cithrin sat down on her divan, scowling up at the man. His arms were crossed over his chest, his mouth pinched. He wasn't really much older than Qahuar Em. Cithrin pulled off one of her shoes and massaged her foot. The sole was filthy. Her dress hung from her as if the cloth itself was exhausted and sweating.

"I didn't sleep," she said. "I can't help her anyway."

"If you say so," Wester said, nodding curtly. He turned to leave, and her sudden rush of distress flooded her. She hadn't known how badly she didn't want to be alone.

"Did everything go well while I was gone?" she said, her voice tripping out of her.

Wester stopped at the head of the stairs.

"Went fine," he said.

"Are you angry with me, Captain?"

"No," he said. "I'm going to go tell the needlemakers' woman that you're too ill to see her. I take it we'll send her a note when you're feeling better?"

Cithrin pulled off her other shoe and nodded. Wester went down the stairs. The door clacked closed behind him. Cithrin lay back. The night had been everything she'd hoped, but the first blue light of dawn had left her exhausted. Her body felt limp and shaky the way it had all those nights with the caravan when sleep had escaped her. She'd convinced herself that those days were over, but she'd been wrong. And now, say it or not, Wester was angry, and she was surprised how much his disapproval stung.

She thought of calling him back, of explaining that she'd allowed herself to be seduced for a reason. That going to Qahuar Em's bed had only been a ploy. The more she rehearsed the words, the worse they sounded. Voices rose up from the floor beneath her. The guards that Wester had hired. From the sound, they were playing at dice. Her spine ached. Someone below her shouted in dismay, and others groaned along in sympathy. She closed her eyes, hoping that being back in her own rooms would relax her enough that she could rest. Instead, her mind jumped and hopped, faster and faster, like a ball rolling down an infinite hill.

Fifteen ships could be split into three equal groups of five or else five of three, so perhaps Qahuar's clan was expecting the merchant ships to divide into three major ports—likely Carse, Lasport, and Asinport. But what if they were expecting the trade to go on past Asterilhold to Antea or Sarakal or Hallskar? Two dozen men in a single ship wasn't a small thing, but would Lyoniean sailors do well in the colder waters of the north? Could she argue, with her ties to Carse, that she'd be able to provide ships more experienced in the native waters? And if she made the argument, would it be true?

And why had Opal betrayed her? And why had God let Magister Imaniel die? And Cam? And her parents? And did Sandr still want her? Would Cary still be her friend? Did Master Kit still approve of who and what she was? What did other people do when they had no friends and their lovers were their enemies? There had to be some better way to do things.

The tears welled up in her eyes and trickled down her cheeks. She didn't feel sad. She barely felt anything at all besides tired and annoyed with herself. She was suffering some sort of little fit, and she could wait until it passed. The dice game shifted, and two men's voices caught up a tune, coming together and apart.

Cithrin forced herself to sitting. Then standing. Then she stripped off last night's clothes and put on a simple skirt and blouse. She tied back her hair until she saw the little bite marks that Qahuar had left on her neck and let her hair back down. She filled the little basin by her bedside, washed her face. The paints Cary had left were there, and Cithrin considered remaking Magistra Cithrin of the Medean bank. She decided against it—she had little enough energy as it was—and went downstairs.

When she opened the door, the company went quiet. The two Firstblood men looked at each other and then away. The paler of them was blushing visibly. The Kurtadam man nodded.

"Sorry about that, Magistra," he said. "Didn't think you were here."

Cithrin waved the concern away.

"Yardem?" she said.

"In the back room, Magistra," the Kurtadam said.

Cithrin walked past the guards to the rear, then through into the darkness. Yardem Hane lay on a long, low cot, fingers laced over his belly. His eyes were closed, his ears folded and soft. Cithrin was just about to turn around, putting the conversation off for another time, when he spoke.

"Help you, ma'am?"

"Um. Yes. Yardem," she said. "You know the captain as well as anybody."

"That's true," the Tralgu said, his eyes still closed and his voice calm.

"I think I may have upset him," she said.

"You wouldn't be the first, ma'am. If it gets to be a problem, the captain will tell you."

"All right."

"Anything else, ma'am?"

The Tralgu didn't move apart from the ride and fall of his chest.

"I slept with a man, and now I'm going to betray him," she said, and her voice sounded as grey and hard as slate. "I have to do it to keep my bank, but I think I feel guilty about it."

Yardem opened one soft black eye.

"I forgive you," the Tralgu said.

Cithrin nodded. She shut the door behind her when she left, then walked back out the street and up her private stair. The voices below her were quiet now, aware that the owner of the house might hear them. She sat at her writing desk, took out the books, and began drafting the proposal that would beat out Qahuar Em.

Geder

Geder couldn't say exactly when they left the dragon's road. At first, it was only that wind and weather had heaped dirt and desert hardpack over the path, even as it passed through a few of the sprawling caravanserais that passed for cities in the Keshet. Then the last of the great meeting places fell away behind him, and the jade of the roadway became rarer, the brown of the earth and yellow-grey of desert grass more common. Then the path was only visible as a stretch where the scrub and weeds were smaller, their roots blocked inches from the surface.

And then it was gone, and Geder was riding through the mountains and valleys at the eastern edge of the world. The trees were thin and twisting, with thick, almost ropey bark that seemed designed to imitate stone. At night, tiny lizards with bright yellow tails skittered across the ground and through the tents. Morning often found one or more dead in the horses' feed sacks. Water became scarce enough that every muddy wisp of a creek meant his five servants would fill everything that would hold moisture, and even so Geder often saw their supply fall to less than half. Every night, he heard the servants talking about bandits and unclean spirits that haunted the empty places in the world. Even though no new dangers appeared, he slept poorly.

Geder had spent most of his life within the limits of Antea.

Travel had meant the journey from Rivenhalm to Camnipol, or along the king's winter hunt to Kavinpol, Sevenpol, Estinport. He'd been Kaltfel, royal city of Asterilhold, once as a boy to watch an obscure relation be married. And he had gone on campaign to Vanai under Lord Ternigan, and then Sir Alan Klin. He'd never imagined himself traveling alone or nearly so in lands so barren and cut off that the local villagers had never heard of Antea or the Severed Throne. But when he came to a stand of shacks clumped around a thin, hungry-looking lake, the wary men who came out to meet him shook their heads and shrugged.

He could as well have told them he'd come from the stars or the deep lands under the earth. It would have meant as much, and possibly more. The mountains' inhabitants were Firstblood, but of a uniform olive complexion with dark eyes and thick wiry hair that made them seem like members of a single extended family. Some few knew the civilized languages well enough to trade with the outposts, but for the greater part they spoke in a local patois that Geder could almost put together from some of the ancient books he'd read. He felt he'd ridden into the dim past.

"Sinir," Geder said. "Are these the Sinir mountains?"

The young man looked over his shoulder at the dozen men who had come from the village and licked his lips.

"Not here," the man said. "East."

On the one hand, everyone he met in the empty, ragged mountains seemed to recognize the word, to know what he meant when he asked. On the other, the Sinir mountains had been just a bit to the east for almost two weeks now, retreating before him like a mirage. The thin, dusty paths snaked through the valleys or along the sides of steep, rocky slopes. They were little more than deer trails, and more than once Geder had found himself wondering if he'd left behind all human habitation, only to find another small, desperate village around the next turning.

"Can you show me?" Geder asked. "Can one of your men take me there? I'll pay you with copper."

Not that copper would have any effect on these people. Coins meant nothing here more than small, particularly bright stones would have done. His black leather cloak would have more use out here, but he didn't want to part with it, and besides, no one he'd met since he left the Keshet for the unmarked lands had shown the slightest interest in his offers. He asked out of habit. Because he had always asked before. He had no real hope that they would accept the bargain.

"Why do you want to go there?" the young man asked.

"I'm looking for something," Geder said. "An old place. Very old. It has to do with the dragons."

The man licked his lips again, hesitated, and nodded.

"I know the place you mean," he said. "Stay here tonight, and I can take you in the morning."

"Really?"

"You want the old temple, yes? Where the holy men live?"

Geder leaned back. It was the first he had heard about a temple or priests, and his heart sped up. There were stories and references in several of the essays on the fall of the Dragon Empire that talked about pods of sleeping dragons lulled into a permanent sleep and hidden in the far corners of the world. This might be a hidden pod of books, scrolls, legends, and tradition. If he could convince the local priest class to let him read the books, or buy copies... He tried to think what he had to offer for trade.

"Prince?"

"What?" Geder said. "Oh, yes. Yes, the old temple. That's

where I'd like to go. Do we have to wait for morning? We could go now."

"Morning, sir," the young man said. "You stay with us tonight."

The village boasted two dozen wooden shacks clustered together in a stand of ash. Perhaps a hundred people lived in the dry, quiet squalor. In the high air above them, hawks called and glided, spiraling up toward the sun. Geder had his squire put his tent beside the lakeshore just outside the radius of the village with each of the servants set to keep watch for a part of the night. Not that five servants would be enough to defend him if the locals turned ugly, but if a little warning was the most he could get, he'd take that.

At sunset, an old woman came to his camp with a bowl of mashed roots with bits of cooked meat in it. He thanked her, gave her a few of his remaining copper coins, and then buried the food without eating a bite. The heat of the day poured up out of the ground, and the chill night air came off the water. Geder lay on his cot, his mind perfectly awake and restless. The long, slow dread waiting for sleep had become the hardest part of his day. The poor food, the mind-killing monotony of the trail, the profound loneliness all grated on him, yes, but in the quiet moments between lying down in the darkness and actual forgetfulness, all the things he was running from seemed to catch up with him.

He imagined what might have happened back in Camnipol. The conspiracy behind the attempted coup might have been rooted out, hung in the streets. That would have been the best hope. Or maybe another wave of hired swords had come and slaughtered half the court. He wondered whether Jorey Kalliam's father had given him the same advice that Geder had taken. What part of the world would Jorey have gone to, if he were avoiding the upheaval?

Geder imagined coming home to a kingdom utterly changed. What if Asterilhold had paid the mercenaries as the first strike of a comprehensive invasion? When Geder turned toward home, there might be no Antea, no Severed Throne, no Rivenhalm. His father might be dead even now.

Or Klin and his men might have come into favor again. Geder pictured himself riding through the eastern gate only to find guards at the ready to arrest him and throw him into the public gaol. He stood on a platform, looking out over a sea of seared, burned faces—Vanai, killed at his order— before he realized that he was finally slipping down into dream.

In the morning, the dreams faded and his servants brought him a double handful of dried apples and a tin cup of water. Half a dozen men had congregated at a trailhead. A low cart squatted beside them, loaded with baskets of dried beans and three freshly slaughtered goats. Offerings, apparently, for the temple. The oldest of the men clapped his hands fast and loud, and the others grabbed thick ropes, pulling the cart across the thin dirt. Geder followed on horseback, the only man in the company riding.

The trail they followed snaked through the hills, clinging to the sides of crevasses and cliffs. The stone itself changed, becoming more jagged and sharp, as if centuries of erosion had failed to soften it. Geder found himself speculating about the relationship of the landscape to the dragon's roads. Could the same endurance also have been given to the broken land here? Was this what marked the Sinir mountains from those around them?

The shapes of some stones was peculiarly organic. There were soft, almost graceful curves, and places where the stones seemed to fit together, articulated like bones. In one meadow they passed through, a collection of curved terraces was marked by borders of a pale, porous rock that matched neither the arid desert stones Geder had become used to nor the new, uneven geography. The effect was as if a giant had died there, leaving its ribs in a jumble on the land. Geder looked up and saw the skull.

The broad forehead alone was as long as his horse. He could have crouched inside the empty eye sockets. The muzzle disappeared into the earth, as if the fallen dragon were drinking from the land itself, and five blade-long teeth still clung to the jaw. Centuries of fierce sunlight had bleached the bone, but wind, sand, and rain hadn't worn it down. Geder pulled his mount to a halt, gaping. The villagers kept hauling their cart, talking to each other, trading a skin of water among them. Geder dismounted and walked to the skull. He hesitated, reached out a hand, and touched the sun-warmed dragon bone. The corpse had lain here for thousands of years. Since before humanity had begun its history.

"Prince?" the young man from the village called, "Come! Come!"

Trembling, Geder lifted himself back into the saddle and trotted along.

The sun hadn't shifted more than a hand's span when the group made a final turn around a high stand of scattered boulders each as large as a sailing ship, and the temple came into view. Carved into the stone of the mountain, the dark holes of doorways and windows stared out into the landscape. Geder had the brief sensation of being stared at by a single, huge insectile eye. A wall as tall as the defenses of Camnipol marked the end of the trail. Huge, towering statues of what had once been human figures were set into the stone along the wall like sentries, their features eroded into knobs and stumps, and a huge spread-winged dragon towered above them all. Great banners shifted in the breeze, one at each of the thirteen statues. Each was a field of a different color—blue, green, yellow, orange, red, brown, black, through thirteen distinct shades—with a pale circle in the center cut by four lines into eight sections.

Its sigil was of cardinal and intercardinal showing the eight directions of the world in which no falsehood could hide. The sign of the Righteous Servant. Tears leapt to Geder's eyes, and something like relief flooded him. Triumph, perhaps. This was the place. He'd found it.

They drew nearer, and the longer it took, the more Geder understood the breathtaking scale of the place. A huge iron gate hung at the front of the wall, imposing and forbidding. Above it, in a brutal script, were the words *Khinir Kicgnam Bat,* each letter as tall as a man. Geder squinted up at them, struggling to make his translation while still half drunk with wonder.

Bound is not broken.

The villagers brought their cart to a stop still fifty yards from the great iron doors. Geder saw now that a section within the door itself was set with a complex of swirling gears. The interlocked teeth clanked once, shifted, and the section of iron parted like a curtain. Six men walked out toward them. They had the same general features as the villagers, though with more roundness to their cheeks and oil sleeking their hair. They wore black robes tied with lengths of chain at the waist and sandals that wrapped their ankles. The men of the village knelt. Geder bowed, but didn't dismount. His horse shifted uneasily beneath him.

The priests looked at one another, then turned to the young man who had led the group.

"Who is this?" the eldest of the priests asked.

"A stranger," the young man said. "He came asking after

the Sinir. We brought him to you, the way the Kleron told us."

Geder urged his horse closer. The grandness of the place had made the beast skittish, but he held the reins tightly. The eldest priest stepped toward him.

"Who are you?" the monk asked.

"Geder Palliako, son of the Viscount Palliako of Rivenhalm."

"I don't know this place."

"I'm a subject of King Simeon of Antea," Geder said. And then when the priest stayed silent, "Antea's a very important kingdom. Empire, really. Center of Firstblood culture and power."

"Why have you come here?"

"Well," Geder said, "that's a long story. I was in Vanai. That's one of the Free Cities, or, really it was. It's gone now. But I found some books, and they were talking about this...Ah...They called it the Righteous Servant or the Sinir Kushku, and it was supposed to have been designed by the dragon Morade during the fall of the empire, and I thought that if I could use the different descriptions of where it was compared with the times when the accounts were made I might be able to...find it."

The priest frowned up at him.

"Have you heard of the Righteous Servant?" Geder asked. "By any chance?"

He wondered what he would do if the man said no. He couldn't bring himself to ride back out. Not after seeing this.

"We are the servants of the Servant," the man said. His voice was rich with pride and certainty.

"That's excellent. That's just what I'd hoped! May I..." Geder's words tumbled over themselves, and he had to stop, cough, and collect himself. "I was hoping, if you have archives... Or if I could speak with you. Find out more."

"You will wait here," the priest said.

Geder nodded, but the man had already turned away. The priests were pulling the cart in through the gap in the iron gate, the village men retrieving another much like it. As Geder watched, the priests vanished into their temple, and the other men, waving at him and smiling, went away down the trail, returning to their homes. Geder stayed where he was, caught between the desire to see the temple behind the wall and the fear of being left alone and unable to find his way back through the mountains. The gears in the gate ground themselves closed. The rope-drawn cart vanished around the stones. Geder sat on his horse, trying not to look at the five servants he'd dragged across the known world and into this emptiness. In the distance, a hawk shrieked.

"Should we set up camp, my lord?" his squire asked.

Night fell. Geder sat in his tent, the walls murmuring to themselves in the breeze. At his little desk, by the light of a single candle, he read the books he'd already read ten times over, his eyes taking in the words without the meanings.

The sense of disappointment, of rejection, of rage were slowly building in his belly with the growing certainty that they weren't going to come out. He'd been left to sit on the doorstep like a beggar until he took the hint and limped away. Back to Camnipol, back to Antea, back to all of the things he'd come from.

He was at his journey's end. He couldn't even pretend a reason to push onward. He had crossed two nations, mountains, deserts, only to be snubbed at the end. He turned a page, not knowing what had been on it, and not particularly caring. He imagined himself at home, telling the tale. The

Jasuru seer, the dragon bones, the mysterious hidden temple. *And then,* they would say. *What then, Lord Palliako?*

And he would lie. He would tell about the degenerate priests and their pathetic, empty cult. He'd write essays detailing whatever perversions came to mind, and ascribe all of them to the temple. If it hadn't been for him, for Geder Palliako, the place would have been utterly lost to history. If they saw fit to treat him this way, he could see that they were remembered any way he saw fit.

And the priests would neither know nor care, so where was the pleasure in that? The morning would come, he would have the tent loaded, and he'd begin the trip back. Perhaps he could find a merchant in one of the cities of the Keshet who would accept a letter of credit and buy some decent provisions. Or stop at the village and tell them the priests had instructed them to give him their goats. That would be almost worth doing.

"My lord! My lord Palliako!"

Geder was out of the tent almost before he heard the words. This squire was pointing at the dark iron gate. The small side door was still closed, but a deeper shadow had formed between the two massive panels, a line of darkness.

A man came out, walking toward them. Then two more, with blades strapped to their backs. Geder waved his and his servants hurried to light the torches. The first man was huge, broad across hips and shoulders. His hair was gone, and the expanse of his scalp glowed in the moonlight. In the torchlight, his robe looked black, though in truth it could have been any dark color. The guards behind him wore the same robes as the priests had before, but of finer cloth, and undrawn swords with hilts and scabbards of iridescent green.

"Are you Prince Palliako who has come to learn of Sinir

Kushku?" the large man asked. Though he spoke softly, his voice had the weight of thunder behind it. Geder felt his blood shift in his veins at the sound.

"I am."

"What do you offer in return?"

I don't have anything, Geder thought. *A cart, some servants. Most of my silver was spent on the way here, and what do you have to buy with it anyway? It isn't as if any of you were going to the market fair...*

"News?" Geder said. "I can give you reports about the world. Since you're so ... remote."

"And do you mean the goddess harm?"

"Not at all," Geder said, surprised by the question. None of the books he'd read had mentioned a goddess.

The big man paused, his attention turning inward for a moment. He nodded.

"Come with me, then, Prince, and let us speak of your world."

Dawson

Summer in Osterling Fells. Dawson rose with the sun and spent his days riding through his lands, tending to the work that his winter business and the intrigues of the spring had left undone. The canals that fed the southern fields needed to be remade. One of the villages in the west had burned late in the spring, and Dawson saw to the rebuilding. Two men had been found trapping deer in his forest, and he attended the hanging. Where he went, his landbound subjects offered him honor, and he accepted it as his due.

Along the roads, the grass grew higher. The trees spread their broad leaves, shimmering green and silver in the breezes and sunlight. Two days from east to west, four from north to south, with mountain tracks to hunt, his own bed to sleep in, and a bowl of perfect blue skies above him. Dawson Kalliam could hardly imagine a more luxurious prison to waste his weeks in while the kingdom crumbled.

The holding itself buzzed with activity. The men and women of the holding were no more accustomed to the presence of the lord during the long days of summer than they were to his absence during the winter months not taken up by the King's Hunt. Dawson felt the weight of their consideration. Everyone knew that he had been exiled for the season, and no doubt the servants' quarters and the stables were alive with stories, speculation, and gossip.

Resenting that made as much sense as being angry at crickets for singing. They were low, small people. They understood nothing that wasn't put on the table before them. Dawson had no reason to treat their opinions of the greater world with more regard than he would a raindrop or a twig on a tree.

Canl Daskellin, on the other hand, he had expected better of.

"Another letter, dear?" Clara asked as he paced the length of the long gallery.

"He's telling me nothing. Listen to this," Dawson said, shaking the pages. He found the passage. "*His majesty remains in poor health. His physicians suspect the weight of the mercenary riot is weighing on him, but expect he will be much improved by the winter.* Or this. *Lord Maas has been most aggressive in his defense of Lord Issandrian's good character, and is making the most of having escaped censure.* It's all like this. Provocations and hints."

Clara put down her needlework. The heat of the afternoon left a beading of sweat across her brow and upper lip, and a lock of her hair had come free of its dressing. Her dress was thin summer cloth that did little to hide the shape of her body, softer than a young woman's and more at ease with itself. In the golden light spilling through the windows, she looked beautiful.

"What did you expect, love?" she asked. "Direct talk, plainly stated?"

"He might as well not have written," Dawson said.

"You know that isn't true, love," Clara said. "Even if Canl isn't giving you all the details of the court, the fact that he's corresponding means something. You can always judge a person by who they write to. Have you heard from Jorey?"

Dawson sat on the divan across from her. At the far end

of the gallery, a servant girl stepped through the doorway, saw the lord and lady in the room, and backed out again.

"I had a letter from him ten days ago," Dawson said. "He says everyone in court is walking quietly and speaking low. Nobody thinks this is over. Simeon was due to name Prince Aster's ward at his naming day, but he's postponed it three times now."

"Why would he do that?" Clara asked.

"The same reason he exiled *me* for Issandrian's treasons," Dawson said. "If he favors us, he's afraid they will take up arms. If he favors them, then we'll do it. And with Canl calling the tunes, I can't say he's wrong to think it."

"I could go and ask Phelia," Clara said. "Her husband's been put in roughly the same position as Canl, hasn't he? And Phelia and I haven't seen each other in ages. It would be good to talk with her again."

"Absolutely not. Send you into Camnipol alone? To Feldin Maas? It wouldn't be safe. I forbid it."

"I wouldn't be alone. Jorey would be there, and I'd take Vincen Coe to keep me safe."

"No."

"Dawson. Love," Clara said, and her voice had taken on a hardness he rarely heard from her. "I let you stop me when there were foreign mercenaries in the streets, but that's passed. And if someone doesn't reach out, the breach will never be healed. Simeon can't do it, poor bear, because it isn't something that can be commanded. You and Feldin can't because you're men and you don't know how. The way this happens is you draw your swords, and we talk about who wore the most fetching dress at the ball until you put them back in their scabbards. Just because you don't feel comfortable with it doesn't mean it's difficult."

"We've gone past that now," Dawson said.

Clara lifted an eyebrow. The silence lasted three heart-beats. Four.

"You need to raise your army, then, don't you?" she said.

"It's forbidden. Part of my season of exile."

"Well, then," Clara said, picking her needlework back up. "I'll write to Phelia this evening and let her know I'd be open to an invitation."

"Clara—"

"You're quite right. I wouldn't dream of going without escort. Would you like to speak with Vincen Coe, or shall I?"

The anger that leapt up in Dawson surprised him. He rose to his feet, throwing the pages of Canl Daskellin's letter to the floor. He badly wanted to take some book or bauble or chair and throw it out the gallery window and into the courtyard. Clara's eyes were on her work, the thin glimmer of the needle piercing the cloth and drawing through, piercing and drawing. Her mouth was set.

"Simeon is my king too," she said. "Yours isn't the only noble blood in this house."

"I'll talk to him," Dawson muttered, forcing the words out through a narrowed throat.

"I'm sorry, dear. What did you say?"

"Coe. I'll talk to Coe. But if he doesn't go with you, you aren't going."

Clara smiled.

"Send my maid to me when you go, dear. I'll have her fetch my pen."

The huntsman's quarters were outside the great granite-and-jade walls of the holding. A long, low building, the roof's thatching laced down by long ropes of woven leather and weighted by the skulls and bones of fallen prey. The courtyard had weeds growing at the sides where the boots of men didn't trample them down and baled hay targets for the archers to practice against. The air stank of dog shit from the adjoining kennels, and a huge shade tree arched above the building's side, snowy with midsummer blooms.

Voices led Dawson to the back of the building. Five of his huntsmen stood or sat around the table of an ancient stump, raw cheese and fresh bread on the wood. They were young men, stripped to their hose in the heat. Dawson felt a moment's deep nostalgia. Once he'd been much like them. Strong, sure of his body, and able to lose himself in the joys of a warm day. And when he had been, Simeon had been at his side. The years had robbed them both.

One caught sight of him and leapt to his feet in salute. The others quickly followed. Vincen Coe was in the back, his left eye swollen and dark. Dawson strode over to them, ignoring all but the wounded man.

"Coe," he said. "With me."

"My lord," the huntsman said, and hurried to Dawson's side. Dawson walked fast down the wide track that led from the holding down toward the pond to the north. The shadows of the spiraling towers striped the land.

"What happened to you?" Dawson said. "You look like you tried to catch a rock with your eyelids."

"Nothing of importance, lord."

"Tell me."

"We drank a bit too much last night, lord. One of the new boys got a bit merry and...made a suggestion I found offensive. He repeated it, and I found myself moved to correct him."

"He called you a catamite?"

"No, my lord."

"What, then?"

In spring, before the start of the court season, the pond

was clear as water from a stream. In autumn, after Dawson's return from court, it could be as dark as tea. He'd rarely seen it in the height of summer, the green of the water building on the reflections of the trees to make something almost emerald. Half a dozen ducks made their way across the water, their wakes spreading out behind them. Dawson stood at the edge where the grass had the dampness of mud beneath it. Vincen Coe's uncomfortable silence became more interesting with every passing breath.

"I could ask the others," Dawson said. "They'll tell me if you won't."

Vincen looked out over water to the distant mountains.

"He impugned the honor of Lady Kalliam, my lord. And made some speculations that..."

"Ah," Dawson said. Sour rage haunted the back of his mouth. "Is he still here?"

"No, my lord. His brothers carried him back to his village last night."

"Carried him?"

"I didn't leave him in fit state to walk, sir."

Dawson chuckled. Flies danced across the water before him.

"She's going back to Camnipol," Dawson said. "She has the idea that she can make peace with Maas."

The young huntsman nodded once, but didn't speak.

"Say it," Dawson said.

"With permission, sir. That's not wise. It's hardest drawing blood the first time, and that's already happened. It only gets easier."

"I know it, but she's determined."

"Send me instead."

"I'm sending you in addition," Dawson said. "Jorey's still in the city. He can give you a better picture of where things stand. You protected me when this all started. I need you to protect her now."

The two men stood together. Voices came from behind them. The kennel master shouting to his apprentice. The laughter of the huntsmen. It all seemed to come from another world. One not so far in the past when things had been better and safer and still right.

"Nothing will hurt her, my lord," Vincen Coe said. "Not while I live."

Three days after Clara left, riding off in the open carriage that had brought them with Vincen Coe riding close behind, the unwelcome guest arrived.

The heat of the day had driven Dawson out of the holding proper and into the winter garden. Out of its season, it looked plain. The flowers that would offer up blooms of gold and vermillion in the falling days of the year looked like tough green weeds now. Three of his dogs lay panting in the heat, dark eyes closed and pink tongues lolling out. The glasshouse stood open. Closed, it would have been hotter than an oven. The garden slept, waiting for its time, and when that time came, it would transform itself.

By then, Clara would have returned. He had spent time away from her, of course. He had court business and the hunt. She had her circle and the management of the household. And yet when she left him behind, the solitude was harder to bear gracefully. He woke in the mornings wondering where she was. He lay down at night wishing she would walk in through the dressing room door, alive with news and insight and simple inane gossip. Between the two moments, he tried not to think of her, or of Feldin Maas, or the possibility of her being used somehow against him.

"Lord Kalliam."

The servant was a young Dartinae girl, new to his service. Her eyes burned in the manner of her race.

"What is it?"

"A man's come asking audience, my lord. Paerin Clark, sir."

"Don't know him," Dawson said, but half a breath later, he did. The pale banker, agent of Northcoast, and seducer of Canl Daskellin. Dawson stood. At his feet, the dogs sat up, looking from him to the servant girl and back while they whined softly. "Is he alone?"

The girl's eyes widened, suddenly anxious.

"He has a retinue, my lord. A driver and footmen. And I think his private man."

"Where is he now?"

"In the lesser hall, my lord."

"Tell him I'll see him in a moment," Dawson said. "Bring him ale and bread, put his men in the servants' hall, and then get me my guard."

The pale man looked up when the doors of the lesser hall swung open and stood when Dawson entered. That Dawson had four swordsmen in hunting leathers behind him didn't so much as raise the man's eyebrows. The bread on the plate before him had a single bite taken from it, the pewter ale tankard might not have been touched.

"Baron Osterling," the banker said with a bow. "Thank you for seeing me. I apologize for arriving unannounced."

"Are you running Canl Daskellin's errands now, or he running yours?"

"I'm running his. The situation in the court is delicate. He wanted you informed, but he doesn't trust couriers and some things he wouldn't want written in his hand regardless."

"And so he sends the puppet master of Northcoast?"

The banker paused. The faintest touch of color came to his skin, and the polite smile he always wore.

"My lord, without giving offense, there are one or two points it might be best if we clarified. I am a subject of Northcoast, but I am not a member of its court, and I am not here at the bidding of my king. I represent the Medean bank and only the Medean bank."

"A spy without a kingdom, then. So much the worse."

"I apologize, my lord," the banker said. "I see I am not welcome. Please forgive the trespass."

Paerin Clark bowed deeply and started toward the door, taking the court and Camnipol with him. *Just because you don't feel comfortable with it doesn't mean it's difficult,* Clara said in his memory.

"Wait," Dawson said, and took a deep breath. "Who's wearing the prettiest dress at the twice-damned ball?"

"Excuse me?"

"You came for a reason," Dawson said. "Don't be such a coward you abandon it the first time someone barks at you. Sit. Tell me what you have to tell."

Paerin Clark came and sat. His eyes seemed darker now, his face as blank as a man at cards.

"It isn't you," Dawson said, sitting across the table and ripping off a crust of the bread. "Not as a man. It's what you are."

"I'm the man Komme Medean sends when there's a problem," Paerin Clark said. "No more, no less."

"You're an agent of chaos," Dawson said, softly, trying to pull the sting from the words. "You're a man who makes poor men rich and rich men poor. Rank and order mean nothing to men like you, and they mean everything to men like me. It isn't you I disdain. It's only what you are."

The banker laced his fingers across his knee.

"Will you hear my news, my lord? Despite what you think I am?"

"I will."

For the better part of an hour, the banker spoke in a low voice, detailing the slow landslide that was happening in Camnipol. As Dawson had suspected, Simeon's unwillingness to commit his son as the ward of any house came from the fear of making waves. The respect for his kingship was failing on all sides. Daskellin and his remaining allies offered what support they could, but even within the ranks of the faithful, unease was growing. Issandrian and Klin remained in exile, but Feldin Maas was everywhere in the city. It seemed as if the man never slept, and wherever he went, the story he told was the same: the attack of the show fighters had been rigged to throw disgrace on Curtin Issandrian in order that the prince not be sent to his house. The implication was that the convenient appearance of the soldiers from Vanai had been part of a great theater piece.

"Arranged by me," Dawson said.

"Not you alone, but yes."

"Lies, beginning to end," Dawson said.

"Not everyone believes it. But some do."

Dawson rubbed his forehead with the palm of his hand. Outside, the day was leaning toward night, the sunlight reddening. It was all as he suspected. And Clara was riding into the center of it. The hope she'd offered before she'd left had sounded risky at the time. After this report, it seemed merely naïve. He would have given his hand to have had the banker come a week earlier. Now it was too late. He could as well wish a thrown rock back into his hand.

"Simeon?" Dawson asked. "Is he well?"

"The hard times wear on him," Paerin Clark said. "And, I think, on his son."

"I think it isn't death that kills us," Dawson said. "I think it's fear. And Asterilhold?"

"My sources tell me that Maas is in contact with several important men in the court there. There have been loans of gold, and promises of support."

"He's raising an army."

"He is."

"And Canl?"

"He's trying to, yes."

"How long before it comes down to the field?"

"No one can know that, my lord. If you're careful and lucky, maybe never."

"I can't think that's true," Dawson said. "We have Asterilhold on one hand and you on the other."

"No, my lord," the banker said, "you don't. We both know I came hoping for advantage, but an Antean civil war won't profit us. If it does come to pass, we won't take a side. I've done what I can here. I won't be going back to Camnipol."

Dawson sat up straighter. The banker was smiling now, and it looked suspiciously like pity.

"You've abandoned Daskellin? *Now?*"

"This is one of the great kingdoms of the world," Paerin Clark said, "but my employer plays his games on larger boards than that. I wish you the best of luck, but Antea is yours to lose. Not mine. I'm traveling south."

"South? What's more important than this in the south?"

"There's an irregularity that needs my attention in Porte Oliva."

Cithrin

Cithrin stood at the top of the seawall, the city spread out behind her and the vast blue of sea and sky ahead. At the edge where the pale, shallow water of the bay turned to deep blue, five ships stood. The towering masts were trees rising from the water. The furled sails thickened the spars. The small, shallow boats of the fishing fleet were rushing into port or else out of the traffic as dozens of guide boats raced out, fighting to be the first to reach the ships and take the honor of guiding them in.

The trade ships from Narinisle had arrived. Five ships, arriving together and flying the banners of Birancour and Porte Oliva. When they had left, there had been seven. The other two might have become separated by storm or choice or scattered in an attack. They might arrive the next day or the next week or never. On the docks below her, merchants waited in agonies of hope and fear, waiting for the ships to come near enough to identify. And then, once the ships were in their berths, the fortunate among the sponsors would board, compare contracts and bills of lading, and discover whether profits were assured. The unfortunate would wait on the docks or in the port taprooms, digging at the sailors for news.

And then, once the captains of the ships had answered their sponsors, once the laborers had begun the long business of hauling the goods from ship to warehouse, once the frenzy of trade and goods and the exchange of coin had passed over Porte Oliva like a wind across the water, it would be time to begin the preparation for the next year's journey. Shipyards would make repairs. The new sponsors would offer contracts and terms to the captains. And Idderrigo Bellind Siden, Prime Governor of Porte Oliva, would consult with the captains and the masters of the guilds, and graciously accept the proposals to change this from one port city among many to the center of trade for a generation to come.

And in her hand, written in green ink on paper as smooth as poured cream, was the letter that forbade her from being part of any of it. She opened it now and considered it again. It was ciphered, of course, but she had spent long enough with Magister Imaniel's books and papers that she could read it as clearly as if it had been in a normal script.

Magistra Cithrin bel Sarcour, you are to cease all negotiation and trade in our name immediately. Paerin Clark, a senior auditor and representative of the holding company, will attend you as soon as can be arranged. Until that time, no further contracts, deposits, or loans are to be made or accepted. This is unconditional.

It was signed by Komme Medean himself, the old man's script jagged and shaking from gout. She had shown it to no one. In the eight days since it had come, she'd wrestled with the order. It was the first she'd ever had from the holding company, and precisely what she'd expected. The auditor would come, just as she'd planned at the start. He would recover the bank's funds, lost from Vanai. All her daydreams of keeping the bank alive, or steering it the way the guide boats were now preparing to lead the trade ships to safety, would end. She would be herself again. Not Tag the Carter, not a smuggler hiding in the shadows, and not Magistra Cithrin. Only without Besel and Cam and Magister Imaniel. Without Vanai.

And so, with respect, she preferred not to.

With a soft breath too slight to call itself a sigh, she ripped the page. Then again, and again, and again. When the pieces were as small as individual numbers and symbols of the cipher, she threw them over the edge of the seawall and watched them spin and flutter.

On the water, the guide boats were crowded around the trade ships. She imagined the voices of the men shouting up to the captains, the captains shouting back. As she watched, the first of the ships began the short, final leg of its annual journey. She turned away and walked back to her bank. The front door stood open to the breeze. As she walked through, Roach jumped to his feet as if she'd caught him doing something. Behind him, Yardem stretched and yawned hugely.

"Where have you been?" Captain Wester said.

"Watching the trade ships arrive, just the same as everyone else in the city," she said. She felt unaccountably light. Almost giddy.

"Well, your coffee brewer sent three people on from the café so far this morning asking after you. They came looking here."

"What did you tell them?"

"That you were busy, but I expected you'd be back in the café after midday," Wester said. "Was I lying?"

"You? Never," she said, and laughed at the suspicion on his face.

Despite the heat, Cithrin wore a dark blue dress with full sleeves and a high collar to the meeting at the governor's palace. Her hair was tucked into a soft cap and pinned in place with a silver-and-lapis hairpin that was from the last of the jewelry she had hauled from Vanai. It would have been more appropriate for a cool day in autumn and left a trickle of sweat running down her back, but the thought of something more revealing in front of Qahuar Em seemed uncomfortable. And of course wearing the necklace or brooch that he'd given her would have been inappropriate.

When he greeted her in the passageway outside the private rooms, his bow was formal. Only the angle of his smile and the merriment in his dark eyes gave a hint of their nights together. He wore a sand-colored tunic with black enameled buttons to the neck, and she found herself aware of the shape of his body beneath it. She wondered, now that they weren't to be rivals any longer, what would become of the attachment. The servant, a pale-haired Cinnae woman, bowed as they went through the doorway.

A single dark-stained table dominated the room, a bank of windows behind it looking out into the branches of a tree. The shifting branches gave the room a sense of shadow and cool that it didn't deserve. The Cinnae mercenary rose to his feet as Cithrin stepped into the room and sat again when she did. The Tralgu woman and the representative of the local merchant houses didn't attend.

"Good year," the Cinnae man said. "Have you been down to the ships, Magistra?"

"I haven't had the opportunity," Cithrin said. "My schedule's been remarkably full."

"You should make the time. There were boxes of the most fascinating baubles this year. Little globes of colored glass that chime when you rub them. Quite lovely. I bought three for my granddaughter."

"I hope the world has been treating you gently, sir," Qahuar Em said. His voice was almost sharp. *Why would he be angry?* she wondered.

"Quite well," the Cinnae said, ignoring the tone. "Quite excellently well, thank you."

The private door slid open and the governor stepped in. His round face was sweat-sheened, but cheerful. When they began to rise, he waved them back to their seats.

"No need for ceremony," he said, easing himself into his own chair. "Can I offer any of you something to drink?"

Qahuar Em shook his head, the Cinnae mercenary doing the same half a moment later as if he'd been waiting to see what Qahuar would do. Cithrin's belly tightened in warning. Something was going on that she didn't understand.

"Thank you both for coming," the governor said. "I very much appreciate the work you have all done, and your dedication to Porte Oliva, to me, and to the queen. I am excited to have such excellent minds turning toward the welfare of the city. This is always the most difficult part, isn't it? Making the decision?"

His wistful sigh said he was enjoying himself. Cithrin answered with a tight smile. Qahuar wasn't meeting her eyes.

"I have been over the proposals very carefully," the governor said. "Either of them would have been, I think, an excellent pathway to the prosperity of the city. But I think the flexibility of the five-year contract offered by the gentlemen here present would better serve than the eight that the Medean bank requires."

Cithrin felt her breath leave her. Despite the heat, something cold settled into her throat and breast. Qahuar Em hadn't been offering five years. It had been ten.

"Eight years is a very long time," the Cinnae mercenary

said, nodding slowly. His grave expression was a poor mask for his pleasure.

"Between that and the somewhat higher annual fees," the governor said, "I am very sorry to turn away your proposal, Magistra Cithrin."

"I quite understand," Cithrin said as if someone else were speaking. "Now that it's settled, might I enquire what rates Master Em offered?"

"Oh, it's a partnership," the Cinnae said. "Not just his clan, you know. We're in this together, he and I."

"I can't think that there's need to go into the details," Qahuar Em said, still not looking at her. His attempts to spare her more humiliation were worse than the mercenary's gloating.

"It isn't as though it won't be known," the governor said. "Out of courtesy and respect, Magistra, the fees asked were ten hundredths without guarantee or fourteen with."

The wrong numbers. They were the wrong numbers. It was supposed to be sixteen and nineteen, not ten and fourteen. The offer she'd found in his office had been a trap, and she had fallen into it.

"Thank you, my Lord Governor," Cithrin said with a nod. "The holding company will very much appreciate your candor."

"There will be no acrimony, I hope," the governor said. "The Medean bank is new to our city, but very much honored."

"None at all," Cithrin said. Given the hollowness in her chest, she was surprised the words didn't echo. This couldn't be happening. "Thank you very much for the courtesy of meeting with me. But I assume you gentlemen have details to discuss."

They all rose when she did, the governor taking her hand in his greasy fingers and pressing it to his lips. She kept her smile amused and world-wise in defeat, a mask of who she wished she had been. She bowed to the Cinnae mercenary and then to Qahuar Em. The emptiness in her shifted, and something painful bloomed in its place.

She walked carefully from the room, down the stairs, and out through the entrance hall to the square beyond. The sky was an opalescent white, the breeze hot as breath against her cheek. The sweat dampened her armpits, her back, her legs. She stood for a few minutes, confused and stunned. She wasn't supposed to be here. She needed to get back inside. There were details she needed to work out, contracts to be signed and witnessed. There was the great project to be done. She wasn't supposed to be out here. She should be inside.

The first sob was like retching: sudden, reflexive, and violent. *Not here,* she thought. *Oh, God, if it's going to happen, don't let it happen here where the whole damned city can watch.* Long, fast strides, her thighs pulling against the fabric of her dress to gain every inch. She reached the mazework streets. She found an alleyway, followed its turns and windings to a shadowed corner, and squatted there on the filthy paving stones. She couldn't stop the sobs now, so she pressed her arm against her mouth to keep them quiet.

She'd lost. All of her expectations, all of her plans, and she'd lost. They'd given her contract to someone else, and left her a stupid, ugly half-breed slut crying herself dry in an alley. How had she thought she could win? How could she ever have believed?

When the worst had passed, she stood again. She wiped the tears and snot on her sleeve, wiped the grime off her dress, and began the walk to her rooms. Humiliation rose on her shoulders and whispered in her ear. How much did Qahuar tell his partners? Did he brag about getting her legs apart? That old Cinnae mercenary had likely had every part of her flesh described to him before she'd walked into the room. Qahuar had known everything she'd done before she did it, planned it. Had his servants been warned not to interfere with her late-night invasion of his office? Had they been watching from the shadows, laughing at the idiot girl who thought herself clever?

At the bank, she heard the voices of the guards — Marcus and Yardem and the new Kurtadam woman — through the door, neither angry nor laughing. The tulips bobbed in the breeze, their petals broken and splayed, the red turning black at the base. She wanted to go in, but her hand would not reach for the latch. She stood for what seemed like hours, willing herself to go in to the nearest thing she had to friends or family or love. Her employees. She wanted Yardem Hane to come out and find her. For Cary to come walking down the street. For Opal to rise from her ocean grave and choke her to death where she stood.

Cithrin went upstairs. She stripped off her dress and sat on the bed in her shift. Her sweat wouldn't dry, wouldn't cool her.

She'd lost. Even now, it didn't make sense. She couldn't quite bring herself to believe it. She'd lost. The weeping was gone now. The pain was gone, though she had the sense that it was only resting, sleeping like a hunting cat after a kill. It would be back. For the moment, she felt nothing. She felt dead.

She'd lost. And the auditor was coming.

The sun traced its arc through the high air. Cithrin sat. The sounds of the street changed, the heat-dazed traffic of the day slowly giving way to the brighter, more energetic voices of evening. She needed to piss, but she put it off. Impossible to think there was any moisture left in her after soaking in sweat and tears. And still, her body performed its functions whether she approved or not. When the urging became too much to ignore, she found her night pot and used it. Once she was in motion, it was easier to move. She pulled off her shift, leaving it puddled on the floor, and found a light, embroidered dress, more attractive because it was already in her hands. She pulled it on, walked down the stairs and out into the street without bothering to lock the door behind her.

The taproom had all the shutters open, the sea breeze passing through it. No candles or lanterns were lit to keep even that slight additional heat away, so the rooms were dim despite the sunlight. The servant girl was one she recognized, thick-faced with night-black hair down to her shoulder blades. A tiny dog pranced nervously around the girl's ankles. Cithrin walked toward the back table, her table. Someone was there, half hidden by the rough cloth.

Qahuar Em.

Cithrin forced herself to walk forward. She sat across from him. A loose shutter clapped against its frame twice and went quiet. The man's expression was mild and rueful. A half-empty tankard of ale rested on the table.

"Good evening."

She didn't answer. He clicked his tongue against his teeth.

"I was hoping I might offer you a meal, a bottle of wine. An apology. It was unkind of the governor to bring you in that way."

"I don't want anything from you," she said.

"Cithrin—"

"I don't want sight or sound of you ever again for as long

as I live," she said, each word cool and sharp and deliberate. "And if you come near me, I will ask my captain of guard to kill you. And he'd do it."

Qahuar's expression hardened.

"I see. I admit I am disappointed, Magistra. I'd thought better of you."

"*You'd* thought better of *me*?"

"Yes. I hadn't imagined you the sort of woman to throw tantrums. But clearly I've misjudged. I would remind you that you were the one who put yourself in my bed. You are the one who crept through my halls. It's mean and small of you to blame me for anticipating it."

You don't know what this was, Cithrin thought. *You don't know what it meant for me. They're going to take away my bank.*

Qahuar stood and placed three small coins on the table to pay the taproom. The light caught the roughness of his bronze skin, making him look older. This summer was her eighteenth solstice. It was his thirty fifth.

"We're traders, Magistra," he said. "I very much apologize that the delivery of the news was unpleasant, but I cannot be sorry that I can take this agreement to my clan elders. I hope you have a more pleasant evening."

He pushed back the bench, wood rasping against the stone floor, and stepped around her.

"Qahuar," she said sharply.

He paused. She gathered herself. The words were cast in lead, almost too heavy to pull up her throat.

"I'm sorry I betrayed you," she said. "Tried to betray you."

"Don't be," he said. "It's the game we play."

Some time later, the taproom's servant came, took up the coins, and cleared away Qahuar Em's drink. Cithrin looked up at her.

"Your usual?"

Cithrin shook her head. Everything from her throat down to her belly felt solid as stone. She lifted her hand, surprised to find her soft cap still there. She pulled it off, let down her hair, and held the silver-and-lapis pin up. It seemed almost to glow with its own light in the gloom. The servant girl blinked at it.

"That's very beautiful," she said.

"Take it," Cithrin said. "Bring me what you think it's worth."

"Magistra?"

"Fortified wine. Farmer's beer. I don't care. Just bring it."

Geder

The high priest—Basrahip or possibly *the* Basrahip, it was hard to tell—leaned back on his leather-and-iron stool. His thick, powerful fingers rubbed at his forehead. Around them, the candles flickered and hissed, their smoke filling the room with the smell of burning fat. Geder licked his lips.

"My first tutor was a Tralgu," he said.

Basrahip pursed his lips, considered Geder, and shook his wide head. *No.* Geder swallowed his delight and tried again.

"I learned to swim at the seashore."

The broad head shook slowly. *No.*

"I had a favorite dog when I was young. A hunting beast named Mo."

The high priest's smile was beatific. His teeth seemed almost unnaturally wide. He pointed a thick finger at Geder's chest.

"Yes," he said.

Geder clapped his hands and laughed. It wasn't the first time the high priest had made the demonstration, but it was always a source of amazement. No matter what the lie, no matter what voice Geder told it in, how he held his body or changed the pitch of his voice, the huge man knew which words were false and which true. He never guessed incorrectly.

"And it's really a goddess that lets you do this?" Geder said. "Because I never came across a reference to that. The Righteous Servant was supposed to have been something Morade created, like the thirteen races and the dragon's roads."

"No. We were here before the dragons. When the great web was strung and the stars hung upon it, the goddess was present. The Sinir Kushku is her gift to the faithful. When the great collapse came, the dragons were fearful of her power. They fought against each other, each wishing the friendship and patronage of the Sinir Kushku for himself. The great Morade pretended an alliance, but the goddess knew when treachery came into his heart. She guided us here, where we might be safe, far from the world and its struggles, to wait until the time came for our return."

"This is totally unlike any account I ever read," Geder said.

"Do you doubt me?" Basrahip asked, his voice low and gentle and with the strange throbbing that seemed to inflect all his speech.

"Not at all," Geder said. "I'm amazed! A whole era before the dragons? It's something no one has written about. Not that I've ever seen."

Outside the small stone room, the stars glittered in the sky and the crescent moon lit the cascade of stones. In the darkness, Geder could almost imagine the great stone dragon above the temple wall moving, turning its head. The odd green crickets that infested the temple sang in shuddering chorus. Geder wrapped his arms around his legs, grinning.

"I cannot tell you how pleased I am that I found this place," Geder said.

"You are an honored man of a great nation," the high priest said. "I am pleased that you have come so far to find our humble temple."

Geder waved the comment away, embarrassed. It had taken the better part of a day to explain that, while he was nobility, *prince* was a particular title where he came from, and couldn't be applied so widely. He'd spent most of his life being called *lord* and *my lord,* and even though it meant the same thing, *honored man of a great nation* left him self-conscious.

Basrahip rose and stretched as, in the distance, a harsh voice screeched out the call to night prayer. Gerder expected Basrahip to make his excuses and hurry out to lead the priests in their rituals. Instead, he paused in the doorway, candles casting shadows over his eyes.

"Tell me, Lord Geder. What was it you most hoped to find here?"

"Well, I wanted to see if I could find the Sinir mountains and some source material about the Righteous Servant for a speculative essay I'm drafting up."

"This is what you *most* hoped to find?"

"Yes," Geder said. "It is."

"And now that you have found it, it will be enough?"

"Of course," Geder said.

The big man's gaze locked on him, and Geder felt a blush rising in his neck and cheeks. Basrahip waited for what seemed half a day, then shook his head.

"No," he said gently. "No, there is something else."

The days since Geder's arrival at the temple had been astounding and rich and unnerving as a dream. For two full days from morning until nightfall, he had stood in the great court between the temple itself and the gated wall. A dozen pale-robed priests with long hair and full beards sat around him as he drew maps and tried to summarize centuries of history. Often when they asked questions of him, he had to admit his ignorance. How had the borders of Asterilhold and Northcoast been set? Who claimed the islands south of Birancour and west of Lyoneia? Why were the Firstblood centered in Antea, the Cinnae in Princip C'Annaldé, and the Timzinae in Elassae when Tralgu and Dartinae had no particular homeland? Why were the Timzinae called *bugs*, the Kurtadam *clickers*, and the Jasuru *pennies*? What names were the Firstblood known by, and by whom were they hated?

They seemed particularly intrigued by the Timzinae. Geder prided himself on knowing a great deal. Having his limits exposed was humbling, but the thirst the olive-skinned men had for every scrap of information made it bearable. Every story and anecdote he gave them, they were fascinated by.

He found himself telling them his own past. His life as a boy in Rivenhalm. His father and the court in Camnipol. The Vanai campaign and how it ended and the mercenary attack on Camnipol, traveling the Keshet.

When the sun grew too hot to bear, the priests brought out a huge half-tent of stretched leather and wide wooden beams that shaded Geder and rose behind him like a gigantic hand. They hauled out wide-mouthed ceramic pots of damp sand that kept the buried gourds of water cool. Geder chewed lengths of dried goat meat spiced with salt and cinnamon, talking until his throat was hoarse. They stopped as the sun slid behind the peaks, answering the harsh, barking call. Geder's servants made camp for him there and slept on the ground beside him. And then, on the third day when he was certain his voice would fail him, Basrahip—the

Basrahip—came to him and motioned that he should follow. The huge man led him up stone stairways worked smooth as glass by generations of leather-shod feet, through the wide passage as much cave mouth as corridor.

He had expected carved stone, but Geder didn't see any sign that the halls had been touched by hammer and chisel. They might have grown this way, as if the mountains had known they would be home to these men. Lanterns of paper and parchment sat in alcoves and spilled their light over the floors and across the curved ceilings. The air smelled rich with something Geder couldn't quite identify, part manure and part spice. The air was so hot it stifled. He trotted through the twists and turns until the passage widened and the high priest stepped aside.

The great chamber was taller than twenty men standing one atop the other. The ceiling was lost in darkness more profound than night. And towering above them, the carved statue of a huge spider covered in beaten gold and lit by a hundred torches. Fifty men at least knelt at its base, all of them turned toward Geder, their hands folded on their shoulders. Geder stood, his mouth slack. No king in the world could boast a grander spectacle.

"The goddess," Basrahip had said, and his voice had echoed through the space, filling it. "Mistress of truth and unbroken ruler of the world. We are blessed by her presence."

Geder barely noticed when the huge man's hand touched his shoulder and began to press him gently but implacably down. When he knelt, it seemed like the obvious thing to do.

After that, he was taken to new quarters within the temple walls. Many of the doors and windows he'd seen when he first came went no deeper than a single room, or at most two, the priests' cells clinging to the side of the mountain.

Geder's squire brought him a basin to bathe in, his books, and the small traveling desk, and lit his lantern. He lay in the darkness that night, a thin wool blanket around him, and sleep a day's ride away. He was too excited to sleep. His only disappointment was that the temple had no library.

On the fourth morning, Basrahip came again, and their conversation began, and it had continued every day since.

I don't understand why you stay hidden."

"Don't you?" Basrahip said.

They were walking down the thin brick-paved path that led to the temple's well.

"The Righteous Servant," Geder said. "It's something that you all have. If you were in the world, you could tell whenever a merchant was lying about his costs. Or when your men were unfaithful. And life in court. God, what you could do there."

"And that is why we stay hidden," Basrahip said. "When we have involved ourselves in the affairs of the world, we have seen the rewards of it. Blades and fire. Those who have not been touched by the goddess live lives of deceit. For them, to hear our voices is to die as the people they were. Her enemies are many, and ruthless."

Geder kicked at a pebble, sending it skittering down ahead of them. The sunlight pressed down on his face and shoulders.

"But you are going to go back out," Geder said. "You said that you were waiting for the time to go back out."

"We will," the high priest said. They reached the edge of the well, a stone-lined hole in the earth with a rope tied to the stake sunk deep beside it. "When we are forgotten."

"That could be any time in the last century," Geder said, but the high priest went on as if he hadn't spoken.

"When the wounds of the old war are healed and we can

walk the world without fear, She will send us a sign. She will sort clean from unclean, and end the age of lies."

Basrahip squatted, taking the rope in his hands and hauling, hand over hand, until it came up wet. The bucket had been copper once, given over now to verdigris. Basrahip tipped it up to his lips and drank, rivulets falling from the corner of his mouth. Geder shifted uncomfortably beside him. The high priest put the bucket down and wiped the back of his hand across his lips.

"Are you troubled, Lord?"

"I'm ... It's nothing."

The wide smile was cool. The dark eyes considered him.

"Listen to me, Lord Palliako. Listen to my voice. You can trust me."

"I'm only ... Could I have a drink of that water too?"

Basrahip lifted the bucket up to him. Geder took it in both hands, drinking slowly. The water was cool and tasted of stone and metal. He handed it back, and Basrahip held it out over the blackness for a moment before he let it drop. The rope slithered as it sped back down. The splash was louder than Geder had expected.

"You can trust me," the high priest said again.

"I know," Geder said.

"You can tell me. Nothing bad will come of it."

"Tell you what? I mean, I'm not sure what you're saying."

"Yes you are," the man said, and started back toward the temple. Geder trotted to keep up. "Why did you come looking for the Sinir Kushku? What was it that drew you here?"

"You mean ..."

"Through the ages, other men have found us here. Stumbled upon us. You came *seeking*. What was it that led you here?"

Two of the younger priests passed them, heading toward

the well. Geder cracked his knuckles and frowned. He tried to remember what had started him. When was the first time he'd heard the legend? But perhaps that in itself didn't matter.

"Everywhere I turn," he said, the words coming slowly, "it seems like things are lies. I don't know who my friends are, not really. I don't know who gave me Vanai. Or who in Camnipol would want me killed. Everything in court seems like a game, and I'm the only one who doesn't know the rules."

"You are not a man of deceit."

"No. I am. I have been. I've lied and hidden things. I know how easy it is."

Basrahip stopped, leaning against a boulder. The wide face was impassive. Almost serene. Geder crossed his arms. A stirring of anger warmed his chest.

"I've been a token in everyone else's game," Geder said. "My whole life, I've been the one they tricked into sitting on sawn boards over the shit hole. I've been the one they laughed at. They burned my book. Alan Klin burned my *book*."

"Did that bring you here?"

"Yes. No. I mean, when I was a boy, I used to tell myself stories like the old histories. Where I led an army into a doomed battle and won. Or saved the queen. Or went to the underworld and pulled my mother back from the dead. And every time I've gone into the world, it's disappointed me. Do you know what that's like?"

"I do," the high priest said. "You didn't come here to write an essay, Lord Geder. You came here to find us. To find me."

Geder felt his mouth in a grim, hard scowl.

"I did," he said. "Because I want to know the truth.

Because I am sick to death of wondering. All the lies and deceits and games that everyone plays around me? I want to be the one man who can cut it away and find the truth. And so I heard about the end of all doubt."

"Would knowing alone be enough? Would it bring you peace?"

"It would," Geder said.

Basrahip paused, listening. A fly whined around them, landed on the big man's wide head to drink his sweat, and flew away again.

"It wouldn't," Basrahip said, hauling himself back to his feet. "That isn't what you want. But you are coming closer, Lord Geder. Much closer."

I heard them talking," one of his servants whispered. "They're going to kill us all in our sleep."

Geder sat in the darkness of his cell. The whispers were supposed to be quiet enough to escape him. If he'd been back in his cot, they would have. Instead, he'd slipped out and padded across the dark floor on silent feet. His back was to the wall beside the doorway, his servants not seven feet away.

"Stop talking shit," his squire said. "You're just scaring yourself."

"I'm not," the first voice said again, higher and tighter this time. "You think they want people knowing where they are? You think they're at the ass end of the world because they want company?"

A third voice said something, but he couldn't make out the words.

"And let them," the first voice said. "What I heard, he burned down Vanai just because he could, and laughed while he did it."

"Keep talking about his lordship that way and it won't be

these sand monkeys in priest robes that kill you," his squire's voice said. "I'll face down a hundred false gods before I cross him."

Geder hugged his knees closer. He expected to feel hurt, but the pain didn't come. Or anger. He rose to his feet, walking without any attempt to be quiet. He heard the silence of the servants outside his door, but he didn't care about them. Not what they thought, not what they were, not if they lived. He found his tunic and a pair of leggings and pulled them on in the darkness. He didn't bother trying to get the stays all tied. Modesty was preserved, and that was enough. Basrahip wouldn't mind.

When he walked out into the starlit dark, his servants were pretending to sleep. He stepped over them, walking the narrow path along the mountainside, the dirt cooling his feet and the stones biting them. In the first cell he reached where a monk slept, he shook the man awake.

"Take me to Basrahip," he said.

The high priest slept deeper in the temple. His rooms were dark, the pallet he slept on hardly big enough to accommodate him. The monk who'd brought Geder set down his candle and backed out of the room bowing. Basrahip tucked one massive leg under himself and sat up. He seemed perfectly alert. Geder cleared his throat.

"I've been thinking. About what you asked. I want to master the court. I want the men who used me to suffer," he said. "I want them to beg my forgiveness. I want them humiliated where the world can point at them and pity them and laugh."

The high priest didn't move, and then, slowly, he grinned. He lifted a massive finger and pointed it at Geder.

"Yes. Yes, that is what you want. And tell me this, my friend. My brother. Would that be enough?"

"It'll do for a start."

The high priest threw his head back and howled with laughter. As he grinned, his teeth shone white as ivory in the candlelight. He stood, wrapping his blanket around him, and Geder found himself grinning too. Saying the words, having them understood, was like taking a stone off his chest.

"I had hoped, Lord Geder," the high priest said. "From the moment I saw you—an honored man from a great kingdom—I *hoped* that this was the time. That you would be the sign the goddess sent, and you are. Brother Geder, you are. You have found your truth, and if you will honor it, so shall I."

"Honor it?"

"Camnipol. Your great city at the heart of your empire. Pledge her a temple there, a first temple in a new age free from lies and doubt. I will return with you myself, and through me..."

The huge man held out his hands, palms up. With the candle on the floor, it was as if he were offering handfuls of shadow. Geder couldn't stop grinning. He felt light and uncomplicated and alive in a way he hadn't since he'd scooped gems from frozen boxes half a year before.

"Through me," the high priest said, "she will give you what you want."

Clara Annalie Kalliam
Baroness of Osterling Fells

M y lady," the Tralgu door slave said, bowing.

"Good morning, Andrash," Clara said, stretching the kinks out of her back. "I can't begin to tell you how good it is to be back in the city. I do love the holding in its own right, but it simply wasn't built for the summer sun. Vincen will be...You remember Vincen? He'll be seeing to the things we brought, if you could find someone to help him?"

"Yes, my lady. Your sons are, I believe, in the summer garden."

"Sons?"

"Captain Barriath arrived some days ago," the slave said.

"Jorey and Barriath in the same house. Well, *that* can't have been pleasant."

The door slave smiled.

"It is good to have you back, my lady."

Clara patted the old man's arm as she left the heat and warmth of their private square for the dim and cool of the mansion proper. She saw at once how things had slipped. The flowers in the hall vases were wilted. The floor had a layer of grit blown in by the wind and not yet washed away. The air was close and stuffy the way it got when the windows had stayed shut for too many days in a row. Jorey had been much too amiable with the house staff. Or else he was growing to be as oblivious as his dear father. Either way, something would have to be done.

She heard the boys' voices before she reached the garden. Jorey's voice was higher, shriller, more demanding. Barriath tended to spit his arguments as if they tasted bad. From the time Jorey had had words, the two had been like fire and rain to each other, but they were devoted to one another. Clara had had much the same relationship with her own sister. *No one can harm her but me, and I shall destroy her.* Love was so often like that.

At the steps down into the summer garden, she paused.

"Because it's *simplistic,* that's why," Jorey said. "There's a hundred things happening, and they all tie into each other. Now that there isn't going to be a farmer's council, are we facing another grain revolt? If Northcoast's really on the edge of another round of succession wars, will Asterilhold be distracted from us? Are the new Hallskari ship designs going to mean more piracy in Estinport and less in Tauendak? You can't take everything like that and press it down into one thing. The world's more complex than that."

"There are fewer choices than you believe, brother," Barriath said. "You won't find someone against the farmers and supporting Asterilhold. If you want one, you take the other. No family will forbid mixing races and also trade with Borja. The king isn't like a sculptor with a fresh stone, able to make whatever he sees fit. He's like a man walking into a sculptor's yard picking from what's already there."

"And you think the prince is the only way he can show his favor?"

"The only one that matters," Barriath said. "If his majesty gave every favor and grant he has to Daskellin, and sent Aster to be the ward of Maas, he'd still be saying that in the long term, the kingdom will be shaped by Maas's vision. That's why Issandrian—"

"But if the king—"

. The two voices intertwined, neither boy listening to other, and the threads of their arguments tangled into a single ugly knot. Clara stepped out into the garden and put her hands on her hips in feigned accusation.

"If this is how you greet your poor mother, I should have fostered you both with wolves," she said.

Her boys both grinned and came to embrace her. They were men now, strong-armed and smelling of musk and hair oil. It seemed like only the week before that she'd been able to take them in her arms. Then they started in again, talking over each other, only now the melee of words seemed to center on her and why she was there rather than the politics of the court. Clara beamed at them both and stepped down into the lush green and pale blooms of the summer garden. The fountain, at least, had been maintained, water splashing down the front of a contemplative if underdressed cast bronze Cinnae woman. Clara sat at the fountain's lip and began pulling off her traveling jacket.

"Your father, poor thing, is gnawing his foot off back at home, and as a favor to him and myself, I have come to keep up some semblance of normalcy. This idiotic bickering has cost me the better part of the season already, and I simply must see dear Phelia."

Jorey leaned against an ivied wall. Arms crossed and scowling, he looked like the image of his father. Barriath sat beside her and laughed.

"I have missed you. No other woman would call the first armed conflict on the streets of Camnipol in five generations idiotic bickering," he said.

"I am just as sorry as anyone about what happened to

dear Lord Faskellin," Clara said, sharply. "But I defy you to call it anything besides idiotic."

"Peace, Mother, peace," Barriath said. "You're quite right, of course. It's only that no one else puts it that way."

"Well, I can't think why they don't," Clara said.

"Does Father know you're going to call on Maas?" Jorey asked.

"He does, and before you start, I am to be guarded the whole time, so please don't bother with the monster stories of Lord Maas and all the terrible thing he's like to do to me."

Her two boys looked at one another.

"Mother," Jorey began, and she cut him off with a wave of her hand. She turned pointedly to her eldest son.

"I assume you've taken leave from the fleet, Barriath dear. How is poor Lord Skestinin and that painted shrew he had the poor judgment to marry?"

The streets of the city were full and busy. Carriage wheels clattered over the cobblestones. In the market, butchers sold meat and bakers, bread. Petty criminals scooped shit out of the alleys and off the pavement, guarded by swordsmen wearing the king's colors if not precisely his livery. The cherry trees that lined the streets sported green fruit with real threats of red. Workmen hung out over the Division, repairing and maintaining the very bridges from which they were suspended. She had not thought it possible that a city could look as it had in better times, sound as it had, smell as it had, and still be bent double under the weight of fear. She had been wrong.

It showed in small things. Merchants too quick to laugh, altercations over precedence and right of way, and the stony expression common to everyone in the city when they thought no one was watching. Even the horses smelled something, their huge, liquid eyes a fraction too wide and their gait just barely skittish.

She'd chosen to take a sedan chair open on the sides with four bearers and Vincen Coe walking beside it. Something had happened to the poor man's eye just before they'd left Osterling Fells, and the bruise had started to seep yellow and green down his cheek. He wore boiled leather studded with steel and both sword and dagger. It was more than a huntsman would sport, and with the recent injury, he looked quite thuggish.

The mansion of Feldin Maas shared a private courtyard with House Issandrian. Both gates were of the same gaudy ironwork, the houses themselves painted and adorned in such rich profusion they seemed designed by a cake maker gone mad. Curtin Issandrian, of course, was exiled just as her Dawson was, and he had taken all his family and servants with him. Her uncle Mylus had suffered a blow to the head when he was young and spent his life with half his face slack and empty. The square reminded Clara of him, all bustle and action on the left and empty as death on the right.

Phelia stood at the top of the front steps. Her dress was purple velvet with silver thread all along the sleeves and collar. It should have been beautiful on her. Clara gave her shawl to the footman and went up to Phelia. Her cousin took her hands and smiled tightly.

"Oh, Clara," Phelia said. "I can't say how much I've missed you. This has been the most awful year. Please, come in."

Clara nodded to the door slave. It wasn't the Dartinae woman she was used to seeing, but a severe-looking Jasuru man. He didn't nod back. She stepped into the relative cool of the Maas front hall.

"Hey! Stop, you!"

Clara turned, surprised to be addressed in so curt a fashion, only to see that the comment had been directed at Vincen Coe. The Jasuru man was on his feet, his palm against Vincen's chest. The huntsman had gone unnaturally still.

"He's with me," Clara said.

"No one goes in armed," the door slave growled.

"You can wait here, Vincen."

"All respect, my lady," the huntsman said, his gaze still fastened to the Jasuru, "but no."

Clara put a hand to her cheek. Phelia had gone pale, her hands flitting one way and another like birds.

"Leave your blades, then," Clara said. And then to her cousin, "I assume we can rely on the rules of hospitality?"

"Of course," Phelia said. "Yes, of course. Of course you can."

Vincen Coe stood silent for a moment. Clara had to agree that Phelia would have been more convincing if she hadn't said it three times over. Vincen's hands went to his belt, undid the clasp, and handed it with sword and dagger still sheathed to the door slave. The Jasuru took it and nodded him through.

"I believe you've lost weight since I saw you last," Clara said, walking at Phelia's side. "Are you feeling well?"

Her answering smile was so brittle it cracked at the sides.

"It's been so hard. Ever since the king sent away Curtin and Alan—and you, of course. Ever since then, it's all been so hard. Feldin hardly sleeps anymore. I wish all this had never happened."

"Men," Clara said, patting Phelia's arm. The woman shied away, and then, as if realizing she ought not, permitted the touch with a nod. "Dawson's been beside himself.

Really, you'd think the world was ending from the way he chews at every scrap of gossip."

"I love the king and God knows I'm loyal to the throne," Phelia said, "but Simeon's handled this all so badly, hasn't he? A brawl goes out of hand, and he sends people into exile? It only makes everyone feel there's something terrible happening. There doesn't have to be."

She turned up a wide flight of well-polished black stairs. Clara followed her. From the end of the hall they were leaving, Clara heard men's voices raised in argument but couldn't make out the words. One of the voices was Feldin Maas, but while the other seemed familiar, she couldn't put a name to it. She caught Vincen Coe's eye and nodded him down the hall.

Go find what you can.

He shook his head once. *No.*

Clara lifted her eyebrows, but by then they'd reached the landing. Phelia ushered them into the wide sitting room.

"You can wait here," Clara said at the doorway.

"If you wish, my lady," Vincen Coe said, and turned to stand with his back to the wall like a guard at his duty and didn't show the vaguest hint of going back down the stairs to investigate. It was all quite vexing.

The sitting room had been redone in shades of red and gold since the last time Clara had seen it, but it still had the low divan by the window that she preferred. And, like a good hostess, Phelia had a pipe prepared for her. Clara plucked up the bone and hardwood bowl and tamped a bit of tobacco into it.

"I don't know what to do any longer," Phelia said, sitting on the divan. She was leaning forward with her hands clasped between her knees like a child. "I tell myself things aren't so terribly bad, but then I wake up in the dark of the night and I can't get back to sleep. Feldin's never there. He comes to bed with me, but as soon as I'm asleep he goes back to his letters and his meetings."

"These are hard times," Clara said. She lit the pipe from a thin silver candle set there for the purpose and drew in the smoke.

"Curtin was going to take the prince on as his ward, you know. But now that he's gone, everyone's been scrambling. I think ... I think Feldin may be named. I may be helping to raise a prince." Phelia giggled. "Can you imagine me raising a prince?"

"Aster's a boy," Clara said. "I've had three of them. One doesn't raise boys so much as try to keep fragile things out of their reach."

"Men aren't any different," Phelia said. "They never think about what might break."

Clara sucked on the stem of the pipe and blew out a cloud of sweet grey smoke before she spoke.

"That is the issue, isn't it? We have a problem, and it's spilled over from our court into Northcoast and Asterilhold. Sarakal and Hallskar are likely taking notice as well."

"I know it."

"Well then, dear," Clara said, keeping her voice light, "how shall we solve it?"

"I don't know why it's all such a concern. There were ages when Asterilhold, Antea, and Northcoast all answered to the High Kings. Everyone's intermarried with everyone else. We're practically a single kingdom already. When you think about it."

"That is so utterly true," Clara said, sitting beside her cousin. Phelia was plucking at her dress with her fingertips now, picking away threads and lint that weren't there.

"I just don't see why there should be any fuss about swords

and bows and such. Nobody can possibly want that, can they? What would fighting gain anyone? It isn't as if we aren't already practically one kingdom."

"Yes, but as long as there's one throne in Camnipol and another in Kaltfel, they'll rattle their swords at one another," Clara said. "It's what they do, isn't it?"

Phelia started. Her eyes were wider than they should have been, and her hands gripped her knees until the blood was all gone from her knuckles. Now *that* was interesting. Clara cleared her throat and went on, pretending not to notice.

"The problem is how to give everyone a way to keep their honor intact without asking very much of them. I know Dawson won't bring himself to see reason unless we can find a path to it that doesn't involve stooping under something. I assume your Feldin's very much the same."

"But he's won. Feldin feels he's won, and if the prince does come to live with us..."

Clara waited.

"You know I admire Dawson," Phelia said. "He's always been so staunch. Even when he was being rude to Feldin, it was more from the way Dawson lives in the world as he would like it to be. I never thought it was out of anger or spite."

"Well, I wouldn't go so far as to call my darling husband a man without spite, but I take your meaning, yes."

Phelia giggled nervously. Her shoulders were hunched like someone braced against a blow.

"Did you hear that Rania Hiren's pregnant?" Phelia asked. Clara debated for less than a heartbeat, and decided to let her cousin change the subject.

"Not again. How many times is this?"

"Eight, if you count the live births. There were three stillborn."

"I'm amazed she has the stamina," Clara said. "And her husband must be a man of some quality. Rania's the dearest soul under the sky, but after the twins, she did start to look a bit like a mop's head. It isn't her fault, of course. It's just her skin."

"I have the same sort, though," Phelia said. "I dread to think what I'll look like after my first child."

"You're young, dear. I'm sure you'll be able to get your figure back. I suppose it's rude for me to ask how work has been on that particular project?"

Phelia blushed, but she also relaxed. Bed gossip and the intricacies of the female flesh might be indelicate, but they were safer than politics and the rumors of war. Throughout the hour, Clara let them talk of nothing in particular, always leaving opportunities for Phelia to return them to the topic of their husbands and the threat hanging over the city like smoke from a fire. At no point did Phelia take the opportunities offered her. That said quite a bit in itself.

When the time came to take her leave, Clara found Vincen Coe precisely where he had been, scowling at the empty air. As they walked down the stairs, Phelia took Clara's arm, leaning into her with each step; the visit seemed to have calmed her as much as it had uneased Clara herself. At the door, Vincen reclaimed his blades from the Jasuru as Clara embraced Phelia in farewell. Her bearers brought the sedan chair to the ready, and Clara took her shawl back from the footman. It wasn't until she was out of the private square that the last of the tobacco ran out and Clara realized she'd accidentally stolen Phelia's pipe. She knocked the bowl clean on the side opposite from Vincen so as to keep the ashes from falling on him.

"You were eavesdropping, I assume?" she said, loudly enough to carry over the noise of the street.

"Not at all, my lady."

"Oh please, Vincen," she said. "I'm not dim. How much did you hear?"

A few moments later, the huntsman shrugged.

"Almost all, my lady. She spoke a bit softly when she was discussing her fertility problems, and you were laughing at the comments about Lord Sonnen's mistress."

"You heard the first part, then. About my husband and hers?"

"I did."

"Why do you suppose she would be concerned about Asterilhold and Antea sharing a common history? Being 'practically one kingdom'?"

"At a guess, my lady, because she expects they may be again."

He glanced at her, and his expression—guarded, calm, grim—told her that they were in agreement. Whatever the intricacies of blood and marriage, precedent and politics, Antea and Asterilhold could never be united while Simeon and Aster lived. And Phelia, never meaning to say it, thought unification possible. Even likely. And Aster was quite likely going to be living under her roof.

It seemed to follow that Feldin Maas and his foreign backers intended to kill Prince Aster.

"Well," Clara said with a sigh. "So much for making peace."

Cithrin

Wind rattled the shutters and hissed at the windows. The morning sun was too bright to bear. By simply existing, the world made Cithrin want to vomit. She rolled over on her bed, pressing her hand to her throat. She didn't want to stand up, and she certainly wasn't walking to the Grand Market. The attempt alone would kill her.

There was a vague uneasiness muttering at the back of her mind, a reason that staying here would be a problem. She was supposed to go to the café because...

Because...

Cithrin said something obscene, then, without opening her eyes, repeated it slowly, drawing out the sounds. She was supposed to meet with a representative of the tanner's guild to talk about insuring their trade when the ships went back out. It wouldn't be long now. Days, perhaps. Not more than two weeks. Then the thrice-damned ships would go out, traveling up the coast while the season still held. They'd make their stops in the north, make what trades they could, and then hunker down for the winter, waiting for the ships from Far Syramys to reach the great island of Narinisle and begin the whole blighted thing over again. And so it would go, on and on and on until the end of all things, whether Cithrin got out of bed or not.

She sat up. Her rooms were in disarray around her. Bottles

and empty wineskins crowded the floor. Another gust pushed against the windows, and she felt the air around her press in and then out. It was nauseating. She stood up slowly and walked across to look for a dress to put on that didn't stink of sweat. Sometime during the night, it appeared she'd knocked against the night pot, because a puddle of cold piss was well on its way to staining the floorboards. The only clothes that didn't look filthy were the trousers and rough shirt she'd worn as Tag the Carter. For what she had to do, they'd suffice. There were still half a dozen silver coins in her purse, and she shoved them into Tag's pocket.

By the time she reached the bottom of the stairs, she felt more nearly human. She stepped out into the street for a moment, then back in through the bank's front door.

"Roach," she said, and the little Timzinae jumped to attention.

"Magistra Cithrin," he said. "Captain Wester and Yardem just left to collect payment from the brewer just north of the wall and the two butchers in the salt quarter. Barth and Corisen Mout went with them. Enen's asleep in the back because she drew night watch, and Ahariel is going to get some sausages and come back."

"I need you to run an errand for me," Cithrin said. "Go to the café and let the man from the tanner's guild know I won't be there. Tell him I'm unwell."

The boy's nictatating membranes clicked over his eyes nervously.

"Captain Wester said I should stay here," Roach said. "Enen's asleep, and he wanted someone awake in case—"

"I'll stay down here until someone gets back," Cithrin said. "I may feel like slow death, but I can still raise a shout if it's called for."

Roach still looked uncertain. Cithrin felt a stab of annoyance.

"I pay Wester," she said. "I pay you too, for that. Now *go*."

"Y-yes, Magistra."

The boy darted out to the street. Cithrin stood in the doorway for a long moment, watching the dark legs scissor and stretch as he ran. Far down the street, he dodged a cart loaded with fresh-caught fish, turned the corner, and vanished. Cithrin counted slowly to twelve, giving him time to reappear. When he didn't, she walked out into the street and pulled the door shut behind her. The wind was against her and kicking up bits of dust and straw, but she squinted her way to the taproom.

"Good morning, Magistra," the keeper said as her eyes adjusted to the gloom. "Back already?"

"Seems I am," she said, fishing the silver coins back out of her pocket. "I'll take what this buys."

The keeper took the coins, lifting and dropping his hand as he estimated their weight.

"Your boys know how to go through wine," he said.

"They don't drink it," she said, grinning. "It's all for me."

The man laughed. It was a new kind of lie she'd only just discovered, telling the bleak truth lightly and letting everyone around her mistake it for a joke. *They don't drink it; it's all for me. Come winter, I'm as likely to be in the stocks as free. Nothing I do matters.*

He came back with two dark bottles of wine and a small tun of beer. Cithrin tucked the tun under her arm, took a bottle in either hand, and waited as he opened he door for her. Now the wind was at her back, pushing her on like it wanted her to get back home. The sky was blue above her with a skin of white clouds high in the air, but it smelled like rain. Porte Oliva autumns had a reputation for rough weather, and summer was in its last days now. A little cloud-burst now and again hardly seemed worth complaining about.

She didn't go back into the main rooms, heading for her own door instead. Maneuvering up the stairs was hard with the tun still under her arm. She hit the corner of the wall at the top with her elbow. The impact was enough to leave her fingers tingling, but she didn't drop the bottle.

She'd forgotten about the puddle of piss, but she was feeling well enough now to open her window and pour the night pot's contents into the alley. She swabbed up the rest with a dirty shift, then threw that out the window too. She'd eaten a link of gristly sausage and a heel of black bread the day before. She knew she ought to be hungry, but she wasn't. She pulled off her carter's boots, pulled open the first of the wine bottles, and lay back on her bed, her back against the little headboard.

The wine was sweeter than she was used to, but she could feel the bite of it. Her stomach rebelled for a moment, twisting like a fish on a fire, and she slowed down to sips until it calmed. Her head throbbed once, the beginning of an ache. The wind paused, leaving her in silence. She heard the voices of the two Kurtadam guards rising from below her.

The woman—Enen—laughed. Warmth and calm slid into Cithrin's blood. She took one last, long drink straight from the bottle's neck, turned, and set the wine on the floor. The darkness behind her eyes was comfortable and deep. The roar of the wind kicking back up seemed to come from a great distance, and her mind, such as it was, sparked and slipped. Connections came together in unlikely, unrepeatable ways.

She had the sense that Magister Imaniel had left her something for Captain Wester. She thought that it had to do with the canal traffic in Vanai connecting to the docks in Porte Oliva, and also with herbs and spices packed in snow. Without drawing a line between awake and dozing or dozing and asleep, Cithrin's consciousness faded to darkness. Time stopped, started when she became vaguely aware of angry voices, very far away, and stopped again.

"Get up."

Cithrin forced her eyes open. Captain Wester stood in the doorway, his arms crossed. The light was dim, the city in twilight and cloud.

"Get out of bed," he said. "Do it now."

"Go away," she said.

"I told you to get out of that God damned *bed*!"

Cithrin pushed up on one arm. The room shifted, unsteady.

"And do what?" she said.

"You've missed five meetings," Marcus said. "People are going to start talking, and when they do, you're done. So stand up and do what needs doing."

Cithrin stared at him, her mouth slack with disbelief and a rising anger.

"Nothing needs doing," she said. "It's done. I'm done. I had my chance, and I lost it."

"I met Qahuar Em. He's not worth pouting over. Now you—"

"Qahuar? Who cares about Qahuar?" Cithrin said, sitting up. She didn't remember spilling wine on her tunic, but it tugged where dried wine had adhered to her skin. "It was the contract. I tried for it, and I lost. I had the world by the hair, and I lost. I failed."

"You failed?"

Cithrin spread her arms, gesturing at the rooms, the city, the world. Pointing out the obvious. Wester stepped closer. In the dim light, his eyes seemed bright as river stones, his mouth as hard as iron.

"Did you watch your wife and daughter burn to death in front of you? *Because* of you?" he asked. When she didn't answer, he nodded. "So it could have been worse. You aren't dead. There's work that needs doing. Get up and do it."

"I'm not permitted. I had a letter from Komme Medean that I'm not allowed to trade in his name."

"So instead you curled up in a mewling ball in his name? I'm sure he'll be thrilled. Get out of bed."

Cithrin lay down, pulling her pillow to her chest. It smelled foul, but she held it anyway.

"I don't take orders from you, *Captain*," she said, making the last word an insult. "You take money from me, so you do what I tell you. Now go away."

"I won't let you throw away everything you've worked for."

"I *worked* to keep the bank's money safe, and I've done it. So you're right. I win. Now go away."

"You want to keep it."

"Stones want to fly," she said. "They don't have wings."

"Find a way," he said, almost gently.

It was too much. Cithrin shouted wordless rage, sat up, and threw the pillow at him as hard as she could. She didn't want to cry anymore, and here she was, crying.

"I told you to get out!" she screamed. "No one wants you here! I am canceling your contract. Take your wages and your men and lock the door behind you."

Wester took a step back. Cithrin's chest went hollow, and she tried to swallow back the words. He bent down, picked up her pillow between thumb and finger, and lobbed it back to her. It landed on the bed at her side with a soft sound like someone being punched in the stomach. He nudged one of the empty wineskins with the toe of his boot and took a long, deep breath.

"Remember that I tried to talk you back to your senses," he said.

He turned. He walked away.

She had anticipated the pain, braced herself for it, so it wasn't the anguish of knowing he would leave her that surprised. The surprise was that even knowing, even being ready for it, the despair could still swamp her. It felt like something had died halfway between her throat and her heart, and was curled there inside her body, rotting. She heard him walking down the stairs, each step quieter than the one before. Cithrin snatched up her filthy pillow and screamed into it. It felt like days, just screaming, her body shaking from hunger and exhaustion and the poison of wine, beer, and ale. The muscles in her back and belly were threatening to cramp, but she could no more stop screaming and weeping than she could choose not to breathe.

There were voices below her. Marcus Wester and Yardem Hane. She heard Yardem rumble something that she recognized form its cadence as *Yes, sir* though the syllables before and after it were a confusion. Then a smaller, higher voice. Roach, perhaps.

They'd all go. All of them.

It didn't matter.

Nothing mattered. Her parents were dead so long ago she didn't remember them. Magister Imaniel and Cam and Besel, all dead. The city of her childhood was burned and broken. And the bank, the one thing she had ever made for herself, would be taken from her as soon as the auditor arrived. She couldn't bring herself to think that a few guards leaving early could matter.

But it did.

Slowly, very slowly, the storm within her stilled. It was full dark now, and tiny raindrops tapped against the window like fingernails. She reached for the wine bottle beside the bed and was surprised to find it empty. But there was still the other bottle. And the tun of beer. She would be all right. She only needed to get her strength back. A few more minutes were all she needed.

She hadn't quite roused herself when the footsteps came. First the steady tramp at the base of the stairway, and then, before it even reached the top, heavier thudding. Something hit the wall of the house, and Yardem grunted. There was a wet sound that might have been rain pouring off the roof, but seemed nearer than that. A light glowed. A lantern in Wester's hand. And behind him, Yardem Hane and the two Kurtadam guards struggling with a copper basin easily four feet long.

"We should have brought it first and filled it later," Enen said, her voice straining.

"We'll know next time," Marcus said.

Through her doorway, she saw the three guards put down the basin. It was as tall as Marcus's knee and it sloshed.

"What are you doing?" Cithrin asked, her voice smaller and weaker than she'd expected it to be.

Ignoring her, Yardem handed a round stone jar to the captain and started lighting the candles and lamps in the main room. The two Kurtadam saluted and went back down the stairs. Cithrin sat up, steadying herself with one hand. Marcus walked toward her, and before she could stop him, he grabbed her by the hair and dragged her off the bed. Her knees hit the floor with a thud and a stab of pain.

"What are you *doing*?" she shouted.

"I tried talking first," Wester said, and pushed her into the basin. The water was warm. "Take those rags off or else I will."

"I am not going to—"

In the growing light of the candles, his expression was hard and implacable.

"I've seen girls before. I'm not going to be shocked. I've got soap here," he said, pressing the stone jar into her hand. "And be sure to wash your hair. It's greasy enough to catch fire."

Cithrin looked at the jar. It was heavier than she'd expected, with a tight-fit lid. She didn't know the last time she'd washed herself. When he spoke again, his voice was resigned.

"Either you do it, or I will."

"Don't watch," she said, and as she did, she realized that she was agreeing to a contract whose terms she didn't yet know. All she felt was relief that they hadn't left her.

Marcus made in impatient sound, but turned to face the stairway. Yardem coughed discreetly and stepped into the bedroom. Cithrin pulled off the carter's clothes and knelt in the basin. The air felt cold against her skin. A carved wood bowl floated beside her, and she used it to rinse herself. She hadn't realized how filthy she'd felt until she didn't anymore.

A familiar voice came from the stairway.

"Is she there?" Cary asked.

"She is," Marcus said. "Just toss it up for now."

The actor grunted, and Marcus moved forward, catching a bundle of rope and cloth out of the air.

"We'll be downstairs," Cary said, and Cithrin's street door opened and closed. Marcus untied the rope and passed a length of soft flannel out behind him. Cithrin took the towel from his hand.

"Got a clean dress here too," he said. "You say when you're decent."

Cithrin stepped out of the bath shivering and dried herself quickly. The water in the basin was dark, a scum of suds floating on the top. Shrugging on the dress, she recognized it as one of Cary's. The cloth smelled of face paints and dust.

"I'm decent," she said.

Yardem came out of her bedroom. He'd fashioned her blanket into a sack and filled it with empty wineskins and bottles. The tun and her remaining bottle were in with the dead. She reached out, ready to tell him to leave those, that she wasn't done with them. The Tralgu cocked an ear, his earring jingling. She let him pass.

"I've got food coming," Marcus said. "You have all the bank's records in here?"

"There's a transaction ledger at the café," she said. "And copies of a few of the contracts."

"I'll send someone. I am posting a guard at the foot of the stairs and under that window. No drink stronger than coffee comes in. You stay in here until you figure out what we're going to do to keep your bank for you."

"There isn't anything," she said. "I've been forbidden from any more negotiation or trade."

"And God knows we wouldn't want to break any rules," Marcus said. "Whatever you need, you say the words. Everyone gets a good self-pitying drunk now and again, but it's over. You stay sober and you do what needs doing. Understood?"

Cithrin stepped in close and kissed him. His lips were still and uncertain, the stubble around them rough. He was the third man she'd ever kissed. Sandr and Qahuar and Captain Wester. He stepped back.

"My daughter wasn't much younger than you."

"Would you have done this to her?" she asked, gesturing at the basin.

"I'd have done anything for her," he said. And then, "I'll have the bath taken away, Magistra. Do you want us to get some coffee since we have to get the books from the café anyway?"

"It will be closed by now. It's night."

"I'll have an exception made."

"Then yes."

He nodded and went back down the stairway. Cithrin sat at her little desk. The sound of rain above her mixed with the voices below. There was nothing to be done, of course. All the best efforts and intentions in the world couldn't change a single number inked in her ledgers. She looked anyway. Yardem and the two Kurtadam came and hauled the basin away again. Roach appeared with a bowl of fish-and-cream soup that tasted of black pepper and the sea. A mug of beer would have gone with it perfectly, but she knew better than to ask. Water was good enough for now.

Her mind felt fragile, a thing that might fall apart at any little jostle, but she tried to imagine herself as the auditor from Carse. What would he see when he looked at all this? She went through the initial listing of inventory that she'd made. Silk, tobacco, gems, jewels, spices, silver, and gold. The pudgy Antean at the mill pond had stolen some, and her estimate of the loss was included, the numbers in black strokes against the cream-colored paper. So there was the beginning. Now to what she'd done with it.

Turning the pages had a sense of nostalgia. The dry hiss

of the paper, and here was another artifact of the golden age that had just passed. The contract and receipt from when she'd bought the rooms from the gambler. The onionskin permit and seal that had marked the opening of the bank. She traced her fingertips over it. It hadn't been a full season since she'd begun. It seemed more than that. It seemed a life-time. Then the agreements of consignment from the spicer and the cloth merchants. Her valuation, theirs, and the final income from sale. The jewelry had always been the problem. She found herself wondering if there might have been a bet-ter way to be rid of it than the one she'd chosen. Maybe if she'd waited until the ships from Narinisle had come in. Or placed them on consignment with a trading house with a heavy export trade. Then she wouldn't have been flooding her own market. Well, next time.

Distant thunder rolled softly through the steady tapping of rain. Roach, soaked to his scales, brought up the lockbox from the café, a huge earthenware mug of coffee, and a note from Maestro Asanpur hoping that she would feel better soon and saying that the café felt too large without her in it. It was almost enough to reduce her to tears again, but that would have confused the Timzinae boy, so she forced herself to keep composure.

The best trade she'd worked had been the horizontal semi-monopoly with the brewer, cooper, and taphouses. Each person in the chain of production was in business with the bank, and so as soon as the grain and water arrived at the brewery, every trade benefited her, and put her in the posi-tion to guarantee business to the next link. If she could make arrangements with a few farmers for dedicated access to their grain crops, it would be a locked-in gold-producing mechanism.

But that would be for the next person, whoever they were.

Cithrin sipped at her coffee. It had been a good thought, though, and well performed. In a year, when the remnants of her parents' investment in the bank came to her, she would have to see if there was some much smaller version of the same plan. It would be painful, she thought, going from Magistra Cithrin bel Sarcour to the bank's ward again for that last year. But once she reached her naming day, and could enter into business for herself...

The skin on her arm puckered, the fine hairs standing up. Her neck prickled. A feeling of cold fire lit her spine. She closed the books she'd written, shoved them aside, and went back to the older ones, written by other hands now dead. The records of Vanai. The small red-inked notation that marked her arrival at the bank. She closed the book with trembling hands.

Captain Wester had been right.

There was a way.

Dawson

"I won't hear it," King Simeon said. The months hadn't been kind to him. His skin was greyer than it had been, his lips an unhealthy blue. Sweat beaded his brow though the room wasn't particularly warm. "God, Dawson. Listen to yourself. You're back from exile for one day—*one*—and already you're back at it."

"If Clara's right and Maas is plotting against Aster's life—"

Simeon slapped his palm to the table. The meeting chamber echoed with it, and the silence that followed was broken only by the songs of finches and the babbling of the fountain outside the windows. The guards around the back wall remained impassive as always, their armor the black and gold of the city, their swords sheathed at their hips. Dawson wondered what they would have said, had they been asked. Someone must be able to talk sense to Simeon, though it clearly wasn't him.

"If I'd listened to your advice," the king said, "Issandrian would be leading a popular revolt against me right now. Instead, he was here yesterday, bending his knee, asking my forgiveness and swearing on his life that the mercenary riot wasn't his plan or doing."

"If it wasn't his, it was someone's," Dawson said.

"I am your king, Baron Osterling. I am perfectly capable of guiding this kingdom safely."

"Simeon, you are my friend," Dawson said softly. "I know how you sound when you're frightened to your bones. Can you put it off until next year?"

"Put what off?"

"Fostering your son. Naming his protector. The closing of the court is three weeks from now. Only say that the events of the season have distracted you from the decision. Take time."

Simeon rose. He walked like an old man. Outside the window the leaves were still green, but less so than they had been. The summer was dying, and someday very soon the green would fade, red and gold taking the field. Beautiful colors, but still death.

"Maas has no reason to wish Aster ill," Simeon said.

"He's in contact with Asterilhold. He's working with them—"

"You worked with Maccia to reinforce Vanai. Lord Daskellin danced with Northcoast. Lord Tremontair is keeping assignations with the ambassador from Borja, and Lord Arminnin spent more time in Hallskar than Antea last year. Shall I slaughter every nobleman with connections outside the kingdom? You wouldn't live." Simeon's breath was fast and shallow. He leaned against the windowsill, steadying himself. "My father died when he was a year younger than I am now."

"I remember."

"Maas has allies. Everyone who loved Issandrian and Klin turned to him when they left."

"Mine turned to Daskellin."

"You don't have allies, Dawson. You have enemies and

admirers. You couldn't even keep Palliako's boy near you when he was the hero of the day. Lerer sent him off to the edge of the world rather than let him take another revel from you. Enemies and admirers."

"Which are you, Majesty?"

"Both. Have been since you flirted that Cinnae girl away from me at the tourney when we were twelve."

Dawson chuckled. The king's smile was almost abashed, and then he was laughing too. Simeon came back and collapsed into his chair.

"I know you don't approve," he said. "But trust me that I'm doing the best I can. There are just so many things to balance, and I'm so tired. I am unbearably tired."

"At least don't give Aster to Maas. I don't care if he is the most influential man at court just now. Find someone else."

"Thank you for your advice, old friend."

"Simeon—"

"No. Thank you. That's all."

In the antechamber, the servants gave Dawson back his sword and dagger. It seemed years since Simeon had insisted on the old formality of coming to private audience unarmed. This was how far they had all fallen. Dawson was still adjusting the buckle when he stepped outside. The air was warm, the sun heavy in the sky, but the breeze had an edge to it. The soft, pressing air of summer was gone. The seasons were changing again. Dawson turned away the footman's assisting hand and climbed into his carriage.

"My lord?" the driver asked.

"The Great Bear," Dawson said.

The whip cracked, and the carriage lurched off, leaving the blocky towers and martial gates of the Kingspire behind. He let himself lean back into the seat, the jolts and knocks sending jabs of pain up his spine. First the journey back from Osterling Fells and then the better half of the day waiting for his majesty to clear an audience for him had worn him down more than it once would have.

When he'd been a young man, he'd ridden from Osterling Fells to Camnipol, stopping only to trade horses, arrived just before the queen's ball, and spent the whole evening until the dawn dancing. Mostly with Clara. It seemed like a story he'd heard told of someone else, except that he could still see the dress she'd worn and smell the perfume at the nape of her neck. He turned the memory aside before his wife's younger incarnation aroused him. He wanted to walk upright when he reached the club, and while he was old, he wasn't dead.

The Fraternity of the Great Bear rose up, its façade the black stone and gold leaf of the Undying City. Coaches and carriages were thick in the street, drivers pushing to position themselves where their particular masters would walk the fewest steps from carriage to door. The air stank of the fresh horse droppings being ground to paste under a hundred hooves. Dawson toyed with the idea of getting out here and walking in just to escape, but it was beneath his station, so he made do with abusing the driver for his slowness and incompetence. By the time the footmen of the club hurried out with a step for him, he almost felt better.

Within, the club was a fabric woven from pipe smoke, heat, and music ignored in favor of conversation. Dawson gave his jacket to a servant girl who bowed and scurried away. When he entered the great hall, half a dozen men turned toward him, applauding his return with varying degrees of pleasure and sarcasm. Enemies and admirers. Dawson cut a bow that could be read as acknowledgment or insult depending on who it was given to, scooped up a cut crystal glass of fortified wine, and stalked to the smaller halls on the left.

A wide, round table sat in the center of one hall, a dozen men around it, many of them talking at once. In among the press of bodies and wit, Issandrian's long hair and Sir Klin's artless face. Issandrian caught sight of him and stood. He nodded to Dawson rather than bow. It might only have been a trick of the light, but the man seemed lessened. As if his exile had actually humbled him. The others at his table began to grow quiet, becoming aware that something was happening around them even if they were too dim to know what. Dawson drew his dagger in a duelist's salute, and Issandrian smiled in what might have been approval.

At the back of the hall were private meeting rooms, and the least of these was hardly larger than a carriage itself. The dark leather couches ate what little light the candles gave. Daskellin sat in a corner where he could see whoever entered. His back was to the wall, and his sword was undrawn, but near his hand.

"Well," Dawson said, lowering himself to the couch opposite, "I see you've squandered everything we had in my absence."

"Pleasure to see you too," Canl Daskellin said.

"How do we go from successfully defending Camnipol from foreign blades to riding behind Feldin Maas? Can you answer that?"

"Do you want the long answer or the short?"

"Will the long be less annoying?"

Daskellin leaned forward.

"Maas has backing, and we don't. I had it. Or I thought I did. Then a balance sheet changed or some such, and Clark lit out for Birancour."

"It's what you deserve for working with bankers."

"It won't happen again," Daskellin said darkly.

It was as close to an apology as Dawson expected to get. He let the matter slide. Instead, he drained his glass, leaned to the door, and rapped against it until a serving girl appeared to refresh his glass.

"Where do we stand, then?" Dawson asked when she'd gone.

Daskellin shook his head, breath hissing out through his teeth.

"If it comes to the field, we can hold our own. There are enough landholders who still hate Asterilhold that it's easy enough to rally them."

"If Aster dies before he takes the throne?"

"Then we fervently pray his majesty's royal scepter's still in working order, because a new male heir is the best hope we have. I've had my genealogist look through the blood archives, and Simeon has a cousin in Asterilhold with a legitimate claim."

"Legitimate?" Dawson asked, leaning forward.

"I'm afraid so, and you can't guess this. He's a supporter of the principle of a farmer's council. We lose the quarter of our support with more sense that guts. The others rally around Oyer Verennin or possibly Umansin Tor, both of whom can also make a claim. Asterilhold backs its man with the help of the group Maas and Issandrian have gathered, we fight a civil war, and we lose."

Daskellin clapped his hands once. The candle above him sputtered. In the halls of the club, a serving girl shouted and a man laughed. Dawson's fortified wine tasted more bitter than it had when he started it, and he put the glass down.

"Could this have been the scheme all along?" Dawson asked. "Was Maas using Issandrian and Klin and all that hairwash about a farmer's council just for this? We may have been aiming at the wrong target all this time."

"Possibly," Daskellin said. "Or it might have been a chance he saw and decided to take. We'd have to ask Feldin, and I suspect he might not tell us the truth."

Dawson tapped the lip of his glass with a finger, the crystal chiming softly.

"We can't let Aster die," Dawson said.

"Everything dies. Men, cities, empires. Everything," Daskellin said. "The timing's the question."

Dawson took his dinner with the family in the informal dining hall. Roast pork with apple, honeyed squash, and fresh bread with whole cloves of garlic baked into it. A cream linen cloth on the table. Ceramic dishes from Far Syramys and polished silver utensils. It could as well have been ashes served on scrap iron.

"Geder Palliako's come back," Jorey said.

"Really?" Clara said. "I don't remember where he'd gone. Not to the south, certainly, with so many people having friends and family in Vanai. You can't expect a decent reception when you've killed a person's cousin or some such. Wouldn't be realistic. Was he in Hallskar?"

"The Keshet," Jorey said around a mouthful of apple. "Came back with a pet cunning man."

"That's nice for him," Clara said. She rang for the serving girl, and then, frowning, "We don't need to throw another revel for him, do we?"

"No," Dawson said.

He knew, of course, what they were doing. Jorey bringing up odd, trivial subjects. Clara burbling on about them and turning everything into a question for him to answer. It was the strategy they always used in dark times to lift him up out of himself. Tonight, the burden was too heavy.

He'd considered killing Maas. It would be difficult, of course. A direct assault was impossible. In the first place, it was expected and so would be guarded against. In the second, failure meant an even greater sympathy for Maas in the court. The idea of challenging him to a duel and then allowing things to go wrong appealed to him. He and Maas had been on the dueling grounds often enough that it wouldn't be an obvious convenience, and men slipped all the time. Blades went deeper than intended. He had to ignore the fact that Feldin was younger, stronger, and had lost their last duel only because Dawson was cleverer. The idea was still sweet.

"Fact is," Barriath said as the serving girl came in, "this boat is sinking, and we're bailing it out with a sieve."

"Meaning what?" Jorey said.

"Simeon's my king and I'll put my life down at his word, the same as anyone," Barriath said, "but he's barely his own master anymore. Father stopped the Edford Charter madness, and now we're looking at plots from Asterilhold. If we stop that, there will be another crisis after it, and another after that one."

"I don't think that's appropriate talk for the dinner table, dear," Clara said, accepting a fresh glass of watered wine from the servant.

"Ah, let him talk," Dawson said. "It's what we're all thinking about anyway."

"At least wait until the help is gone," Clara said. "Or who knows what they'll think of us in the small quarters."

The servant girl left blushing. Clara watched the door close after her, then nodded to her eldest son.

"Antea needs a king," Barriath said. "Instead it's got a kindly uncle. I hate to be the one to bring the bad news, but it's all through the navy. If it weren't for Lord Skestinin encouraging the captains to lay on the lash and drop troublemakers for the fish, we'd have had a mutiny by now. At least one."

"I can't believe that," Clara said. "Mutiny's such a rude, shortsighted thing. I'm certain that our men in the king's navy wouldn't stoop so low."

Barriath laughed.

"Mother, if you want truly inappropriate dinner conversation, I can tell you something about how low sailing men stoop."

"But Simeon is the king and Aster's still a boy," Jorey said. It was, Dawson thought, a brave attempt to keep the subject from veering again. "You can't expect them to be different people than they are."

"I agree with you, my boy," Dawson said. "I wish I didn't."

"Best thing," Barriath said, "would be for Simeon to find a protector with a spine to watch over Aster, and then abdicate. A regency could last eight or ten years, and by the time Aster took the crown, the kingdom would be in order."

Jorey snorted his derision, and Barriath's face went hard.

"Spare me," Jorey said. "A regent who could solve all the kingdom's conflicts in a decade wouldn't be likely to give up his regency. He'd be king."

"You're right," Barriath said. "And that would be just terrible, would it?"

"That's starting to sound awfully like the people we're working against, brother."

"If you two are going to start fighting, you can leave the table now," Clara said. Barriath and Jorey looked at their plates, muttering variations on *I'm sorry, Mother*. Clara nodded to herself. "That's better. Besides, it's a waste of effort to argue about the problems you don't have at the expense of the ones you do. We simply have to convince Simeon that poor Feldin really has gotten himself in too deep with those terrible Asterilhold people."

"It isn't as easy as that," Dawson said.

"Certainly it is," Clara said. "He's certain to have letters, isn't he? That's what Phelia said. That he was always off at his meetings and letters."

"I don't think he'll be writing to his foreign friends with detailed accounts of treason, Mother," Barriath said. *"Dear Lord Such-and-so, glad to hear you'll help me slaughter the prince."*

"He wouldn't have to say it, though. Not outright," Jorey said. "If there was evidence he was corresponding with this cousin who'd lay claim to the throne, it might be enough."

"You can always judge people by who they write to," Clara said with satisfaction. "There's the inconvenience of actually getting the letters, of course, but Phelia was so desperately pleased to see me last time, I can't think it will be particularly difficult to arrange another invitation. Not that one can rely on that, of course, which is why I've sponsored that needlework master to come show us his stitching patterns. Embroidery seems simple just to look at, but the more complex work can be quite boggling. Which reminds me, Dawson dear, I'm going to require the back hall with the good light tomorrow. There will be about five of us, because after all it seemed a bit obvious to only bring Phelia. That won't be a problem, will it?"

"What?" Dawson said.

"The back hall with the good light," Clara said, turning her head to him and raising her eyebrows without actually looking up from cutting her meat. "Because really needle-work can't be done in gloom. It—"

"You're cultivating Phelia Maas?"

"She lives with Feldin," Clara said. "And with the close of court coming so soon, waiting seems unwise, don't you think?"

There was a glitter in her eye and a dangerous angle at the corner of her mouth. Dawson found himself quite certain that his wife was enjoying herself. He found his mind dashing to keep up with hers. If Phelia could be convinced to allow access to the house for a few men...

"What are you doing, Mother?" Barriath asked.

"Saving the kingdom, dear," she said. "Eat your squash. Don't just move it around on the plate and pretend you've done anything. That never worked when you were a boy, I can't imagine why you still try it."

"He won't believe us," Dawson said. "After all the objections I've raised, Maas will claim forgery. But it might be enough to sway Simeon from giving Aster over."

"More swaying from the king?" Barriath said. "Is that really what we need? Move him to decisive action, or stay back."

"Someone else could take them," Jorey said. "Someone who isn't particularly allied with us or Maas."

"What about the Palliako boy?" Clara said. "I know he seems a bit frivolous, but he and Jorey are on good terms and it isn't as though he were part of your inner circle."

Dawson ate a bite of pork, chewing slowly to give himself time to think. In truth, the meat wasn't bad. Salt and sweet and something like pepper heat under it all. Quite good, in fact. He felt the smile spreading across his lips, becoming aware that it had been some time since he'd smiled.

"I don't know about that," Jorey said, but Dawson waved the words away.

"Palliako was useful ending the Vanai campaign. And he was here to stop the mercenary riot. He's been an apt tool before," Dawson said. "I can't think why this time would be different."

Geder

The banner spread out over the table, vermillion cloth flowing down to puddle on the floor. The dark eight-fold sigil in the pale center had bent onto itself, so Geder leaned in and plucked it straight. Lerer stroked his chin, walking first close and then back and close again before stopping at his son's shoulder.

"Among my people, this is the standard of your race," Basrahip said. "The color is for the blood from which all races of mankind came."

"And the compass rose in the middle there?" Lerer asked.

"That is the symbol of the goddess," Basrahip said.

Lerer grunted. He walked forward again, touching the cloth with careful fingertips. Geder felt his own fingers twitch toward it, mirroring his father. Basrahip had told him how the priests harvested spider silk and learned to dye it. The banner represented the work of ten lifetimes, and running his hands over it had been like touching the wind.

"And you wanted to hang this at...ah...Rivenhalm?"

"No," Geder said. "No, I was thinking it would be at the temple here in Camnipol."

"Oh. That's right," Lerer said. "The temple."

The road home from the hidden temple of the Sinir mountains had been a thousand times more pleasant than the journey out. At the end of each day, Basrahip would sit at the fire with him, listening to whatever anecdotes and tales Geder could remember, laughing at the funny ones, becoming pensive at the tragic. Even the servants, initially unable to hide their discomfort at the high priest's company, calmed well before they reached the border between the Keshet and Sarakal. Somewhat to Geder's surprise, Basrahip knew the rough track of their journey. The priest had explained that though the human world had remade itself, collapsed, and begun again countless times since the temple of the spider goddess had withdrawn from the world, the dragon's roads hadn't changed. He might not know where one country bordered another or even the path of a river as those things changed over time. The roads were eternal.

When they'd stopped in Inentai to rest the horses and reequip themselves, Basrahip had wandered the streets like a child, his mouth open in astonishment at every new building. It occurred to Geder at the time that in some fashion, he and the priest were not so dissimilar. Basrahip had lived a life with tales of the world, but never the world itself. Geder's life had been much the same, only his personal, private temple had been built with books and carved out from his duties and obligations. And still, in comparison, Geder was a man of the world. He had seen Kurtadam and Timzinae, Cinnae and Tralgu. Basrahip had known only Firstblood, and in fact only those who looked like himself and the villagers nearest the temple. Seeing a Firstblood with dark skin or pale hair was as much a revelation to the priest as a new race.

Watching him move first tentatively and then with greater and greater sureness through the streets and roads, Geder had some vague understanding of what his own father had meant by the joy of watching a child discover the world. Geder had found himself noticing the things he'd overlooked and taken for granted only because they astounded his new friend and ally. When, at the trailing edge of summer, they reached Camnipol again, Geder was almost sorry to see the journey's end.

Add to which, his father seemed oddly uncomfortable with his discoveries.

"I don't suppose you've picked a site for this new temple? Lost goddess and all."

"I was thinking someplace close to the Kingspire," Geder said. "There's the old weavers' guild hall. It's been empty for years. I'm sure they'd like someone to take it off their hands."

Lerer grunted noncommittally. Basrahip began to refold the temple banner. Lerer nodded to the priest, put a hand on Geder's elbow, and steered him gently out to the corridor, walking casually. Geder hardly noticed that his father was separating him from Basrahip. The dark stone ate the daylight, and the servants found themselves suddenly needed elsewhere.

"That essay," his father said. "You're still working on it?"

"No, not really. It's outgrown itself. It was supposed to be about finding a likely area to be associated with Morade and the fall of the Dragon Empire. Now I've got the goddess and the history of the temple and everything. I've barely started making sense of it all. No point writing any more until I know what I'm writing about, eh? What about you? Is there any fresh news?"

"I was looking forward to that essay," Lerer said, half to himself. When he looked up, he forced a smile. "I'm sure there's fresh news every day, but so far I've been able to keep from hearing any of it. These bastards and their court games.

I could live until the dragons come back and I still wouldn't forgive what they did to you in Vanai."

The word tightened Geder's stomach. The lines at the corners of Lerer's mouth were sorrow and anger etched in skin. Geder had the surreal urge to reach out his thumb and rub them smooth again.

"Nothing bad happened in Vanai," Geder said. "I mean, yes, it burned. That wasn't good. But it wasn't as bad as it's made out. It's all right, I mean. In the end."

Lerer's gaze shifted from one of Geder's eyes to the other, looking into him. Geder swallowed. He couldn't think why his heart would be beating faster.

"In the end. As you say," Lerer said. He clapped his hand on Geder's shoulder. "It's good you're back."

"I'm glad to be here," Geder said, too quickly.

With a quiet cough to announce himself, the house steward stepped into the corridor.

"Forgive me, my lords, but Jorey Kalliam has arrived asking after Sir Geder."

"Oh!" Geder said. "He hasn't seen Basrahip yet. Where is he? You didn't leave him in the courtyard, did you?"

Lerer's hand dropped from Geder's shoulder. Geder had the sense that he'd somehow said the wrong thing.

"His lordship is in the front room," the steward said.

Jorey rose from the chair by the window as he came in. The season in the city had put some flesh back into the man's face. Geder smiled, and the two of them stood looking at each other. Geder read his own uncertainty—should they clasp hands? embrace? make formal greeting?—in Jorey's expression. When Geder laughed, Jorey, smiling sheepishly, did too.

"I see you're back from the wild places," Jorey said. "The travel agrees with you."

"Does it? I think I just about wept when I could sleep in a real bed again. Going on campaign may be a string of discomfort and indignity, but at least I never worried about being killed by bandits."

"There are worse things than a good, honest bandit. You were missed here," Jorey said. "You heard what happened?"

"Exile all around," Geder said, trying to affect a jaded tone. "I don't know that I could have helped. I barely had any part except when we held the gate from closing."

"That was the best part to have in the whole mess," Jorey said.

"Probably so."

"Well."

The silence was awkward. Jorey sat again, and Geder walked forward. The front room, like all of the Palliako rooms in Camnipol, was small. The chairs were worked leather that time had stiffened and cracked, and the smell of dust never left the place. The sounds of hooves against stone and drivers berating one another came from the street. Jorey bit his lip.

"I'm here to ask a favor," he said, and it sounded like a confession.

"We took Vanai together. We burned it together. We saved Camnipol," Geder said. "You don't have to ask favors of me. Just tell me what you need me to do."

"That's intended to make this easier, isn't it? All right. My father believes he's discovered a plot against Prince Aster."

Geder crossed his arms.

"Does the king know?"

"The king is choosing not to know. And that's where you

come in. I think we can get evidence. Letters. But I'm afraid that if I take them to King Simeon, he'll think they're forged. I need someone else. Someone he trusts, or at least doesn't distrust."

"Of course," Geder said. "Absolutely. Who is the traitor?"

"Baron of Ebbinbaugh," Jorey said. "Feldin Maas."

"Alan Klin's ally?"

"And Curtin Issandrian's, for that, yes. Maas's wife is my mother's cousin, which God knows doesn't sound like much of a toehold, but it's what we have to work with. She—the wife, I mean. Not my mother. She seems to know more than she's saying. There's no question she's frightened. My mother has her at a needlework master's knee as we speak in hopes of winning her confidence."

"But she hasn't confessed anything? Told you for certain what's going on?"

"No, we're still well in the realm of suspicions and fears. There's no proof. But—"

Geder put up his hand, palm out.

"I have someone you should meet," he said.

The last time Geder had been to the Kalliam mansion, it had been dressed for a revel in his honor. Without the flowers and streamers and crepe, the austerity and grandeur of the architecture came through. The servants in their livery had the rigid stance of a private guard. The glass in the windows sported no dust. The women's voices that came from the back hall sounded genteel and proper, even without any individual word being audible. Basrahip sat on a stool in the corner. His broad shoulders and vaguely amused expression made him seem like a child revisiting a playhouse he'd outgrown. The austere cut and rough, colorless cloth of his robes marked him as not belonging to the court.

Jorey was sitting at a writing desk, fidgeting with pen and ink without actually writing anything. Geder paced behind a long damask-upholstered couch and wished he liked pipes. The occasion seemed to call for the gravity of smoke.

The choir of feminine voices grew louder, and the hard tapping of formal shoes came from the doorway, louder and then softer as they passed. They hadn't come in. Geder moved toward the door, but Jorey waved him back.

"Mother will be seeing the others out," he said. "She'll be back in a moment."

Geder nodded, and true to Jorey's word, the footsteps returned, the voices reduced to a duet. When the women stepped into the room, Jorey rose to his feet. Basrahip followed suit a moment later. Geder had danced with the Baroness of Osterling Fells at his revel, but between the months and the whirl of drink and confusion that time had been, he wouldn't have recognized her. He could see how her own features had influenced Jorey's, especially around the eyes. Surprise touched her expression and vanished again, less than the flutter of a moth's wing. Behind her, a sickly-looking woman with a pinched face and dark eyes had to be Phelia Maas.

"Oh, excuse me," Clara Kalliam said. "I didn't mean to intrude, dear."

"Not at all, Mother. We were hoping you'd join us. You remember Geder Palliako?"

"How could I forget the man who held the eastern gate? I haven't seen you at court this season, sir, but I understand you've been traveling. An expedition of some sort? Let me introduce my cousin Phelia."

The dark-eyed woman came into the room and held her hand out to Geder. Her smile spoke of relief, as if she'd been dreading something that she thought she'd now avoided. Geder made his bow and saw Lady Kalliam's eyebrows rise as she noticed the priest in the corner.

"Ladies," Jorey said. "This is Basrahip. He's a holy man Geder brought back from the Keshet."

"Really?" Lady Kalliam said. "I hadn't known you were collecting priests."

"It came as a surprise to me too," Geder said. "But please, won't you ladies sit?"

According to his plan, Geder sat Phelia Maas on the couch with her back toward Basrahip and then took his own place across from her. Jorey resumed his place at the writing desk, and his mother took a chair near that happily didn't block Geder's view of the priest.

"Maas," Geder said, as if recalling something. In truth, he'd planned precisely what to say. "I had an Alberith Maas serving under me in Vanai. A relation of yours?"

"Nephew," Phelia said. "My husband's nephew. Alberith has mentioned you often since his return."

"You're the Baroness of Ebbinbaugh, then?" Geder asked. "Sir Klin was my commander in the Vanai campaign. He and your husband are friends, yes?"

"Oh yes," Phelia said with a smile. "Sir Klin is a dear, close friend of Feldin's."

Behind her, Basrahip gazed into the middle distance, his face impassive as if listening intently to something only he could hear. He shook his head once. *No.*

"There was a falling-out, though, wasn't there? I'm sure I heard something like that," Geder said, pretending a casual knowledge he didn't have. The woman's face went still, except for her eyes, which clicked from Geder to Lady Kalliam and back. There was fear in the way she held her hands and the corners of her mouth. Geder felt a slow, pleasant warmth growing in his chest. It was going to work. At his side, Jorey's mother considered him with interest.

"I'm sure you misunderstood," Phelia said. "Alan and Feldin are on excellent terms."

No.

"I always liked Sir Klin," Geder said for the simple pleasure of being able to lie to a woman who couldn't lie to him. "I felt terrible when I heard he'd been blamed for the riot. Your husband didn't suffer for that, I hope."

"No, no, thank you. We were very fortunate."

Yes.

"Sir Palliako," Lady Kalliam said, "to what do we owe the pleasure of your company today?"

Geder looked at Jorey, then at Lady Kalliam. He'd meant to ask a few innocuous questions, get what insight he could, uncover what could be uncovered. He'd meant to move slowly. The way the woman held herself tighter and tighter, the fragility of her smile, and the scent of fear that came from her like the sweet from roses argued against. He couldn't scare her so badly she left, but he could scare her badly. He smiled at Lady Kalliam.

"Well, the truth is I was hoping for an introduction to Baroness Ebbinbaugh here. I had some questions for her. I haven't spent all the season traveling," he said pleasantly. "I've been looking into the riot. Its roots. And its aftermath."

The color had gone from Phelia Maas's face. Her breath was fast and shallow, like a hand-caught sparrow about to die from fright.

"I can't imagine what there is to look into," she said, her voice thready and faint.

Geder found it was easier to smile kindly when he didn't mean it. Outside, a wind chime was singing to itself in random, idiot percussion. Jorey and his mother had both gone perfectly still. Geder laced his fingers over his knee.

"I know everything, Lady Maas," he said. "The prince. The riot. The Vanai campaign. The woman."

"What woman?" she breathed.

He didn't have the first idea what woman, but no doubt there was some woman involved somewhere. It didn't matter.

"Say anything," he said. "Pick any detail. Even things you don't imagine anyone else could know, and I'll tell you if they're true."

"Feldin isn't involved in any of it," she said. Geder didn't even need to look at Basrahip.

"That isn't true, Lady Maas. I know you're frightened, but I'm here to help you and your family. I can do that. But I need to know I can trust you. You see? Tell me the truth. It doesn't matter, because it's all things I know already. Tell me how it started. Just that."

"It was the ambassador from Asterilhold," she said. "He came to Feldin a year ago."

No.

"You're lying to me, Baroness," Geder said, very gently. "Try again."

Phelia Maas shuddered. She seemed like a thing made of spun sugar, almost too delicate to support her own weight. She opened her mouth, closed it, swallowed.

"There was a man. He was going to be part of the farmer's council."

Yes.

"Yes. I know who you mean. Can you tell me his name?"

"Ucter Anninbaugh."

No.

"That wasn't his name. Can you tell me his name?"

"Ellis Newport."

No.

"I can help you, Baroness. I may be the only man in Camnipol who can. Tell me his name."

Her dead eyes met his.

"Torsen. Torsen Aestilmont."

Yes.

"There," Geder said. "That wasn't so hard, was it? Do you understand now that you and your husband have no secrets from me?"

The woman nodded once. Her chin began to spasm, her cheeks flushed, and a heartbeat later she was bawling like a child. Jorey's mother swooped to her side, putting an arm around her. Geder sat, watching. His heart was beating quickly, but his limbs were loose and relaxed. When he had denied Alan Klin the secret wealth of Vanai, he'd felt excited. Gleeful. When he'd come to the decision to burn Vanai, he'd felt righteous anger. Maybe even satisfaction. But he wasn't sure that ever in his life before now—before this moment—he'd felt sated.

He rose and walked over to Jorey. The man's eyes were wide. Impressed almost past the point of believing. Geder spread his hands. *You see?*

"How did you do that?" Jorey whispered. "How did you know?" There was awe in his voice.

Basrahip was fewer than three paces away. The bull-huge head was still bowed. The thick fingers bent around each other, hand clasping hand. Phelia Maas's sobs were like a storm on the sea, and the murmured lullaby of promises and comfort from Lady Kalliam had barely thrown any oil on that water. Geder went to leaned so close his lips brushed the huge man's ear.

"I will build all the temples you want, forever."

Basrahip smiled.

Clara

On one hand, they had seriously misunderstood who and what Geder Palliako was. But on the other, he appeared to be on their side. For the time being, at least.

Still, Clara's heart ached for Phelia.

The bedroom was darkened, heavy curtains pushing the daylight away. Phelia lay on her back, the salt tracks of dried tears marking the corners of her eyes. Clara sat beside her, stroking her shoulders and arms the way physicians did when someone had taken a blow to the head or received shocking news. When Phelia spoke, the hysteria was gone. There was no more room for pretending that things could end well, and Clara could hear in the woman's voice that losing that hope had been a relief.

"Will he really keep Feldin safe?" Phelia asked. "If I give him the letters, will Palliako really see that Simeon doesn't kill him?"

"That's certainly what he said," Clara said.

"Do you trust him?"

"I barely know him, dear."

They lapsed again into silence.

"If the king already knows anyway," Phelia said. "If he only wants to see who in the court of Asterilhold was involved...I mean, with all that Palliako already knew, Aster was never in any real danger. Not really."

"That's one way to see it."

For the better part of an hour, Geder Palliako had coaxed Phelia into admitting everything. Feldin's complicity in the mercenary riot, his connections in Asterilhold, his alliances within the groups fighting for a farmer's council. Any one would stand as treason. Together, Clara didn't see room for mercy. Which wasn't what Phelia needed to hear now.

"How did it all get so out of hand?" Phelia asked the darkness. She sighed. It was a small, hard sound. "Tell him I will. I'll take him to Feldin's private study. I have a key, but there will be a guard. And he has to swear that it will only be exile."

"All right."

Phelia took Clara's hand, holding it like it was the only thing that kept her from falling down a cliff.

"You won't make me go alone, will you? You'll come with me?"

There was nothing Clara wanted less. Phelia's eyes glittered in the twilight of the room.

"Of course, dear," she said. "Of course I'll come."

In the smoking room, Clara found the men waiting with such anxiety she imagined herself as a midwife come to deliver news of a birth. Dawson stopped his pacing as she walked in. Geder and Jorey looked up from a game of cards they were only half playing. Only the quiet priest seemed unconcerned, but then she supposed unnatural serenity was part of his work. Even Vincen Coe was there, brooding in the shadows the way he so often did. The air was close and hot, like every sip had already been breathed once before.

"She's agreed to take Lord Palliako to the letters," Clara said, "but only if he swears Simeon won't have Feldin executed and if I'm with her when they go."

"Absolutely not," Dawson said.

"She will lose her nerve, husband," Clara said. "You know what she's like. I'll take Vincen with me, and we'll be fine. The four of us—"

"Five," Geder said, "with Basrahip."

"I'm going too," Jorey said.

"Of course you aren't, dear," Clara said. "Feldin only allows me because I'm a woman and he finds me feckless and charming. Vincen's a servant. Lord Palliako and…"

"Basrahip," the priest said.

"Yes, that. Phelia was here for the needlework and had an example she wanted to show me, so I went home with her. Along the way, we bumped into Lord Palliako and his friend and Phelia invited them along so we could hear stories of his summer travels. Perfectly innocent."

"I don't see why I couldn't be part of that," Jorey said. "Or Barriath."

"Because you are your father's sons, and I am only his wife. You have a great deal to learn about the place of women. Now, I suggest we do this before Phelia has a change of heart, poor thing."

Walking out to the carriage, Clara felt proud of Phelia. The way she held herself. The polite nod she gave to Dawson as they pulled away. The autumn sun was already near the horizon, the flame seeming to dance on the rooftops as the driver threaded his way through the streets. The city seemed clearer than usual, the sounds of wheels and voices sharper and more real than she was used to. The buildings they passed had rich textures in the stone of the walls. They passed a young Tralgu pushing a cart piled high with grapes, and Clara felt she could have counted each individual fruit. She felt as if she'd woken up twice without going to sleep in the middle. She wondered if it was how soldiers felt on the morning of a battle. It seemed likely.

Geder Palliako smiled at everything. She still thought of him as the pale, pudgy boy who'd ridden off to war in her son's company. In truth, his travels had left him leaner and darkened by the sun. And more than that, his eyes had changed. Even when he'd returned from the city he'd killed, there had been a shyness to him. It wasn't there any longer, and she thought he looked less handsome for the loss. She found herself wondering what he had really been doing all those weeks he pretended to have been in the Keshet. When his priest caught her staring, he smiled. She turned away.

The private courtyard wasn't half dead any longer. As many lanterns and candles were glowing in the windows of Curtin Issandrian's mansion as in Feldin Maas's. The carriage jolted to a stop and a footman ran out with a step for them. Phelia first, and then herself. Geder Palliako, the only man of blood. Vincen Coe and the priest paused, unsure for a moment, and then the priest smiled and waved the huntsman on.

The door slave was a different man, Firstblood this time, but so thick with muscle he might have been the priest's twin. Vincen and Geder turned over their swords and daggers. The priest had no weapons.

"The baron wanted to see you when you came," the door slave said. "He's in the rear hall."

No honorifics, no *my lady*. He might have been speaking to anyone for all the respect in his tone. Clara wondered what sort of men Maas had been taking into service, and then instantly answered her own question. Mercenaries. Fighters. Sword-and-bows. The sort of men who kill for pay. And she was going into the enemy camp. Stepping over the threshold, she faltered. Phelia looked at her, alarmed. Clara shook her head and bulled on. She refused to accept support and comfort from someone in her cousin's position. It would be rude.

In silence, Phelia led them down the wide corridor toward the room where she'd received Clara the last time she'd been. Fresh-cut flowers and garlands of autumn vine left the air smelling rich. The candlelight softened the corners and warmed the colors of the tapestries and the carpeted runner. Geder coughed. A nervous little sound.

At the base of the stair, Phelia turned right, and they all followed her. A short hallway that jogged at the end. Fewer candles were lit here. The shadows thickened and pressed in against them. At the far end of the hall, a thin servant's staircase rose up and a wider set of doors stood closed. They wouldn't have to go so far.

"Who's that?" a man's voice said.

In a recess, a man in hunting leather stood up from where he'd been sitting. The guard.

"My husband sent for me," Phelia said. "They said he was in his private office."

"He ain't," the guard said. "Who're these?"

"The people my husband asked me to bring," Phelia said tartly. Clara could hear the fear in her voice, the despair. She felt a surge of pride for the woman's courage.

"He is here," the priest said. His voice had an odd, unpleasant throbbing quality. "You've made a mistake. He's in the room behind you."

"No one in there, I'm telling you."

"Listen. Listen. You've made a mistake," the priest said again. "He's in the room behind you. Knock on the door and he'll answer."

From the look on the guard's face, Clara was fairly sure anyone beside the lady of the household would have already been knocked to the ground and reinforcements shouted for. Instead, the man turned to knock on the oaken door and Vincen Coe stepped up behind him, wrapping an arm across the guard's neck and lifting him. The man choked and kicked, his hand clawing at Vincen's arm. Clara closed her eyes, and the sounds alone were worse than the sight. After entirely too long, the guard went slack. Vincen lowered the body to the floor and stood with the guard's drawn sword in his hand. Phelia drew a key from her sleeve, fitted it to the lock, and a moment later they were in Feldin Maas's private study.

Vincen brought a candle in from the hallway, and by its light he found and lit the lamps. The room slowly grew lighter, taken by a dark, sullen sort of dawn. Shelves of dark wood and a thin writing desk with a brass inkwell and a white fluff of a feather quill. It was a larger space than Clara had expected. There were no windows, and a lattice of dark and light against one wall led her to think the room had once been used to store bottles. Phelia walked to the shelves like she was walking in her sleep. From amid the clutter of scrolls and codices, she took a simple wooden box, its top fastened with a hook and hinged with leather. She held it out to Geder Palliako.

"They're ciphered," she said. "I don't know the code."

Geder took the box, grinning like a boy with an unexpected present. As soon as it left her hand, Phelia closed in on herself, as if her bones had gone soft and smaller.

"Thank you, dear," Clara said. "It was the only way. You know it was the only way."

Her shrug was painful to watch.

"I don't know how it came this far," she said. "I truly don't. If I could have—"

The roar was inhuman. Anger and wildfire and murder made sound. Clara screamed even before she knew what it was.

"What in hell is this?"

Feldin Maas stood in the doorway, a bare blade in his hand. His face was flushed almost purple with rage. Two more men stood behind him, blocked from entering. *If he closes that door,* Clara thought, *we're trapped. And if we're trapped, we're dead.*

"No, Feldin," Phelia said, walking forward. "It's the right thing. It's what we have to do. Lord Palliako's promised mercy. He knew everything anyway."

"You *brought* them here? *You* betrayed *me*?"

"I—"

Maas's sword reached out swift and sudden as a lightning strike. Clara, behind her cousin, didn't see the blade strike home, but she heard it. She saw the horrible play over Feldin Maas's face: surprise, horror, grief, rage. Even before the blood, Clara knew the woman was dead.

Vincen Coe boiled past her, shouting and swinging his stolen blade like a scythe in a meadow. Maas fell back into the hallway from the sheer animal force of the attack. For a moment, the doorway was clear. Geder Palliako stood over the fallen woman, his jaw slack and his face pale. Clara pushed him, moving him toward the door.

"Go!" she shouted. "Before they seal us in!"

Geder and the priest hurried out. The sound of blade against blade almost made Clara pause. *I'll surrender,* she thought. They wouldn't harm a woman. It was an idiot's thought. A reflex. Against all instinct, she ran out toward the fighting.

If the corridor had been wider, Feldin and his two guards would already have gotten around Vincen and cut him down. Instead, the huntsman swung hard and fast, his blade filling the space, holding them at bay. Sweat was pouring down his face, and his breath was fast. Feldin waited with a duelist's eyes, looking for an opportunity.

"Run!" Vincen shouted. "I'll win you what time I can!"

Geder Palliako needed no more urging. He turned, sprinting down the hall toward the staircase and double doors. She caught a glimpse of the wooden box still in his hand. She took four steps after him, but turned back. The priest moved just behind her, retreating from the fight, but not fleeing. Vincen's shoulders worked like a laborer's.

"Oh," she heard herself say. "Oh, not this. Not this."

Feldin's blade swung high and hard, batting Vincen's swing aside. The guard to Feldin's left thrust past him, and Vincen grunted, leaping back. There was blood on the guard's blade. Vincen's blood, spilling on the floor.

"You can't win," the priest said, his voice loud and throbbing. Clara looked up at him, tears in her eyes, but he smiled and shook his huge head. "Lord Maas, listen to my voice. Listen to me. You cannot win."

"I will see your guts," Maas shouted.

"You won't. Everything you love is already gone. Everything you hoped for is already lost. You can't win. The fight is over. You've lost everything already. You have no reason to fight."

Feldin surged forward, but even Clara could see the change in his stance. His swing was more tentative, his weight on his back foot, as if reluctant to engage the fight he had just been winning. Vincen drew back, limping badly. His leathers were red and wet. Feldin didn't step forward.

"You saw her die, Lord Maas," the priest said. "You saw her fall. She has gone, and you can't bring her back. Listen to my voice. *Listen* to me. The fight's lost. Nothing you can do here matters. You can feel that. That thickness in your throat. You feel it. You know what it means. You cannot win. You cannot win. You cannot win."

One of the guards moved forward, his blade before him, but his gaze kept cutting back to Feldin. Feldin, whose eyes were caught on nothing. Vincen started to close with the man, but Clara rushed forward, put her hand on his arm, pulled him back.

"You can feel the despair in your belly, can't you? You feel it," the priest said. His voice was sorrowful, as if he regretted every word. Each syllable throbbed and echoed within itself. "You feel it in your heart. You're drowning in it, and it will never end. There is no hope. Not now. Not ever. You cannot win, Lord Maas. You *cannot* win. There is nothing for you. You've lost it all, and you know it."

"Lord Maas?" his guard said.

The point of Feldin's blade lowered to the floor like he was drawing a vertical line in the empty air. In the candlelight, it was hard to see, but she thought there were tears on his mask-empty face. The guards looked at each other, confused and unnerved. Feldin dropped his sword to the ground, turned, and walked away down the corridor. Clara trembled. The huge priest put one hand on her shoulder, one on Vincen Coe's.

"We should leave before he changes his opinion," the priest said.

They backed down the hallway, leaving a track of blood. The guards took a few uncertain steps toward them, then back toward their retreating lord. They reminded Clara of nothing more than hunting dogs given two conflicting commands. When they reached the double doors, Vincen stumbled. The priest lifted him up, slinging him over a shoulder. It took them minutes to find a door that led out, what seemed half the night to negotiate the darkened gardens and reach the edge of Maas's estate. A thick hedge marked the border, and the priest knelt by it, rolling Vincen Coe's body to the ground. There were voices in the night. Shouting and calling. Searching, Clara thought, for them.

"Under here," he said. "Watch over him. I'll bring a cart."

Clara knelt, pushing herself in through the twigs and leaves. The hedge had little space beneath it, but there was some. Vincen Coe dragged himself in after her, digging his elbows into the litter of dead leaves and old dirt. His face was ashen, and everything from his belly down was wet and slick. In the darkness, the blood wasn't red, but black. She pulled him in close to her as best she could without proper leverage. She had the sudden visceral memory of being thirteen, hiding in her father's gardens while one of her uncles dashed about pretending he didn't know where she was. She shook her head. The memory was too innocent for the moment.

Vincen rolled onto his back with a groan.

"How bad is it?" she whispered.

"Unpleasant," Vincen said.

"If Maas uses his dogs, we're as good as found."

Vincen shook his head, the leaves under him making the softest crackling sound.

"By now, I'm sure everything on the estate stinks of me," he said. "Take them till morning to find which blood's freshest."

"Still feeling well enough to joke, I see."

"Yes, my lady."

Clara struggled to rise, squinting through the leaves. There was more shouting now. And, unless she was mistaken, the crash of swordplay. She felt sure she heard Jorey's voice raised in command. In the close confines of their shelter, she felt the huntsman's fast, shallow breath as much as heard it.

"Be strong a bit longer," she said. "Just a bit longer."

When he reached his hand to her, she thought it might be the last gesture of a dying man, but his fingers curled around the back of her neck, drawing her toward him with a definite strength. His lips were rough against hers, surprising and intimate and strong. Clara was shocked, but then gave a little internal shrug. The young man might be dead in the next few minutes, so really where was the harm?

When he released her, his head dropping the inch back to the ground, Clara wiped her mouth with the back of a well-soiled hand. Her lips felt pleasantly bruised, her mind by turns scandalized, flattered, and amused.

"You forget yourself," she said reprovingly.

"I do, my lady," the huntsman said. "With you, I often do."

His eyes fluttered closed. His breath remained painful and quick, and Clara lay in the darkness, willing it to continue until she heard voices she knew as her own household, and started shouting for help.

Marcus

Qahuar Em scratched his chin, his head tilted at a considering angle. Marcus kept his expression bland. The table they sat across was polished oak with a burned-in knotwork pattern. It didn't have the green banker's felt that Cithrin used. Marcus had expected that it would, but perhaps the customs were different in Lyoneia. The tiny box that sat on the table was black iron with a lid that hinged on the side and the image of a dragon on the front. If there was some significance to the design she had chosen, he didn't know it.

"I'm sorry," Qahuar Em said. "This is confusing."

"Nothing odd about it," Marcus said. "Banks and merchant houses hold items of interest for each other all the time, I'm told."

"When they're closely allied, and one has people in a city where the other doesn't," Qahuar said. "Neither of those applies here."

"Strange circumstances."

"Which you aren't going to explain to me."

"I'm not," Marcus agreed.

Qahuar reached over and picked up the little box, cupping it easily in one palm. The lid opened with a clank, uncovering a brass key shorter than a finger bone. Marcus scratched his ear and waited for the man to speak.

"Why do I think this is going to be connected to something disagreeable and embarrassing?" Qahuar asked, making it clear from his tone that an answer would be welcome but wasn't expected.

"I'm authorized to sign a statement that it's here at the request of Magistra bel Sarcour," Marcus said. "Press the key into wax and I'll put my thumb across it so there's no question we're talking about the same one. Anything you like."

The box closed again. The near-scaled fingertips tapped the oak with a sound like the first hard drops of a thunderstorm.

"I'm prepared to take no for an answer," Marcus said.

"The magistra and I didn't part on the best of terms," Qahuar said, pronouncing his words carefully. "She sent you rather than come herself. I find it hard to believe she's come to trust me."

"There's ways you can trust an enemy you can't always trust a friend. An enemy's never going to betray your trust."

"I think she would say I'd betrayed hers, and I can argue she did mine."

"Proves my point. You two were being friendly back then," Marcus said with a smile they both knew he didn't mean.

A soft knock came at the meeting room door. A full Jasuru woman in robes of grey and scarlet nodded to both men.

"The men from the shipyard, sir."

Qahuar nodded, and the woman retreated, closing the door behind her with a soft click.

"Going well, that?" Marcus asked.

"Well enough. It will take a year at least to have everything in order, but time moves both ways. Actions can have effects long before they themselves happen."

"Angry letters from the king of Cabral, for example?"

"Sometimes I wish I'd lost," Qahuar said. And then, "For more reasons than one. Captain, we're men well acquainted the world. I think we understand each other. Would you answer a question?"

"You won't mind if I lie?"

"Not at all. You're a man whose name is known all through the west. At the head of a private army, you could command any price you ask, but you're working guard captain for a branch bank. You aren't open to bribery. And — forgive me — you don't like me very much."

"None of that's a question."

"Are you in love with her?"

"I've loved a lot of people, and the word hasn't meant the same thing twice," Marcus said. "The job is to protect her, and I'm going to do the job this time."

"This time?"

Marcus shrugged and kept quiet. The bastard had gotten him to say more than he meant already. Marcus had to give it; Qahuar was good at what he did. The half-Jasuru stood up, his lips pursed. Slowly, deliberately, he put the box in the pouch at his belt.

"I hope I'm not going to regret this," he said.

"I expect it won't matter to you one way or the other," Marcus said. "For what it's worth, though, I appreciate your taking it on."

"You know it's not as a favor to you?"

"Do."

Qahuar Em held out a broad hand. Marcus rose to his feet and took it. It was an effort not to squeeze a little hard, just to show he could. The man's bright green eyes looked amused. And maybe something sadder as well.

"She's a lucky woman," Qahuar said.

God, let's hope so, Marcus thought but didn't say.

Autumn had come to Porte Oliva overnight. Trees that had been lush and full were dropping leaves that were still green in the center. The sunset winds were loud with their skittering. The bay had turned the color of tea, and stank at midday like a compost heap. The queensmen patrolling the twilight streets wore overcoats of wool and green caps that covered their ears. Marcus walked the narrow streets near the port, feeling the first bite of night's chill, and decided maybe he liked the city after all.

He found Master Kit and the others in a torchlit courtyard between a taphouse and an inn. Smit and Hornet were still putting the last adjustments on the stage supports while Master Kit barked instructions to them, not even in costume yet. A young woman was pacing behind them. She was fairhaired with large eyes that left Marcus thinking of babies and a tight-bound dress that showed her figure. Her hands were knotted before her, fingers wrestling one another like fighters in a melee.

Marcus walked over to Master Kit. Instead of saying hello, he nodded to the woman.

"New one?"

"Yes," the old actor said. "I have hope for this one."

"Had hope for the last one too."

"Fair enough. I have expectations of this one," Master Kit said. "Calls herself Charlit Soon, and I find she rehearses wonderfully. Tonight we'll see how she does with an audience. If she stays through tomorrow, I think I've found my full company."

"And she's what? Twelve years old?"

"Cinnae blood some generations back," Master Kit said. "Or that's the story, anyway. She believes it, and it may even be true."

"But you don't believe it?"

"I withhold judgment."

As if she'd heard them, the new actor glanced over at them and then away. Sandr jumped out the back of the cart and waved to Marcus. Either his fear had faded or he was a decent actor. Marcus waved back. Mikel, thin and weedy as ever, came out from the taphouse with a bucket of sawdust, Cary following behind with a broom.

"I heard rumor you might be leaving Porte Oliva."

"It's one possibility," Master Kit said. "We've played here almost an entire theatrical season. I think cities can get full on plays. Show too many, and I believe people become complacent I don't want what we do to lose its magic. I was thinking of taking the company up to the queen's court at Sara-su-mar."

"Before the winter, or after?"

"I'll know more after Charlit's been onstage for a few nights," Master Kit said. "But probably before. When the ships leave for Narinisle."

"Well, do what's right, but I'll be sorry to see you go."

"I take it you're staying for the foreseeable future?" Kit said. Mikel began spreading the sawdust on the flagstone paving of the courtyard to soak up the damp, Cary sweeping along behind him. It seemed like an odd thing to do. The yard was only going to fill up with mud and piss and rain again.

"I can count the foreseeable future in days," Marcus said. "Weeks at best."

"You'd be welcome to travel with us," Master Kit said. "Yardem and Cithrin too. I think we all miss being caravan guards, just a little. It wasn't a role we'd ever had before, and I don't expect we will again."

"Master Kit?" Sandr called from behind the cart. "One of the swords is missing."

"I believe it's with Smit's bandit robe."

"It isn't."

Master Kit sighed, and Marcus clapped him on the shoulder and left him to his work.

Lantern flames and barn heat made the interior of the taproom warmer than the streets. The scent of roasting pork and beer competed with the less pleasant smell of close-packed bodies. Marcus kept one hand on his coins as he walked through the press. With so many distractions and people in so small a space, he'd have been shocked if there wasn't at least one cutpurse looking for a little luck. He saw Yardem first, sitting at a back table, then as he got closer, Enen and Roach, Cithrin and...Barth. That was his name. The Firstbloods were Corisen Mout and Barth, and Corisen Mout had the bad front tooth. Feeling unaccountably pleased with himself, Marcus sat at the table.

Cithrin raised her eyebrows, asking.

"It's done," Marcus said. "You? Things went well with the governor?"

"Fine," Cithrin said. "Paid the fee, left the box."

"The receipt?"

"Burned it," Cithrin said. "There won't be a trail back. As long as the governor doesn't get curious and force the lock, we're as ready as we're likely to get."

A servant hurried over, put a tankard of ale on the table in front of Marcus, and reached to take Cithrin's away. She stopped him, and he nodded his bow and darted away.

"What are the chances that the governor's baser instincts will get the better of him?" Marcus asked instead of *How much have you drunk?* If she were in danger of losing herself, Yardem would have stopped her. Maybe already had.

"Life is risk," she said as Roach, sitting beside her, sipped ale from his own tankard.

"Yardem was just telling us about the shapes of people's souls," Barth said. "Did you know your soul's a circle?"

Marcus shot a pained look at Yardem. The flick of an ear was the closest he got to an apology.

"Don't listen to anything he says, Barth. He's religious. It makes him nervous when things are going well."

"Wasn't aware they were going well, sir," Yardem said dryly.

Over the next hour, Marcus drank his tankard of ale, ate a plate of roast pork with a black sauce hot enough to bring tears to his eyes, and listened to the talk around the table. Barth kept on Yardem about souls and destiny, but Enen and Roach and Cithrin chewed on more practical matters: how many payments would be coming to the bank proper and how many to the room at the café, how to assure that no one attacked whoever carried the café payments across the city, whether to make arrangements with the queensmen to help enforce their private contracts. All the business and consideration of a bank's owner to her people. Cithrin spoke like a woman sure of her fate, and Marcus admired her for that.

The banging of a stick on a tin pan interrupted them.

"Show's to start!" Mikel's voice threaded through the noise of the taproom. "Come and watch the show! Show's to start!"

Marcus dropped a few coins on the table, rose, and, half joking, offered Cithrin his hand.

"Shall we?" he asked.

She accepted his support with a mocking formality.

"It's what we've come here for," she said. Marcus led her and the members of his new company out to the pleasant cool of the courtyard to watch his old one. The crowd was good. Easily fifty people, and more likely to stop as they went in or out. When Master Kit strode out on the boards, his wiry hair pulled back and a sword strapped to his hip, a few people applauded, Marcus among them. Sandr came out a moment later, pretending to pick his teeth with a blunted dagger.

"You, Pintin, have been my second in command these many years," Master Kit said, thrusting out his chin in parody of heroism. "From the moments of my highest glory and the depths of my despair, you have followed me. Now once again the hounds of war are loosed, and we must fly before them. The armies of dark Sarakal descend upon the city tomorrow."

"Best we get out tonight, then," Sandr said. The crowd chuckled.

"Indeed, ours is not to stand and fight the doomèd fight. The city surely shall fall, and before it does, Lady Daneillin—last of her house and gentlest beauty of Elassae—must be taken safe away. That is our great work, Pintin. Our company is to fly this night with the great lady in our charge."

"Yeah, problem with that," Sandr said in his Pintin voice. "The men were on the city wall seeing who could piss the farthest. Seems the magistrate thought it was raining. They're all in the city gaol."

Master Kit paused. The self-importance in his jaw melted.

"*What?*" he shrieked in comic falsetto. More people laughed. They were warming to it.

Marcus leaned toward Yardem Hane.

"I'm not like that, though," he said. "All that high dramatic talk and sucking my gut in. That's not what I'm like."

"Not at all, sir," Yardem said.

Two days later, Cithrin sat across the café table from him. A light rain pattered outside the open doors and windows, the stones at the entrance of the Grand Market darkened almost black. Behind him, two Kurtadam men were talking about the latest news from Northcoast. Another war of succession seemed almost certain. Marcus told himself he didn't care, and for the most part that was true. The world smelled of coffee and raindrops.

"If we have the free coin, I'm thinking about sponsoring one of the Narinisle ships next year," Cithrin said.

Marcus nodded.

"There's going to be uncertainty about the new fleet idea. Especially at first. If it's a success, even just for the first couple of years, it's going to increase the traffic through Porte Oliva. That could be a very good thing for us, so long as we're in position. Known to everyone. Trusted."

"All that assuming," Marcus said.

Cithrin swallowed. She'd lost weight in the last weeks, and her skin, while always pale, was growing pallid. It was odd to him that none of the men who came asking her patronage for a loan or offering to deposit their wealth with her for a discreet return appeared to notice that the anxiety was eating her. She wasn't sleeping enough. But she wasn't drinking herself to sleep either. That counted as strength enough for him.

"All that assuming," she agreed. And then, "Do you ever wish we'd run? Filled our pockets and just...gone?"

"Ask me again once the auditor's left," Marcus said.

She nodded. The ancient, half-blind Cinnae man limped in from the back. The rain seemed to have no good effect on his hips. Cithrin raised her empty cup, and Maestro Ansanpur nodded with a knowing smile and turned back around.

"Magister Imaniel always said that waiting was the hardest thing," she said. "That the easiest way to lose was to get impatient. Do something for the sake of doing something and not because it's right. That always sounded obvious when he said it. He and Cam were the nearest thing I had to parents. I was with the bank almost as soon as I could walk. He knew everything about money and risk and how to appear one way when you're actually something else."

"He'd have made a good general, sounds like," Marcus said.

"No," she said. "I don't know. Maybe. He didn't like soldiers, though. He didn't like war. I remember he used to say that there are two ways to meet the world. You go out with a blade in your hand or else with a purse."

"Really? And here I thought there was money to be made from war."

"There is," Cithrin said. "But only if you're standing in exactly the right place. In the larger sense, there's always more lost in the fight than there is won. The way he said things, it sounded like we were all that kept the swords in their scabbards. War or trade. Dagger and coin. Those were the two kinds of people."

"Sounds like you miss him."

Cithrin nodded, then shrugged, then nodded again.

"I do, but not the way I thought I would. I thought it would all be about wanting to ask him what he knew, but most times when I think of him, it's just that it would be nice to hear his voice. And I don't even think of him as often as I'd expected."

"You've changed since you saw him," Marcus said. "That's one of the things Yardem used to tell me that actually made sense. He said that you don't go through grief like it was a chore to be done. You can't push and get finished quicker. The best you can do is change the way you always do, and the time comes when you aren't the same person who was in pain."

"And did that work for you?"

"Hasn't yet," Marcus said.

Maestro Asanpur returned with a fresh cup in his trembling hand. He placed it before Cithrin with a faint clink of fine ceramic. She blew across the surface of it, scattering the steam with her breath. When she sipped it, her smile lit the old Cinnae's face.

"Thank you, Maestro," she said.

"Thank *you*, Magistra," he said, and limped forward to close the shutters against the chill.

The patter of the raindrops grew heavier, the splashes like little detonations of white against the grey. She was right. Waiting for battle was the hardest part. Unless you got a dagger in your gut during the battle. Then that was hardest. Or you got through just fine and saw your men dead around you. Then that was.

Yardem appeared at the far side of the square, a darker shadow in a world made from them. He didn't run, didn't even hurry. Marcus watched the Tralgu endure his way past the queensmen and the market. With each step, he seemed to grow more solid. More real. He ducked his head as he came in the door.

"Sir."

"All right," Marcus said, his throat and chest tight. "All right."

Cithrin stood up. She looked calm. It would have taken

living with her for the better part of a year to see the fear in her eyes and the angle of her chin.

"The auditor's come, then?" she said.

Yardem flicked his ears and nodded.

"He has, ma'am."

Cithrin

Paerin Clark.

Sometime during her years in Vanai, she must have heard the name. The syllables had a familiarity without detail, like a name from history or myth. Drakis Stormcrow. The Risen Guard. Aesa, Princess of Swords.

Paerin Clark.

Cithrin plucked at her skirt, keeping the lines of it neat and straight. Her heart pounded against her ribs like a trapped bird. Her belly was a solid knot that veered between cramping and nausea. She wanted something to drink. Something powerful that would loosen her muscles, calm her, give her courage. Instead she held herself the way Master Kit had taught her, her shoulders low and back, her spine loose, and prayed that she looked like a woman in full possession of her powers instead of a half-grown girl in her mother's clothes.

The mild-looking man sat at her desk, in her rooms, with his legs crossed and his fingers laced across his knee. His hairline was receding. His shoulders were narrow. He could have been anybody. He could have been no one. His notebook lay open on the table, a steel pen across it, but he didn't write notes. Not even ciphered ones. He asked his questions gently, and smiled when she spoke. His Northcoast accent was soft at the corners. Where other men's words hissed, his shushed.

"Magister Imaniel had no part in this, then?"

"No, none," Cithrin said. "The intention was solely that we should take the bank's Vanai assets to Carse. As far as Magister Imaniel knew, we were doing just that. If the snows hadn't come early to the pass at Bellin, we would have followed that plan."

"And the decision to divert to the south?"

"That was Captain Wester's."

"Tell me more about that."

No voices came from below them. Captain Wester and the guards were gone, sent out of the house by Clark. A dozen sword-and-bows that he'd brought with him had taken their place. The silence seemed wrong. Eerie. The rain pattered against the windows like a thousand tiny fingers poking at her, and the thunder muttered ominously in the distance. Cithrin recounted everything she could in the detail she could manage. Being intercepted by the Antean forces, smuggling the cart into Porte Oliva, hiding in the salt quarter.

"And only Captain Wester and his Tralgu were acting as guard at this point?"

"I don't know that I'd call Yardem 'his Tralgu.' "

"They were the only two guards?"

"Yes," Cithrin said.

"Thank you."

She told about the attack by Opal, about Marcus's fears of leaving the city and his fears of staying. She was careful, when she described forging the documents, to keep her tone calm and matter-of-fact. Magister Imaniel had always said that appearing guilty gave them the impression there was something to feel guilty for. When she admitted to filing false papers with the governor of Porte Oliva, the auditor didn't comment or even change expression. Once she was past the history of founding her false branch of the bank and began to outline her investments, loans, consignments, and commissions, she felt herself starting to relax.

She talked for the greater part of the evening. Her voice grew hoarse, and her back began to ache from sitting too long in one position. If Paerin suffered the same, he didn't show it.

"How much did Captin Wester advise you on these strategies?"

"He didn't," Cithrin said. "He didn't try, and I didn't ask him to."

"Why not?"

"He's not a banker. I gave him a budget that I thought was appropriate for the protection of the gold we kept here and for the moving of any substantial amounts within the city, but that's all."

"I see. Well. Thank you, Mistress bel Sarcour. That was the most interesting story I've heard in some time. I assume all the books and records are here?"

"Yes," she said. "I've also taken a room at a café by the Grand Market, but all of those records have been brought here."

"Excellent."

"I would also like to make a suggestion? If I may."

Paerin Clark raised his eyebrows. Cithrin took a deep breath.

"Due to circumstances," she said, "I have been identified closely with the bank here in the city. With the branch being so recently established, I think it wouldn't be in anybody's interest to change that. Once you've completed your audit, I hope you'll consider keeping me on as the public face of the branch."

Clark took up his pen and closed the still-unmarked notebook.

"I think you have misunderstood the situation," he said. "This...let's call it misadventure...has embarrassed the Medean bank in general and Komme Medean in particular. It has disrupted negotiations in Herez and Northcoast, and taken resources, myself included, away from some profoundly important situations. From what you've told me, I expect you've been taken in by a mercenary captain for reasons I haven't fathomed yet. But I am very, very good at what I do. If there's anything here you haven't told me, I will find it. I'm going to spend as long as it takes to review every transaction you've made. I already have three men going through the city asking about your activity. If there's anything that's not in these books, I'll find that too. And public gaol in Porte Oliva is far from the worst thing that can happen from here.

"Now, before I get started, I have one last question. I will ask you this only once. If you tell me the truth, I am in a position to see you're treated mercifully. If you lie, I can make your life unbearable. You understand?"

She should have been frightened. That was what Clark intended, certainly. Instead, an odd peace flowed into her. He was bullying her. He was condescending to her. He was underestimating her. And so her last reservations were laid to rest. The man was an ass, and anything she did to him would be justified.

"I understand," she said. She saw him hesitate, hearing something in her voice he hadn't expected. She smiled. "What was your question?"

"What aren't you telling me?" he asked

That I'm going to beat you, Cithrin thought. *That I am going to win.*

"If you have any questions, Master Clark, I am at your disposal," Cithrin said. "But my numbers balance."

For the next week, she lived in exile, sitting in the café or walking through the city streets during the days, sleeping at night at an inn not far from her bank. The auditor called upon her daily with lists of questions and clarifications: Why was the rate of interest specified in this contract, but not in another? Why was a particular sum withdrawn from the bank's reserves, and when would it be returned? Why was this loan accepted when another apparently of greater merit was refused? Cithrin sat in her rooms—*hers*, dammit—and allowed herself to be subjected to the examination. She knew every answer, and after a few days, it became something of a game to watch Clark try to catch her out. He was smart, and he knew his business. She even found herself respecting him. He had been doing this work since Cithrin was a hardly more than a child.

But then, so had she.

The ships left for Narinisle. They carried pressed oil, wine, cotton cloth, and the dreams and hopes of the merchant houses of Porte Oliva. But they didn't carry any agreements of capital from the Medean bank in Porte Oliva, because the audit was still progressing. Next year, maybe.

Cithrin stood on the seawall and watched the ships depart, towed out past the dangers of the bay, and then sails rising up and filling like spring flowers in bloom. She stood silently until they faded into the grey between sea and sky, and then she watched the haze. Seagulls called and turned in the wide air, complaining or celebrating. At her side, Captain Wester crossed his arms.

"Another one came to the café this morning," he said. "Your brewer lady and her son."

"What did you tell them?"

"Yardem talked with them. He said the same as the others. The audit's normal for a new branch, and please to go along with whatever the man asks. She wasn't happy. Wanted to talk with you. Didn't like it when he said that the two of you comparing notes would only make the auditor's job harder. Accused Yardem of accusing her of something."

"I'm sorry about that," Cithrin said. "I'd stop this all if I could."

"I know."

Cithrin pulled her cloak closer around her and turned away from the limitless sea back toward the city. Her city. She wasn't sure when it had become hers.

"With luck, we'll be back to normal before long."

He fell in at her side. She couldn't say if she matched his stride or if he matched hers.

"You still have the option of walking away," he said. "I can go get the key back. You can reclaim the box from the governor's palace. It wouldn't be so bad. Carse is a decent enough city. Even if there is trouble with the succession, you'd be safe there. No one tries to put Carse under siege. Give it a year, take your money. You could do anything."

"I couldn't do this," Cithrin said.

"Fair point."

They walked down long, whitewashed steps and along the wall toward the salt quarter. Somewhere along the way, they passed the spot where Opal had died, but she didn't recognize it and she didn't ask. A small wire-haired dog trotted by, yipped at them, and sped away when Marcus pretended to reach down for a rock to throw.

"Notice you haven't been drinking," he said.

I would drown a small child for a bottle of wine, Cithrin

thought, *but I am going to need my wits, and there won't be any warning.*

"I don't miss it," she said.

"You haven't been sleeping."

"Don't miss that either."

The inn that had become their home while the bank itself remained under occupation sat at the corner of two of the larger of Porte Oliva's narrow streets. Its white walls and wooden roof looked cold under the low clouds. As they came near, a man stepped out of the doorway. She saw Marcus become alert without changing his stride. She felt a low burning in her throat.

The man came toward them. One of Paerin Clark's guards.

"He wants to see me?" Cithrin asked.

"Same as always, miss," the guard said. "I think he's finished up."

Cithrin took a deep breath. The time had come.

"May I bring the captain along?"

"Don't see why not."

The walk back to the bank was short, but Cithrin felt every step of it. It occurred to her that the dress she was wearing was the first she'd bought when she came to Porte Oliva, the one she'd invented Hallskari salt dyes for in exchange for a five-coin reduction. The dress of a truly dangerous woman. She tried to take it as a good omen.

A Kurtadam boy walked by selling paper funnels with honeyed almonds, and Cithrin stopped to buy one. She popped two in her mouth, gave one to Marcus. Paerin's guard waited, and she tipped the paper toward him. Smiling, he took two. So he was willing to accept gifts from her. That meant he was either a cold bastard to the bone, or the news from the auditor was good. No, she thought, it meant the guard *believed* it was good.

For twenty days, she had been denied her room. Walking back up the stairs, she was prepared to choke down outrage, but when she reached the top, everything was precisely as it had been. Paerin Clark might have been a ghost for all the trace he left of himself.

The man sat at her desk. He was writing now, the illegible symbols of cipher coming from the nib of his pen without need of a code book. He nodded to Cithrin and then to Marcus, finished the line of script, and turned to them.

"Mistress bel Sarcour," he said. "I had one last question for you. I hope you don't mind."

His tone had changed markedly. She could hear the respect in it. That was fair. She'd earned it.

"Of course."

"I'm fairly sure I've guessed the answer, but there's a sum placed aside in the most recent books. Six hundred twelve weight of silver?"

"The quarter's profit for the holding company," she said.

"Yes," the auditor said. "That's what I thought. Please, have a seat both of you."

Marcus gave her the stool, choosing to stand behind her.

"I have to say, I am impressed with all this. Magister Imaniel trained you very, very well. We have, of course, suffered some loss. But in the main, the contracts you've made seem sound. The city fleet project was, I think, ill-advised, but since they refused your offer we don't have to concern ourselves with that."

Cithrin wondered what it was about the fleet that the auditor found problematic, but he was still speaking.

"I am making my report to the holding company now. My primary finding is that what you have done here was honestly intended to be in the interests of the bank as a whole. We are, unfortunately, obligated to a length of contract in Porte Oliva that doesn't match what we'd like, but I know you were doing the best you could. And while some aspects of your behavior were certainly outside the law, I see no advantage to seeking any legal redress."

"He means we got away with it?" Marcus asked.

"He does," Cithrin said.

"Good to know."

Paerin tapped his fingertips against the top of the desk, the deep lines of a frown marking his high forehead.

"I don't want to be forward, and I can't, of course, make any guarantees," he said, "but there may be a position for a woman with your talents in Carse. I would need to discuss it with Komme Medean and some of the other directors. But if you would like to make a career as a banker, I think you could find a start there."

You still have the option of walking away, Marcus had said less than hour earlier. She still did. It was time to burn that hope.

"I would prefer to have a start here," Cithrin said. "Have you considered my proposal?"

Paerin Clark looked at her blankly. Then, embarrassed for her, he nodded.

"Yes, that. No. We will be putting a recognized member of the bank in charge of the branch until it can be dissolved. Keeping you in your present position isn't possible."

Marcus chuckled.

"Does it make me a bad man that I was hoping he would say that?" he asked.

Cithrin ignored him. When she spoke, she sat straight and looked the auditor in the eye.

"You've overlooked something, sir. There's a record book

from Vanai that isn't among these. It's an old one, though. It doesn't touch directly on your audit."

Paerin Clark shifted his chair to face her. He crossed his arms over his chest.

"It is the book that records my status as ward of the bank," Cithrin said. "It shows my legal age, and the date upon which I can begin to sign legally binding contracts. That would be next summer."

"I don't see how that—"

Cithrin gestured to the books, the piles of paper and parchment, the entire mechanism of her bank.

"None of these contracts is legal," she said. "I am not legally permitted to enter into any agreement. I'm ten months too young."

Paerin Clark's expression was the same bland smile he'd worn the first day he'd come. It might only have been her imagination that he was a shade paler. Cithin swallowed to loosen the knot in her throat.

"If the information in that book becomes public," she said, "the bank will have to resort to direct appeal to the governor to either enforce the contracts anyway or reclaim the sums that were given out. I've met the governor, and I think that he is unlikely to take money away from his citizens to give to a bank that's in a hurry to abandon his city."

"And the book in question is where?" Paerin Clark asked.

"In a strongbox deposited with the governor under my name privately and separately from the bank. And the key to the box is in the keeping of a man with no incentive to see the bank succeed here. If I tell him what it unlocks, you can burn all these papers to light your cookfires."

"You're bluffing. If this comes out, you're guilty of forgery, theft. Misrepresentation. You'll be in gaol for the rest of your life, and all we'll lose is money."

"I can get her out of here," Marcus said. "A city's complement of queensmen half incapacitated from laughing at you? I can get her out of Birancour and in a decent house by midwinter."

"We are the Medean bank," Paerin Clark said. "You can't outrun us."

"I'm Marcus Wester. I've killed kings, and I'm lousy at bluffing. Threaten her again, and —"

"Stop it, both of you," Cithrin said. "Here's my offer. Keep the branch as it is, but install a notary from the holding company. We say it's to help with the workload. I'm the face and voice, but the notary oversees all the agreements."

"And when I refuse?"

She wanted a drink. She wanted a warm bed and man's arms around her. She wanted to know for certain that she was doing the right thing.

"I burn this branch to the ground," she said.

The world balanced on the edge of a blade. The auditor closed his eyes, leaned back in his chair. *Ah well,* Cithrin thought. *Life as a fugitive wasn't so bad last winter. At least this time I can wear my own clothes.* Paerin Clark opened his eyes.

"You sign nothing," he said. "All agreements are signed by the notary and the notary alone. Negotiations don't happen without the notary present. If you're overruled, you accept it. Control rests with the holding company. You're a figurehead. Nothing more."

"I can live with that," she said. And also, unspoken: *Until I can change it, I can live with that.*

"And you return the missing book with evidence of your age to me. Before I leave the city."

"No," Marcus said. "She gives you that, she's got no purchase. You could go back on everything, and she'd have nothing."

"She'll have to trust me."

Cithrin swallowed. She wanted to vomit. She wanted to sing.

She nodded. Paerin Clark was still for a long moment, then he picked up the papers he'd been writing, sighed, and ripped them into small squares.

"It seems I have a somewhat different report to write," he said, smiling wryly. "Congratulations on your new bank, Magistra."

Geder

The funeral rites of Phelia Maas were somewhat over-shadowed by the execution of her husband. Geder, given the choice, had opted for the execution, as had the majority of the great names at court. King Simeon's throne sat on a raised dais. Aster sat beside him in a smaller chair of the same design. King and prince both wore black ermine. Then there was the broad expanse of the chamber, Feldin Maas kneeling in its center. His ankles and wrists were bound with wire, and even from the gallery behind the woven rope, Geder could see the bruises on the man's legs and the long black scabs across his back. Ten executioners stood in a rough circle around the prisoner. Their masks were steel and made to look like snarling animals, and their blades were dull and rusted.

A single drum beat out its dry call. It was the only sound apart from some idiot whispering at the back the crowd. Geder tried to ignore the people and focus on the spectacle. Even though he'd arrived late, the assembled nobles had made room for him, so he had an excellent view just at the edge of the gallery. Dawson Kalliam and his two sons stood next to him. Geder was wearing his black leather cloak from Vanai, but the cut of it was all wrong now. His body had changed shape over the summer, and it hung loose on him.

He wished he'd thought to get it recut. Everyone who wasn't watching Feldin Maas die seemed to be looking at him.

King Simeon, gray in the face and severe, lifted his arm. The drum went silent. The mass of people in all three levels of the gallery took in their breath. Even the idiot at the back stopped talking.

"You have the courtesy of a final statement, traitor," the king said.

Feldin Maas shook his head slowly. *No.*

The king's arm fell. The executioners moved in, each man sinking the point of his blade hard into the man's flesh. Geder had been led to believe that the blades were fairly dull, and the force each of the killers used reinforced the idea. Maas cried out once, but only once. When the executioners stood back, he lay in a spreading pool of blood, the ten blades sticking out of his body. The assembly around him let its breath out with a sound like wind through trees.

King Simeon stood. Behind him, Prince Aster looked like a statue of himself carved from pale stone. Geder wondered what it would be like for a boy just past his ninth naming day to know that a grown man had been plotting to kill him and then watch the man die brutally.

"This is the right and proper fate of all who swear false loyalty to the Severed Throne," he said. "Let all who stand witness to this justice carry forth the word that all traitors to Antea will suffer and all will die."

The applause and shouts of approval burst forth all around. Geder joined in, and Dawson Kalliam leaned close to him, shouting to be heard.

"This is yours too, Palliako."

It was a kinder way of putting it than he'd used before the ceremony started. Then he'd said, *You've given Simeon a spine at last.*

The drum began again, and king and prince turned and walked out in solemn procession. Servants dressed in red came to carry out the body. Maas was to be displayed, swords still in place, for seventeen days. What was left after that would be thrown into the Division with the kitchen scraps and sewage, and anyone who tried to pull it out for a more respectful burial would be hung. Somewhere behind Geder, hidden by the nobles of Antea, the doors opened. With the king gone and the ceremony finished, conversation rose to a deafening roar. Geder couldn't make out what anyone was saying over the noise of everyone else, so he just followed the subtle movement of the crowd and made his way out.

In the great halls of the Kingspire, the nobility of Antea broke into a hundred small groups. Dispersed, the din of the talk was less deafening if not particularly more comprehensible. He saw people pretending not to look at him, and he had some idea what they were saying: *Palliako claims he was wandering the Keshet, but he came back knowing all about the plot on Prince Aster* and *burning Vanai was all part of his plan* and *I told you his bringing loyal soldiers back just before the mercenaries tried to take the city was no coincidence.* He walked through the hall slowly, bathing in it.

"Sir Palliako. A word."

Curtin Issandrian and Alan Klin walked up to him looking like bookends in the library of the damned. Geder smiled. Curtin Issandrian put out his hand.

"I've come to thank you, sir. I owe you a great debt."

"You do?" Geder asked, leaving the man's hand floating in the air between them.

"If it weren't for you, I would still be in alliance with a secret traitor to the crown," Issandrian said. "Feldin Maas was a friend, and I let that friendship blind me to his nature.

Today has been a terrible day for me, but it has been necessary. And I thank you for it."

Geder wished Basrahip had been there, just to know if Issandrian were what he pretended to be. Another time, though. There were months and years still to come when he and his Righteous Servant could ferret out every secret in the court. A little magnanimity now wouldn't hurt anyone. He took Issandrian's hand.

"You're a good man, Geder Palliako," Issandrian said, speaking just loudly enough to be overheard. "Antea is fortunate to have you."

"Thank you, Lord Issandrian," Geder said, matching him. "It is a strong man who can admit he was misguided. I respect you for it."

They dropped hands, and Alan Klin came forward, his own hand extended. Geder grinned and took it, pulling the man close.

"Sir Klin!" he said, grinning. "It's been too long."

"It has. It truly has."

"Do you remember that night on the march to Vanai when I got drunk and burned that essay I showed you?"

"Yes. Yes, I do," Klin said, laughing as if they were sharing a nostalgic moment.

Geder laughed too, and then let the amusement drain from his face.

"So do I."

He dropped Klin's hand, turned, and walked away feeling like the ground itself was rising to meet his footsteps. Outside, the day was blue skies and chill winter wind. His father stood near the steps that led down to the carriages, watching the chaos of horses, wood, and wheels. He held a pipe in his hand, but there seemed to be no fire in it.

"So did the political process come to its logical end?" Lerer asked.

"Didn't you watch?"

"I'm too old for blood sports. If the thing needs doing, then do it, but don't make a theater piece out of it."

"But the king has to make an example, doesn't he? He's trying to keep Asterilhold from interfering with us," Geder said. He felt hurt that his father hadn't watched Maas die. "They were going to *kill* Prince Aster."

"I suppose," Lerer said. "Still. I'll be damned pleased to be home, get the stink of Camnipol off my skin. We've been away from Rivenhalm too long."

If we are to understand the freedom of humanity, we must first understand its enslavement. The root of all races—even the Firstblood—exists in the reign of dragons, and the end of that reign must by necessity mark the beginning of a peculiarly human history. It is not an exaggeration to say that the last breath of the last dragon was the first moment of the age of humanity in all its variety. But like all freedom, it was bounded and defined by that which came before. Our knowledge of the Dragon Empire is imperfect at best, but I contend that the discovery of the cave-palaces beneath Takynpal gives us our best view into what I have chosen to call the Age of Formation.

Geder flipped ahead, rereading pages he had translated before. The paper was brown with age, and fragile. He disliked handling it for fear that the pages would crack and flake away in his fingertips, but he needed to get as close to the original texts as he could. It seemed to him that there had to be something—some word or phrase that could have been translated in more than one way—that would mention the existence and history of the goddess.

The door of his sitting room swung open and Basrahip came in. He still wore his robes from the temple in the mountains, but he'd accepted a pair of leather-soled boots for walking on the cobbled streets of Camnipol. Among the rich red tapestries and soft upholstered chairs of the Palliako room in Camnipol, he looked entirely out of place. A desert weed in an arrangement of roses. He smiled at Geder and bowed.

"Been walking again?" Geder said.

"I knew tales of the great cities of the world, but nothing I had imagined could be so grand and so corrupt," the priest said. "A child not more than seven summers old lied to me. And for no reason."

"What did he say?"

The huge priest lumbered to a chair just across from Geder and lowered himself into it, the wood creaking under him as he spoke.

"That he could tell my future for three copper coins. He knew it was untrue. A child."

"He was a beggar," Geder said. "Of course they're trying to cheat you. They need the money for food. I think you should be careful where you walk, though. There are parts of the city that aren't safe. Especially after dark."

"You live in an age of darkness, my friend. But this city will be beautiful beyond measure when it is pure."

"Have you been to the temple?"

"I have," Basrahip said. "It is a beautiful building. I am looking forward to the day when I can make it my own."

"The paperwork shouldn't take long. Before the close of court, certainly, and that's less than a week now. But there's not much to do in Camnipol over the winter months."

"I have tasks enough."

"So I've been reading," Geder said, "and there's something bothering me."

"Yes?"

"The goddess is eternal. She was there at the birth of the dragons. She was there all through the Dragon Empire, but the only references I see to the Righteous Servant or the Sinir Kushku come at the very end, during the final war. And then they talk about it as if Morade created it, the way Asteril made the Timzinae or Vailoth made the Drowned. I just don't understand how that can be right."

"Perhaps then it cannot," the priest said. "You should put less trust in written words, my friend. They are the stone eggs of lies. Here. I will show you. Read something from your book there."

Geder flipped the pages, fingertips shifting across the words until he found a passage that was easily rendered.

"*It was the fourth century of the Dragon Vailoth's rule when these policies changed.*"

"Is that true?" the priest asked him. "Is it untrue? Do you mean what you say? No, old friend. It's neither. Your voice carries nothing. They are only words you repeat emptily. To write a thing down is to kill it. Only in the living voice can the truth be known. My brothers and I have listened to one another, passing the voice of the goddess down from generation to generation, and with every new speaking from the start, we have known what we heard to be true. These books you have? They are ink on paper. Objects. Soulless. You would be wiser not to put your faith in them."

"Oh," Geder said. "That's...I'd never looked at things that way. Does that—?"

"Geder?"

Lerer Palliako stood in the doorway. His tunic was the

blue and gray of House Palliako, formally cut with silver buttons on the sleeve. His hand clutched the doorway, as if he needed it to keep himself steady.

"What's the matter, Father?"

"We have a visitor. You should come with me."

Geder rose to his feet, alarm tightening his skin. Basrahip looked from the doorway to Geder and back.

"Stay here," Geder said. "I'll come back as soon as I can."

Lerer walked in silence through the halls. The servants, usually buzzing through the rooms like bees in a meadow, were gone. At the door to the private meeting chamber, he stopped. For a moment, Geder thought he would speak, but instead he shook his head, opened the door, and stepped in.

The private chamber had been designed for comfort. Candles glowed from polished silver sconces, doubling their light and filling the room with the scents of honey and heat. A fire grate sat unlit and soot-blackened in its corner. Light spilled from the western window, and the pale silk chairs caught it, seeming almost to glow. A boy in a grey tunic looked up at him solemnly, and Geder felt he should have recognized the face. On the far wall, a huge painting the size of a standing man showed a green-scaled dragon towering above figures representing the thirteen races of man. And looking up at the painting, King Simeon.

The king turned.

Lerer bowed and said, "Your Majesty." Geder bowed a moment later, quickly and with the sense of trying to catch up. The boy was the prince. Prince Aster and King Simeon.

"I am pleased to meet you at last, Geder Palliako," the king said. Geder took the use of his given name as permission to stand.

"I...Um, thank you. It's a pleasure to meet you too, Majesty."

"You are aware that tradition calls for the prince to be taken in by a house of the highest reputation and nobility. A family that will swear to protect him should the need arise."

"Ah," Geder said. "Yes?"

"I have come to ask you to fill this role."

"My father, you mean? Our house?"

"It's not me he wants," Lerer said. "It's you."

"I...I don't know how to raise a boy. All respect, Your Majesty. I wouldn't have the first idea what to do."

"Keep him safe," the king said. His voice didn't sound commanding. It didn't sound formal. It sounded like a man on the edge of begging or prayer. "Just keep him safe."

"Right now everyone in court loves you or fears you, my boy," Lerer said. "Half of them are saying you're the first hero Antea's seen in a generation, and the other half won't mention you for fear of drawing your attention. I'm not sure it's a good reason to take the title of protector."

"I'm not doing it," Geder said. "I'm no one's protector. It'd be you, Father. You're the Viscount of Rivenhalm."

"But you are the Baron of Ebbinbaugh," King Simeon said.

"Ebbinbaugh?" Geder said.

"Someone has to take Maas's holdings," Lerer said. "Seems that's you."

"Well," Geder said, a grin spreading across his lips. "*Well*."

Prince Aster rose and walked to Geder. He wasn't a large boy. Geder had always thought he was taller. He had the gray eyes and serious face of the dead queen, but his father's jaw.

"I owe you my life, Lord Palliako," the boy said. The cadence of his voice made the phrases sound rehearsed. "I would be pleased to have you as my protector, and swear that I should do honor to you as your ward."

"Do you want to?" Geder asked. The boy's formal expression faltered. Tears appeared, glistening in his eyes.

"They say I can't stay with Da anymore," he said.

Geder felt himself starting to tear up as well.

"I lost my mother when I was young too," he said. "Maybe I could be like an uncle? Or an older brother."

"I don't have any brothers," Aster said.

"See? Neither do I," Geder said. Aster tried to smile. "We'd probably need to visit your father a lot, though. And mine. God, am I going to have my own holding? Father, I'm going to have my own holding."

"You will," Lerer said. "I think his majesty didn't want to be the only one in the room losing a son."

Geder barely heard him. This morning, he'd been a hero. Now he had a barony of his own and a place in court that men fought and sometimes died to get. Sir Alan Klin would soil himself when he heard that he'd made an enemy of Prince Aster's protector.

"Thank you, Your Majesty. I accept this duty and honor, and I'll make sure Aster's kept safe. I swear it."

The king was weeping, tears streaking down his cheeks, but his voice didn't waver when he spoke.

"I put my trust in you, Lord Palliako. I will...I will make the announcement at the close of court. I'll see you're seated appropriately for your new station. This is a brighter day for the kingdom. And I thank you for that."

Geder bowed. He wanted to run out in the streets, capering and singing. He wanted to go brag to all of his friends, starting with Jorey Kalliam and...

"Can I borrow the prince?" Geder asked. "Just for a few minutes? There's someone I want him to meet."

In the sitting room, Basrahip had moved to Geder's chair. The huge hands turned the pages slowly, the broad face twisted with disdain. Geder cleared his throat. The priest looked up, his eyes shifting from Geder to the prince standing at his side.

"Basrahip, high priest of the goddess, may I introduce my new ward Prince Aster. Prince Aster, this is Basrahip."

The prince walked forward, stopped the appropriate distance away, and bowed his small head. He looked like a kitten greeting a bull.

"I am very pleased to meet you, sir," the prince said.

Basrahip smiled.

"No," he said, softly. "You aren't. But give it time, young prince. Give it time."

Entr'acte

The Apostate

The apostate groaned, rolling over on his thin mattress. The first bare light of dawn outlined the stable door, and in his blood, the spiders shuddered and danced, agitated as they had been for weeks now. In the twenty years he had traveled the world, the taint in his blood had never troubled him as much as these last weeks. Around him, the others still slept, their deep and regular breath reassuring as a thick wool blanket. The stables were warm, or warmer at least than sleeping in the cart would have been. He wouldn't have to break a skin of ice off the water bucket before he drank. When he sat up, his spine ached. Maybe from the coming winter, maybe from the years weighing down his shoulders, maybe from the restlessness of the creatures that lived in his skin.

One of the horses snorted in its stall, shifting uneasily. From the shadows, there was a tiny gasp. He went still, straining to hear.

"I won't finish," a familiar voice whispered. "I swear I won't finish."

The apostate closed his eyes. It never changed. All through the world, likely all through the ages and epochs of humanity, some things simply never changed. He swallowed, readying his voice. When he spoke, the words carried through the stables and out into the yard.

"Sandr! If you get that girl pregnant, I will be sorely

tempted to tie off your cock with a length of wire, and I swear it will not improve your performance."

The voice that had gasped squeaked in alarm, and Sandr rushed into the dim light, pulling at his tunic to cover himself.

"There's no one here, Master Kit," the boy lied. "I don't know what you're talking about."

"Which performance do you mean?" Smit asked in a sleepy voice. "Seems to me that if you're talking about stagecraft, tying yourself down might be a decent exercise in concentration."

"Help him play a hunchback," Cary said through a yawn.

"There's no one here," Sandr said again. "You're all imagining things."

The scrape of a board at the stable's back marked the girl's escape, whoever she was. The apostate rose to sitting. Hornet lit a lantern, the warm light chasing away the darkness. With groans and complaints, the company came to life. As they always did. Charlit Soon, the new actress, was looking daggers at Sandr. Yet another irritation the apostate would have to soothe. He wondered, and not for the first time, how anyone without the spiders could keep an acting company together for any length of time. But perhaps they couldn't.

"Up," he said. "I'm sure there's work to be done that will make us more money than lying here in the dark. Up, you mad, beautiful bastards, and let us once more take the hearts and dreams of Porte Oliva by storm."

"Yes, Mother," Cary said, rolled over, and fell back to sleep.

The first time he'd met Marcus Wester, the apostate had given him a private name: the man without hopes. In the last year, the despair had faded a bit, but sometimes Wester would still make his little jokes—*I'm too stubborn to die* or *You don't need love when there's laundry to wash*—and the people around him would chuckle. Only the apostate knew how deeply the man meant what he said.

It was what made the mercenary captain interesting.

The taproom near the bank had the advantage in these cold months of keeping food and a warm fire. Cary and Charlit Soon would set up in the common room some nights, singing songs from the lighter comic operas and making between them enough to feed the whole company for three days.

"Always best to keep your political assassinations discreet," Wester said. "Really, that was where I went wrong. Well, it's not the first place I went wrong."

"One of the places, sir," Yardem Hane said.

"Will it keep Northcoast from violence, do you think?"

"They poisoned a man so he'd vomit himself to death," Marcus said. "That's violence. But with his claim disposed, I don't see any swords taking the field, no. So that's good for the Narinisle trade. And apparently Antea's decided not to descend into civil war either."

"I didn't know they were on the dragon's path," the apostate said, taking a sip of his ale. During winter, they kept it in the alley under guard, so it was as cold as the rooms were warm.

"Didn't either. This new notary gets reports from everyplace, though. It's one of the advantages of being part of a bank where the bank people know about you. Anyway, it seems the only thing that kept the court in Camnipol from turning on each other like a pack of starving dogs was a religious zealot from the Keshet."

"Really?"

"Well," Wester said, "he's a real Antean noble, but apparently he spent time in the Keshet and came back with a bad case of the faith. Exposed some sort of plot, turned the court on its ears, and built a temple just down the street from the Kingspire to celebrate."

"There's nothing sinister about building temples, sir," Yardem said. "People do it all the time."

"Not in celebration," Wester said. "People go to God when they've got trouble. Things are well, there's not much point sucking after the divine."

Yardem flicked a jingling ear and leaned toward the apostate.

"He says these things to annoy me."

"Always works."

"It does, sir," the Tralgu lied.

"And the Goddess of Round Pies seems especially dim."

"Round pies?" the apostate asked.

"The cult's got a symbol. Big red banner with a white bit in the middle, and what looks like eight bits of pie all stuck together."

"Eight points on a compass," Yardem said.

No, the apostate thought, dread pouring into him like dark water. *No, the eight legs of a spider.*

"You all right, Kit?" Wester asked. "You're looking pale."

"Fine," the apostate said. "Just fine."

But in his mind there was a single thought:

It's begun.

Acknowledgments

Writing a book is never as solitary a job as I expect. This project especially has benefited by the time and attention of people besides myself. I owe debts of gratitude to Walter Jon Williams, Carrie Vaughn, Ian Tregillis, Vic Milán, Melinda Snodgrass, and Ty Franck, who were there when the lightning struck, and Jim Frenkel, who did what he could. Also my agents Shawna McCarthy and Danny Baror, who have been better than gold on this as on everything. And I would especially like to thank the crew at Orbit. My editors Darren Nash and DongWon Song have made working on the project a joy, and the deep professionalism and consideration I've seen from everyone on staff in New York and London have continually impressed. This would be less of a book without each of them.

Any errors and infelicities are entirely my own.

extras

about the author

Daniel Abraham is the author of the critically acclaimed Long Price Quartet. He has been nominated for the Hugo, Nebula, and World Fantasy awards, and won the International Horror Guild award. He also writes as M.L.N. Hanover and (with Ty Franck) James S. A. Corey. He lives in New Mexico. Visit his website at www.danielabraham.com

Find out more about Daniel Abraham and other Orbit authors by registering for the free monthly newsletter at www.orbitbooks.net

if you enjoyed
THE DRAGON'S PATH

look out for

THE BLACK PRISM

Book One of the Lightbringer trilogy

by

Brent Weeks

Chapter 1

Kip crawled toward the battlefield in the darkness, the mist pressing down, blotting out sound, scattering starlight. Though the adults shunned it and the children were forbidden to come here, he'd played on the open field a hundred times – during the day. Tonight, his purpose was grimmer.

Reaching the top of the hill, Kip stood and hiked up his pants. The river behind him was hissing, or maybe that was the warriors beneath its surface, dead these sixteen years. He squared his shoulders, ignoring his imagination. The mists made him seem suspended, outside of time. But even if there was no evidence of it, the sun was coming. By the time it did, he had to get to the far side of the battlefield. Farther than he'd ever gone searching.

Even Ramir wouldn't come out here at night. Everyone knew Sundered Rock was haunted. But Ram didn't have to feed his family; *his* mother didn't smoke her wages.

Gripping his little belt knife tightly, Kip started walking. It wasn't just the unquiet dead that might pull him down to the evernight. A pack of giant javelinas had been seen roaming the night, tusks cruel, hooves sharp. They were good eating if you had a matchlock, iron nerves, and good aim, but since the Prisms' War had wiped out all the town's men, there weren't many people who braved death for a little bacon. Rekton was already a shell of what it had once been. The alcaldesa wasn't eager for any of her townspeople to throw their lives away. Besides, Kip didn't have a matchlock.

Nor were javelinas the only creatures that roamed the night. A mountain lion or a golden bear would also probably enjoy a well-marbled Kip.

A low howl cut the mist and the darkness hundreds of paces deeper into the battlefield. Kip froze. Oh, there were wolves too. How'd he forget wolves?

Another wolf answered, farther out. A haunting sound, the very voice of the wilderness. You couldn't help but freeze when you heard it. It was the kind of beauty that made you shit your pants.

Wetting his lips, Kip got moving. He had the distinct sensation of being followed. Stalked. He looked over his shoulder. There was nothing there. Of course. His mother always said he had too much imagination. Just walk, Kip. Places to be. Animals are more scared of you and all that. Besides, that was one of the tricks about a howl, it always sounded much closer than it really was. Those wolves were probably leagues away.

Before the Prisms' War, this had been excellent farmland. Right next to the Umber River, suitable for figs, grapes, pears, dewberries, asparagus – *everything* grew here. And it had been sixteen years since the final battle – a year before Kip was even born. But the plain was still torn and scarred. A few burnt timbers of old homes and barns poked out of the dirt. Deep furrows and craters remained from cannon shells. Filled now with swirling mist, those craters looked like lakes, tunnels, traps. Bottomless. Unfathomable.

Most of the magic used in the battle had dissolved sooner or later in the years of sun exposure, but here and there broken green luxin spears still glittered. Shards of solid yellow underfoot would cut through the toughest shoe leather.

Scavengers had long since taken all the valuable arms, mail, and luxin from the battlefield, but as the seasons passed and rains fell, more mysteries surfaced each year. That was what Kip was hoping for – and what he was seeking was most visible in the first rays of dawn.

The wolves stopped howling. Nothing was worse than hearing that chilling sound, but at least with the sound he knew where they were. Now . . . Kip swallowed on the hard knot in his throat.

As he walked in the valley of the shadow of two great unnatural hills – the remnant of two of the great funeral pyres where tens of thousands had burned – Kip saw something in the mist. His heart leapt into his throat. The curve of a mail cowl. A glint of eyes searching the darkness.

Then it was swallowed up in the rolling mists.

A ghost. Dear Orholam. Some spirit keeping watch at its grave.

Look on the bright side. Maybe wolves are scared of ghosts.

Kip realized he'd stopped walking, peering into the darkness. Move, fathead.

He moved, keeping low. He might be big, but he prided himself on being light on his feet. He tore his eyes away from the hill – still no sign of the ghost or man or whatever it was. He had that feeling again that he was being stalked. He looked back. Nothing.

A quick click, like someone dropping a small stone. And something at the corner of his eye. Kip shot a look up the hill. A click, a spark, the striking of flint against steel.

The mists illuminated for that briefest moment, Kip saw few details. Not a ghost – a soldier striking a flint, trying to light a slow-match. It caught fire, casting a red glow on the soldier's face, making his eyes seem to glow. He affixed the slow-match to the match-holder of his matchlock and spun, looking for targets in the darkness.

His night vision must have been ruined by staring at the brief flame on his match, now a smoldering red ember, because his eyes passed right over Kip.

The soldier turned again, sharply, paranoid. 'The hell am I supposed to see out here, anyway? Swivin' wolves.'

Very, very carefully, Kip started walking away. He had to get deeper into the mist and darkness before the soldier's night vision recovered, but if he made noise, the man might fire blindly. Kip walked on his toes, silently, his back itching, sure that a lead ball was going to tear through him at any moment.

But he made it. A hundred paces, more, and no one yelled. No shot cracked the night. Farther. Two hundred paces more, and he saw light off to his left, a campfire. It had burned so low it was barely more than coals now. Kip tried not to look directly at it to save his vision. There was no tent, no bedrolls nearby, just the fire.

Kip tried Master Danavis's trick for seeing in darkness. He let his focus relax and tried to view things from the periphery of his vision. Nothing but an irregularity, perhaps. He moved closer.

Two men lay on the cold ground. One was a soldier. Kip had seen his mother unconscious plenty of times; he knew instantly this man wasn't passed out. He was sprawled unnaturally, there were no blankets, and his mouth hung open, slack-jawed, eyes staring unblinking at the night. Next to the dead soldier lay another man, bound in chains but alive. He lay on his side, hands manacled behind his back, a black bag over his head and cinched tight around his neck.

The prisoner was alive, trembling. No, weeping. Kip looked around; there was no one else in sight.

'Why don't you just finish it, damn you?' the prisoner said.

Kip froze. He thought he'd approached silently.

'Coward,' the prisoner said. 'Just following your orders, I suppose? Orholam will smite you for what you're about to do to that little town.'

Kip had no idea what the man was talking about.

Apparently his silence spoke for him.

'You're not one of them.' A note of hope entered the prisoner's voice. 'Please, help me!'

Kip stepped forward. The man was suffering. Then he stopped. Looked at the dead soldier. The front of the soldier's shirt was soaked with blood. Had this prisoner killed him? How?

'Please, leave me chained if you must. But please, I don't want to die in darkness.'

Kip stayed back, though it felt cruel. 'You killed him?'

'I'm supposed to be executed at first light. I got away He chased me down and got the bag over my head before he died. If dawn's close, his replacement is coming anytime now.'

Kip still wasn't putting it together. No one in Rekton trusted the soldiers who came through, and the alcaldesa had told the town's young people to give any soldiers a wide berth for a while – apparently the new satrap Garadul had declared himself free of the Chromeria's control. Now he was King Garadul, he said, but he wanted the usual levies from the town's young people. The alcaldesa had told his representative that if he wasn't the satrap anymore, he didn't have the right to raise levies. King or satrap, Garadul couldn't be happy with that, but Rekton was too small to bother with. Still, it would be wise to avoid his soldiers until this all blew over.

On the other hand, just because Rekton wasn't getting along with the satrap right now didn't make this man Kip's friend.

'So you *are* a criminal?' Kip asked.

'Of six shades to Sun Day,' the man said. The hope leaked out of his voice. 'Look, boy – you are a child, aren't you? You sound like one. I'm going to die today. I can't get away. Truth to tell, I don't want to. I've run enough. This time, I fight.'

'I don't understand.'

'You will. Take off my hood.'

Though some vague doubt nagged Kip, he untied the half-knot around the man's neck and pulled off the hood.

At first, Kip had no idea what the prisoner was talking about. The man sat up, arms still bound behind his back. He was perhaps thirty years old, Tyrean like Kip but with a lighter complexion, his hair wavy rather than kinky, his limbs thin and muscular. Then Kip saw his eyes.

Men and women who could harness light and make luxin – drafters – always had unusual eyes. A little residue of whatever color they drafted ended up in their eyes. Over the course of their life, it would stain the entire iris red, or blue, or whatever their color was. The prisoner was a green drafter – or had been. Instead of the green being bound in a halo within the iris, it was shattered like crockery smashed to the floor. Little green fragments glowed even in the whites of his eyes. Kip gasped and shrank back.

'Please!' the man said. 'Please, the madness isn't on me. I won't hurt you.'

'You're a color wight.'

'And now you know why I ran away from the Chromeria,' the man said.

Because the Chromeria put down color wights like a farmer put down a beloved, rabid dog.

Kip was on the verge of bolting, but the man wasn't making any threatening moves. And besides, it was still dark. Even color wights needed light to draft. The mist did seem lighter, though, gray beginning to touch the horizon. It was crazy to talk to a madman, but maybe it wasn't too crazy. At least until dawn.

The color wight was looking at Kip oddly. 'Blue eyes.' He laughed.

Kip scowled. He hated his blue eyes. It was one thing when a foreigner like Master Danavis had blue eyes. They looked fine on him. Kip looked freakish.

'What's your name?' the color wight asked.

Kip swallowed, thinking he should probably run away.

'Oh, for Orholam's sake, you think I'm going to hex you with your name? How ignorant is this backwater? That isn't how chromaturgy works—'

'Kip.'

The color wight grinned. 'Kip. Well, Kip, have you ever wondered why you were stuck in such a small life? Have you ever gotten the feeling, Kip, that you're special?'

Kip said nothing. Yes, and yes.

'Do you know *why* you feel destined for something greater?'

'Why?' Kip asked, quiet, hopeful.

'Because you're an arrogant little shit.' The color wight laughed.

Kip shouldn't have been taken off guard. His mother had said worse. Still, it took him a moment. A small failure. 'Burn in hell, coward,' he said. 'You're not even good at running away. Caught by ironfoot soldiers.'

The color wight laughed louder. 'Oh, they didn't *catch* me. They recruited me.'

Who would recruit madmen to join them? 'They didn't know you were a—'

'Oh, they knew.'

Dread like a weight dropped into Kip's stomach. 'You said something about my town. Before. What are they planning to do?'

'You know, Orholam's got a sense of humor. Never realized that till now. Orphan, aren't you?'

'No. I've got a mother,' Kip said. He instantly regretted giving the color wight even that much.

'Would you believe me if I told you there's a prophecy about you?'

'It wasn't funny the first time,' Kip said. 'What's going to happen to my town?' Dawn was coming, and Kip wasn't going to stick around. Not only would the guard's replacement come then, but Kip had no idea what the wight would do once he had light.

'You know,' the wight said, 'you're the reason I'm here. Not here here. Not like "Why do I exist?" Not in Tyrea. In chains, I mean.'

'What?' Kip asked.

'There's power in madness, Kip. Of course . . .' He trailed off, laughed at a private thought. Recovered. 'Look, that soldier has a key in his breast pocket. I couldn't get it out, not with—' He shook his hands, bound and manacled behind his back.

'And I would help you why?' Kip asked.

'For a few straight answers before dawn.'

Crazy, and cunning. *Perfect.* 'Give me one first,' Kip said.

'Shoot.'

'What's the plan for Rekton?'

'Fire.'

'What?' Kip asked.

'Sorry, you said one answer.'

'That was no answer!'

'They're going to wipe out your village. Make an example so no one else defies King Garadul. Other villages defied the king too, of course. His rebellion against the Chromeria isn't popular everywhere. For every town burning to take vengeance on the Prism, there's another that wants nothing to do with war. Your village was chosen specially. Anyway, I had a little spasm of conscience and objected. Words were exchanged. I punched my superior. Not totally my fault. They know us greens don't do rules and hierarchy. Especially not once we've broken the halo.' The color wight shrugged. 'There, straight. I think that deserves the key, don't you?'

It was too much information to soak up at once – broken the halo? – but it *was* a straight answer. Kip walked over to the dead man. His skin was pallid in the rising light. Pull it together, Kip. Ask whatever you need to ask.

Kip could tell that dawn was coming. Eerie shapes were emerging from the night. The great twin looming masses of Sundered Rock itself were visible mostly as a place where stars were blotted out of the sky.

What do I need to ask?

He was hesitating, not wanting to touch the dead man. He knelt. 'Why my town?' He poked through the dead man's pocket, careful not to touch skin. It was there, two keys.

'They think you have something that belongs to the king. I don't know what. I only picked up that much by eavesdropping.'

'What would Rekton have that the king wants?' Kip asked.

'Not Rekton you. You you.'

It took Kip a second. He touched his own chest. 'Me? Me personally? I don't even own anything!'

The color wight gave a crazy grin, but Kip thought it was a pretense. 'Tragic mistake, then. Their mistake, your tragedy.'

'What, you think I'm lying?!' Kip asked. 'You think I'd be out here scavenging luxin if I had any other choice?'

'I don't really care one way or the other. You going to bring that key over here, or do I need to ask real nice?'

It was a mistake to bring the keys over. Kip knew it. The color wight wasn't stable. He was dangerous. He'd admitted as much. But he had kept his word. How could Kip do less?

Kip unlocked the man's manacles, and then the padlock on the chains. He backed away carefully, as one would from a wild animal. The color wight pretended not to notice, simply rubbing his arms and stretching back and forth. He moved over to the guard and poked through his pockets again. His hand emerged with a pair of green spectacles with one cracked lens.

'You could come with me,' Kip said. 'If what you said is true—'

'How close do you think I'd get to your town before someone came running with a musket? Besides, once the sun comes up . . . I'm ready for it to be done.' The color wight took a deep breath, staring at the horizon. 'Tell me, Kip, if you've done bad things your whole life, but you die doing something good, do you think that makes up for all the bad?'

'No,' Kip said, honestly, before he could stop himself.

'Me neither.'

'But it's better than nothing,' Kip said. 'Orholam is merciful.'

'Wonder if you'll say that after they're done with your village.'

There were other questions Kip wanted to ask, but everything had happened in such a rush that he couldn't put his thoughts together.

In the rising light Kip saw what had been hidden in the fog and the darkness. Hundreds of tents were laid out in military precision. Soldiers. Lots of soldiers. And even as Kip stood, not two hundred paces from the nearest tent, the plain began winking. Glimmers sparkled as broken luxin gleamed, like stars scattered on the ground, answering their brethren in the sky.

It was what Kip had come for. Usually when a drafter released luxin, it simply dissolved, no matter what color it was. But in battle, there had been so much chaos, so many drafters, some sealed magic had been buried and protected from the sunlight that would break it down. The recent rain had uncovered more.

But Kip's eyes were pulled from the winking luxin by four soldiers and a man with a stark red cloak and red spectacles walking toward them from the camp.

'My name is Gaspar, by the by. Gaspar Elos.' The color wight didn't look at Kip.

'What?'

'I'm not just some drafter. My father loved me. I had plans. A girl. A life.'

'I don't—'

'You will.' The color wight put the green spectacles on; they fit perfectly, tight to his face, lenses sweeping to either side so that wherever he looked, he would be looking through a green filter. 'Now get out of here.'

As the sun touched the horizon, Gaspar sighed. It was as if Kip had ceased to exist. It was like watching his mother take that first deep breath of haze. Between the sparkling spars of darker green, the whites of Gaspar's eyes swirled like droplets of green blood hitting water, first dispersing, then staining the whole. The emerald green of luxin ballooned through his eyes, thickened until it was solid, and then spread. Through his cheeks, up to his hairline, then down his neck, standing out starkly when it finally filled his lighter fingernails as if they'd been painted in radiant jade.

Gaspar started laughing. It was a low, unreasoning cackle, unrelenting. Mad. Not a pretense this time.

Kip ran.

He reached the funerary hill where the sentry had been, taking care to stay on the far side from the army. He had to get to Master Danavis. Master Danavis always knew what to do.

There was no sentry on the hill now. Kip turned around in time to see Gaspar change, transform. Green luxin spilled out of his hands onto his body, covering every part of him like a shell, like an enormous suit of armor. Kip couldn't see the soldiers or the red drafter approaching Gaspar, but he did see a fireball the size of his head streak toward the color wight, hit his chest, and burst apart, throwing flames everywhere.

Gaspar rammed through it, flaming red luxin sticking to his green armor. He was magnificent, terrible, powerful. He ran toward the soldiers, screaming defiance, and disappeared from Kip's view.

Kip fled, the vermilion sun setting fire to the mists.

Chapter 2

Gavin Guile sleepily eyed the papers that slid under his door and wondered what Karris was punishing him for this time. His rooms occupied half of the top floor of the Chromeria, but the panoramic windows were blackened so that if he slept at all, he could sleep in. The seal on the letter pulsed so gently that Gavin couldn't tell what color had been drafted into it. He propped himself up in bed so he could get a better look and dilated his pupils to gather as much light as possible.

Superviolet. Oh, sonuva—

On every side, the floor-to-ceiling blackened windows dropped into the floor, bathing the room in full-spectrum light as the morning sun was revealed, climbing the horizon over the dual islands. With his eyes dilated so far, magic flooded Gavin. It was too much to hold.

Light exploded from him in every direction, passing through him in successive waves from superviolet down. The sub-red was last, rushing through his skin like a wave of flame. He jumped out of bed, sweating instantly. But with all the windows open, cold summer morning winds blasted through his chambers, chilling him. He yelped, hopping back into bed.

His yelp must have been loud enough for Karris to hear it and know that her rude awakening had been successful, because he heard her unmistakable laugh. She wasn't a superviolet, so she must have had a friend help her with her little prank. A quick shot of superviolet luxin at the room's controls threw the windows closed and set the filters to half. Gavin extended a hand to blast his door open, then stopped. He wasn't going to give Karris the satisfaction. Her assignment to be the White's fetch-and-carry girl had ostensibly been intended to teach her humility and gravitas. So far that much had been a spectacular failure, though the White always played a deeper game. Still, Gavin couldn't help grinning as he rose and swept the folded papers Karris had tucked under the door into his hand.

He walked to his door. On a small service table just outside, he found his breakfast on a platter. It was the same every morning: two squat bricks of bread and a pale wine in a clear glass cup. The bread was made of wheat, barley, beans, lentils, millet, and spelt, unleavened. A man could live on that bread. In fact, a man *was* living on that bread. Just not Gavin. Indeed, the sight of it made his stomach turn. He could order a different breakfast, of course, but he never did.

He brought it inside, setting the papers on the table next to the bread. One was odd, a plain note that didn't look like the White's personal stationery, nor any official hard white stationery the Chromeria used. He turned it over. The Chromeria's message office had marked it as being received from 'ST, Rekton': Satrapy of Tyrea, town of

Rekton. It sounded familiar, maybe one of those towns near Sundered Rock? But then, there had once been so many towns there. Probably someone begging an audience, though those letters were supposed to be screened out and dealt with separately.

Still, first things first. He tore open each loaf, checking that nothing had been concealed inside it. Satisfied, he took out a bottle of the blue dye he kept in a drawer and dribbled a bit into the wine. He swirled the wine to mix it, and held the glass up against the granite blue sky of a painting he kept on the wall as his reference.

He'd done it perfectly, of course. He'd been doing this for almost six thousand mornings now. Almost sixteen years. A long time for a man only thirty-three years old. He poured the wine over the broken halves of the bread, staining it blue – and harmless. Once a week, Gavin would prepare a blue cheese or blue fruit, but it took more time.

He picked up the note from Tyrea.

'I'm dying, Gavin. It's time you meet your son Kip. – Lina'

Son? I don't have a—

Suddenly his throat clamped down, and his chest felt like his heart was seizing up, no matter that the chirurgeons said it wasn't. Just relax, they said. Young and strong as a warhorse, they said. They didn't say, Grow a pair. You've got lots of friends, your enemies fear you, and you have no rivals. You're the Prism. What are you afraid of? No one had talked to him that way in years. Sometimes he wished they would.

Orholam, the note hadn't even been sealed.

Gavin walked out onto his glass balcony, subconsciously checking his drafting as he did every morning. He stared at his hand, splitting sunlight into its component colors as only he could do, filling each finger in turn with a color, from below the visible spectrum to above it: sub-red, red, orange, yellow, green, blue, superviolet. Had he felt a hitch there when he drafted blue? He double-checked it, glancing briefly toward the sun.

No, it was still easy to split light, still flawless. He released the luxin, each color sliding out and dissipating like smoke from beneath his fingernails, releasing the familiar bouquet of resinous scents.

He turned his face to the sun, its warmth like a mother's caress. Gavin opened his eyes and sucked in a warm, soothing red. In and out, in time with his labored breaths, willing them to slow. Then he let the red go and took in a deep icy blue. It felt like it was freezing his eyes. As ever, the blue brought clarity, peace, order. But not a plan, not with so little information. He let go of the colors. He was still fine. He still had at least five of his seven years left. Plenty of time. Five years, five great purposes.

Well, maybe not five *great* purposes.

Still, of his predecessors in the last four hundred years, aside from those who'd been assassinated or died of other causes, the rest had served for exactly seven, fourteen, or twenty-one years after becoming Prism. Gavin had made it past fourteen. So, plenty of time. No reason to think he'd be the exception. Not many, anyway.

He picked up the second note. Cracking the White's seal – the old crone sealed everything, though she shared the other half of this floor and Karris hand-delivered her messages. But everything had to be in its proper place, properly done. There was no mistaking that she'd risen from Blue.

The White's note read, 'Unless you would prefer to greet the students arriving late this morning, my dear Lord Prism, please attend me on the roof.'

Looking beyond the Chromeria's buildings and the city, Gavin studied the merchant ships in the bay cupped in the lee of Big Jasper Island. A ragged-looking Atashian sloop was maneuvering in to dock directly at a pier.

Greeting new students. Unbelievable. It wasn't that he

was too good to greet new students – well, actually, it *was* that. He, the White, and the Spectrum were supposed to balance each other. But though the Spectrum feared him the most, the reality was that the crone got her way more often than Gavin and the seven Colors combined. This morning she had to be wanting to experiment on him again, and if he wanted to avoid something more onerous like teaching he'd better get to the top of the tower.

Gavin drafted his red hair into a tight ponytail and dressed in the clothes his room slave had laid out for him: an ivory shirt and a well-cut pair of black wool pants with an oversize gem-studded belt, boots with silverwork, and a black cloak with harsh old Ilytian runic designs embroidered in silver thread. The Prism belonged to all the satrapies, so Gavin did his best to honor the traditions of every land – even one that was mainly pirates and heretics.

He hesitated a moment, then pulled open a drawer and drew out his brace of Ilytian pistols. They were, typical for Ilytian work, the most advanced design Gavin had ever seen. The firing mechanism was far more reliable than a wheel-lock – they were calling it a flintlock. Each pistol had a long blade beneath the barrel, and even a belt-flange so that when he tucked them into his belt behind his back they were held securely and at an angle so he didn't skewer himself when he sat. The Ilytians thought of everything.

And, of course, the pistols made the White's Blackguards nervous. Gavin grinned.

When he turned for the door and saw the painting again, his grin dropped.

He walked back to the table with the blue bread. Grabbing one use-smoothened edge of the painting, he pulled. It swung open silently, revealing a narrow chute.

Nothing menacing about the chute. Too small for a man to climb up, even if he overcame everything else. It might have been a laundry chute. Yet to Gavin it looked like the mouth of hell, the evernight itself opening wide for him. He tossed one of the bricks of bread into it, then waited. There was a thunk as the hard bread hit the first lock, a small hiss as it opened, then closed, then a smaller thunk as it hit the next lock, and a few moments later one last thunk. Each of the locks was still working. Everything was normal. Safe. There had been mistakes over the years, but no one had to die this time. No need for paranoia. He nearly snarled as he slammed the painting closed.